When Hearts Awaken

Victoria Lum

When Hearts Awaken

By Victoria Lum

Published by Eternal Hearts Publishing

Cover Design Copyright © 2025 Y'All That Graphic

Editing by Theresa Leigh and Amy Briggs

Proofreading by Virginia Tesi Carey

ISBN (Paperback): 979-8-9900169-5-8

ISBN (E-Book): 979-8-9900169-4-1

Author's Note

There are heavy topics discussed in this book and your mental health is paramount to me. For a list of potential areas of sensitive content, please visit:

https://www.victorialum.com/sensitive-content-information

Timeline Information: My books are written as standalones and can be read out of order. For readers familiar with my backlist and are wondering where in the timeline this story falls under, Part One occurs after the ending but before the epilogue of *When Hearts Ignite,* and Part Two occurs after the epilogue of *When Hearts Surrender.*

For those of you who have experienced the unspeakable, you're a fighter and you matter.

Get help at the RAINN website: https://rainn.org/
The National Sexual Assault Hotline is available 24/7 (United States): Telephone: 800.656.HOPE (4673)
Online chat: online.rainn.org

DEDICATION

For the readers who like a good touch her and die moment, let me introduce you to Charles Vaughn.

RELATIONSHIP TREE
THE KINGSLEYS AND EXTENDED FAMILY
(LA HEARTS SERIES)

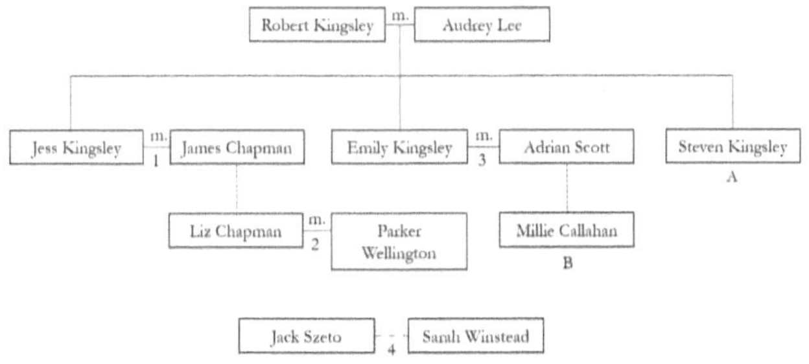

THE ANDERSONS AND FRIENDS
(THE ORCHID SERIES)

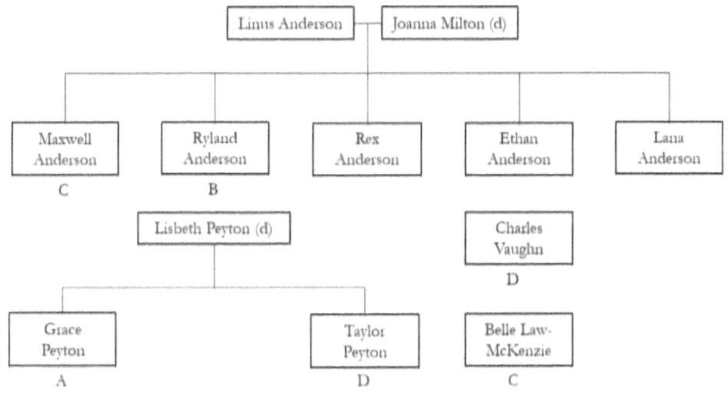

Legend

—— Family ······ Siblings - - - In Relationship   m. Married   (d) Deceased

Books

1 – *The Sweetest Agony* 2 – *The Coldest Passion* 3 – *The Harshest Hope* 4 – *The Brightest Spark*
A – *When Hearts Ignite* B – *When Hearts Collide* C – *When Hearts Surrender* D – *When Hearts Awaken*

Disclaimer: Only main characters are included. Awesome side characters including children are not in this tree.

PLAYLIST

"Let the World Burn" – Chris Grey
"Sirens" – Fleurie
"Wonderful Nothing" – Glass Animals
"Survivor" – 2WEI
"Pain's My Only Home" – Zevia
"Swan's Theme" – Pyotr Ilyich Tchaikovsky (from the ballet, *Swan Lake*)

Cast of Characters

The Andersons are a large family, but their stories are all standalones and can be read in any order. If you're new to their world or diving back in, here's a list of the main characters you'll encounter:

The Anderson Family:

- Linus Anderson – The patriarch of the family and retired from Fleur Entertainment.

- Maxwell Anderson – The eldest son and CEO of Fleur Entertainment; fraternal twin to Ryland. Broody and burdened, he carries the weight of the world on his shoulders.

- Ryland Anderson – The second son and former COO of Fleur Entertainment; fraternal twin to Maxwell. Now a full-time professor.

- Rex Anderson – The third son and CMO of Fleur Entertainment. A self-proclaimed playboy extraordinaire.

- Ethan Anderson – The fourth son and CFO of Fleur Entertainment. Quiet and introspective; an old soul with secrets.

- Lana Anderson – The youngest sister in the main Anderson family line and the Chief of Public Relations at Fleur Entertainment. Sophisticated and fiercely loyal.

- Grace Peyton-Anderson – The older half-sister of the Anderson siblings and a finance guru.

- Taylor Peyton-Anderson – The younger half-sister of the Anderson siblings. A gothic, take-no-prisoners ballerina.

Other Important People:

- Steven Kingsley – Grace's significant other, set to join Fleur Entertainment as COO after Ryland vacates the role.

- Charles Vaughn – Best friend of the Anderson brothers and Steven, CEO of the Bank of Columbia, and currently being driven insane by Taylor.

- Millie Callahan – Ryland's significant other, a PhD student with dreams of changing the world.

- Belle Law-McKenzie – Maxwell's significant other, the belle of the ball who loves rescuing animals and is a fashion designer.

- Olivia Lin – Taylor's friend, a psychiatrist specializing in anxiety and addiction disorders. Observant, smart, and fiercely loyal.

Part One

The White Swan

PROLOGUE

I WAS TEN YEARS old when I fell in love.

For the first and only time in my life.

Mommy pulled me out of recess time in school and snuck me into the backstage of the Met Opera. I remember gaping at the towering archways and the enormous wall of glass lit up by thousands of bright lights.

I thought I was going to Mount Olympus, and the gods were waiting for us behind those doors—we'd just learned about Greek myths in class that day. My little heart pounded as my breathing thinned in anticipation.

I knew my life was going to change forever.

"Today is a magical day," she told me as she led me through a side door. A harried looking woman beckoned us inside, all the while looking surreptitiously around as if we were criminals she wasn't supposed to be letting in.

My older sister, Grace, would get the occasional special days when Mommy would take her to the bookstore, and I'd get the random magical ones. Mommy said it was because she worked all the time, and this was her way of making it up to us. She told me she knew someone at the Met Opera, and she wanted me to see professional ballerinas on stage. Mommy said I was just like her—bitten by the performance bug and born to dance.

I remember hiding backstage behind the thick velvet curtains and feeling the heavy weight of the disapproving stares from adults towering over me.

I bet they could smell the stench of the week-old hot dog I had for breakfast, see the holes in my favorite rainbow leggings, or the frayed edges of my beloved pink ballerina T-shirt. Or perhaps they were looking at Mommy, whose eyes were unusually bright, lipstick fire-engine red, wearing the slinky black, glittering mini dress required for her work at the dance club.

She squared her shoulders and glared right back at them. Then she gently squeezed my hand in reassurance.

We didn't belong there, that was obvious enough, but at that moment, I didn't care.

Because I saw *them*.

The ballerinas on the stage—beautiful fluffy tutus so white, I imagined they'd never get dirtied like my well-worn sneakers. They were fairies dazzling under the bright spotlights.

But none of them were as beautiful as *her*.

Odette, the white swan.

She was twirling on the stage, each spin so graceful, so breathtaking, I couldn't look away. Jenny from school must be wrong. Magic did exist in the world because this...this gorgeous princess gliding across the stage *had* to be magical.

I remember the feeling of bubbles forming in my chest, my muscles clenching with giddiness. The world around me faded into black until all I could see was her wearing her glorious white dress, delicate white feathers in her hair, moving so effortlessly on her tiptoes she appeared to be floating.

She was dancing with her prince, her one true love.

She looked at him like he held her world in his hands, like he hung the moon in the skies just for her.

It was then I fell in love right alongside them.

Tumbled into it, head over heels.

It was as magical as Mommy described. Mommy believed in love—she used to tell me she was drunk on it. Grace would roll her eyes and tell me she thought Mommy was silly, but I'd always thought that was impossible. Because what would make an adult feel this way? What would make someone as smart and kind as Mommy want to risk everything over and over again even though she'd secretly cry in the dark when she thought we were asleep because the men would ultimately disappoint her?

I had the answer then. That day at the Met Opera.

The butterflies flapping their wings in my stomach. The lightness of my breath. My body coming alive. I felt like I could soar high in the skies, that everything in the world would be okay as long as I was in this moment, surrounded by this *feeling*—dancing with them, knowing everything would be all right as long as the other person was by your side.

This had to be it—why Mommy was in love with love.

But then the unthinkable happened. Odette died at the end of the ballet with her prince, because the evil black swan, Odile, and her villainous sorcerer father schemed against them.

The glorious white swan didn't survive, only the ugly, scary black one did. There was no happily ever after. I bawled my eyes out, unable to stop the sobs tearing from my throat despite others trying to shush me because I was causing a scene. I didn't care. Mommy always said holding in your emotions wasn't healthy. My little heart clenched in pain, not understanding why something so magical could end so tragically.

"It's not the true story, little Tay," Mommy whispered, tugging me to her side as we rode the subway back to our dingy apartment in the Bronx.

I clutched the beautiful white swan figurine to my chest. Mommy caved and bought it for me, even though I was sure it meant we'd be eating instant noodles for a week. But it was beautiful, one of those dolls that'd twirl and there was even a small compartment to store knick-knacks.

"It isn't?"

She shook her head, her warm eyes crinkling at the corners, but there was sadness in them—sadness she tried her best to hide. "You see, in the *real* story, there once was a beautiful white swan named Odile, and she loved her older sister Odette so, so much. However, they had an evil father, one who couldn't be there for them, but he was all they had left because their mother had passed away."

I shifted in the hard plastic seat and leaned against her chest, listening to the steady drums of her heartbeat blending with the rumbling of the subway train on the tracks.

She continued, "Odile wanted a better life for her and Odette, because she knew they couldn't count on their father. So, she worked really hard to be the smartest and the strongest swan. She'd catch the largest fish, swim the fastest, and protect the other little swans in the flock. But some of the male swans were jealous of her abilities. You see, they thought she was taking their jobs away from them."

My breath stalled, dread coiled in my throat. "What happened?"

Mommy frowned, her eyes unfocused. "One day, they cornered her while she was hunting. They backed her into a patch of grass so tall it blocked them from view of the other swans. Ruthlessly, they pecked at her and plucked her beautiful white feathers off, one by one. She fought hard, but there were too many of them, and after all, she was just one female swan. Everything hurt and as she laid on the ground, bleeding from her wounds, she watched the dark red blood stain her skin. At that moment, she thought she was going to die. But then, if she did, who was going to protect Odette?"

My lips wobbled. Tears blurred my eyes. This story was sad and horrible. I wanted the fairytale—the poor princess getting her happy ending; a prince riding by in his golden carriage and sweeping her off her feet.

Mommy took my hand and squeezed it. "It was her strength and willpower that led her to recover. But this time, when her feathers grew back, they became black. As beautiful and inky as the night-time sky. She realized she didn't need to be the graceful white swan because she was the warrior black swan all along. She was a fighter. She vowed to become even more powerful and no one would ever hurt her or Odette again."

Mommy yawned, her hand flying to her mouth. A few of her dark tresses had slipped out of her glittery updo—all part of her costume for work. Her dark eye circles were stark against the harsh fluorescent lights and thin lines appeared between her brows, but she was still the most beautiful person I'd ever seen...aside from the white swan I saw at the Met Opera.

My chest pinched. I hated seeing her so exhausted. But I knew if I told her that, she'd give me a sad smile and tell me everything was fine.

"Because it's just us girls against the world," she'd say. Maybe Mommy was the black swan in her story.

I shifted in my seat, raking in a breath of stale air, then closed my eyes. "I'm tired, Mommy. I'm going to take a nap. Can you finish the story of Odile later?" Maybe she'd sleep and get some rest too.

"Yes, sweetheart." I heard the smile in her voice and slowly felt her relax next to me, her soft snores soon filling the air.

I wasn't tired. Not one bit. My mind was filled with images of the fierce black swan, her shiny black feathers glinting like the sharpest blades under the pale moonlight—her armor against the world because the other swans ravaged and took from her.

Stole. Hurt. Maimed.

All her beautiful white feathers *gone*.

I decided then I didn't like Mommy's story. I wanted to be the perfect white swan dancing with her prince, even if they didn't survive in the end. At least she got to be happy for a moment. She was *beautiful*.

It was magic.

Mommy never did finish telling me her story of Odile before she passed away years later, and I never asked, because I didn't think I needed to know the ending, since come hell or high water, I was going to be Odette.

But I never thought there'd be a day when I'd finally understand what she was trying to tell me.

Because I end up becoming the black swan.

CHAPTER 1

Charles

LITTLE FIREFLY FLYING AGAINST the wind, buzz, buzz, buzz, I'll never let it win...

The nursery rhyme Grandma used to sing hammers incessantly inside my mind like a broken record playing on repeat. Sitting next to the bed, I close my eyes.

The overhead lights are dimmed, a faint smell of lavender filling the air. I know if I opened my eyes, I'd see the silk comforter on the bed, the thousand thread count sheets, and floor-to-ceiling windows overlooking the glittering skyline of Manhattan. Luxury at its finest—the best money could buy.

But the stench. The acrid smell of antiseptic agents no fragrances could dispel. The incessant beeping from the monitors. The icy chill in the room.

There's no comfort in the hospital.

"Little Firefly," I rasp. Opening my eyes, I gently twine her hand in mine—her warmth the only thing telling me she's still alive. "If you can hear me, please wake up. Everything is a fucking mess. Liam is on another bender. He still won't talk to me, and the company...*fuck!*"

Breathing in deeply, I attempt to calm myself. Emotional outbursts are useless. But right now, I wish I could let it all out, punch the wall, or break a window.

Keep calm and carry on, Charles. You aren't like them...your parents.

It's the one thing I've vowed never to become. Never to be a slave of my emotions—to let them sweep me away into madness, oblivious to the chaos I'd cause to others around me.

Even so, I wish I wasn't alone in this, that I had someone by my side.

I run my hand through my hair, not caring I'm ruining it for the emergency board meeting later today to deal with the biggest scandal in the company's history. The headlines swarm in my head: "Married CFO of Bank of Columbia accused of sexually assaulting a barely legal college intern at the Halton Financial Summit," "Bank of Columbia—a breeding ground for predators?," "The worst sex scandal in the banking industry—multiple victims have come forward."

Dammit, Patterson. What the fuck were you thinking? A heavy sense of shame creeps inside me. I should've known about this. I'm the CEO and I see the bastard weekly. I should've seen something. Even if he was a trusted employee Grandma hired, a mentor I trained with when I worked up the ranks in the company. I shouldn't have let down my guard and let him have free rein, assuming he was trustworthy.

But it isn't the first time I've been so buried in my work I've missed something alarmingly obvious.

"Have you been paying attention, Charles?" Liam yells, his eyes full of hatred. "Or have you been so self-absorbed in the company—your precious fucking legacy—that you forgot everyone else?"

The bank, which Grandma's family started and is world-renowned for its sterling reputation. *Not anymore, and on your watch too.*

Not to mention, this scandal following our announcement of a philanthropic initiative to raise awareness of sexual violence toward women is nothing short of ironic.

Now I have to fix this mess—if I haven't fucked it up too much already.

"At least you have a chance to repair things," Firefly's imaginary voice whispers in my mind. She always knew what to say.

The lump swells in my throat and I squeeze her limp hand. I miss her so much.

"If only I can fix everything, Little Firefly," I whisper. *If only I can fix you.*

"If you were here… you'd get a kick out of the official PR strategy to get us out of this mess," I murmur.

"You got your wish. I'm going to immerse myself in the ballet world." The company has recently sponsored the American Ballet Corporation, otherwise known as ABTC, and we'll be donating proceeds of ticket sales to victims' organizations. "If you were here, I'd be able to spend more time with you. Things are different now."

I swallow. "I'd put you and Liam first in everything. I'd—"

I stop myself. Wishful thinking doesn't do shit in the real world.

I trail my gaze over Firefly's still figure on the bed, the place she has called home for the last six years. She looks gaunt. I miss her laughter. I miss her snarky remarks and teasing grins. She was the glue that held Liam and me together.

I miss our summers in the Hamptons.

Staring past her to the large window, I take in the darkening clouds hanging low—a heavy, oppressive weight.

I think back to another day with overcast skies and gloomy weather. Everything was different then.

"Liam, you are so dead, you asshole! Next time, I'm putting a snake in your underwear drawer," she shrieked, chasing after him, holding some shredded fabric in her hands, her strawberry blonde tresses billowing in the wind. The clouds were quickly sweeping in, warning us of an incoming storm, but the scene before me sparkled with life.

"Got to catch me first, pipsqueak!" His laughter traveled up to the second-story window of our sprawling Victorian summer home in the Hamptons.

"Oh my God, grow up already! I'm sixteen and you're twenty, dude!" She shook her head. "Pipsqueak? I can take you down with my eyes closed."

I chuckled at their crazy antics.

"Charles, you ready?" Grandma asked from behind me.

"As ready as I'll ever be." I curved my lips into a smile I'd practiced in front of the mirror a million times before—warm enough to disarm, but not so big as to look like a deranged idiot or a people-pleaser. Excitement and nervousness tremored through me. It was the moment I spent my entire life preparing for.

Her eyes glimmered with pride. "You'll do fine. I had my first press conference at twenty-six too. I never thought I'd live to see the day when I could hand the reins of the bank to you. I was worried it'd have to go to your father…"

Grandma winced, but she didn't need to finish her sentence. My parents were the last people who should take over the company. She cleared her throat. "You were always the right person for it—calm, collected, smart, my perfect darling boy."

Reaching up, she patted my cheek and headed toward the door. Her shiny heels clicked loudly against the parquet floors. She paused and turned around. "Charles, remember what I told you before. Vaughns live with honor. Business with integrity. And…" she swallowed, "we stay away from The Association."

I frowned. This wasn't the first time she mentioned the organization to me. But she never told me more, other than I should stay away from it. I glanced out the window one last time, watching Liam and Firefly screeching and laughing in the sprawling green lawn below. I smiled. Maybe after my press conference, I could join them.

Ten years—it's been ten fucking years. How did everything change so much?

"Mr. Vaughn. Sir. Sir?"

A warm voice shakes me out of my trip down memory lane and I see Julie, the brunette daytime nurse, striding in with a clipboard.

Clearing my throat, I stand up and strain a wide smile. "Julie, you're looking energetic today." I wink. "And how many times have I asked you to call me Charles? How are your boys? Just started kindergarten, right?"

She flushes. "You remembered. Time flies. I can't believe the twins are already five."

"I know. I met you when you were still pregnant with them."

A flash of pain jars my insides, but my smile doesn't waver. People don't like to see negative emotions—they make them uncomfortable. Making people comfortable is second nature to me—it's the first step of establishing trust, which is paramount in business.

I met Julie when Firefly was admitted. Back then, we were hoping she'd wake up. But now, the twins are in kindergarten, and Firefly's still lying like a beautiful statue on the bed. Frozen in time.

And I'm still here, wishing I'd made a million different choices.

Something must've given my thoughts away, because Julie's eyes soften in sympathy before she squeezes my suit-clad arm. "She's very stable, no news. But sometimes, no news is good news, you know?"

After six years of no news, I can't help but think that's bad news.

Her forced optimism sounds like screeching nails against a chalkboard, but I maintain the mask on my face. If I smile enough, maybe I can chase away this guilt inside me.

"Well, you know me. Always hopeful. She'll wake up one day, I know it." *Aren't you tired of pretending everything is okay when it isn't?* I squeeze Julie's hand back and she brightens, no doubt thinking her reassurance worked on me.

She cranks up the volume of the flat-screen TV playing the *CBC* noon newscast. She told me she liked to turn on the TV for Firefly in case she could hear us and wanted to know what was going on in the world.

"We were all talking about your award at the nurses' station! Best CEO under the age of forty-five! I wish I could attend a fancy event like that."

My attention flickers to the clip they're playing, me striding to the podium for *Forbes's* annual CEO awards held at the Kensington Hotel two months ago, the spotlight highlighting the deep blond of my hair, the practiced smile on my face, my jawline covered in just the right amount of scruff, the tailored navy suit fitting me like a glove. I looked every inch the charismatic, successful CEO the public knows me for.

A perfectly curated image.

It was fucking hot in that room, and I *hated* every second of it.

I glance at Julie, taking in her wistful gaze at the screen. "Thank you. It was a fun night. Next time, if I get invited to something similar, I'll see if I can get some extra tickets for you. Nurses should be pampered, not CEOs," I murmur.

"Oh my God, I was totally joking! You're too kind." Julie giggles and shakes her head. "We're taking good care of her, don't you worry." She straightens, her voice sobering. "If anything changes, you'll be the first to know."

"Thank you."

She traipses over to the door and gently closes it behind her.

My smile slips off my face as I take in Firefly again. Brushing her brittle hair away from her face, I let out a deep sigh.

"Why didn't you go to her?" Liam screams. "I told you to. What the fuck is wrong with you? Is the company the most important thing to you?"

My tie chokes my breath and with a rough yank, I tug it loose. I straighten up the items on Firefly's nightstand and replace the wilted daisies with the fresh ones I brought with me. Tidiness and order—the perfect balm for the rioting emotions in my gut.

Calm. Keep calm, Charles. I keep myself busy for God knows how long until I find the room spotless, everything in its place, a pristine castle waiting for her sleeping princess to wake up.

A noise draws my attention to the TV.

A striking ballerina is dancing on the screen—her motions flawless, controlled, her midnight black hair arranged like a halo on top of her head.

A dark angel.

My pulse quickens for some unknown reason and for a moment, I forget about the guilt eating away at me, and instead am drawn into the world the dancer on the screen has created.

Her eyes are haunted—the sorrow in them eviscerating, and my chest clenches. Those eyes have seen pain—I'd bet my fortune on it. She stares at the camera—I feel like she could gaze into my soul.

Who is she?

The clip cuts away to another news segment, but my attention remains riveted to the screen.

Firefly would've loved to see her dance. *If she weren't laying on the bed in a coma.*

Fisting my hands tightly, I tear my gaze away from the screen. My eyes burn as I carefully reach into my breast pocket and pull out a small present, gift-wrapped in red, her favorite color.

I open the drawer of her nightstand, filled with the personal belongings they found on her that day—her wallet, her phone, her earrings, and her favorite bracelet. Shifting those items to the side, I set the gift next to five other pristine, unopened ones.

"Happy birthday, Little Firefly."

With my heart ripped out of my chest, I walk to the door, only for it to suddenly swing open, and someone I don't expect barges in.

"Ethan?" I stare at the tall dark-haired man in front of me, whose eyes look reddened, his gaze far away like he's deep in thought. His tie is crooked, collar unbuttoned. He doesn't look like the usual put together, quiet younger sibling of the illustrious Anderson family I'm fortunate enough to call my friends.

Ethan startles. "Charles," he murmurs before clearing his throat and straightening up, his face completely devoid of the earlier emotions.

"You're still visiting her." An observation, not a question.

"Always." A few seconds pause, then he adds, "I promised Liam."

He doesn't say more, but then again, he doesn't need to. He's lying and I don't call him out on it. We all need lies to hide behind, so we don't have to face the truth.

Clasping his forearm, I give it a squeeze before pasting on my fake smile and slipping out of the room.

CHAPTER 2

The September evening chill sweeps through the open French doors of the rooftop studio at the opulent historic building housing ABTC just off Central Park West. I breathe in the humid air, a sure sign that rain is around the corner.

Stark moonlight streams in from the arched windows, joining the dim glow of the two kerosene lamps I brought with me. The studio is dilapidated—some windowpanes are missing or cracked, the lightbulbs hanging from the ceiling broken. Most dancers avoid coming up here.

But it's my haven. Me and the moonlight. My spot of brightness in the dark.

I stare at my reflection in the mirror as I spin and spin, each rotation giving me the highest of highs. Grinning, I close my eyes, letting my body take over, my limbs long and strong, practicing the moves I know as well as breathing.

I'm in my element. Ballet. Dance. Pure control.

Thirty-two fouetté turns. That's what the famous black swan dance in Act III of *Swan Lake* calls for. It's when you hear the audience cheer at the ballerina for spinning like those rotating dolls in the toy store.

Thirty-one. Thirty-two. I count the rotations in my mind, but I don't stop.

I can do more. I'm much stronger than that.

My toes pinch, my calves burn, but the pain grounds me and I push forward, the high in my veins and determination in my lungs driving me.

"You're one of the best Odiles out there," Madame Renoir said in the past.

The best.

All those late night hours practicing when the world was asleep, the strict diets and tiresome exercises, Mom and Grace working extra hard to make money to put me through dance lessons even though we had barely enough to survive on.

The best fucking ballerina.

My lungs heave out panting breaths as I slow down and stop. Forty-five turns. But the last three were too unstable. I need to work on that.

I walk to the corner of the room and dislodge the third floorboard from the wall. Biting my lip, I survey the items in the hiding place. A small metal box for things I've collected over the years—ballet ticket stubs, my first pair of pointe shoes, and the doll Mom gave me. I've always thought these items would give me luck if I store them here, hidden away in the lauded institution of dance.

Carefully, I take out the doll and twist the dial, watching the faded porcelain ballerina twirl, the gems on its tutu sparkling under the moonlight. A wistful longing tugs inside my chest as I think back to that day long ago at the Met Opera, when everything was different.

When I was different.

Blowing out a breath, I play a new song on my phone.

Now, it's time for *the* challenge. The one role I haven't been able to master since I was sixteen because of what happened. The only role I've ever wanted to dance since I was ten. The role that's a prerequisite for promotion to principal ballerina.

Odette, the white swan, typically danced by the same ballerina portraying the black swan.

Looming shadows flicker and twist against the walls as the chilly wind taunts the flames inside the lamps.

Closing my eyes, I will my battering heart to calm and my tensed muscles to relax. Tchaikovsky's emotional music streams through the speakers. Placing my body into position, I wait for the starting point of Odette's solo in Act II.

And I fly.

The evocative sweeps of the string instruments and the somber sounds of the oboe carry through the abandoned space as I dance in the company of the lonely moonlight.

Por de bras, développé, arabesque—I glide through the poses. I'm the graceful white swan I saw that magical day when I was ten. It's my white feathers sparkling now, effervescent, luminous under the cloak of the night.

But, as it has been every single time in the past, the story shifts and the mood deteriorates. Instead of delicate movements, my limbs won't cooperate. My muscles tense, but I push through. I persist. *I'm the white swan. The fucking white swan.* The frustrated motions come out stilted and sharp, nothing like the effortless poise of Odette. Nothing like the beautiful ballerina from all those years ago.

"Graceful, Taylor. Why do you dance like you're angry at the world?"

"Gentle. You're in love, but you're afraid to lose it. Have you ever *been in love?"*

Madame Renoir's voice rings in my head, chasing away the ethereal notes of Tchaikovsky's music.

Love. What is love? It's nothing but pain and betrayal. The first time I felt the emotion was when I watched *Swan Lake* with Mom.

The second time I came close to the elusive emotion was six years ago—well, that was when I realized how wrong I was.

Images of Camden barge through my consciousness—his light auburn hair reminding me of my favorite food, carrots; his boyish smile; the intensity in his green eyes when he told me he'd wait until I was ready to say the three little words back to him and to sleep with him for the first time because he knew I was a virgin then.

"I love you, Tay. I'm the luckiest guy on earth to be your boyfriend."

Lies. Pathetic lies. Gut-wrenching pain I still feel today, many years later, especially after what happened. I remember the day he broke up with me vividly.

He stared at me with revulsion, his face flushed. "You *disgust* me."

I recoiled in horror, tears welling in my eyes. "Camden... I w-was forced. I tried to stop them...I really did! I c-couldn't m-move and—"

He curled his lips into a sneer. "You know, I saw you that night. I saw you with him...with *them*." He spit out the last word. "It didn't look like you weren't enjoying yourself."

Betrayal punched a hole in my heart. I shook my head. I thought he was different. Different from Mom's horrible rich ex-boyfriends who gave her black eyes and bruised lips. Camden said he loved me and I thought I was falling for him.

I thought I was safe because he was the sweet boy next door, not one of those rich assholes. He was the boy who shared the same ballet dreams as me.

"I just can't look at you the same way ever again. You're...ruined," he gritted out.

I'm not fucking ruined, you asshole.

Angry at myself for thinking of the past, I dance harder, stretching my limbs higher and farther, making up for my lack of focus with effort. I ignore my aching muscles, the blistering pain of my swollen toes from cramming them into old pointe shoes—shoes I should've tossed a week ago, but fuck, they're expensive to replace at the rate I go through them.

My body fights back, refusing to obey my mind. My positions don't land, my footwork missing a few beats.

"I'm so proud of you." Excitement and pride shone through Mom's voice when I told her I got accepted into ABTC last year. There was relief in her statement, like she'd achieved the purpose of her life, and she died soon afterward in a tragic car accident.

Gritting my teeth, I hurl myself into another move. A pirouette I complete too quickly.

It's supposed to be slow. Controlled. But I'm unraveling, as I always do in this role.

"This is atrocious, Taylor. And you want to be promoted to principal this year?" That's what Madame Renoir would say if she were here, watching me butcher one of the most beautiful dances in the ballet.

You're not worthy of Odette, Taylor. You're soiled.

Fuck. Go away, Lochness Monster. Giving my inner negative voice a ridiculous name often helps with these thoughts.

"I *will* be a principal dancer," I yell, the words shrill, slicing through the night like an assassin's blade.

"Have you ever been in love?" Madame Renoir's words echo inside my mind, and my eyes burn.

Never again. Love isn't for me. But that doesn't mean I can't master this dance or reclaim my body.

I let the anger always lying dormant in the base of my spine flicker alive and surge up my body—violence to offset the sorrow.

"Gentlemen, I didn't disappoint did I?" The monster's dark voice ghosts inside my brain, followed by a glimpse of blond hair.

A flash of light eyes—were they blue? Green? I can't remember. A streak of red glints in my vague memory. The pulsing between my legs that night.

Sharp pain sears my knees and calves as I collapse onto the floor. Biting back a groan, I feel a familiar warm stickiness seeping from the scrapes. Blood. My breathing is ragged as I turn over to lie on my back.

Shadows of men in suits, but their faces hidden, flicker on and off like a broken television screen. They star in my nightmares, depriving me of sleep.

Fuckers, you can't control me. Not anymore.

It's been years. The past is in the past and it can't hurt me anymore. While I'm no longer the naive girl thinking the world is my oyster and somewhere out there, I have a prince waiting for my Odette. I'm twenty-two and a damn good ballerina at the top ballet company in the country.

Fly Harriet.

The monster's voice whispers words I don't understand, followed by the pulsing sensation between my legs. *It's not real. These are trauma flashbacks.* I know this from the self-help books I've read over the years.

I reach down between my legs and twist the small metal piercing through my tights. A VCH piercing I got for pain, not for pleasure. Tears spring into my eyes at the sharp pain radiating from my core. I don't cry. I haven't been able to since I was sixteen.

Better. Much better now. I rake in harsh pants of frigid night air. The shameful heat has receded, replaced with reassuring agony.

Pain as punishment. Pain I can control. It's a grounding technique for me.

I control my body. No one can hurt me anymore.

My breaths are white puffs against the darkness, the icy gale from the outside sweeping in.

Slowly, I close my eyes, my fists balling against my sides.

I'm the white swan...Odette, I repeatedly chant to myself. But all I can see are the grotesque, black feathers sprouting from my skin.

Dirty. Inky blackness. Permanent. A chilling howl travels into the empty room as the music fades into silence.

I'm the white swan and I *will* be promoted to principal ballerina.

Because my sacrifices...my family's sacrifices, can't be in vain.

CHAPTER 3

HALF AN HOUR LATER, I drag myself down to the basement locker room to wash up before my tutoring session with the trainees. My footfalls echo against the aged gray tiles, my mind still reeling from my failure of a practice just now.

"Taylor, are we still on for tonight?" a sweet voice asks from behind me.

"We're so excited!" another voice chimes in.

I stop and turn around, seeing the familiar blonde hair and wide grin of Ainsley and the shy smile and dark brown tresses of her best friend Maddy. They remind me of better days—me and Alexis roaming the halls, wreaking havoc.

Their twin smiles falter when they see the cuts on my knees. These fifteen-year-olds miss nothing.

"Are you okay?" Maddy asks.

I swallow a wince. "I'm fine—fell during practice earlier. This is nothing. But this might not be the year for me to get picked to be Odette/Odile." *Swan Lake* is an annual performance for us and I hope to get the main role, but it's obvious I'm not ready.

Maddy frowns. "You're one of the best dancers I've seen. You'll get it someday, I know it." She purses her lips then hesitantly asks, "So um... Are we're still on?"

I nod and watch the tension melt from her shoulders. Ainsley and Maddy are trainees, both here on scholarship. They show a lot of promise but need help outside the regular curriculum to polish the rough edges in their technique.

"Great! Thanks for tutoring us on the side. I know you're busy with your practices and everything." Ainsley grins.

"Don't mention it. But you guys better work your asses off—I won't be taking it easy on you." I nod toward the locker room. "I'm going to change and I'll head over shortly."

"Yes, ma'am." Ainsley mock salutes and dashes away, dragging her best friend with her.

Maddy looks back and gives me a hesitant wave before disappearing down the hall.

My lips twitch into a smile, my earlier dark mood receding. They remind me of myself when I was younger—eager, hardworking, hope emanating from them that poverty couldn't stifle.

I'd do anything to preserve that spark in their eyes. A warmth settles into my chest as I push open the rusted metal door to the locker room.

A group of dancers huddling by the antique boiler stops talking the moment I step inside, their eyes narrowing into slits as they take in my tattered state, and my mood immediately sours.

"Look what the cat dragged in...an orphaned stray." Carla, their bitchy blonde leader and my nemesis, snickers and her group of lemmings giggles behind her. "Can't afford new tights and shoes, Tay Tay? Why don't you get yourself a sugar daddy?"

She pauses, no doubt for dramatic effect. "But then, who'd want an extra for a vampire movie as a sugar baby? You'd probably murder him in his sleep." The girls cackle loudly.

"Shut your mouth before I shut it for you," I growl and yank open my locker, watching in dismay the contents inside tumbling out onto the floor.

Dammit. Grace always told me to organize my things as opposed to living in a tornado.

"How do you thrive in chaos, Tay?" She giggles and nudges me before heading off to work. "Aren't ballerinas supposed to be disciplined?"

I smirk. "Chaos breeds inspiration, Grace. I'll have you know, I use all of my discipline in my art. Outside of dance is when I can let go. And I bet the authors of those sappy romance books you read live in chaos too."

"Hey! No book-shaming allowed here."

The girls snort as I pick up my belongings—papers, overdue bills, food wrappers, and God knows what. *Ignore them, Taylor. They're bullies and want a reaction from you.* I sniff a balled up towel—a little threadbare but still smells fresh enough—and toss it over my shoulder.

"God, she's so gross. Who knows what Madame Renoir sees in her."

"More talent in my asshole than in your entire being," I mutter, shoving the rest of my stuff back inside the rickety locker. The low pendant lamp swings from the ceiling, casting long shadows across the room—probably because of the kids pounding down the stairwell next door.

"Say it to my face, bitch." Carla's voice sounds closer. "You don't belong here. Ballet is for the upper class, not for poor, motherless bitches like you."

Anger churns through me as my temper gets the better of me. Fuck it. Restraint is overrated—why hold everything in when you can unleash it on those who deserve it? It feels fucking good too.

"Oh, *I'll* say it to your face, you spoiled brat." Squaring my shoulders, I spin around to face Carla and her goons and crack the joints in my neck. At five-foot-seven, I'm no shorty, and I've picked up some skills over the years to krav maga them flat on their asses.

"Hold your horses, Tay. Seriously, you're going for a promotion. Don't get into a fight now." I smell the sweet scent of lavender before I see Lisa, my only friend here, other than Devon. Lisa is tiny, but her personality more than makes up for it.

She glares at the mob. "Carla, don't you have something better to do you with your time? Picking on Tay won't get you promoted."

Carla snorts and flicks her dainty, manicured fingers in my direction. "As if I'd get my hands dirty." She arches a thin, blonde brow. "Seriously,

Lisa, why are you hanging out with her? You're old money. Your parents are on the board."

Lisa rolls her eyes and tosses her shiny brown hair over her shoulders. Ignoring her, she turns toward me. I smother a smile at the fierce lioness expression on her face.

She leans in and whispers, "Have you heard the rumors?"

"What rumors?"

"Change in management. The bigwigs are coming. Going to shake things up. At least, that's what I overheard when Dad left his door open during his board meeting last week. Everyone is talking about it."

I frown. "I haven't heard a thing. But then again, I'm usually the last person to know anything. Will this impact us?" *And my upcoming promotion evaluation?* Cold sweat breaks down my back.

Lisa shrugs. "I have no clue. But apparently, it's something about some alignment with some big corporation for some philanthropic endeavor. Something about an international ballet tour too!"

"That's a lot of 'somes' in one sentence."

She grins. "You're *hilarious*. Har har har. You should be a comedian instead. By the way, you going out with Dev and me today? We're trying a new club in SoHo. Lady of the Night."

I arch my brow. "Let me guess. A hip, new place named after a flower. Is this a Fleur establishment?"

Lisa's eyes brighten at my recognition of the largest entertainment and hospitality company in the world, famously headed by the Anderson family—royalty in New York, if not the entire country.

Ironically, it turns out I'm actually related to them. Grace found out a few months ago our missing-in-action-since-birth father is Linus Anderson, the patriarch. Apparently, he and Mom had a passionate affair a long time ago, but they broke up because he believed in some ridiculous family curse about the eldest son not being able to fall in love or else his woman would die. To say I'm baffled by this turn of events is an understatement.

So, this little 'motherless bitch' is now an Anderson. Fates are the ultimate jokesters. If only Carla knew—she'd shut her big mouth then.

But the masochist in me doesn't want to tell her or the others at ABTC. Or perhaps it's pride. It's the Anderson family money, not mine. I've done fine my entire life without the Anderson influence.

"Come out with us. It'll be the old gang at IBA together again." IBA was the ballet academy we were all at before Lisa and I got accepted into Petite Jeté, a feeder school for ABTC, then eventually joining ABTC.

My eyes snap to Lisa's and she falters, clearly realizing her mistake. *The old gang.*

"I-I'm sorry, that didn't come out right. I mean, I know Alexis isn't here, and Camden is an asshole, but—"

"Alexis left us and fuck Camden." My jaw works. In some ways, the pain of my best friend ditching me far outweighs my boyfriend dumping me at the same time.

They left because they knew what happened to me. People can't be trusted.

Lisa blanches and pats me awkwardly on my shoulder. She never knew why Alexis and Camden left. After what happened, I couldn't bring myself to tell anyone else. To Lisa, she thought Camden and I had a run-of-the-mill breakup, and Alexis and I had some sort of falling out.

I strain a smile, ignoring the pinch in my chest from the invisible scars. "Anyway, I can't go out tonight. I'm tutoring the trainees in half an hour. They have a recital coming up and you haven't seen them, Lisa. They're a mess. They need all the help they can get. Then, I'm going home to watch *Scream if You Dare.*" I clap gleefully, thinking about the over-the-top gory slasher film and the comfy sofa that's waiting for me.

God, I love horror movies. They're always a fun ride and the bad guy usually dies at the end.

She laughs, the color returning to her face, and shakes her head. "I don't know how you watch these things." Leaning in, she pokes me on the side. "And you're a softy underneath all the prickliness, Tay. I see you."

"I'm just doing what I wish someone did for me when I was younger. Ballet is a lifeline for these kids—their only way out of poverty. They get to see the world, join us on tours—it's an opportunity of a lifetime for them."

"See? That's what I mean. You don't have to do any of this and yet you do it without anyone asking. Like I said. A secret softie."

I roll my eyes, fighting a twitch on my lips as warmth spreads through me. Lisa follows me when I head over to the sink.

After washing my face, I reapply a thick coat of my usual black eyeliner. Heavier makeup to draw attention away from my dark eye circles courtesy of my restless sleep at night. Adjusting my nose ring—a black skull today, because of the pissed off mood I'm in—I take in my appearance in the large and slightly tarnished mirror.

Raven-black hair piled high in a messy bun. Pale skin—no shit, since I spend all my time indoors practicing, full lips, and large, slate-gray eyes I now know are an Anderson characteristic.

Fly Harriet. Little beauty.

The ghost of my past whispers in my ears and I flinch, my face leaching of color. Acid sloshes in my stomach. I want to scratch my reflection in the mirror or tattoo something across my face. *What did he mean by that?*

I'm no one's little beauty.

Releasing a shaky inhale, I turn to Lisa. "Have fun with Dev. You guys deserve a night out. Practice has been brutal this week."

She grins, no doubt thinking about her doting boyfriend, the top male dancer in the company. "Fine. Don't work too hard, Tay."

"I won't. Go. Get drunk. Have crazy sex."

Lisa blushes before leaning in and whispering, "You can have crazy sex too if you date, Tay Tay. Maybe you need to come out with us so you can actually meet guys!"

Rolling my eyes, I shoo her away before turning back to the mirror. I wish I could be like her—date men, enjoy sex, and bask in love.

But nope. Love is definitely not in the cards, but I'll reclaim my body and sex one day.

I snap on the thin silver cuff Alexis gave me a long time ago. Somehow, I couldn't bring myself to throw it away when she left. As much as I hate to admit it, I miss her. We were four years apart, and she was like my older sister in ballet. I looked up to her and as I grew up, she became my best friend until she betrayed me. I miss being able to trust people—to believe someone's love for me can be unconditional.

Fly Harriet.

I watch the invisible black feathers sprout from my skin. I scrub at them, but they're still there.

CHAPTER 4

I TAKE A SIP of whiskey, my mood stormy from the protesters who parked in front of the building earlier. The words written on their signs were loud and clear.

"We won't be silenced anymore!"

"Stop hiding and make a statement!"

"Just because you're rich doesn't mean you get to buy our voices!"

Security had to escort me into the building. Other patrons looked at me in pity. I had to stay silent at the recommendation of our PR and legal departments and our crisis management firm until we have an official press release out.

But goddamn it, I wanted to say something. I wanted to tell the masses out there I'm not protecting our disgraced CFO, that what Patterson did isn't what the Bank of Columbia stands for.

"How's my favorite nephew doing? Stealing the hearts of all the ladies and leaving none of them for me?"

Shaking my head, I bite down my frustration and turn away from the oak bar table at MacGregor's Whiskey Library inside The Orchid, the most exclusive establishment in Manhattan and the pinnacle of Fleur Entertainment. It's the place where all our dreams can be fulfilled—great food, luxurious living, concierge services, companionship of all kinds.

"Uncle Ian." I force out a grin, pulling him in for a hug. "It's been awhile. Sorry to bring you in for such circumstances."

He waves me off as if it's no bother he flew in from Paris, where he's currently working in the top ballet company there, just to save my ass and Bank of Columbia from the scandal. But that's who my uncle is. A good man, someone who puts his family first, a much better man than me. I nod to an attendant and they take us to a small table in the darkened corner of the lounge.

"What did I say about that? Call me Ian. The whole 'uncle' thing makes me feel old and ruins my bachelor image. And I was going to come visit for Christmas. What's three months early, anyway?"

We settle into our seats and I take another look at the man who's more like a father to me than my dad ever was. Uncle Ian looks good—his blond hair a few shades lighter than mine, eyes the same sky-blue that runs in our family. If it weren't for the fine lines marring his forehead and the white hairs at his temples, he could probably pass as my older brother.

"ABTC. Moving back here. Are you sure?" I ask after a waitress comes and takes our orders.

"I'm ready for a new challenge after I wrap things up in Paris. Your timing works perfectly."

Sighing, I nod. "I'm sure you saw the protesters out front. They somehow knew I was going to be here today."

He grimaces and I continue, "I talked it over with our people. They recommend announcing our sponsorship of ABTC and kicking off an international ballet tour at the same time. All proceeds from the tour will go toward victims of sexual assault. The public needs more than the standard apology statement and we can't pussyfoot around this scandal."

Ian rubs the scruff on his face, appearing deep in thought. "Do you think it'll work? This tour? I'll help any way I can to make sure it's the best damn tour anyone has ever seen."

"Oh please. Having one of the top choreographers in the world as our artistic director is already a selling point. And you're known in the dance circles for being an ally to assault victims. It's a cause you believe in. You're the perfect person to bring on board for this."

Something flashes across Ian's face, too quickly for me to discern, his expression solemn. I swallow and murmur, "You know you don't have to do this. This tour will be linked to the scandal. You don't need to tie your name to it." It's another source of guilt that's been bothering me for a while. If this tour doesn't do well, I don't want to taint his hard-earned reputation with it.

I fucked up. I should be the only one to bear the consequences.

"I'm a Vaughn first, choreographer second." A muscle tics in his jaw, and he reaches over and pats my hand. "Can't leave my nephew to swim with the sharks alone. Your grandmother would skin me alive if she were still here."

I laugh, a twinge of sadness mixing with merriment. She would have, but unfortunately, she passed away not long ago, and man, do I miss that ball busting woman.

He adds, "Plus, you're like the son I never had. I need to look out for you even though you're thirty-six and a grown ass man. God knows you've been missing a paternal figure in your life."

Because my parents have never looked after me.

The words are left unsaid, but judging from the grimace on his face, he's thinking the same thing. The old wound hidden deep beneath the layers of thousand-dollar suits aches. It's pathetic to still feel this way about them.

"Have you seen them? Last I heard, they were in Lyon for their fourth, no fifth wedding vows renewal." After another public spat that landed in the headlines: "Trouble in Vaughn paradise...again? Lovers' spat got ugly in France."

It was only the tip of the iceberg for what we had to put up with growing up in the Vaughn household. The embarrassment I had to face at school growing up, knowing gossip about my parents was plastered on the front pages of newspapers. I'd force myself to smile at my classmates, pretending I didn't give a shit. The painful reality of being invisible to the two people who were supposed to love you more than anything else in the world because Peter and Martha Vaughn's lives only revolved around themselves.

Some would say we were neglected. Abandoned. Left to starve for emotional connection. I'd say fuck them and fuck emotions. That's what made Peter and Martha the way they are.

I swirl the contents of my tumbler and stare at the amber liquid. Suddenly, I've lost my appetite.

"Charles, you know your parents. Utterly wrapped up and besotted with each other. I'm sure they miss and care about you guys."

I snort. It doesn't matter anymore.

Ian drops the subject. "This goes unsaid, but you're doing your best with the company. Better than I could've done in your shoes." There's an uncharacteristic hardness in his tone, but when I look up, he shrugs nonchalantly. He's probably feeling guilty for not being in the family business.

"It's fine. The world would be deprived of your art if you worked at the bank. And I like work." Most of the time. I enjoy the numbers and analytics. Meeting new people I'm usually fine with.

Smiling at the fake shit spewing out from their lips?

The bane of my existence.

"*Fy machgen*, don't be too hard on yourself."

My boy. In our ancestral tongue. "It's been years since you called me that, and I still can't speak Welsh. I'm also a few years shy of forty, so I don't think 'boy' describes me anymore."

He harrumphs. "You'll always be a boy in my eyes."

A lump forms in my throat as I stare at him—visions of my childhood spent going to the ballet with him and Firefly, late nights watching old movies in the empty estate as Liam and Firefly bicker nearby, trips to the zoo—all things my parents instead of Ian should've done with us.

"You would've been a good father. Why didn't you ever settle down?" I ask.

He stiffens before letting out a sigh. "This and that. Life is unpredictable that way. You win some, you lose some, Charles." He takes a sip from his tumbler.

"But aren't you lonely?"

Ian laughs and shakes his head. "I'm fifty-two years old and trust me, I get plenty of company." Leaning forward, he frowns at me. "The question is, Charles, why are *you* alone?"

I clutch my drink in a death grip as a barrage of emotions assault me—anger, resentment, bitterness, too many for me to name.

Taking a deep breath, I remind myself that volatile emotions have no use in my life.

I don't answer him.

Or perhaps I don't want to have an answer for him.

CHAPTER 5

"DAMN, WHAT'S GOING ON outside?" I sidle next to Lisa, who has her nose smashed against the second floor window, which is cracked open a smidge. She's no doubt looking at the commotion happening downstairs by the front entrance.

"Bigwigs are here. Charles is getting out of the car and people are pissed off."

"Charles?"

"Bank of Columbia's CEO. You really need to read the news, Tay. The scandal is crazy!" Lisa exclaims, then proceeds to tell me how the public is rightfully outraged at the crimes committed by a top executive at the bank.

Countless women have stepped forward with horrid tales of unwanted sexual advances—daughters, wives, sisters of everyday hardworking folks who fell victim to a monster at the company. Flames spark in my chest as Lisa recounts all the stories she's read about so far. All those women whose lives are turned upside down. Women who'll probably experience traumatic flashbacks like me.

Anger swims inside me and I eye the picket line and the angry mob gathered around a black town car as this man, Charles, steps out.

His muscular body is poured into a formfitting suit, his presence radiating with arrogance and prestige.

Like he doesn't give a crap about the lives ruined under his watch at a company he leads.

Charles turns toward the reporters and the crowd. "I have no comment at this time regarding the *alleged* crimes being reported." His face is flushed, and I notice his hands clench into tight fists as if he doesn't believe a word coming out of his mouth.

Outrage and fury roar from the crowd, and I feel the same ire in my veins.

Alleged? From what Lisa just told me, there was nothing alleged about any of it. These bigwigs only care about saving their asses and lining their pockets, legal words and whatnot.

They never believe the women, just like how no one believed me.

Charles flashes the reporters what I'm assuming is a self-deprecating "I'm caught in a tough place, woe is me" expression and I grit my teeth. He unleashes a half-smile and says, "Bank of Columbia and ABTC are combining forces to raise awareness about sexual assault and to advocate for survivors. This will be an exciting partnership for us and I'm thrilled about what's coming. Now, please excuse me, I'm late for a meeting to kick off this partnership and to discuss how we can positively impact this cause."

"Wow, that is the most top-notch BS maneuvering that I've ever seen…and I've seen a lot from Dad and his business partners." Lisa lets out a low whistle.

I bite down a growl and fist my hands by my sides. The fake as shit motherfucker.

Another validation for my aversion to rich men in suits—Mom's exes, the monsters from my past, and even my birth dad, who I haven't forgiven for abandoning Mom and us.

I excuse myself to go to the bathroom before heading into the rehearsal room for Madame Renoir's meeting, which no doubt is to announce this partnership with ABTC and other smaller sponsors. I need to splash some water on my face to cool down. After feeling like I have my wits about me, I step out of the bathroom to head to the meeting.

I pass by a few older men in suits.

"They didn't make them like this back in my day," the bald one mutters under his breath, his lecherous eyes roving over my leotard-clad body.

Keep walking, Taylor. Keep walking. Don't stir up trouble at ABTC.

His buddies chuckle and I see them turn toward a newcomer, their comments dropping in volume.

"Checking out my dancers, John? Not without my permission." A new voice floats to my ears, and I fight a shiver at the rough timbre—powerful and masculine—currently laced with humor.

"Charles, just because you're the largest sponsor doesn't make them yours. Get in line." More laughter. *Ugh. So gross.*

I can't resist looking back as I enter the rehearsal studio. I see the back of the newcomer, a tall man, golden hair shining under the spotlight like a crown. That motherfucker I saw outside just now. Charles, the misogynistic, fake as shit pig. I really hope I don't run into him in the future because I might not be able to help myself and give him a piece of my mind.

Once inside the room, I force my mind to focus on the white swan dance I'm trying to master instead. We have fifteen more minutes before the meeting. I might as well practice. I need to figure this out—push through this block I have with the role. Keep my eyes on the prize—the promotion dangling within reach. Maybe once I get it, I'd feel better about everything that happened.

Maybe I'd feel more...whole.

I take a deep breath and slip into my ballerina persona—perfect, poised, graceful. Calm even as the world riots around me. My hands and feet move on their own accord—the warm-ups easy. I practice my pirouettes, each spin pushing down the anger until it's packed tightly at the base of my spine.

Calm. I'm calm. I'm Taylor, the ballerina now.

After a few more minutes of practice, I blow out a breath.

Then I sense someone staring at me. A man's gaze, I'm sure. It's distracting. Menacing. Unnerving.

The pressure in my chest increases, the hairs on the back of my neck stand like a cat's would in the presence of predators.

Ignore him, Taylor. You're Odette. The white swan is the queen and doesn't care about the peasants watching her.

Temps levé arabesque. Leap. Extend the back leg. Leap again. Soft and vulnerable, gentle like a swan.

My mind refuses to settle and I feel my ballerina persona slipping. I come down from what must've been at least the hundredth leap today and my ankle protests. I've pushed myself too hard after my injury in the rooftop studio.

"Fuck!" I grit out. "What the hell, Taylor. That is the shittiest performance ever."

At this rate, I'll be lucky to keep my current position as a soloist in the company. A promotion will definitely be out of the question.

Frustration lances through me and I bite back a growl before I perform the last leap again, my movement exaggerated with the generous pizzazz of the black swan. I even add a shake at the end for the heck of it.

If I'm going to fail Odette again, at least I'm going out as badass Odile. *Fuckers!* I imagine giving a middle finger to the world because I can't do that in front of everyone in practice. I snort, laughing at my petty act of rebellion.

You are nuts, Taylor.

I plop on the floor and stare at my fellow dancers, still hard at work.

Bethany McLean, our reigning principal dancer, executes the sequence I failed just now. There's no frustration, no torture, no agony. There's only the wistful vulnerability of a cursed swan who fell in love with a handsome prince.

She's everything I can never be.

My nose burns and I tear my gaze away. Desperate to distract myself, I pick up my cell phone from the ground. A few messages await me.

Grace

Meet up at Corazón tonight, ladies? My treat. I'm craving spicy sushi and tequila. *Hearts emoji x5*

Millie

> Someone is in a good mood today! I can't be-
> lieve you're opening your own consulting firm
> soon. Ms. Overachiever making us all look bad. A
> hot boyfriend. Check. Girl boss. Check. Winning
> in life. Check. *winking emoji*

Grace

> Aww, stop it. You're next. I know it. You'll find
> your man and then I'll make fun of you. And I'm
> only starting a business. You're going to get a
> PhD and change the world. You're the one win-
> ning in life.

My lips twitch as I read the messages from my sister and my girl-friends. Grace went through some hell last year, but she's now happily settled down with her financial titan boyfriend, Steven Kingsley. My sister, Irish twins as others call us since she's only ten months older than me, deserves all the happiness in the world.

Belle

> Ugh. I'm a failure all around then lol. Not only
> do I have to deal with my slimy boss every day,
> there are no hot men in my vicinity. No hot
> boyfriend. Check. Not acing my career. Check.

Grace

> How's that possible? You work in the fashion in-
> dustry. How are there no hot men?

Belle

> Okay, I amend that. No hot *straight* men. And
> wait a minute, why are we talking about me?

I snort before grinning, my earlier frustration lessening. Annabelle Law-McKenzie, known to friends as Belle, is the only child of a fashion empire, but unlike other rich kids, she's working her way up from the bottom at her family's company and is one of the sweetest and most down-to-earth people I know.

Millie

> Sorry to disappoint, but I can't go tonight. My asshole of a professor gave us a lot to do. I'll be holed up in the apartment for the foreseeable future.

Millie

> Tay, you're still going to the open house at The Orchid with Grace next week to check out their new amenities, right?

Grace

> The Rose floors! *Devil emoji* You should come with, Millie.

Millie

> Um. No, thank you.

Grace

> You never know. Maybe you'll find your kink there.

I groan at the idea of going to that exclusive establishment for the rich and famous, but on a whim, I promised Grace I'd go with her after I read the newest therapy book I bought—*The Wonderful and Terrifying Year of Yeses*—a book recommended online about saying yes to new experiences and living without fear.

I'm about to type my response when I feel the menacing stare from earlier again. Only this time it's more potent, more laser focused.

A frisson of unease slithers through my body. More messages ping through on my cell phone, but I can't focus. I feel like I'm crawling out of my skin.

Just as I'm about to search for the asshole who's staring at me, someone claps loudly, interrupting the lively activity in the studio.

"May I have your attention, please!" Madame Renoir announces to the crowd.

A hush descends in the room. We turn toward the double doors where Madame Renoir is standing.

My gaze sweeps over the large space, past the other demi-soloists and the corps de ballet, the company musicians with their instruments huddling in one corner, when my eyes inadvertently land on the second floor balcony.

And I see *him*.

The asshole who's making me uncomfortable with his intense scrutiny.

It's the arrogant CEO, Charles.

He was striking from the earlier glimpses of him, but nothing could've prepared me for the sight of him from the front. The earlier charismatic demeanor is gone, and in its place is something far more formidable.

I notice his startling eyes first. An angry forcefulness radiating from them that steals my breath. A pair of eyes on a face so compelling, I can't seem to look away.

Cold daylight shines down from the skylight above him, bathing his figure in a stark aura. His stunning blond hair appears almost white under the bluish light. His square jawline with an enticing divot on his chin and just enough scruff gives his stately appearance an edge of roughness.

A streak of danger.

He looks older than me by at least ten years. Madame Renoir drones on, but my mind can't seem to compute her words as I'm locked in this strange staring contest with him.

Heat crawls up my neck, every nerve ending standing at attention. My body is priming to fight or flee, and I know I'm blushing like an innocent coed, which I'm anything but, but I refuse to look away.

From this predator, because that's who he is. There's no way he's the prey. Then I'm reminded of his response to his buddies outside the bathroom and his comment to the crowd downstairs.

Rich assholes. How typical. *Not all rich men are assholes, Taylor. You don't even know him.*

I know that. Logically, I understand that. But they say first impressions are lasting.

And clearly, judging from the way this Norse god of thunder is staring at me, he doesn't seem to like me much either.

In fact, he looks at me with murder in his eyes.

CHAPTER 6

SHE WAS BUTCHERING THE dance. A bloody massacre. Killing the beautiful swan in front of my eyes.

I recognized her the moment I laid eyes on her. She was the dancer I saw on TV in Firefly's room a few weeks ago. The alluring woman with the haunted eyes so captivating, I couldn't look away. My breath quickened when I spotted that raven hair, and for a brief second, I was breathless with anticipation.

She took me away from my dark thoughts when I was in Firefly's room. What magic would she wield for me today? Could she distract me from the damn mess I found myself in?

But no, I was clearly mistaken before. The woman on the TV was a beautiful mystery—multi-layered and fascinating and this woman here...

She was a volcano threatening to level everything and everyone around her.

My blood pressure rose inside me as I watched her flail her arms and legs out like she wanted to strangle the white swan with her bare hands. Instead of drawing me away from the guilt threatening to eat me alive, I was consumed with useless what-ifs.

Firefly would've hated this. Her favorite ballet, reduced to a toddler's tantrum. If she were here, she would've done justice to the role. She would've taken it seriously.

Then the minx twisted her ankle and tripped.

Her entire persona changed from a fierce ballerina to a goth brat throwing a fit in public. She wiggled her ass, muttering what seemed to be a litany of curses, then plopped down to the ground and started texting.

Like she didn't care. Like she didn't know how important dancing the role of Odette in *Swan Lake* was for a world-renowned ballet company.

Because not everyone got to have that chance.

Maybe Firefly would be the one dancing Odette if you'd made a different choice back then. If you'd only—

The goth brat smirked at her phone and I wanted to smear her dark lipstick and wipe that damn smile off her face.

Calm down, Charles. You know what happens to people who are too emotional. They become unstable. They become irresponsible.

And now she's staring at me, her gaze widening with something...shock? Terror? Somehow, seeing that frightened expression sends a thrill through my veins. No one has ever reacted this way to me in public—I'm the charismatic CEO everyone loves. The golden prince.

It's like she could see through me.

And something about that makes my skin sizzle with awareness.

The air crackles with intensity. The minx narrows her eyes and juts out her chin, her body rigid and defiant, as if daring me to go down there and give her a piece of my mind.

My fingers clench—if she were a sub in one of the kink clubs inside The Orchid, I'd discipline her because of that insolent expression on her face. My jaw twitches, and an unfamiliar fire gathers at the base of my spine as the air gets sucked out of the cavernous room.

Suddenly, she gets up and walks toward the front of the group. I know I should be down there too because they're making introductions soon. But I can't seem to move. My heart is racing—from anger, frustration, unsettling arousal—a barrage of strange and unwanted sensations hitting me from all sides.

It doesn't make any sense.

Or maybe it does. *After all, Charles, you are your parents' child. Maybe instability runs in your blood.*

Fuck.

Ignoring the heated stare from that asshole, I smooth my damp palms on my leotard and stand beside Madame Renoir in front of the room. The businessmen from earlier are also gathered there and I swallow the revulsion rising in my throat when the bald one doles out a sleazy grin.

Bethany smiles at me, still very much a picture of angelic grace. It'd be easy to hate her if she weren't so nice. I quickly nod at her and force out a smile.

"As I was saying, it's been an honor to be in this position for the last ten years, and I'm proud to have seen such growth from everyone. But alas, it's time for me to retire. Fortunately, with Bank of Columbia's sponsorship of ABTC, they've brought on the world-renowned artistic director and choreographer, Sir Ian Vaughn, to take over my position in a year and a half after he completes his current contract in France. Please welcome Sir Ian with your warmest applause."

Cheers and clapping erupt in the crowd as folks recognize the name of the mysterious director behind the recent popularity of modern ballet in Paris. I follow suit, wondering if I'll get along with my new boss, if he'll support me in the promotion. I try to ignore the pinch of concern about him being a man. This is a professional setting, after all.

I should be fine.

Then the suits move to the side, letting a lean, middle-aged man with aristocratic bearing through.

Time freezes as the world spins around me.

My stomach drops to the floor and the sudden disorientation makes me want to throw up the contents of my breakfast.

Blond hair. Light eyes. That jawline.

No. No, no, no. It can't be.

I shake my head, cold sweat forming on my neck. My breathing ratchets up into desperate gasps as I clutch my leotard, unable to tear my eyes away from the man striding toward us with a wide smile on his face, saying hi to the people around him.

"Are you okay, Taylor? You look pale," Bethany whispers as she discreetly holds onto my arm, and I realize I'm trembling.

I couldn't answer her.

Because I'm seeing things I shouldn't be seeing. Hearing things I shouldn't be hearing.

"Fly, Harriet."

"*Merci beaucoup*, Mademoiselle Renoir," Sir Ian speaks.

The unmistakable raspy voice.

The man I remember in my tattered memory—the blurry and ever-changing visage of the monster who's haunted me since I was sixteen. *No. I'm healed already. I have everything under control. The past is in the past, and I'm in the present, moving on. Stop it, Lochness Monster!*

"No one would miss you, little beauty," the ghostly voice whispers.

Sir Ian scans the room before his gaze lands on me. He beams and extends his hand.

A distinct whiff of peppermint reaches my nose. The same smell from that night.

The world spins around me, the thundering pounding of my racing pulse eclipsing the sounds in the room. My chest heaves.

It can't be him. Do you even remember what he looks like? You were drugged.

I can't breathe. Fuck. *Why can't I breathe?*

The people in the room morph into menacing dark shadows, and every atom in my body screeches at me to leave. The looming shadows move toward me.

Danger. I need to run. To escape them. *Not again.*

Screaming, I dart forward, desperate to flee from the monsters, my blood frenzied and hot, when suddenly someone grabs my wrist and holds on tightly.

I can't move. Again.

The room fades away and I'm thrusted into the nightmare of my horrid memories.

Darkness cloaked me, my limbs feeling heavy. I could barely keep my eyes open, but whenever I'd open them, I'd see lights and colors streaking across my vision. I was so dizzy. Disoriented.

Everything came in fragments. Sounds of belt buckles clinking, zippers wrenching down, low grunts and raucous laughter. My dress ripping.

Their large hands. Two of them. No four. Or was it more? How many of them were there?

Heaviness. Pressure. Lots of pain. *No, I don't want this. I don't want any of this!*

My body wouldn't obey me as my mind slowly caught up to what was happening to me.

I'm not here. I'm nowhere. This is a nightmare, and I'd wake up at any second.

"My beautiful Harriet. Fly, Harriet." The same voice again. Then something happened. A strange sensation between my legs—the fire morphing into something else. I tried to speak, but only a moan slipped out.

"We're just having fun, little beauty."

Stop it. I don't want this. Stop. No words would come out. A flash of red winked at me. I focused on it.

Blond hair. Light eyes. Were they green? Blue? Gray? A masculine jawline.

I'm not here. I'm far, far away.

"Look at her thrashing. She's going to come, isn't she?"

Peppermint. It smelled like peppermint. Like Christmas.

Wake up! My wrist throbs and someone is shaking me hard. I open my mouth to scream and this time my voice works.

"No! Get away!"

Bright lights sear into my eyes as the pain in my wrist wrenches me away from that dark place. My heart rams itself against my rib cage, threatening to give up on me.

My vision swirls—I'm in the eye of the tornado—and I finally see the large masculine hand gripping my wrist and I go ballistic.

"Let go of me, asshole!" My body finally regaining function, I swing my free arm at my assailant, a punch landing in a hard smack. Gasps and screams of horror and shock ring out in the room.

My assailant lets go of me and I heave in a sigh of relief. Then, another face pops into my vision—blond middle-aged man with light eyes. Peppermint. Sir Ian.

My eyes widen in horror. "T-The smell...it's the same smell," I whisper.

Panic slams through me, and I scream before shoving him hard. He staggers back a few steps before a few dancers catch him. "It's been six years! I'm over this. The past is in the past!" Nonsensical words flow out of me, my mind still half-suspended in a flashback so real, so terrifying, I can't reorient myself.

A sudden whiff of lavender reaches my nose. "Tay, Tay! Snap out of it, oh my God. Tay, calm down!"

Lisa.

Expelling deep breaths, I close my eyes and listen to the roaring sounds of my heartbeat. Lisa wraps me tightly in her arms and my legs nearly give out from underneath me. After a few seconds, which seems like minutes, I open my eyes.

Slowly, the room comes back into focus—businessmen and dancers, Madame Renoir, her hand covering her mouth in horror, a wall of mirrors, wooden floors, daylight.

I'm in the dance studio.

Acid churns in my stomach as my heart rate slows. *What have I done?*

Sir Ian stares at me with concern and I flinch as I take in his appearance again. My mind screams for me to leave, that the man in front of me is dangerous. He steps forward and I hold up my hand. "S-Stop. Stay away from me!"

"What the *fuck* is wrong with you?" a deep voice growls from my right.

I slowly turn toward him, my heart quaking in my chest. I take in the expensive, shiny dress shoes, expertly tailored pants and suit, a muscle twitching on a masculine jaw—a jaw and lips that are currently red from where I punched him earlier.

Murderous sky-blue eyes. Blond hair like a crown on a king. *Oh shit.*

I smacked him. Charles. The sponsor of the ballet company. The man keeping the lights on in this place. The man I need to depend on for my livelihood.

What have I done?

CHAPTER 7

Acid churns in my stomach, each wave higher than the last. I'm seasick on dry land as the god of thunder hurls lightning bolts at me with his stormy eyes.

"Taylor! Apologize to Sir Ian and Mr. Vaughn *at once*! What has gotten into you? This is unacceptable and we at ABTC do not condone this behavior! I'm afraid I'll—"

The tsunami of her words crashes over me, the tiny voice inside my mind finally piercing through the craze. *No. No. Please don't fire me. Oh God, I haven't had a flashback that intense for years. Why now? Why the fuck now?*

My pulse bangs against my ears, panic making my vision blurry, and I feel sick to my stomach again. I need to fix this. I need ballet—the only thing I have left.

I need to apologize.

Staring at the furious man whose blistering stare is rendering me immobile, I mutter, "I...I'm...I'm sorry. Please...Please don't..."

I can't get the words out. A heavy sense of shame washes over me—why am I apologizing? He grabbed me first—he didn't let me leave.

He didn't know you had a flashback because Sir Ian reminded you of the monster, the man you don't really remember because your mind was too drugged up that night.

I finally notice the notes of cedarwood and bergamot in the air—his scent—and I realize how close we're standing. I quickly stagger back a few steps.

"You *will* apologize to my uncle as well," he commands in that deep, raspy voice. Goosebumps flicker to life on my arms.

His uncle. This intimidating asshole is Sir Ian's nephew. I feel light-headed as I sneak a glance over at the man himself, an involuntary tremor of fear rushing through my body.

I shake myself—I'm going insane. It can't be him. I don't even remember what he looks like, right? But still, my mind is fighting the apology at the tip of my tongue. I shake my head. I can't apologize to him when fear is all I'm feeling whenever I look at him.

"I can't," I whisper. "I can't."

Charles recoils at my words, his eyes darkening. A muscle twitches in his jaw.

"Charles—" Sir Ian says, but the looming god in front of me holds up his hand.

"This is unacceptable," Charles grits out, his eyes pinned on me.

Someone tugs on my shoulder. A reassuring scent of lavender. Lisa, the voice of reason, trying to save me yet again.

She rises to her tiptoes and whispers in my ear, "Whatever it is, it isn't worth your career. Everything you've worked for! They're going to fire you! You hit our sponsor in the face!"

Her words are like a fire extinguisher to the fiery rage incinerating my body and what remains is bone-deep fear.

Everything I've worked for. My sacrifices. Grace and Mom's sacrifices.

My gaze becomes unfocused and nausea comes roaring back in full force.

I can't breathe. Lisa is right. Just apologize and get out of here, Taylor. Sweat gathers on my forehead. I stare in Sir Ian's direction, not meeting him in the eye. "I-I'm s-sorry, sir."

The room breathes a collective sigh of relief, as if we've averted a crisis, but I don't feel any relief at all. My fingers tingle. My skin itches. I want to claw myself. I want the pain, tons of it.

I can't breathe. My lungs rattle from exertion. *I can't breathe.*

I need to go home. I need to—

"Look, young lady. Obviously, there's been some misunderstanding. We've all made mistakes before and I don't fault you for it," Sir Ian begins, his voice still sending shivers down my spine.

I shrink further into my mind.

Lisa clutches my shoulder tightly and I'm never more grateful for her presence than now.

"But I really haven't met you before. I'm not sure what's going on, but whatever it is, you're mistaken."

Unshed tears blur my vision as I grip my wrist, trying to stem the shudders from showing.

I won't cry for him. For them.

Glancing up, I finally take in Sir Ian's concerned face. His blue eyes are crinkled as if he's sincerely concerned by this turn of events. Charles stands slightly in front of him, his arms crossed—a formidable sentry—like he's afraid I'm going to finish what I started and he'll protect his uncle with his life.

Sir Ian smiles softly. "I don't want my career here to begin on a bad note. Let's start over, shall we? I'll forget about this if you can. And I'm sure Charles will forgive and forget too." He looks at his nephew.

My heart hammers inside my chest. I stare at those blue eyes again. Clear. Innocent eyes. Could I've been mistaken? After all, I was drugged. *Were his eyes really blue? Wasn't it dark, Taylor? You couldn't even describe him to a sketch artist.*

Doubts rain in my mind.

"Charles?" Sir Ian murmurs.

Charles stares at me, the fire burning hot in his eyes. His head dips into the barest of nods.

My lips tremble as I finally take in the rest of the room—my colleagues whispering furtively to each other, Ainsley and the other trainees' faces crumbling with obvious concern. My skin heats and I swivel my attention to Madame Renoir, who looks like she's about to have an aneurysm.

Hanging my head, I whisper again, "I'm sorry."

I flee from the room.

Half an hour later, I trap myself in the bathroom of my tiny studio apartment in the Theater District. Murky steam from the shower fogs up the mirror. I watch as the vapors swirl and slither, foreboding, much like the darkness that has tainted my soul that fateful night.

A sentient being intent on ruining me.

My pulse is rioting in my veins as I rake in deep inhales. *It was a flashback, the worst flashback I've had in years. It's not reality. I'm safe now. No one will hurt me anymore.*

I repeat my affirmations. All the self-help books recommend this. But I still feel like a thousand ants are crawling on my body.

I need pain. I need control. The past is in the past. Not the present. *I'm calm. I'm in control.*

With trembling hands, I pull open the top drawer of the bathroom counter and grab an unassuming plastic box—my lifesaving kit for sanity. Flicking the lid open, I pull out a large-gauge needle. Just the needle, no syringe, no illegal substances. I haven't sunk to that level yet. I glance at my reflection under the florescent lights again.

Bloodless, pale skin—lifeless like my soul. Messy, black strands I've tugged again and again on my subway ride back home. Red-rimmed eyes that look haunted.

Everything is okay, Taylor. Pain. You need pain to ground you. We've been through this before. Regression is okay. It's normal.

Holding my breath, I slide the needle underneath my skin on my inner thigh, away from the veins, and flinch from the searing pain as I twist it inside my wound. I watch my blood drip out slowly.

One drop. Two drops. Three drops.

The darkness spreading on the white floor.

The initial gutting pain calms the jitters in my body. *Focus on the pain, Taylor. Control it. Everything else doesn't matter.*

Closing my eyes, the muscles in my shoulders slowly loosen and I take in my first real breath since my outburst at the studio.

I shouldn't be doing this. This isn't healthy.

Logic beckons me to listen to it. Imploring me to let the past go. Hurting myself now won't ever erase my trauma—it just prolongs the agony. But I don't know any alternative. It's the only thing keeping me going. It's my ritual when flashbacks get this bad.

After that horrible night, I tried the cops, who took one look at me and said I had no evidence because I washed everything away. I tried therapy, but I couldn't make the words come out. I remember sitting in the tiny room, staring at the annoying fly buzzing near the ceiling, the therapist latching onto the fact I couldn't remember everything. And I couldn't afford anything out of pocket—too fucking expensive.

I was mute. Silenced.

You're better than this, Taylor. You're stronger. A fighter. Plenty of women have suffered worse and they have their shit together.

My mind refuses to listen, and instead, those voices barge into my mind again.

"Fly, Harriet."

"Let's have some fun, shall we?"

More unwanted memories barrel in, crashing through the uneasy calm. The needle isn't enough. I need more. *I got this.* I breathe in and out for a count of five.

Tossing the needle to the floor, I scramble inside the shower, wincing as the piping hot water singes my skin. My mind on autopilot, I reach for the body wash and rub it over myself, then I grab my loofah and scrub. My ritual. *I can do this.*

Scrub. Scrub. Scrub.

My pale skin turns flushed, then pink. Raw. I still feel disgusting. Dirty.

I pinch the piercing on top of my clit—more grounding pain. I crave it.

I curl up in the corner and bury my face in my hands. My eyes burn as much as my skin does. It's like my chest is being torn apart fiber by fiber. My lungs rake in a deep inhale. I can breathe now.

Feel the pain. Welcome the pain. Purge your thoughts.

It's just a flashback. You're safe now.

I shudder and hold my knees tighter against me, all the while letting the hot water wash away my shame, my darkness, mourning a loss I thought I'd put behind me.

I remember a little girl falling in love for the first time, dreaming about a future where anything is possible.

I remember the warm embrace of a boy I thought loved me, not an ounce of fear inside me as I watch him brush a lock of hair from my face.

I remember dancing on the stage, donned in pure white, angelic with grace, as my instructor marveled at the beauty of my Odette.

Why did I react that way to Sir Ian? Was it him all those years ago? But he didn't act like he recognized you.

My mind swirls in confusion—I don't know what's up or down anymore.

My immediate impulse is to quit everything and run away—to hide from all unpleasant memories and sensations. But as I breathe in the moisture in the shower and feel my muscles slowly relaxing, logic beckons at the door.

I've worked hard to get to where I am, one step away from reaching the pinnacle of my career. I don't know what happened today and why I reacted that way, but until I know more, I can't make rash decisions.

It's okay. I have time. He isn't coming for another year and a half. Maybe I'll remember something by then. Maybe...maybe I'll finally be able to put the past behind me.

Heaving out an exhale, I relish the scalding hot water lashing on to my skin. *Focus on the pain.*

"*Fly, Harriet.*"

I'll never be able to fly again. My wings are clipped.

But I'll survive, just like the black swan from Mom's story.

CHAPTER 8

THE SULTRY MUSIC THUMPS in my ears. It's an eclectic mix of jazz and hip-hop, sensuous and raw. I'm surprised to find myself actually enjoying the glitzy surroundings.

I take a sip of the carrot vodka flambé the bartender recommended when I first arrived at the rooftop bar in The Orchid for its invite only open house.

Grace settles next to me, a fruity drink in her hand. She eyes my cocktail and arches her brow. "Carrot again?"

"You know it." I waggle my brow.

Shaking her head, she sighs. "I miss this, Tay. You and I never go out anymore. You're busy with ballet and I'm busy with work."

"And your boyfriend." I snort, watching her flush a pretty pink. It's almost sickening how much she and Steven are in love with each other.

I ignore the small twinge in my chest. It's also very sweet.

"And Steven." She chuckles.

"You know you have an open invite to watch *Stalk Me if You Dare* later tonight!" I wink, knowing she'll give me shit about it. "I can't believe they made three back-to-back movies to be released one after the other. Marketing brilliance. Heaven is listening."

Grace shudders in mock horror. "How are we even related? I like my swoony romance and you and your blood and gore."

"It's satisfying. Gets the heart pumping. What do you say? I'm ordering pizza like the old days."

She laughs. "Ah, the good ol' days. I always had to hide in the bedroom while you watched that crap. Call me if you want to watch *The*

Notebook afterward. That I can get behind." She lets out a satisfied sigh. "Do you remember when we were kids, we'd walk past this building, wondering if we'll ever get in?"

I grin, thinking back to our childhood. Sometimes, when Mom was at work, Grace and I would ditch high school and wander on Fifth Avenue, eyeing all the expensive clothes costing more than our rent, the hordes of tourists snapping photos of the most famous street in New York City. We'd always make it a point to stop in front of the fifty-plus story building housing The Orchid.

We'd stand there in the sweltering heat, dressed in ripped jeans and thrifted T-shirts, jaw slacked at the chrome and glass exteriors of the building rumored to have everything anyone could ever dream of—top Michelin restaurants, spas, suites, bars, gyms, and other amenities. We'd even tried entering one time, only to be kicked out by the security decked in their suits and ties.

Grace vowed to me then she'd make it one day on her own and be rich and powerful enough to get one of these exclusive invitations even money couldn't buy.

"It's funny how things turned out, don't you think?" She smiles.

"I'm happy for you, sis." I nudge her gently on the side.

It *is* funny how things turned out. The girl who didn't want love because she didn't want to depend on anyone ended up being hopelessly in love with a wonderful man who treats her like the queen.

And the girl who wished she could find her prince and dance with him until the end of time ended up...

Broken.

The pinch in my chest becomes a throbbing ache. *None of that shit, Lochness Monster! Go away!*

"Ladies, glad to see you here," a deep voice murmurs and we turn to see Ethan striding toward us with a few of our half-siblings and Steven in tow, looking like stock photos for handsome, powerful businessmen in their tailored suits and shiny shoes.

"Wouldn't miss it for the world. You guys are unveiling a few new lounges and spaces in here. So exciting!" Grace smiles at him as Ethan pulls her into a side hug.

He grins, a dimple appearing on one side of his face, and the transformation is almost astonishing. Even though he's the second youngest in the Anderson sibling pecking order, Ethan is serious and sharp, part of what makes him a great CFO.

"I approve. I was afraid of my sisters being boring like someone over here," Rex quips, waggling his brows at Ethan, who rolls his eyes heavenward.

"How are you older than me, C? Are our birth certificates wrong?" Ethan mutters, referring to his older brother by a year with his middle initial.

Apparently, there were too many Anderson offsprings, so their parents alphabetized their middle names—Maxwell, the eldest with the middle name Angus, Ryland with Benedict, Rex with something he won't tell us, but it starts with a C. Then Ethan with Delaney, and Lana with Elise.

It turned out Mom secretly continued the tradition with our middle names. Grace is Felicity and mine is Gianna.

Maybe our lives would've turned out differently if we discovered our lineage earlier. The Andersons are a rare breed—even I have to admit they have good heads on their shoulders despite hailing from one of the richest and most powerful families in the country.

"So, have you checked out the new spaces yet? I spent a lot of time working with the designers on them." Rex arches his brow expectantly.

"He only worked on one of them," Ethan murmurs. "Because interior design is *not* part of the business of our chief marketing officer. He only butt in because he's going to take advantage of that space."

"Which space?" I ask.

The brothers stare at each other, and just as Rex is about to answer, another person joins us.

"The Sanctuary on the Rose floors, which you ladies will *not* visit," Ryland announces, referring to the few floors in the building dedicated to pursuits of a more lustful nature.

"Why not? We're adults." I scowl at my second-eldest brother, the Prince of the USA as the media calls him, the more charismatic half of the brooding Anderson fraternal twins. He's the powerhouse of the family—chief operating officer by day and college professor by night.

Ryland smirks. "Barely legal. Nope. Not happening."

"Stick to bossing your students around, Ryland, not us," Grace quips as Steven slides up to her and pulls her to his side. The king of Wall Street loosens his tie and unleashes a devastating smile as Grace melts into his embrace.

"She's got a point, Ryland. They aren't your students. They're modern, independent women who can decide for themselves." Steven presses a soft kiss on my sister's lips.

Like I said—disgustingly besotted with each other.

"Sellout, Steven. You're a sellout," Ethan mutters, his dark eyes twinkling.

"Who's selling what? You guys aren't giving me another PR nightmare to deal with, right?" Lana, our older sister, sweeps in, her long brown hair tied up in a ponytail. She's the head of PR at Fleur.

"Ryland thinks as women, we can't visit the Rose floors," Grace volunteers, doling out an evil smile at Ryland.

Lana narrows her eyes. "As if! Stick to bossing your students around!" Grace gives her a high five.

Ryland chuckles and rakes his fingers through his perfectly coiffed hair. "A smart man knows when to shut up when he's outnumbered."

"Where's Maxwell?" Grace asks, looking for our oldest brother.

"In his cave, as usual—painting and brooding. Couldn't drag him out."

"But he's the CEO. Shouldn't he be here?"

"The frigid king doesn't attend *commoner* events. This is why we have our prince here." Rex claps Ryland on the shoulder and Ryland lets out an exasperated sigh.

Steven tips Grace's chin up and whispers, "You want to stay for longer? I've cleared my plans for the evening. We can do some exploring."

Grace flushes and bites her bottom lip, looking like she's down for any exploring Steven has in mind. Suddenly, she freezes, and I know she's thinking about me, because she looks my way with a question in her eyes. *Do you want to come with us?*

I shake my head and strain a smile. There's no way I'll be a third-wheel. "I have ballet practice. You guys have fun."

"You sure?"

I nod and Grace pulls me into a light hug. "Okay, don't work too hard, our next principal ballerina! Don't be too good or everyone will hate you. No one likes a showoff." She winks before sinking back into Steven's embrace.

"Pssh. Competition only makes you work harder. They can eat my dust." I dole out a lazy wink, pushing down a pinch of guilt for not telling her about what happened and my resulting demotion. Madame Renoir told me despite ABTC's zero tolerance policy toward violence, Sir Ian really wanted to forget the snafu and they decided to give me another chance. But I was demoted from soloist to demi-soloist, which was lucky, all things considering.

It's better to keep Grace in the dark. She'd ask questions if she knew. Questions I don't want to answer because she still doesn't know what happened to me that night. Maybe it's pride. Maybe it's PTSD from what Camden and Alexis did, or what the cops and therapist didn't do. I don't want her to look at me differently or handle me with kid gloves. I don't want her to see me as damaged. I want to be the Taylor Peyton I used to be in her eyes. Maybe if she sees me as that person, then...

That person would still exist.

She cackles. "That's my badass ballerina."

Waving goodbye to my siblings and Steven, I head toward the elevators, the ball in my throat growing by the minute.

"Have you visited The Sanctuary?" a woman standing in front of the elevators asks her friend.

"I haven't. Definitely planning to, though." Her companion giggles. "Anything new on the Rose floors is always worth checking out. I tell you—the Anderson men are gentlemen in public but beasts in the sheets."

I almost vomit in my mouth at the idea of my half brothers being anything in the sheets, but my ears prickle at the mention of the Rose floors. Grace told me they have rooms for every kink there—a voyeur lounge, a faux outdoor forest for doing the deed outside, glamorous strip clubs, private suites with special equipment and toys. There's also a companionship service—men and women who sign nondisclosure agreements and provide anything from fake dates to the entire boyfriend/girlfriend experience with happy endings.

More hushed laughter echoes in the elegant foyer, and I glance at the ladies as we step into the spacious marble elevator. They eye my attire—bleached jeans and a black T-shirt—in distaste and look away as if they know I shouldn't be here mingling with the likes of them.

But too bad for them. Being an Anderson earns me a lifetime ticket to do as I please. So screw them. Ah, the irony—my distrust for rich people before, but now I'm one of them.

Even so, pettiness feels so good.

Crossing my arms over my chest, I stare them down until they shift uncomfortably and look away. The elevator dings, indicating we've reached the ground floor. Hiding my smirk, I glance at the button panel as the doors open and the women scurry out. I follow them.

"Anything new on the Rose floors is always worth checking out." Their words vibrate in my mind. My feet stutter to a stop.

I think back to the therapy books I've read over the last six years—putting myself out there, having a year of yeses, exposure therapy, overcoming tragedy and all the rainbows and butterflies to follow. It's been six years. It's time for me to reclaim my body and sexuality.

My skin breaks out in hives as cold sweat beads on my back. *Saying yes to new experiences doesn't mean checking out the Rose floors when you're a survivor. Don't be an idiot, Taylor.*

The elevator doors start closing, and I stick my hand out to block them from shutting.

"Look at this slut asking for it. Let's have some fun."

My breath catches. I'm tired of it—of the past haunting me, never letting me go.

Visions of Grace smiling at Steven with hearts in her eyes. The way they fold into each other's embrace.

Don't you want what they have? To be with a man without fear? Even if it's just for sex?

Phantom hands graze my body and my skin itches. My pulse rams into my ears like a freight train.

"You'll never be free of me," the imaginary voice whispers, a ghostly menace filling the elevator.

No. I refuse. The past won't define me. I'm in charge of my future. I might not want to trust men or open myself up emotionally again after Camden, but I *will* take back control over my body—to be with men without breaking out in hives.

To experience sex. Sex that I consent to.

Heaving in a deep breath, I retreat into the elevator and press the button for The Sanctuary.

The doors quietly slide closed with a click and I'm on the move.

CHAPTER 9

I REGRET MY DECISION the moment I step into the lobby of The Sanctuary. Heat rushes to my face and my hands grow clammy. The lobby is tasteful, unassuming, and elegant. Everything is decorated in dark beige and black leather, with soft recessed lighting shining on a lady in a red minidress working behind a chrome receptionist's desk.

But I know what has to lie beyond the dark double doors behind her.

Sex. Debauchery.

And from what I'm hearing in stray conversations of couples and groups gathered in front of the receptionist...

BDSM.

My skin feels sensitive, like the barely visible wounds from my maladaptive needle poking behavior has been ripped right open. *What am I thinking? Being here? Why did you think this would be a vanilla, run-of-the-mill sex club? This is the last place a person like you should be in.*

I turn toward the exit. I want to throw up.

You were trying your year of yeses again.

Fuck that damn book. I'm sure *The Wonderful and Terrifying Year of Yeses* wasn't written for someone with messed up post traumatic disorder. I might as well give it to someone else. Maybe Belle. She could use some excitement in her life.

Mired in my thoughts, I don't pay attention and plow into a willowy person who wobbles on her feet from my impact.

"Oh my God, I'm so sorry." I quickly reach out and steady her before she topples over.

A black-haired Asian girl wearing a gray dress suit, looking completely out of place just like me, stares back, clearly bewildered. I grin, sensing kinship immediately—she doesn't belong here anymore than I do.

"It's okay." She smiles, and her expressive brown eyes behind her stylish glasses look me up and down before she leans in and whispers, "You nervous too?"

I bite my lip. "That obvious?"

She nods. "I'm a psychiatrist. I'm good at identifying tells. You're gripping your arm and flushed...not in a good way too."

I groan to myself. "This is so stupid. What was I thinking—"

"Want to go inside with me?" She motions toward the double doors.

I blanch and shake my head. "S-Sorry, I'm not, you know, into women. Not that I think chicks aren't cool, I just am not—"

She laughs. "No, no, no, that's not what I meant. I'm straight and into men too, but I'm nervous about going in there by myself and figured you must be here for a reason, so we might as well psych each other up."

My shoulders relax and I let out an exhale. "Oh."

"You'd be doing me a favor, really. I'm here purely for professional reasons."

I arch my brow. *That's a new one.* "How is going to a BDSM club a professional visit?"

She purses her lips before extending her hand. "I'm Olivia, by the way. Olivia Lin. My practice specializes in anxiety disorders and addiction. Of which, a common one is sex addiction. I have a few patients who frequent establishments such as these and I want to better understand them. So," she motions to the dark space, "field trip."

Olivia looks up at me imploringly. She's tiny and I feel like a giant next to her. "Please? Help me, yeah?"

She reminds me a little of Belle and Millie combined—sweet, sassy, intelligent. I relent, her plea giving me the small amount of confidence boost I need to do this.

I'm not here for me this time. I'm here for a new friend. *And you're a badass. Let's not forget that.*

Swallowing, I shake her hand. "Taylor, but friends call me Tay."

Olivia beams and we head over to the receptionist, who gives us the lay of the land behind the closed doors. Consent is paramount. We're one hundred percent safe in there. There's a two drink maximum policy. There are open group spaces and private quarters. Protection is required unless we have signed waivers and health consents. Security will patrol the place and if we feel threatened, we can press a small button on the silver bracelet she gave each of us, and help will be on the way.

I feel a little better—it sounds like I'll be safe in there. My palms grow sweaty.

"Ready?" Olivia whispers as we pause in front of the double doors.

"Never." I take a deep breath, my pulse kicking up. "But here goes."

We push through and step into a large, modern room lit up with soft recessed lighting, highlighting the circular tables with wraparound black leather sofas spaced throughout. At a quick glance, one would *almost* think they're at a run-of-the-mill high-end lounge.

But then I notice the groups sitting in the leather booths. One table has a scantily clad woman in leather lingerie, her mouth gagged with a black ball, and three men in suits flanking her. Another corner has a man tied to the table, his ass exposed, and he's writhing as another man stuffs something up his backside.

Heat blooms on my face and nausea appears violently in my stomach again.

Sounds of skin slapping against skin. Harsh groans and lewd moans. *"Look at that slut, asking for it,"* that voice whispers in my mind.

I push the thought out of my mind. *Leave me the fuck alone!*

"Whoa, this is um. Interesting. Hey," someone snaps her finger at me, "hey, Tay! You okay?"

Dazed, I glance at a flushed Olivia who is frowning at me with obvious concern.

I force out a smile, but I have a feeling it doesn't work on her because she just cocks her head to the side, her eyes sharpening. Damn my luck for making a new friend who is a psychiatrist.

"You want to leave? You know, you don't need to do this until you're ready," she says. She doesn't ask me what's wrong, which I appreciate. Her voice is soothing, and I try to focus on it.

I have a feeling she's using her doctor voice on me.

"N-No. I can do this." I give her a shaky nod.

She stares at me for a few more beats and then nods. "Stay here. I'll get some water for you. That can help." She leaves before I can stop her and tell her I don't accept drinks I haven't gotten for myself.

"Hey beautiful, looking for a Dom for the night?" a low voice rasps in my ear a few seconds later.

I jump in place and stifle a scream. Turning toward the man, I blanch when I take in his towering frame clad in a suit. He's too close—standing way too close to me. His eyes gleam with nefarious intent.

"You're gorgeous. I'll take good care of you," he murmurs, his voice dripping with fake charm I'm sure will work on other women.

Not me. Not anymore.

I back away, shaking my head vigorously. My heart beats violently and I curse myself for trembling in his presence.

"S-Stay away from me. Stay away, asshole."

He holds his hands up, his eyes narrowing. "No need to go crazy, you frigid bitch. You should be lucky—"

I don't stay for the rest of his words as I walk away, as fast as my legs can carry me, not paying attention to where I'm going. The sounds of moaning and screams of pleasure burrow into my ears the farther I go—shit, I'm heading in the wrong direction.

The lustful noises are louder now, but they don't sound pleasurable to me. They sound like torture.

My mind blanks as my strides quicken. I want to escape, to be anywhere but here.

But aren't you trying to get over your fear? Don't you want to control your body? To have sex like a normal human being?

Don't you want to dance Odette? How can you dance her when you're so angry all the time?

The questions are bullets to my mind, hitting me from all directions. I break into a jog, my sneakers squeaking against the floor as I hurry past private booths and alcoves decorated with glass and velvet curtains, past more couples in the throes of sexual release, the sound of skin slapping against skin making me want to retch.

Finally, I find my way to a quieter space. It's darker here, almost like the abandoned dance studio I call my second home, and my tense muscles slowly relax. I can almost imagine myself back on the rooftop of ABTC, dancing under the pale moonlight.

Breathing a sigh of relief, the cold AC sweeps across my sweaty skin, and I shudder from the sudden onslaught. This was a bad idea. Maybe I should just resign myself to a loveless and sexless life and be a kickass cat lady. That's safer. Much safer.

Huffing a disappointed chuckle, I walk toward the entrance when I hear it.

Slap. Slap. Slap.

"You want to be punished like this, huh?" a barely audible voice whispers.

"Yes." A soft moan.

Slap. Slap. Slap.

"More." The woman's voice grows desperate.

"See? This is how you punish her for disobeying you. None of the gentle slaps. Let her have it," the man murmurs, and I hear another man respond with a grunt.

"You need to see it again?" the first man asks.

I assume the answer is in the affirmative because I hear a collision of slapping noises again, each one louder than the other.

The woman screams, her cries loud and piercing. My heart slams into my throat.

My instinct is to run away, but something about the first man's voice draws me—commanding, dominant, and yet...the way he asks the woman for her permission, I couldn't get that out of my mind. My breathing is thready, my pulse louder than the beats of the sultry music, and I slowly peek past the half-opened curtains of a private room.

A woman is held down on the couch by a dark-haired man. Sweat pours down her face as her breasts thrust against the air. Her skin is red, and tears are streaking down her cheeks.

Horror streaks through me.

I've made a mistake.

She's crying out in pain.

A light-haired man stands next to her, a whip in his hands.

My feet stay rooted in place and memories of that horrible night assault me again. I break out in a sweat, my breathing coming out in quick pants.

"More?" the blond man asks.

The woman cries out something, but the pulse in my ears drowns out her response. *No.* I shake my head. *No, I can't let this happen. Not to her. No.*

"I'll show you one more time, Colt." The blond sets the whip down on the table, takes off his gray suit jacket, and flings it to the side. Then, I watch in horror him taking out his cufflinks and slowly rolling up his sleeves, showing his muscular forearms.

He grabs the whip again.

"No! Stop it!" I scream.

They turn toward me, and I find myself at a loss for words because the blond man staring back at me, his sky-blue eyes burning like the hottest fire, is none other than Ian Vaughn's nephew.

The angry god of thunder. Charles.

His eyes widen in shock as his hand tightens his grip on the whip.

Then he prowls toward me.

CHAPTER 10

She's shaking like a leaf, terror rolling off her lithe frame in waves.

"N-No." The minx hastily scrambles back, her long legs barely keeping her upright. "Stay away from me."

Her eyes widen in fear as they dart to the whip in my hand, then back to my face, then back to my hand again. Sweat glistens on her forehead.

"S-Stay back!"

I frown, and the unease I felt at ABTC last week when she screamed at Uncle Ian comes roaring back. I was furious then at how an opportunity to dance Odette was squandered by the likes of her, someone who didn't even seem to care about the craft. Then she solidified herself on my shit list when she socked me in the face and had the audacity to insult the only parental figure in my life.

But now, seeing those stormy eyes flash with terror, her earlier fierce countenance nowhere to be seen, a flicker of concern gathers in my gut. Something is wrong. If she were a sub here, and I'm sure she isn't because I've never seen her on the Rose floors before, these would be red flags of someone barreling past their limit.

I step toward her, wanting to do something. *Comfort her? Hold her? Tell her everything is okay? Fuck, why the hell do I care about this hellion? She's not your sub.*

My fingers grip the whip for support—anything to tether myself to reality and calmness. I wonder if merely standing next to a hurricane will make you seasick.

But the gentleman in me can't let a woman—even one I despise—be in this state of terror.

"Are you okay?" I move toward her.

"No!" she screams. "P-Please. St-top." She eyes my hands, panic in those gray pools.

I freeze and slowly drop the whip from my hand. It clatters to the floor like a gong and she flinches. *What the fuck happened to her? Did someone hurt her before?*

The thought sends a torrent of anger up my chest, and I don't know why.

"Taylor," I murmur, and her eyes snap up to mine, clearly surprised I know her name. Well, of course I had to find out after her crazy outburst at ABTC. "No one is hurting you."

She lets out a shaky exhale, her eyes bright with fear.

"You are fine. We're all adults here...just having some fun."

Taylor gasps. Then her entire posture changes as if my words woke up something inside her. Her nostrils flare, her hands balling into fists, and she straightens up.

There's my fierce minx.

What? I recoil at the direction of my thoughts.

"You rich men are all the same. You guys think you can use women because we're physically weaker than you." Her words are murderous, laced with venom. She darts a glance at Kristi behind me, who I'm sure, along with Colt, is gaping at this ridiculous turn of events.

Taylor's face turns redder and her body vibrates—this time, not from fear. I can practically see the flames sparking from her eyes. "It's *disgusting* and sick how you guys get off on hurting women, just like—"

I reach her in two strides and her eyes widen as I tower over her.

Leaning down, I rasp, "Say that again. I dare you. Words have consequences."

I'd never maliciously hurt a woman. Never raise a hand on them in anger. Even in BDSM, the pain I dole out is only to give my partner pleasure—while I love the ability to control their orgasms, the women hold all the power in the scenes. It's also for me to let go of my carefully curated image and embrace the darker desires inside me. But I'd hurt myself before hurting another woman. It's something I firmly believe in.

I fucking despise abusers.

My mind flashes to when Dad would slap Mom across the face when they got into yet another heated argument, how she'd cry as she pulled me into her arms, the rare moments when somehow I was in her orbit again...useful, a child to comfort her.

"I *dare* you," I grit out, leaning further down, so close I could smell the sweet scent of alcohol drifting from her parted lips, once again painted in dark purple.

Her breathing comes in quick pants. Her smooth, pale skin flushes pink as her eyes dart across my face like she doesn't know what to look at first. A pulse flutters rapidly in her neck and it's like a beacon drawing out the beast I've tethered tightly within me. I have the strangest compulsion to touch it. To wrap my hand around that slender neck and feel her pulse hammer into my fingers.

What's wrong with me?

Maybe you're your parents' child.

I rear back and she lets out a huge breath.

"Hey, I'm fine. I really am," Kristi's soft voice sounds from behind us. She obviously senses Taylor's terror too. "Charles is just teaching my husband a few tricks as a Dom. I'm fine. We're all good here."

I see the moment when her words click for Taylor, when she realizes she has misread the entire situation. She rakes her hand through her hair.

"I...I see," she whispers before swallowing, a flush creeping up her face. "Shit. Shit. Shit."

I curl my fingers into my palm to stop myself from doing something insane, like reaching out and shaking her for sending me on a maddening rollercoaster of unsavory emotions.

Instead, I can't help myself and say, "Are you done here? You barged into a private scene."

Taylor's lips flatten and her eyes narrow into slits. Stiffening, she turns her attention back to me and sneers, "I'll never understand twisted men like you. Can't get hard without hurting women?"

With that parting backhand, she spins around and glides out of the room like a fucking queen.

"Fuck," I mutter under my breath, my pulse rioting in my veins. I feel out of control. This woman drives me insane, and I've only met her twice.

"Well, that was wild," Colt comments. The entire mood of the scene is completely ruined.

"Sorry, guys." I let out a halfhearted chuckle and turn back to my friends. "On behalf of her, I apologize for ruining your night."

Kristi grins and buttons her shirt—well, the buttons Colt didn't rip off earlier. "Don't worry about it, Charles. Seriously, who is she? I've never seen anyone set you off like this before."

"Or anyone who doesn't like Charles." Colt snorts before pulling his wife to his side.

My forced smile twitches on my jaw. "I have no clue."

No fucking clue.

CHAPTER 11

Charles

THE RAIN LASHES AGAINST the windows in a torrent of violence, the weather warning us winter is around the corner. I look at the traffic far below, a blur of navy speckled with red and white lights, before taking out my cell phone and scrolling to my photos app. It's been another long day of meetings after a late night in the office yesterday.

My thumb hovering over the icon, I wonder what the hell I'm doing. Why I am even entertaining this ridiculous nonsense.

But I can't stop thinking about her. Taylor Peyton. The fiery, contradictory minx who looks like she'll fall apart one second and rip out my guts the next. She's like the weather in Tibet—sunny one moment, pouring rain the next—calamitous and unpredictable.

A fucking hurricane blowing through my calm and orderly life.

The fireplace crackles, providing more warmth inside the luxurious confines of the gentlemen's club within The Orchid, where I'm waiting for the rest of the guys to show up for drinks.

"It's been six years! I'm over this! The past is in the past!"

"I'll never understand twisted men like you. You can't get hard without hurting women?"

Her vicious words and haunted eyes float to the surface again. The way she stared at Ian in horror. The fear in her eyes at ABTC and at The Sanctuary. She's out of her fucking mind and I shouldn't pay her any attention, but a niggle of doubt bothers me like a phantom itch I can't scratch.

What if?

"You never listen to us! You always think we're overreacting! Look what that got us, Charles! Look what happened to Firefly!" Liam shoved me and I staggered back, collapsing on the pavement, the storm drenching my clothes.

I blow out a heavy breath. What if I didn't listen this time? But that doesn't mean I need to entertain the whiplash moods of someone clearly disturbed.

"Charlie, it hurts," Little Firefly cried as she burrowed her face into my side. The little pipsqueak was so short, she barely reached my chest.

I ruffled her sunset strands. "Just a skinned knee. Next time, don't go climbing on the monkey bars without someone with you. You're too short for them."

"Will you come with me next time?"

Smiling, I gave her the biggest hug—my bear hug, as she liked to call them. "Of course. I'll always be here for you."

My broken vow to her. One that'll haunt me the rest of my life if she doesn't wake up.

My throat is parched as I scroll through my photos app—I don't take a lot of pictures, so there aren't many to go through before I get to the ones from six years ago.

I smile at the images of Firefly—her grinning at the camera, her smile teeming with life, a pile of books gathered in her arms. One of the three of us back at the Hamptons—the last time we were there as a trio—her waving her hand in hello, her silver bracelet flashing under the afternoon sunlight, Liam throwing his head back, his sleeve of tattoos on full display, and me staring at the two of them, a smirk twisting my lips.

Then, there are the photos Uncle Ian sent me back then. Snapshots of him in Paris, teaching ballet in his academy there, him relaxing on vacation in the Mediterranean. I distinctly remember making fun of him for not being back stateside, claiming the hot European women must've kept him busy. I click the social media app and scroll through his posts from that time. Everything was in Europe, just like I remember.

He wasn't here. He wasn't in New York. Whoever hurt Taylor, Ian had nothing to do with it. But whoever it was, I suspect it was something physical to elicit such a vehement reaction at The Sanctuary last weekend.

The thought of someone snuffing out her spark makes me want to punch something, and the sudden burning rage rising inside my chest terrifies me.

I close my eyes and take a deep breath. And another. I won't turn out like my dad.

"Why are you gripping your phone like it's your worst enemy?"

Startling, I turn around, noticing Maxwell leaning against the doorframe, his charcoal eyes narrowing at me pensively.

"What?" A forced chuckle escapes my lips as I slide my cell phone back into my pocket. "You're overthinking. I was just waiting for you guys, although I expect Rex to be late. No doubt he'll have some women troubles to entertain us with."

"Hm." The oldest Anderson sibling doesn't appear convinced. I walk to the wet bar and pour him a whiskey—single malt, neat, the way he usually likes it.

"Thanks," he murmurs. "Of course you know my favorite drink."

Maxwell's gray eyes, reminding me of a certain angry ballerina, fix on mine again, and I fight to maintain the grin on my face.

"You don't let anyone in, Charles. You know we're here for you, right?"

I huff out an exhale and stare into my tumbler. "I guess we have that in common, don't we? Aren't you 'the reclusive billionaire?'" It's one of the nicknames the press has given him over the years.

"At least I don't hide my true self. You hide under your charming smiles and golden prince persona."

Taking a sip of the alcohol, I wince from the burn. "Maybe it's part of the curse of being the oldest sibling in the family." Except he's loved by his siblings and I'm just a fucking failure in that department.

Something dark flashes in his eyes and he stiffens before looking away. I've hit a nerve, but the man is as locked down as Fort Knox, and until he's willing to share his secrets, no one will know them.

Maxwell lets out a grunt. Apparently, that day isn't today. "Maybe. But it isn't healthy, bottling up your emotions. I have art and racing as outlets. What about you? I don't see you pursuing any interests outside of work, nor do I see you with women. That can't be healthy."

I have my occasional subs. But I don't bother mentioning that weak ass argument.

I press my lips together as a sudden hollowness appears inside my chest.

An outlet?

I'm thirty-six and single, with nothing going on other than my job. Yes, I have lots of friends and am well liked in the business community. But my brother hates me, and Firefly is in the hospital because of me. I've had a few superficial relationships with women, and have tried pursuing women I admire—emotionally intelligent, kind, gentle women, everything Mom isn't—but somehow, they've always ended up choosing other men.

Perhaps other men who could give them their whole hearts. I can't say I blame them.

I don't want a passionate relationship, one like my parents', whose every living moment is fire and brimstone—intense love, hate, and all the emotions that end up burning everyone around them to cinders. But I do want a genuine one.

But am I capable of that?

Until I figure that out, all I have is Grandma's company. Her pride and joy, and protecting it the best I can because it's the one thing I'm proud of...contributing to her legacy and adding my mark to it.

"Who has time for all that shit when running a company and battling PR scandals is a full-time job? Not everyone can multitask like you, Maxwell," I reply.

He opens his mouth to say something, but the door bursts open and in strides the rest of the guys—Steven leading the pack in his three-piece black suit, but unlike his former workaholic self, his tie is loosened. It seems like being in love has finally softened his hard edges.

He's laughing with Ethan, who's shaking his head in amusement. Ryland is frowning at a stack of papers in his hands. Rex trudges in a few minutes later, his hair in disarray. He heads straight to the wet bar.

"Remind me never to take women on dates again," Rex mutters.

"What happened? They expected...*commitment* from you?" Ethan gasps in mock horror.

"You know what they say, the higher the mountain, the more people want to scale it. I don't do relationships and these girls don't seem to get it."

We settle in the living room area and face the roaring fireplace.

"Aren't you tired of it? Flings and one-night stands?" Ethan asks, his voice turning serious.

Rex shrugs and stares at the fire, a sudden heaviness on his frame. "It's all I'm good for. Not everyone is cut out for relationships...*requited or not*." He pins Ethan with a penetrating stare.

Ethan's nostrils flare and the two have a silent stare down, seeming to communicate something we outsiders can't seem to understand.

"Touché," Ethan murmurs. "I swear, someday, I'll get you to admit this playboy persona of yours is just an act."

Rex curves his lips in a half-grin, the spark not reaching his eyes. "You'll be waiting for a long time then." He turns to his older brother. "What about you, Ryland? What's got you smiling like an idiot over there? What are you reading?"

Ryland jolts upright in his blue tufted armchair, and stuffs his papers to the side. His amused smile turns into a scowl. "I'm grading papers, you idiot."

Rex waggles his brows. "Papers, eh? Any hot coeds in class? Ohhh, Professor Anderson, I'll do *anything* to pass this class," he says in a fake high-pitched voice.

Ryland rolls his eyes and sits back in his chair. "Unlike someone, I'm capable of controlling myself. I teach ethics, you dimwit."

Steven mutters under his breath, "He's not saying there's no one."

The guys guffaw and Ryland's glower darkens, a vein throbbing on his temple. He takes out the papers again and his red pen flies across the page. There's something going on with him.

"What about you, Charles? You look off today. Something bothering you?" Steven asks, and everyone turns toward me.

"What did I say? We know you too well to buy into your bullshit," Maxwell mutters under his breath.

I hide my annoyance by taking another sip of my drink, which buys me a few seconds to come up with an answer that'll hopefully fool some of the smartest people I know. After all, Fleur Entertainment's exponential growth isn't because they have idiots as management.

Something occurs to me—a misdirection. "I'm sure you've heard of the sexual assault scandal at the bank."

The guys nod.

I tell them about the plan—the international ballet tour, Uncle Ian joining ABTC as the artistic director. And how I'll even need to oversee parts of the tour myself because my trust in my team is lacking at the current moment.

"Hey, you said ABTC? Have you met our half sister yet?" Rex quips.

I frown. Half sister? Isn't that Grace? I glance over at Steven and cock my brow in question.

"Grace has a younger sister who is a ballerina at ABTC. Taylor Peyton. Black hair, same eyes as these idiots," he supplies.

I jolt. *What the fuck? They're related?* Heat creeps up my neck. "Pissed off all the time, likes dark makeup, wears an equally dark piercing on her nose, and pale as a snowflake? Yeah, I've met her."

Unfortunately.

Rex leans forward in, clearly interested. "That's a lot of description from you, Charles. What? You interested in our sister?"

"You're fucking insane. That woman is as approachable as a feral cat."

He throws his head back and laughs. "She's a ball buster. That's why she's my favorite sister. She doesn't mean any harm. Don't sweat it."

"Don't let Lana hear you." Ethan smirks.

My brows pinch as I survey the room. The guys don't appear at all concerned about Taylor. Perhaps because they've only recently connected as siblings, they don't know her well enough yet? I glance at Steven, finding him furrowing his brows at me in confusion, like he knows I'm withholding something from him.

But it isn't my place to tell them what happened with Taylor at ABTC or The Sanctuary.

I return Steven's gaze with a shrug of my own.

"Did you see the bloodbath on the market yesterday?" Ethan asks.

"Can't believe Canterbury Pharmaceuticals went down in a few hours. Someone's engineered that," Steven comments. I think all of our investment portfolios went down at least fifteen percent yesterday. It's not every day you see a Fortune 500 giant go up in flames.

"Rumor has it Senator Townsend is behind it. He's allegedly part of The Association." Ethan frowns.

"I'd avoid that mess with a ten foot pole," Maxwell comments, his eyes darkening.

My ears perk up at the organization Grandma mentioned all those years ago, but I bite my tongue, remembering Grandma's warning, which seems to be confirmed by Maxwell's ominous comment.

My mind trails to a woman the epitome of lightning in the skies—awe-inspiring yet lethal, who's apparently related to my best friends. *No fucking way.* I shove my thoughts to the side.

I couldn't care less about a certain ballerina with hair the color of midnight magic and eyes that seem to shimmer and transform with her moods.

I couldn't care less about a woman at least a decade younger than me, a woman who's too volatile, a ticking time bomb waiting to explode and take down everyone in her vicinity.

A swirling heat gathers in my gut and spreads to the rest of my body and I gnash my teeth together.

I don't care about her. I most definitely don't like her.

Not one bit.

PART TWO

THE BLACK SWAN

One and a Half Years Later

CHAPTER 12

"How are you feeling about it?" Grace's voice travels through the speakers of my laptop during our video chat.

Her dark blue eyes glint violet under the golden rays of the afternoon light, her hair mussed up by the wind. She's curled up in her favorite chair on the patio of the new place she bought with Steven on the Upper West Side.

But nothing can dim the beauty of a blushing bride—well, almost bride, that is. She and Steven are getting married in two months in August. In a spectacular fashion, Steven proposed to Grace on top of the Eiffel Tower last year, and of course, my sister said yes to him.

As I stare at her beaming face, a ball of happiness gathers inside my chest. Mom would be so happy to know Grace has found someone to love and cherish her the way she deserves.

"Tay? Hey, earth to Tay! Stop munching on that carrot stick." She waves at the camera.

I take an exaggerated bite of the carrot, my lips twitching when she sticks her tongue out at me like we were still kids. To this day, she can't fathom why I love this vegetable so much.

I think it has something to do with this snack being the last thing I remember tasting and enjoying before that night. Perhaps it's the one thing that remains untainted. A person can change, memories can be distorted, but a favorite taste in a happy moment will forever be associated with that time.

It stays with you.

"Of course, I'm excited. I've had to grovel my way back to the understudy position." I shove a bunch of therapy books off my bed—I don't want Grace to see them and ask why I'm reading enough books to sit for a med school exam—books I've dog-eared, highlighted, spilled ketchup on in the late night hours when I couldn't sleep, my mind heavy from grief or manic from nightmares of that night.

Healing is a journey, and I'm in the driver's seat. Another mantra I hold on to.

"*Swan Lake*! It's a big deal! That's what you were obsessed about when we were kids! You know, I'm still jealous Mom took you to the ballet and never me."

"You don't even like ballet! You said you were bored because there was no speaking or singing."

Grace purses her lips and shakes her fingers at me. "That's not true! I like ballet when it's you dancing on the stage. Although, I always have to research the plot beforehand to understand what's happening. It's like reading CliffsNotes of *Pride and Prejudice* before I dig into the book. Why the hell would I want to do that?"

"It's about the beauty in the movements—conveying emotions without words. Because sometimes, there are no words to describe what you're feeling." I swallow as a sudden heaviness forms on top of my chest.

Grace cocks her head to the side and squints at me. I cough into my fist. "I'm talking to a rock. Anyway, yes, it's a popular ballet—a classic. So, it's no surprise the company went with this ballet for the international tour. It'll have the biggest draw."

The infamous international part of the Bank of Columbia apology tour is kicking off in a few weeks. It's actually genius timing to have the tour a year and a half after the allegations came out, because the actual trial for the former CFO is going on right now, and press coverage has been nonstop. This tour will generate some positive news for the bank.

Madame Renoir has prepared us as much as she can. She is now officially retired and Sir Ian will start next week to oversee the last legs of preparation before our first performance at the Met Opera at the end of the month. Apparently, the two of them worked on the choreography and vision together.

"It was kind of harsh, demoting you for a year, don't you think? I mean, sure, you had some words with that bitch, Carla, but she bullied you first." Grace waves her fists, her face flushed at the mention of my nemesis.

She still doesn't know what happened, and it appears Charles never told Steven or the guys, or else I'm sure I would've gotten an earful from Grace. I never thought I'd be thankful for that asshole.

"Eh, fuck it. At least Madame Renoir bumped me back up to soloist before she left." As Madame Renoir packed up her things in her old-fashioned, stuffy office, she also told me I had a gift and she'd hate for it to go to waste.

"But you have to tame your anger, Taylor, or else it will destroy everything, including your art."

All I could do was smile at her then, all the while feeling the ever-present flames singeing my skin. She told me I'd have another shot at a promotion—if I do well on the international tour. She had put in a good word with Sir Ian for me.

But I'd have to work for it.

Impress a man who still makes me uneasy whenever I come across articles online about his imminent return to the Big Apple. No new memories have popped up. Just those glimpses of blond hair, light eyes, fragments of sounds and sentences.

I still don't know why my body reacted so strongly that day at ABTC.

Maybe I'll figure it out once I see him again.

The ballet community is aflutter with excitement—the king is returning home and will bring glory to the art stateside. The press is eating it all up—Sir Ian Vaughn, champion of women and assault victims, working with the disgraced Bank of Columbia in a charity ballet tour. Tons of good press for Charles, no doubt.

Unfortunately for me, Charles is a permanent fixture in our lives now, with him being close friends with Steven and our siblings. While I've gotten to know my half-siblings more, begrudgingly like them a lot, and have even hyphenated my last name with theirs, my relationship with Charles hasn't thawed one bit.

We make it a point to avoid each other at events. Whenever we are in proximity to each other, like at Grace's celebration event at The Orchid for the grand opening of her consulting firm or when Maxwell and Belle got married half a year ago in this prime time drama worthy of an arranged marriage, we'd inevitably butt heads. I can't stand the fake smiling golden prince persona he wears in public.

I've seen the darkness lurking behind the mask—the angry glares he levels my way, the fake-ass smile he uses at press conferences, his harsh commands when he used his whip on his friend in The Sanctuary, the clench of his jaw whenever I point out his inconsistencies. I'm sure he hates me because I don't put up with his bullshit.

But I tolerate him because the people I care about love him and I'm sure he does the same with me. And so, he gets to be the warm fucking sun and I'll happily be the lonely moon in the dark skies as long as he stays out of my way. It's gotten to a point where the girls make fun of our mutual hatred of each other.

"Anyway, what are your plans today?" Grace asks as I hear the sliding door next to her open.

Steven pops into the screen wearing a simple T-shirt, his black hair tousled. He grins and murmurs, "Tay," before pressing a soft kiss on his fiancée's forehead.

Grace flushes and reaches up to cradle his jaw. My heart pinches; the same sensations I've had more this past year as I witness my girls being paired off one by one make a reappearance. Millie with Ryland, her professor—apparently the two have history going back a few years ago. Belle with Maxwell, and, of course, my sister with Steven.

I look away and swallow the lump lodged in my throat, feeling like an intruder in their private moment.

"I'll see you at the performance, Tay. Break a leg," Steven says. "You're going to kick ass."

The backs of my eyes burn unwittingly. From the outside, I look like I have everything I want. Family who loves me, even though I miss Mom and her whimsical romantic thoughts daily. A career in ballet, even though I haven't reached the pinnacle yet. Financial security, being a Peyton-Anderson now, that is the envy of most people in the world.

But I'm hollow inside. A thousand shipwrecks have capsized inside my chest. I'm left adrift, barely clinging on to life in the dark abyss.

And no one sees me.

I shake myself—the Lochness Monster has been visiting more frequently these days and I suspect it's because of all the changes happening, but I'll fight like hell before I get sucked in. Maybe I'll give Olivia a call tonight—she's single, great company, and likes slasher movies too. She says it's fun to psychoanalyze the serial killers. I smirk inwardly; the idea sounds better and better by the second. Pizza and bingeing on *Netflix*. Plotting murders of fictional serial killers. We've become good friends since that night at The Sanctuary, even though I had to grovel my way to her good graces after I ran off that day.

Clearing my throat, I say to the happy couple, "I have to go back to the ABTC to practice. Every second counts now." *And Sir Ian wants to see me.* My shoulders tense at the thought, but I brush it away.

My hand moves to close my laptop, but Grace's voice stops me.

"Hey Tay, you know you don't have to worry about the performance, right? As much as I don't understand ballet, I believe in you. That Sir Ian will love you because you're so talented. You can do this!" She beams widely at me.

I strain a smile before shutting the laptop lid.

Sir Ian wants to see me.

The memory of that disastrous first meeting floats to the forefront.

Why was I so scared that day? Will it happen again when I see him?

Nausea churns inside me, and suddenly, I want to puke.

CHAPTER 13

"Come in," the raspy voice from my nightmares commands behind the closed door.

Acid roils in my stomach and I grip the doorknob, steeling myself before entering Sir Ian's office at ABTC.

Can I do this? Face this man my body seems to fear?

Work closely with him in the foreseeable future and impress him so I can finally get promoted?

Maybe my reaction was a fluke. After all, I don't remember my monster. It was probably some subconscious stress triggering a vivid flashback.

It's a conversation I've had many times in my head, to no avail. But I know this—I'm not jeopardizing my career at the country's best ballet company unless I know something definitively wrong about this man.

Drawing in a shallow inhale, I twist the doorknob and step inside. My eyes dart around the spacious room, doing everything I can to delay looking at the man himself.

Sir Ian has already put his stamp into the space. Gone are the feminine touches of fresh floral arrangements and brightly colored cushions. The office now radiates with masculine appeal. Dark wood paneling and intricate coffered ceiling frame the large windows overlooking Central Park. Golden plaques and trophies, no doubt from the accolades he has accumulated over the years, beckon at me from the walls and shelves, as if to say, how can someone so talented and respected in the community be a monster?

The man himself sits behind a grandiose oak desk in the center of the room. I knot my hands in my shapeless black sweater. I'm sweating faster than I can wipe the moisture away.

"S-Sir Ian." I hate how I stammer in his presence. I straighten up. *Fuck. What's wrong with me?*

He sets a fountain pen on the desk, sits back in his plush leather chair, and observes me. I'm caught by surprise at how much he looks like Charles. Less imposing, definitely thinner, but the same nose and eyes. But unlike his nephew, whose presence only makes me want to get up in his face, Sir Ian puts every atom of my body on alert, ready to run away.

I stare back, forcing myself to smile in his presence, even though I'm sure I look like I'm grimacing instead.

After a few seconds of terse silence, made even more uncomfortable by the unusual stillness in his figure and shrewd eyes, his lips curve up in a smile. "I hope you're doing well, Ms. Peyton-Anderson. Do you mind if I call you Taylor?"

I let out a stale breath. I nod. "Taylor is fine."

He motions to the seat in front of him.

I hurry forward and take a seat at the edge of the chair, my tote bag on my lap. Placing my hand at the opening, where a pepper spray is within reach, I force myself to take even breaths.

Citrus. I take a deeper whiff. *Yes, citrus, like oranges.*

Not peppermint. *See? It was probably all in your head that day.*

My body relaxes marginally.

Sir Ian clears his throat. "The reason I asked for this meeting is to make sure you're fine with this arrangement."

I frown. "Arrangement?"

"Me working here. You being one of my dancers," he explains, his voice gentle. "I know I shouldn't mention the unusual circumstances in how we met," he pauses and stares at me, and my skin heats, "but I wouldn't be a good boss if I don't make sure any concerns are aired out before my employment here begins."

Sir Ian leans forward, and I shrink back, slowly pushing the chair farther away from the desk. My fingers automatically inch toward the pepper spray.

He says, "I've reviewed tapes of your past performances. You're talented, Taylor, one of the most promising dancers I've seen in a long time. Obviously, you have issues dancing Odette, but your Odile... It's frankly one of the best Odile's I've seen in a while."

I grip my handbag tightly and the leather crinkles under my nails.

Issues dancing Odette. That's the understatement of the century—I'm afraid I'll never be able to master the role of the white swan. How can I perform a role that's the epitome of innocence and grace, of the sanctity of love?

"I'd like to keep you on, but only if you'll respect me as your artistic director. I can't afford to have any disruptions like at our first meeting. There's too much at stake for both ABTC and for Bank of Columbia," he concludes and settles back in his seat.

I breathe a sigh of relief at the distance.

"Your nephew's company."

He grabs the fountain pen on his desk and twirls it in his fingers. I stare at the ruby on it instead of looking at him. It glints like blood in the cold daylight.

He replies, "It's my family's company. My mother started it and Charles has done a wonderful job so far." Something in his voice gives me pause, but when I look at him, he's smiling warmly. He obviously loves his family. That is something I can identify with. Unease still prickles me, a background noise that seems louder in the presence of this man, but I feel more comforted right now. *A monster won't love his family, right?*

"I'd like to reiterate, I don't know what you went through in the past, but I have nothing to do with it. I haven't met you before ABTC." His fingers still—his pen poised in his grasp. "Do we have a problem with each other, Taylor? Or are you okay with working under me?"

A quiet intensity radiates from him as he waits for my response.

My skin itches again, and I fight the impulse to scratch at it or to run home and take a scalding hot shower.

One second drags to two, then to three, but Sir Ian doesn't waver. He calmly sits there, a serene smile on his face, as he patiently waits for me to answer him.

He hasn't made any inappropriate remarks. He hasn't even tried to touch me. He's been professional and even...kind.

It can't be him all those years ago.

But why does it feel so real? Why is my gut telling me this man isn't all he appears to be?

But you have no evidence. No basis in reality, Taylor. Even you aren't sure. Don't sabotage yourself.

I knot the straps of my tote around my fingers and pull, relishing the lash of pain as the leather digs into my hand. The pain grounds me. The pain tells me everything is under my control.

"I don't have a problem, sir."

Sir Ian nods and stands. I follow suit. He motions to the door. The meeting is over. "Enjoy the rest of your evening and I'll see you Monday for practice."

"Y-Yes, sir."

My feet carry me as fast as I can out of the office and I collapse against the door after I shut it, my legs trembling, sweat rolling down my back.

I hope I didn't make the biggest mistake of my life.

CHAPTER 14

AFTER MY MEETING WITH Sir Ian, I spend an hour working out and practicing in the rooftop studio, needing to do something with the nervous energy flooding my insides. By the time I leave ABTC, the sun dips low in the late afternoon sky, finally releasing the world from the suffocating heat on this early June day.

I take a few steps down before turning around to admire the building. Sinewy shadows thrash with the muted orange rays against the facade of the historical structure, which sticks out amid the modern skyscrapers with its baroque exterior of wraparound wrought iron gates and stained glass windows.

I remember dragging Mom here on our magical days and sitting on the steps, watching willowy dancers—the girls graceful like swans, the boys refined—stride through those double doors. Mom would tell me the acceptance rate was less than one percent. Only the best of the best may walk in these lauded halls.

It was my dream—our dream—for me to be part of this institution, for me to become one of those elegant ballerinas to inspire the next generation of dancers.

It was *my* way of contributing to the family, *my* way of taking us out of poverty.

And now, I'm here—a soloist, the second highest ranking under the principal dancer. I'm an Anderson with a trust fund. Mom isn't here anymore, but this dream with her...this dream is still alive.

This dream is all I have left, and it's well within reach.

But I feel this cavernous hollow in my chest I can't seem to fill.

A loud noise interrupts my morose thoughts. Turning around, I bite back a groan when I see the familiar, towering silhouette of Charles getting out of a town car with two other businessmen, including the balding man with lecherous eyes I remember from our first meeting at the studio.

"What's one pussy when I can get two, you know?" The balding creep clasps his meaty hand on Charles and laughs at his own joke. *Still as gross as before, I see.*

"You must be an HR nightmare, John." The other lanky man in a suit chuckles at his friend's lewd comment. These two men are older than Dad and probably have children my age.

Revulsion churns through me and I throw up a little inside. But I find my attention riveted not on dumb and dumber, but on the imposing man whose hair gleams like molten gold—an archangel descending on humankind.

Charles smirks, slapping his hand on John's shoulder, his low laughter sending shivers up my spine. But something about his grin seems forced. "As long as all parties are happy, who am I to judge?" He winks and the men laugh some more.

Ugh. Disgusting pigs. Reason one hundred and one why I hate Charles Vaughn and everything he stands for—entitled rich assholes. Except for my brothers and Steven, I haven't met one who hasn't disappointed me yet.

I must've made a noise because Charles suddenly turns toward me, his eyes sharpening before narrowing. And that's when I see it—the pulse hammering across his temple, the stiff tension in his shoulders which I normally don't see when he's with my siblings.

The fake-ass smile that doesn't reach his eyes. *Huh. He's hiding behind his mask...again.*

The men quiet, clearly wondering how much I've overheard, and slowly make their way toward me.

"Taylor, you remember our sponsors, John Finkle and Chris Larkey from Legions Capital," Charles murmurs when they stop a few feet before me.

John bares his teeth as his eyes rove over my face, then down my body like he's undressing me in front of him.

I clench my hands and fight the urge to run away. A charring heat burns up my insides.

How dare they disrespect me this way?

"My eyes are up here, gentlemen," I grind out. "Plenty of women don't appreciate your attentions."

John's eyes widen and his buddy huffs out a disgruntled breath. No doubt they aren't used to women calling them out on their BS.

"You b—" John scowls and steps toward me.

I flinch and curse myself for the automatic reaction when Charles clamps a hand on John's shoulder, his fingers digging into the fabric.

"John was just admiring your outfit today—all black ensemble on a summer night, quite the choice, don't you think? Embodying the black swan already, Ms. Anderson?"

My eyebrow arches at him dropping the first half of my last name, but Charles doesn't look at me. Instead, he's doling out another fake smile to John, which is incongruous with how white his knuckles are on the man's shoulder.

The man is a walking contradiction.

"Anderson?" John asks.

Charles slowly relaxes his grip, letting his hand drop to his side. I see him discreetly flex his fingers before responding, "Yes. Fleur Entertainment's Andersons. Taylor is Linus's youngest daughter. She's the understudy for the Odette and Odile roles for the tour."

The men blanch at that revelation. I guess there are advantages of being an Anderson other than the money. No one wants to cross my family, especially when they own half the city.

"W-Why didn't you say so earlier, Charles?" Chris says. "We weren't aware the Andersons had a dancer in the family."

"An obvious oversight on my part," Charles comments wryly, his lips tilted in that annoying smirk again. "Why don't you head on inside? Sir Ian's waiting. I'll be there shortly."

The men take another look at me, this time keeping their eyes on my face, then walk into the building.

"I didn't need you to rescue me," I mutter as Charles sidles up next to me. His cologne of cedarwood and bergamot wafts to my nose and I take a discreet step to the side.

He's too tall, too large, too close to me.

His eyes flicker down at my feet, obviously noticing my movement. He arches his brow, but thankfully doesn't comment further.

"But I *do* need to rescue my tour. They are fronting the expenses for the first two stops and I don't need you to fuck it up before we kick it off."

I snort and cross my arms. "Of course, that's what you were doing. God forbid you were actually putting the pigs in place."

He leans down, and I fight every urge to step back a few more paces. He already noticed I moved away from him and damn if I'd let him see me scurry away again. From this distance, I see pale gold flecks in his startling glacial eyes—arresting, beautiful, completely wasted on a man like him.

Charles murmurs, "I didn't want you to think I did that for you."

I scoff. "Please, I would *never* think that. You don't have a good bone in your body."

He snickers. "On what basis, since you know me so well?"

"On the basis that every inch of you is fake as shit. I don't know why no one sees that."

That damn sardonic arch of brow makes another reappearance. "Oh?" His voice drops to a ghostly whisper, and I shiver. "I can rest assure you, plenty of my inches are very real."

I swallow as my eyes automatically dart to the bulge behind the fly of his pants.

"My eyes are up here, minx."

Flames erupt on my face, and I scowl at him. But whatever I want to say fades away when I take in those startling eyes once more. They are darkening, mirroring the deep navy chasing away the afternoon glow in the skies.

My breath freezes in my throat as my gaze trails to his full mouth and the shadow of his carefully groomed scruff. An insane thought runs through my head.

How would his scruff feel against my skin?

Charles unleashes a smile lighting up his entire face, his eyes trailing down to my lips, which I belatedly notice are parted. I quickly shut them, cross my arms over my chest again, and lift my chin. I've gone nuts, probably from the heat. Maybe it's not a good idea to wear black on a hot summer day.

"You know, it's a sign of low EQ to erupt at people whenever they say something you don't want to hear," he says.

His body heat radiates from his tall frame, and my skin is hot to the touch. But I nevertheless remain rooted in place. In this game of chicken, I won't be the one to lose.

"I hate to break it to you, Charles. It's a sign of low *IQ* to hang out with the scum of mankind."

Tossing my hair over my shoulders, I smile inwardly when some of the black strands whip him across his face. I pat my hand on his suit jacket and say, "But I don't expect you to understand that. Not all of us are born with honor. You know, it isn't good to bottle everything up inside you, right? Can't be healthy."

I spin around, intending to leave him in the dust, but suddenly, his hand grips mine. My pulse leaps in my ears as he touches me and I swallow a gasp.

"Let go of me," I command, but he doesn't budge.

"Be careful, little girl. It isn't wise to poke the bear." His words carry a steely edge, the same thread of danger I saw when I first met him, the same dominance in his voice when he was at The Sanctuary. But this time, beside the anger simmering beneath the surface, there's something else in his voice—a spiciness feeling more like a sultry caress disguised as a warning.

He looks like he wouldn't mind using the whip he held that night on me.

Goosebumps prickle my arms and I try tugging my hand away, but he grips it tighter—not to the point of pain, but enough to show who he believes has the upper hand in our dynamic.

I don't think so, asshole.

Baring my teeth, I pivot, raise my foot, and stomp the heel of my boot on his fancy leather shoe, watching in satisfaction when he winces in pain. His eyes flare, but he quickly drops my hand.

"I told you to let go. I don't give warnings twice. Maybe you should take your own advice." I walk down to him and stab his chest with my finger—his damn muscular chest—for emphasis. "Don't. Poke. The. Bear."

Without waiting for a response, I make my way down the steps and head toward the subway station, his raw and raspy laughter echoing in my ears.

My lips twitch, bubbles simmering inside my chest.

Taylor one, Charles zero.

Then, I freeze, belatedly noticing the spark of amusement, the rush of satisfaction at my rejoinder and not bowing down before him. And it's then I realize, despite him being so close to me just now, I didn't feel afraid.

CHAPTER 15

BACKSTAGE AT THE MET Opera is a study of controlled chaos. A frenetic energy hums through the wings in between Acts III and IV of *Swan Lake*. It's the inaugural performance kicking off the international tour and also Ian's debut as the artistic director of ABTC. Naturally, everyone is on edge. A faint smell of sweat and perfume permeates the air and the rushed footsteps of dancers and stagehands dashing across the floor remind me of standing in the middle of Grand Central Station during rush hour.

I silence my phone, but the buzzing still comes through—no doubt updates on the Patterson trial and financial reporting I'm expecting from my finance team. Despite the mountain of work waiting for me in the office, I have to be here today for the inaugural performance. Along with accompanying the ballet company for the first few international stops, I promised I'd be here to show my support when we announced the tour as part of the response to the scandal.

I glance at our family's empty private box, front and center of the Parterre level, and a twinge of sadness prickles my chest. I've avoided that box and instead am watching the performance from backstage because of the feelings it evokes in me. Grandma wasn't a fan of ballet—she loved opera and musicals more. Liam wouldn't be caught dead sitting through any of the performances.

Firefly was the only person who would've enjoyed this night. I think back to the excited glow in her blue eyes when she grabbed my arm during the last performance we saw together—*The Nutcracker*—three years before she ended up in the hospital.

"Glad I don't have to march into the office to drag you here, you workaholic." She winked before settling down into her seat. "I wish we could do this more often."

I huffed out a laugh. "Don't be so dramatic. I'll always make time for you."

Liar.

For the next three years, I'd never accompanied her to another performance. There were always other obligations—work, networking, business dinners.

I always assumed I'd have more time with them.

Regret is a corrosive poison—once in your system, it slowly eats away at you little by little, until every movement causes pain.

I swallow, looking away.

"Taylor, will you grab another pair of pointe shoes for Bethany?" Ian asks. "The ribbon tore in her current pair—she has a few extras on her table."

"Yes, sir."

The bane of my existence jolts to attention and scurries away from her spot across the wings, where she was staring forlornly at the stage. She's wearing yet another baggy sweatshirt and sweatpants, looking completely out of place in a field of glittering costumes and bright colors. Her arms are hiked across her chest. I frown—it's not the first time I've seen her wrap her arms around herself like that, and I can count with one hand how many times I've seen her in anything that's not ill-fitting or in funeral colors.

It's like she's trying to protect herself or make herself invisible.

But that's impossible. Her willowy frame, the innate elegance in her features punctuated by the angry countenance hovering over her most days, the pale skin marred by dark makeup and her ever-changing nose piercings.

Can the moon ever blend in with the dark night? I don't think so.

Really, Charles? Moon and dark night? I'm slowly being driven crazy by her. That's the only rational explanation.

"Don't. Poke. The. Bear."

Flames radiate from my chest when I think back to that day on the steps of ABTC. The woman never backs down, even when it's good for her. Every time I saw her in the last year and a half, we'd always end up in some strange bickering match over everything. She'd have opinions about my single status, which she said was because women were too smart to fall for my shit, which I'd return with a backhand about her lack of boyfriends, a comment I'm still not proud of today. Then there were countless barbs about my fake smile, my questionable business partners—pretty much if I were to say the sun is yellow, I'm sure she'd have an opposing viewpoint.

The woman fucking hates my guts, that much is obvious.

She tries my patience and drags me down to her level, daring me to erupt—to lash out with no care about my surroundings.

But you like it even though you won't admit it. Why else would you want to murder the assholes from Legion when they were being their usual lecherous selves?

Fuck that. I won't engage in this train of thought.

But the most annoying thing about the minx was how she'd shut down whenever I mentioned my uncle. Her face would pale and her snappy barbs wouldn't come then. It unsettles me.

Ian strides over, his fingers tugging the tie around his neck. He forces out a smile.

"The performance is going very well," I comment.

I know he's nervous. After all, this is a homecoming performance. Meaningful.

"It's acceptable. Bethany is flawless as Odette, but her Odile leaves a lot to be desired." He frowns as the stagehands transform the scenery into the moonlit lake, where Odette and her prince will meet their tragic ending. "You know your ballet, Charles. Taylor would've been better suited for Odile. There's a fire and power in her that'd show well on the stage. Too bad the roles are typically danced by one person."

I think back to her haunted eyes when I saw her at The Sanctuary almost two years ago. That fire was missing then.

It was pure terror.

Even to this day, that memory bothers me. I'd rather bicker with her than to see that haunted look on her face.

Ian sneaks a glance at me, his lips twitching. "It doesn't hurt that she's beautiful too. I see how you stare at her."

I flinch. *No fucking way.* "In hatred, you mean."

"Why do you hate each other so much?"

Turning toward him, I frown. "She's the definition of unstable and immature. Did you forget how she socked me in the face the first time we met? How that punch was meant for you? Her vague accusations?"

Someone runs over and hands a document to Uncle Ian and he takes out his jeweled pen and signs on it before responding.

"That makes her interesting. Let me ask you this, Charles. If you had to choose, would you eat stale crackers or spiced curry for the rest of your life?"

"Huh?"

He stares at the stage, his lips hiked up in a smile. "Stale crackers taste like cardboard—no kick, no personality. Spiced curry, on the other hand, tests your taste buds—gives you a dash of pain and then rewards you with a creamy aftertaste. I'd pick curry any day."

As if on cue, Taylor runs back over, her eyes scanning backstage before they land on me. Her lips are flattened, like she's unimpressed or displeased with the world—Firefly used to tell me this is called "a resting bitch face." She's directly under the spotlight now, and I see a white graffiti design splattered across her black sweatshirt that reads:

"Go away. I'll bite. I'm not your babe, your honey, or your sweetheart."

I arch my brow at her, motioning to her outfit.

"Nice clothes. Very mature," I mouth.

I don't know why I'm taunting the brat. She brings out the worst in me. I swear, in her presence, I don't feel like I'm approaching forty. I either feel like a goddamn hormone-ridden teenager, wanting to rile up the girl I find to be interesting just to see how she'd respond, or I'd wish I were in The Sanctuary and could punish this little brat the way she deserved.

What would it be like to get her all worked up, all traces of impudence spanked out of her, to see her eyes glazed over in pleasure as she kneels before me?

My cock twitches in my pants. It's completely maddening.

Is it because she sees past the mask I wear? Because she approaches life with a gumption I don't have? Because she wears all her emotions on her face while I tether mine closely to my chest?

She flicks me the middle finger before rushing over to Bethany and handing her the shoes. Bethany says something to Taylor, and the minx beams—fucking beams at her.

This woman is an infuriating, perplexing conundrum—bratty and spiteful one moment, which is no surprise given our age gap, and a somber, calming presence the next. A tornado in everyday life that'd become an ethereal calm whenever she'd step into her role as a ballerina. Fire and brimstone mixed with aching vulnerability.

An onion with multiple layers, and all of them would make you cry.

I pride myself on being able to read people in a few seconds—it makes me good at what I do and why I'm one of the most well liked CEOs in society.

But I can't read her. And damn, does that annoy me.

Ian laughs next to me. "I see you like curry too."

CHAPTER 16

Sʜᴇ's ᴇxᴏ̨ᴜɪsɪᴛᴇʟʏ ᴘᴇʀꜰᴇᴄᴛ.

I watch with bated breath as Bethany and Dev move together—the devastated Odette and her prince in the last moments before their deaths. Tchaikovsky's famous melody is steeped in sorrow, the haunted notes echoing in the darkened stage as the lone spotlight shines on the tragic couple.

They reach for each other—a series of pirouettes and lifts—their movements restrained, yet desperate at the same time.

My heart swoops and falls with them, desperately wishing they could find another way out even though I've seen this ballet a hundred times and know the ending by heart. God, if Grace knew about this, she'd call me a secret romantic.

The last few weeks under Sir Ian's tutelage have yielded no additional clues. He has been completely professional. Faultless. But my sleep has been destroyed, marred with nightmares where I wake up bathed in sweat—my mind and body still fighting with each other. It's like my body is trying to tell me something my mind can't remember.

It's unsettling and annoying. I haven't felt this way in years.

Dev lifts Bethany in the air, followed by an achingly tender embrace. My heart clenches in wistfulness and longing.

I'm thrown back to a time when I was with Alexis at IBA.

"You have that look on your face," Alexis snickered as we peered at the stage where a *Swan Lake* rehearsal was taking place.

"Shhhhh. This is my favorite part." I nudged her. "And what look?"

Her sharp blue eyes twinkled with laughter as she leaned in. "The look of love and heartbreak. Like you're Odette."

I pursed my lips. "How aren't you moved by this? Undying love, life and death, all performed without words."

"I am." Her voice quieted as we stared at the prince carrying Odette toward the lake to their deaths—because they couldn't break the curse the sorcerer placed on Odette and would rather die than be apart. "You'd make a great Odette someday, Tay. I know it in my gut."

There was a wistfulness in her voice, and I tore my gaze away from the stage to look at her. Her eyes had a faraway look. Our friendship bangle dangled from her slim wrist.

She smiled. "You have what it takes to make it to the top. Grit. Talent. Even the teacher said you captured Odette's essence so well. You'll be unstoppable once you have the technique down."

Oh Alexis, how wrong you were. A weight settles on my chest and I touch the cool metal of the bangle around my wrist.

"That's what you're missing, you know." Charles's deep voice interrupts my thoughts, and a pillar of heat appears by my side.

Rolling my eyes, I mutter, "Why are you even here, Charles? Don't you have work or whatever you CEOs do?"

"My uncle's first performance. I can't miss it." He shuffles closer to me, staring at Dev and Bethany. "Your Odette is missing the vulnerability and all the nuanced emotions that make her role a classic. Your version will march up to the prince, slap him across the face, and come up with some scheme to kill the sorcerer. This is why you keep having issues dancing the role."

Amusement laces his voice as he straightens his suit jacket. He probably thinks he has me all figured out—he has no fucking clue why I can't dance the vulnerability required for Odette.

You don't know shit, Charles.

"Shut up."

The smirk falls off his face and he arches his brow. "What did you just say?"

I glower at him. "You don't know what you're talking about. You're the *last* person to talk to me about this."

His shoulders stiffen and a lock of blond hair falls across his face. That damn annoying mask he wears all the time falls off his face. "What on earth is *wrong* with you? Can't take criticism?"

"No, I have no problem taking criticism, but it's rich coming from you. A man with no dance qualifications to speak of, standing here telling a woman how she's wrong for a role she's a professional in."

My breathing comes out in rapid pants as if a runaway train is barreling toward a head-on collision, its brakes cut, unable to stop. "And how *dare* you ask me what's wrong with me? Why don't I ask you what's wrong with you? How is someone who doesn't even have the guts to tell the world what he's thinking even qualified to lecture another person on vulnerability, love, and heartbreak?"

"What the fuck?" he grits out.

Charles's countenance turns stormier, and in this moment, I can't hear anything other than the blood pumping in my ears. The poison is overflowing inside me and it needs to come out.

The vague silhouettes of business suits that fateful night barge into my mind.

That fake charm at the bar I fell hook, line, and sinker for, followed by pain. Lots of pain.

"Rich men like you just know how to take what's not yours. Because you guys can get away with it. You're all one dimensional. So how dare you lecture me on emotions!"

My pulse roars in my ears, my skin hot to the touch. I clap my hand over my lips, belatedly realizing how much I just spewed out—the lack of sleep from the recent resurgence of my nightmares must be getting to me.

And I took it out on the wrong man, who's standing next to me and saying the wrong thing at the wrong time. Guilt slashes through me, and I swallow.

It's not right. "I-I'm so—"

"You're talking in riddles again. If you have an accusation, say it. If you think I did something, call me out on it. Don't pussyfoot around this shit. You had nothing on my uncle back then and now you have nothing on me." Charles's nostrils flare as he stares at me, his chest rising and falling rapidly. His lips twitch in fury—his entire body is vibrating with restrained anger.

Someone hushes us. I look around, finding everyone in the ten foot radius glaring at us, and I realize we are causing a scene.

I am causing a scene.

I look at Charles again and something shifts in his gaze. He frowns, his eyes sharpening as they cascade over my face. Perhaps he sees the guilt or the regret. Perhaps he's noticing my dark eye circles. But something registers in those arresting eyes of his, and now they're reflecting a new emotion.

Pity.

The last emotion I want from anyone, least of all...him.

He pulls me into a darkened corner farther away from my colleagues, and I swallow my gasp when I see Charles looming over me. He's flushed, a muscle pulsing in his jaw.

"You don't know *anything* about me," he rasps.

He leans down some more, obliterating the inches between us. The heat from his body singes me and I fight the urge to back away.

"You don't know the first thing about men like me because you know what, Taylor? I bet you don't even know yourself." Those crystal blue eyes sear into me, like they can see through to my soul.

Applause rings through the audience, and I startle, my attention temporarily drawn to the closing drapes—the performance has ended. But there's commotion—more commotion than usual.

People dash across the stage and I see Dev carrying a distressed Bethany toward Sir Ian. She's clutching her foot as strained sobs tear from her lips.

Something is wrong, but I barely notice, because all I could think of was Charles's accusations.

Charles straightens to his full height, his eyes darting toward the crowd gathered around Bethany and Sir Ian. He takes a few steps in their direction, his jaw clenching, but he stops himself.

Turning toward me, he says, "You go about lashing out at everyone—myself, my uncle, whoever you deem unworthy, even when you don't have a shred of evidence the person you're attacking with your words deserves them."

My nostrils flare as a ragged breath slips out of my throat.

His eyes soften, the fury from earlier slowly receding into the background. He's picking up his mask from the floor and putting it back on.

He murmurs, "I bet the person you want to hate is yourself. So before you accuse others of hiding their emotions, why don't you hold up a mirror and take a good look and figure out why you're lying to yourself."

He spins around and stalks away.

The person you hate is yourself.

His words ring in my ears, a sucker punch to the gut, and I curl into myself, clutching my sweatshirt tightly as an ache sears into my chest.

Closing my eyes, I slide down to the floor, my head hanging between my knees as my breathing becomes shallow.

A sticky sense of shame seeps inside me, weighing me down.

Alexis is gone. Camden left. My dreams are tainted. My future is uncertain. In the last few weeks, my journey to recovery has regressed a few steps. And now I'm an angry shell of a person who's trying to put on a brave face every day.

Aren't you wearing a mask too, Tay?

I'm the world's biggest hypocrite.

Identifying the problem is step one to resolving it. This is good. This is progress. And progress is never linear. I recite the words I've read in my self-help books and slowly feel my mind calming down. It's painful now, but once I get past this, I'll be stronger, one step closer to reclaiming myself.

I lift my head up and look at my colleagues gathered around Bethany. Medical staff have arrived, alarm clear on their faces. Charles and Ian are in a heated discussion, their frustration and concern evident.

Charles turns toward me, his penetrating eyes snaring mine. He swallows as regret and something undecipherable flashes across his face. I hold his gaze—finding a strange power in them, like someone finally sees me. The real me, scars and all.

And for a split second, I feel less lonely.

CHAPTER 17

Charles

"THERE'S NO OTHER CHOICE?" I rub the bridge of my nose and toss the stack of newspapers on to the dark coffee table in Uncle Ian's office.

The headlines of the financial section are seared into my memory. "Amid the Patterson trial, Bank of Columbia's apology tour comes to a grinding halt," "Pledges to non-profits to be revoked with ballet tour at risk?," "Disaster on stage—ABTC lead ballerina hurt in premiere," "Even Sir Ian can't save Bank of Columbia."

Bethany fractured her ankle during the ending scene of the ballet last weekend—a mishap with her shoes caused her to plummet right as the curtains closed.

She won't be dancing again anytime soon.

"This is a disaster," Ian mutters, raking his hand over his disheveled hair. "But I don't see any other choice—there's only one understudy for her role—Taylor. She isn't ready."

My jaw twitches at the mention of the minx and an uncomfortable heat swirls in my gut at the memory of our terse exchange before disaster struck.

The hatred in her voice, the fire in her eyes. The flash of pain, followed by the completely blown out of proportion response when I mentioned how she was wholly unsuitable to dance Odette.

She's completely wrong for the role. A walking disaster.

And now she's supposed to save the tour? Most likely, we'll be met with angry mobs requesting refunds after the performances.

"Fuck. Sponsors will pull out if this tour goes under." I pace the room. "And God knows what'll happen if we can't fund the pledges to the sexual assault organizations—not with the cash tied up for other purposes. The press will eat us alive if that happens."

A years-long assault committed by a high-ranking management member of the bank is hard to overcome as is. Then, the same bank renouncing on donation commitments to the very victims' rights organizations?

A catastrophe.

Even Uncle Ian and his reputation for being a champion of women's rights in the arts won't save us. Not to mention, with the trial going on, we're appearing in the news daily. We need some good to offset the bad.

I need this tour to go well.

"I've called Taylor over. She's on her way up."

As if on cue, a knock sounds from the door. My shoulders stiffen and muscles tense—every inch of me preparing to go to battle against this hellion.

"Come in," Ian commands before heaving another heavy exhale and settling into his desk chair.

Taylor strides in, her posture stiff but head held high. She's wearing another ill-fitting ensemble—an oversized gray sweatshirt and black leggings this time. She startles when she notices me, her stormy eyes flashing with ire. I sit back on the sofa and force my body to relax—not wanting to give away the pulse of heat surging up my insides at the spark of challenge in her gaze.

She fucking drives me crazy.

Taking a seat in the armchair across from me, she ignores me and addresses Ian. "You asked for me, sir?"

"I have Charles here because, as you know, with Bethany injured, you'll need to step into the roles of Odette and Odile for the rest of the tour." My uncle leans forward and clasps his hands on the desk. "This tour is important to me, to ABTC, and to Bank of Columbia. And I don't need to remind you what is at stake for you."

Taylor freezes, a pink flush slowly crawling up her neck. "The promotion?" she whispers.

My uncle nods. "This tour will be the ultimate test for you. If the tour is well received, I will allow you to sit for the evaluation for the principal position." He stands up and prowls around his desk toward her.

Taylor's eyes widen at his approach, her complexion suddenly paling. A pulse batters against her neck and her breathing quickens. I'm thrown back to the fear in her eyes the day when I first met her and how I don't *ever* want to see her like that again.

"You won't mess this up for me." I slap my knees and draw her attention away. *Look at me instead.*

Her eyes are wild as her gaze darts from Ian to me, then back, then finally settling on me again. She blows out an exhale.

"This is more important than your promotion. The success of this ballet will impact the bank—my family's legacy, and you better not mess this up. If it were up to me, you wouldn't be dancing this role because you're completely unsuited for it."

The familiar fire in her eyes sparks again, and a crushing sense of relief washes over me. The fiery minx is back. "Your family's legacy is none of my business, so don't you try to pin this on me. It's not my fault *someone* was so oblivious he let a sexual predator work under him this entire time without noticing."

Guilt slices through me. The minx seems to know where the weakest parts of my armor are. Taylor stands up and glares at Ian, then at me.

Ian arches his brow, a sharpness in his eyes.

"Ballet is my life. I live and breathe it. I will do my part."

Taylor strides in front of me and I'm hit with a whiff of patchouli and vanilla. A spark of awareness lights up my gut. Slowly, I rise from my seat, enjoying the way she needs to arch her head back to glare at me.

The defiance in her eyes awakens the inner beast I struggle to control, tempting me to unleash the turbulent emotions I've kept restrained, to overpower and tame my prey.

"You better not disappoint me." I watch in fascination the way her pulse jumps when I speak.

She gasps, the little sound fanning the flames in my chest and I lean down a fraction, just to drive her crazy.

She narrows her eyes, her voice taking on a throaty tone. "I'm *not* dancing for you, Charles."

The sultry image of her writhing her lithe body in those ballet shoes *for* me has me almost rearing back in horror.

Slowly, she rises to her tiptoes and whispers, "I'm dancing for myself. Your opinion doesn't matter. You can take your misogynistic attitude and *shove it*."

The fire is now burning hot inside my chest. My nerves spark alive at our proximity. Time slows to a crawl and I clench my fingers, fighting an irrational impulse to reach out and feel the rapid pulse feathering her neck.

How will it feel to have her burn me alive?

To feel the flames at the source?

Complete insanity.

CHAPTER 18

MY HEART HAMMERS RAPIDLY in my rib cage as I stomp down the third floor corridor, only lit by two wrought iron sconces.

That strange moment in Sir Ian's office just now. Charles towering over me, his navy three-piece suit barely restraining his raw masculinity. The way those glacial eyes of his become incandescent.

How the oxygen was sucked out of the room with every inch he closed between us, his head dipping down in those very tiny increments.

He didn't look like the charming golden prince.

He looked like a ravenous lion, and I was his next meal.

Instead of panicking or my pulse clamoring in fear, my first instinct was to lean into him, to close the remaining inches between us and see what he'd do.

A sensual heat pulses between my legs—a sensation so strange, I almost don't recognize it.

Until I do.

There's no way I'm attracted to that arrogant asshole.

A shocked gasp emits from my lips.

No fucking way.

I throw open the stairwell door and fly down the stairs. I can't be so messed up, my body is reacting to the type of men I've always avoided since I was sixteen. Rich, arrogant men with fake charm who see women as nothing more than pussy and sex.

The same fake mask. Insincerity in his voice.

But the common sense doesn't stick. I can still smell Charles's cologne and feel his body heat so close to mine. I think back to that evening at The Sanctuary—him rolling up his sleeves, doling out one harsh command after another, the crack of a whip hitting skin—the violence in his eyes and voice.

The throbbing heat continues to gather between my legs, the sensation climbing as my underwear rubs against my piercing with every step I take. This isn't supposed to happen. The piercing is supposed to be painful—pain I can control.

There's no way the pulsing sensation between my legs is attraction. No fucking way.

I bite back a frustrated growl as I reach the basement and bank a right, eager to take a scalding hot shower to stop this madness.

"No way," I mutter. Stepping into the room, I beeline for the showers, not caring I don't have a change in clothes or my towel with me.

I slam into someone.

"Sorry, I—"

"Watch it, bitch!" Carla's shrill voice jolts me from my thoughts.

She has a towel wrapped around her body and is sneering at me like a tyrant would to her captive.

I roll my eyes. "We have to stop meeting like this." I move around her.

"Cheater."

Gasps ring out in the locker room and I feel a dozen pairs of eyes staring at me.

"What did you say?" Heat suffices my face. Fuck, this bitch messed with the wrong person today. Slowly, I turn back to her.

Carla taps her feet, her lips twisted in a sneer. "I'm just saying what everyone is thinking. You want to be Odette. We all saw you salivating over the role since the day you got here."

She steps forward and pokes me in the chest. "But you aren't good enough. Bethany is so much better than you. Worthy of the role, unlike trailer trash like you."

"You better watch what you're going to say next."

Carla ignores me and raises her voice. "We all saw you hand over the pointe shoes to Bethany. The faulty shoes. Because that's the only way you'll ever be Odette—if Bethany is taken out of the picture. If you're going to cheat, then at least be brave enough to admit it!"

A murmur rises in the room, the girls whispering to each other, their fingers pointing in our direction. I'm appalled. There's no love lost between us, but even she must know I won't resort to cheating to get what I want.

"I had nothing to do with Bethany's accident. I never wanted to get the role this way."

She snorts. "You think because you're an Anderson now, you're somehow different? That you can cheat and steal and get away with it? Well, you can't. We won't let you. And we'll find proof you sabotaged Bethany, and that'll be the end of your ballet career." I'm once again reminded why I didn't want the world to know I'm an Anderson—but that ship has long sailed when the paparazzi caught whiff of our existence a year ago.

I reach out and grab her towel, pulling her toward me, the venom barely disguised in my voice. "I am not a cheater, bitch."

Carla arches her face up. "Go ahead. Hit me. End your career now. I don't give a fuck who your family is. I'll sue the shit out of you and it'll be splashed all over the news. Hit me, cheater. Go ahead."

My hands tremble, and the pressure builds inside my chest. It'll feel so good to hit her, to smack that smirk off her face, but what will that do?

Carla sneers, the whites of her teeth taunting me.

This is what she wants. Don't fall for it, Taylor. Be the best damn Odette so no one can say anything anymore.

My fists tighten on her towel, but slowly, I release my grip. Huffing out a deep breath, I wipe my hands on my leggings.

"No, you're not worth my energy or time." I look around the room, making sure I make eye contact with everyone staring at me. "You just wait and see—I'll be the best damn Odette you've ever seen."

I'll start by finally taking action on unraveling what happened that night. If my overblown reactions at the premiere were any sign, those monsters from my past won't rest until I find out what happened. The cops abandoned me back then—a poor girl with no connections. But everything is different now.

I have influence and resources as an Anderson. I'll fucking help myself.

Brushing past her, I pull out my phone and pull up my text messages.

Taylor

Grace, can you get me the info for the private investigator you hired back when you were trying to find the identity of our dad?

CHAPTER 19

NERVOUS ANTICIPATION SIZZLES THROUGH me as my cell phone buzzes inside the hidden pocket of my bridesmaid gown. *Please tell me it's him.*

I quickly take it out and swipe to the message.

Emerson

> I won't lie and tell you this is going to be easy—the trail has most likely gone cold, but I'll take the case.

My fingers shake as I type out a response.

Taylor

> Thank you. Please keep this between us.

Emerson

> That goes without saying. Privacy is a requirement in my line of work.

A few dots appear on the screen.

Emerson

> And Taylor...I'm sorry about what happened to you. We will get the bastards.

A lump forms in my throat as I stare at the message from him and I grip my phone tightly in my hands and rake in a ragged inhale.

It's the first time anyone has ever acknowledged what happened to me without doubt, suspicion, or derision.

He's not like Alexis or Camden, the cops or that shitty therapist. He didn't reject me.

I was expecting the pain of dismissal and rejection from Emerson Clarke, the private investigator who helped Grace in the past and is one of the best in his field. I thought he'd take one look at the paltry information I'd gathered and brush me off.

A glimmer of hope flickers inside me. Maybe luck is finally on my side, because he's going to find out what happened all those years ago.

"Tay, you okay? You look like you've seen a ghost." Millie tucks a lock of dark brown hair behind her ear as she stares at me with concern.

I wipe away my expression. "What? Oh, nothing. I'm just thinking about walking around in this getup." I smirk and gesture at our deep burgundy bridesmaid gowns—all designs from McKenzie's Atelier, because there's no way Belle would let us wear any other brand. "This is not exactly my style."

"Come on—they are gorgeous! I picked them out specifically for you guys!" Belle complains and pouts at me, but her eyes are shining with laughter. "Millie gets the sexy thigh high slit that'll drive Ryland insane. I get the sweetheart neckline with the hidden bustier because I don't have massive boobs like you guys."

She points to her chest for emphasis. This woman must be delusional because she is gorgeous with her perfectly proportioned curves, her porcelain skin, and straight black hair, thanks to her mom, who's an Asian supermodel.

Belle then narrows her eyes at me. "And you, Ms. Badass Ballerina, you get the boatneck gown with sleeves since I know you like to cover yourself up, which makes no sense to me because why wouldn't you flaunt that?" She gestures to my body and sighs. "But never fear. McKenzie's designs are gorgeous, no matter the cut, and you look ravishing. Too bad there isn't a guy you're trying to impress." She snorts.

A flash of blond hair and intense blue eyes barrels into my mind.

It has to be the love in the air impacting common sense because there is no way I'm trying to impress Charles Vaughn even if he were the last man on earth.

"Tay is trying to impress someone? Is that what I hear?" Grace sweeps into the living room of the bridal suite inside The Orchid and we all gasp in surprise.

"You look so beautiful!" I marvel.

Tears spring into my eyes as I take in my sister, who looks otherworldly in her cream-colored silk wedding dress—an elegant A-line silhouette with gentle pleating and a long train reminiscent of royal brides. Her hair is pinned up in a low, twisted chignon bun with springs of baby's breath pinned as decoration.

The girls fuss over her, all exclaiming how gorgeous she is, but all I can do is stand before her, rooted to the ground, my heart pounding with so many emotions, I'm afraid they'll all explode from me at the same time.

Mom, if you're looking down at us, you must be so happy. Your beautiful, intelligent daughter is getting married to a man who worships the ground she walks on. It's everything you would've wanted for her.

I press my lips together in a tight smile at Grace, fighting a tremble that threatens to make itself known—the impulse to cry, to laugh, to pull her into my arms, emotions swirling together into something indecipherable.

At least one of us got our happily ever after.

The women in my family haven't been lucky in love—Mom with her string of broken relationships before she died and me...well, I don't think love is in my cards. But I'm glad that isn't the case with Grace.

Grace seems to sense my thoughts and I see the same unshed tears in her eyes as she glides forward and pulls me into her arms. "I wish Mom were here," she whispers.

I sniffle, my heart full of love for her and also battling with the wave of unexpected grief hitting me from the side. My voice is thick as I whisper, "She *is* here. I can feel her. I'm so happy for you, Grace. So, so happy. You deserve all the love and joy in the world."

She hugs me tighter. "And so do you, Tay. I know you hold your cards close to your chest, and don't think I don't see past the grumpy persona of yours. You're the best sister a girl could ever ask for."

My vision blurs as I pull back, seeing her smiling at me. I let out a ragged exhale before rubbing my nose piercing—a red heart today. "Damn right I am. I don't wear a red dress and give out hugs just for anyone."

Grace laughs and a stray tear leaks from her eyes, which she quickly wipes away. She takes my hand and squeezes it gently, her expression sobering. "*Nothing* will change between us. Sisters forever."

The lump in my throat grows as I watch Belle and Millie pull her toward the window, shrieking about her ruining her makeup.

I stand there, looking at the three women I love the most in the world, the joy radiating from their faces almost contagious. All three of them are so in love with their men, wonderful men who are equally enthralled with them.

And I feel bereft.

Things are going to change now. Even if they say it won't.

Soon, they'll be talking about pregnancies and kids and I'll still be here, unable to form a meaningful connection with anyone, unable to move on.

I'm being left behind.

The thoughts immediately crush me. Wordlessly, I open the door to the suite and slip away.

Invisible.

CHAPTER 20

STEPPING OUTSIDE, I BREATHE in the sweet fragrance of flowers, the tightness in my chest slowly dissipating. I continue on the cobblestone path leading to the courtyard where Steven and Grace will have their ceremony in an hour, followed by a dinner reception at the rooftop lounge.

Unlike most high society weddings, they've opted to have a smaller, intimate gathering with close family and friends in attendance instead.

Laughter reaches my ears and I stop under a stone arch lining the hidden courtyard. Guests are dressed in their finest—most are already seated facing a gothic-style dark gazebo in the center of the space.

Lush greenery and ivy line the walls. Ancient oak trees with their gnarly branches hang low, providing shade for the guests. The perfume of the flowers is stronger here, with the courtyard being surrounded by arrangements of burgundy roses and orchids, the colors matching our gowns.

But what catches my attention isn't the beautiful space, which Grace once told me is the very courtyard Steven once stood in under the pouring rain to convince her to give him a chance.

It's the children.

Ainsley, from ABTC, is grinning with Maddy while they're practicing a dance with five adorable little girls in cotton candy pink tutus. Steven has sponsored a few scholarships for underprivileged dancers at various ballet companies—he tells me it's his way of taking care of the other little Graces and Taylors in the world. As a thank you, the girls and the kids are performing at the reception.

"Hands up! Yes! That's perfect. Stop wiggling your butts." Ainsley's words are met with giggles, and my lips hike up in a smile.

"Maddy and I won't call you guys graceful ballerinas anymore. We're calling you all dancing elephants instead."

The kids laugh harder and shake their bottoms in the air. Maddy barks out a laugh and shoves Ainsley on the shoulder. "It's your fault, Ains! Bad influence! What will Mr. Kingsley think?"

Ainsley laughs and pokes her friend back. "I'm a bad influence, but you love me for it!"

The smile slips from my lips as I remember Alexis saying something very similar that night.

"Do we really have to go to the lounge? They won't even let us in, right? I'm sixteen." I stared at Alexis curling her fiery hair into perfect waves, all the while humming a song on repeat.

She glanced at me in the mirror and winked. "It's a celebration! And unofficial networking with the suits. You know we're expected to attend. Don't worry, there's no age limit tonight. It'll be fun! Maybe you can take some photos to store in that memento box of yours in your secret stash."

"It's not a secret if you know about it." I grin. But of course she knows about my hiding spot in the rooftop studio. She keeps trying to take over it, saying she has ballet secrets and dreams she wants to embed within the floors of the company too.

"It's because you love me, Tay Tay. You won't say it, but I know you do!" she singsonged.

I laughed at her ridiculousness as excitement about the night of adventures ahead filled my veins. Grace and I were too poor to go out, so a night on the dime of the ballet company would be a treat. I eyed my reflection in the mirror—my black hair also curled in voluminous waves, my makeup natural except for a red lip—Alexis always told me my gray eyes and delicate features didn't need tons of makeup to stand out. *Show everyone your beauty*, she'd say.

"Fine! But let it be said if anything happens, it's all your fault. You're such a bad influence." My lips twitched, but I did my best to maintain a straight face.

Alexis laughed and threw her head back, her hair a fiery brand in the air. "But you love me for it, bestie."

The children's joyful shrieks draw my attention back to the present and a pinch tugs at my chest. I blow out a deep breath and look at a decorative gilded mirror hanging on the stone wall. My signature thick eyeliner, deep purple lipstick, and a nose piercing.

I bet she wouldn't recognize me now.

Then, I stare at roses adorning the space. My heart pinches at the sight of my favorite flowers, all their thorns shorn off. I trace the smooth stems with my fingers.

No one likes the thorns. People only want the beautiful flower.

Suddenly, my skin prickles to attention and I sense a heated intensity directed my way. Looking up, I see *him* mingling with the boys inside the gazebo.

Charles stands tall to the right of Steven, who's laughing at something Ryland is saying. Maxwell smirks ncxt to them, his hands in his pockets. I barely notice my brothers, my attention drawn to the golden-haired archangel with the heart of a devil.

My eyes drift up from his shiny leather shoes, tailored pants highlighting his long legs, to his muscular torso straining against the confines of his black tux jacket. It's like the tux was invented for him to showcase the ideal masculine physique. My skin heats as I continue my pcrusal and I know the exact moment when he turns his attention to me again, because every nerve ending in my body comes alive.

Swallowing, I drag my gaze up to his face and I find his arresting eyes snared on mine, and even from this distance, I can feel the glacial chill radiating from them. My first instinct is to scowl at him or look away. To ignore the man who seems to be the only person seeing the dark storms plaguing my mind.

But I can't. Perhaps it's the turbulent emotions consuming me all day, the feeling of being invisible despite being surrounded by people, or the heady love in the air—a stark contrast to the loneliness carving a bottomless hole inside me.

He's caught me in a weak moment.

In this moment, I don't want to lose the only attention directed at me, the woman behind the forced smiles. The person who's forced to confront a future she'll never have—a collision of bittersweet sentiments. Dreams shattered. Futures altered.

I want to be seen.

My breath stutters, my heart quickening, and soon I'm dizzy. Disoriented. Like I've been staring at the sun for too long.

His eyes darken, and I see his throat rippling as he swallows.

I have given myself away.

And I don't want to give any more of my broken pieces away to anyone, least of all him.

Charles cocks his head to the side, just slightly, barely noticeable. The afternoon sun shines a beam on him, his hair glowing. This infuriating man looks too damn hot for his own good.

He furrows his brows, his gaze intent, and a muscle pulses in his jaw.

"Are you okay?" he mouths. He takes a small step toward me.

I see sincerity in his eyes and can almost hear him asking me the question with concern in his voice, and it makes me uncomfortable, the tightness in my chest worsening.

I feel raw and exposed under his scrutiny.

My heart is now drumming up a storm inside me.

He takes another step toward me.

"Charles?" Maxwell asks before following Charles's gaze and turning his head my way. My brother's eyes darken with concern.

Quickly, I look away and force my lips into a bright smile. "Girls, how's the dance coming along?" I holler to Ainsley and their group.

"Something is coming all right! A herd of elephants!"

The girls cackle, and I hurry over to join them, ignoring the penetrating heat of Charles's gaze.

CHAPTER 21

THE PIANIST SWAYS HIS body as he plays Claude Debussy's "Clair de Lune" and the bridesmaids slowly make their way down the aisle. As I stand there inside the gazebo next to Steven, as his best man, I watch Belle, followed by Millie, glide up the cobblestone path, both of them a vision in dark red, before they stand to the other side of the officiant. Glancing at the men next to me, I find Maxwell and Ryland's gazes affixed on the women, love shining from their eyes.

Maxwell's lips move as he mouths a few words to Belle, who looks like she wants to run into her husband's arms.

I love you.

Those were the words he murmured—I'm sure of it.

My heart hitches at the obvious affection—enough to melt the normally cold exteriors of the Anderson twins.

What would it feel like to let someone in and have her love all parts of you, including the parts you hide?

I breathe in. Would I turn into my parents, so madly obsessed with each other, no one else matters in life? Not their responsibilities, their families...their children?

A few kids giggle and I see the little girls in tutus pointing at the bridesmaids, their eyes wide with wonder. My lips twitch as I remember how excited they were moments ago when they were practicing a dance with Taylor.

"That's good! You were wonderful!" Taylor clapped, her face radiant with joy.

My heart skipped several beats as I took in the happiness in her eyes, the brilliance of her smile.

"But Tay Tay, what if I forget how many times to spin?" one of the kids asked. "What if I'm too scared to move?"

Taylor tapped her chin, like she was considering their plight seriously. She kneeled to the ground and beckoned the girls closer. "Then you wiggle your booty like elephants!" She tickled the girls, and they squealed.

I swallowed the chuckle threatening to erupt because the boys were standing next to me.

"When I was your age, I always forgot my steps too. And you know what the secret is? You just pretend you know what your next steps are as you make them up, because no one else knows the dance. Only you do." She winked and the girls gaped at her like she was Yoda.

Taylor was so good with the kids. So patient, fun, and kind. I had a feeling this sweetness was hidden inside her all along.

I flinch at the direction of my thoughts and I refocus my attention on the scene before me.

The wistful strains of the cello sweeps through the air. I recognize the wedding processional music the happy couple chose—Camille Saint-Saën's famous musical piece, "Le Cygne."

Otherwise known as "The Swan."

It was a favorite of Grandma's. She told me it represented the impermanence of beauty, but it stayed with you long after it was gone.

It's a heartrending sentiment.

The mesmerizing violin wraps the intimate space in its thrall when Taylor walks in.

Every atom in my body freezes, suspended in time, as I watch her float toward me like the beautiful swan of this musical piece. My breath hitches as I stare at her, unable to look away.

The impermanence of beauty. No, I'm afraid this image will be emblazoned in my mind forever.

The burgundy gown drapes over her lean frame as she holds her head high—the innate poise of a ballerina. The late afternoon sunlight bathes her elegant frame in a golden caress, illuminating those expressive dark eyes of hers, the mirrors into her soul, her plump lips, a perfect cupid's bow.

Even though she tries to hide behind her dark makeup and lipstick, I can see through it. The sweetness, the softness, the same loneliness I recognize in myself. And an untold pain she's holding inside her, the reason she's lashing out at the world.

My pulse rushes in my ears as she moves toward me.

One step. Two steps. Three steps.

I swear I smell her distinct scent of vanilla and patchouli and my mouth waters. I'm tempted to close my eyes and draw in a deeper inhale to savor every single note of this intoxicating fragrance.

She looks up, her eyes locking with mine, and she stumbles, her luscious lips parting. Her gray eyes widen and I'm thrown back to the moment I witnessed half an hour ago, when she was standing in the shadows, looking so alone, with utter heartbreak and devastation in her eyes.

When I wanted to rush toward her and pull her into my arms.

The brief second seems to stretch forever, and I slowly clench my hands into fists. The same impulse makes a reappearance—the need to go to her and pull her into my arms. To tell her she's not alone.

Because she has me.

Madness. You've lost your mind, Charles. She's a brat, the very definition of instability you try to avoid.

Then she wipes her face clean of expression, her shoulders squared, head held high, and breaks our connection before making her way to the girls. The music switches to Felix Mendelssohn's famous "Wedding March," and everyone stands as Grace walks in with Linus Anderson, who has tears in his eyes. No doubt he'd never expected the daughter he recently reunited with would let him walk her down the aisle.

The crowd murmurs with apparent excitement—smiles and joy abound—but I can't pay attention.

Instead, I find myself glancing at Taylor, standing a mere few feet away from me.

She's smiling at her sister, but her eyes are shining with sad tears.

And my heart breaks a little inside.

CHAPTER 22

LOUD CHEERS AND THUNDERING applause erupt inside the rooftop lounge as Steven sweeps Grace into a low dip to end their first dance together as husband and wife. The clinking of silverware against plates soon follows, the crowd ravenous for a display of affection from the normally cold king of Wall Street.

Steven chuckles, the whites of his teeth blinding as he stares at a blushing Grace, who's hiding half her face behind her hand. He leans down and murmurs something into her ear and I don't think it's possible for my sister to flush any redder, but apparently there's no limit tonight.

Gently, he pries her hand off her face. The smile slips off his lips and the cold king is back—but this time, the smolder in his eyes is burning hot. Steven clasps the nape of Grace's neck and kisses her like we're not here.

He kisses her like it's the end of the world and he can die a happy man with her in his arms.

What would it feel to have someone look at me like that?

Wolf whistles and laughter ring in the room, but it all sounds so far away—like I'm underwater. Even if I were to find out the truth about that night, I don't think I'm capable of letting anyone in—my walls are so high, even I can't scale them. Frankly, I have no desire to let anyone into my heart. Camden's betrayal haunts me to this day—that someone who claimed to love me could abandon me at the lowest point of my life.

I'd never put myself in that position again.

I focus my attention on the glittering skyline of Manhattan, unrivaled in its beauty. The wedding is perfect—everything Grace deserves.

The food is scrumptious, and Ainsley and Maddy did a phenomenal job leading the little dancers into a short, but lovely ballet inspired by *The Nutcracker*.

Even the skies are clear tonight. I swear I even see a shooting star or two. My lips twitch in a smile—Grace has an obsession with shooting stars. She believes they're magical, that the gods will grant wishes.

If only it were that simple—wishing upon a star.

The crowd's excited laughter and murmurs reach my ears and while I'm surrounded by a room full of people, I've never felt so alone before in my life.

I'm happy for Grace. Truly. She deserves Steven and all the love in the world. But in these moments, when their ardent love is in my face, it hurts like a sucker punch aimed at my broken heart.

It's not their fault. It's not my fault. I understand why I'm feeling this way.

But I hate it. This selfishness, jealousy, envy, and loneliness don't belong in a beautiful night such as this.

The DJ switches the music to a faster song and couples join the newlyweds on the dance floor. Millie pulls a brooding Ryland into the crowd, but as soon as she curls her arms around his neck, a beautiful smile appears on his lips. In a darkened corner away from the commotion, I see Maxwell holding Belle tightly in his arms, clearly lost in the sensations of each other, oblivious to the world around them.

My breath hitches and my legs bounce under the table.

Screw this shit. It's a beautiful evening and the Lochness Monster can't come and screw it up. I'm going to request some fast songs and dance like nobody's business.

Filled with renewed determination, I make my way over to the DJ before a familiar voice stops me.

"Tay!"

My eyes widen as I see Olivia waving at me from the back of the room. Tonight, I almost don't recognize her, since she's wearing contacts and a slinky black dress instead of her usual glasses and business suit.

"What are you doing here?" I ask, making my way over. "I didn't know you know Grace."

We usually hang out outside of The Orchid bingeing movies, browsing bookstores, or even visiting a bar or two. She's easy to talk to and I'm thankful she doesn't psychoanalyze me, because let's not open that can of worms. I've been meaning to introduce her to Grace and the other girls, but haven't had a chance yet. I think they'll like her too.

"I wanted to say hi at the ceremony, but you were too busy." She pulls me into a light hug. "Actually, I'm a guest of Steven's and I also know Maxwell."

She pauses but doesn't say more and suddenly something clicks in my mind.

"*Hold on a second*...you're the same Dr. Lin that Maxwell is seeing?"

Olivia shrugs, a mischievous smile on her face. "Can't confirm or deny that. You can ask your brother, though."

Holy shit. She's the expert who helped Maxwell with his severe social anxiety and panic attacks. I almost fan-girled at the idea of her when I heard how Maxwell's doctor turned his life around with therapy and medication.

"I'm not a hugger, but I want to hug the fucking shit out of you," I blurt out. "You saved Maxwell and because you helped him get his shit together, he and Belle are so, so happy now. And they deserve it. God, do they deserve it after everything they went through." Those two went through life and death situations not long after they got married and came out on the other side.

Olivia chuckles and swats me away. "I love my job. So," she eyes me quizzically, "we're both not on the clock tonight and I presume...dateless. We should party it up. Us single girls need to stick together in this sea of nauseating love."

I bark out a laugh. "Hear, hear. Are you sure you're supposed to say this? Aren't you supposed to be all hell-bent on healthy commitments and all that shit?"

"Well, Ms. Peyton-Anderson," her voice drops into a soothing tone I know is her psychiatrist voice, "Dr. Lin would also tell you weddings may be hard on single people because folks often reflect on milestones then and it's only natural for us to compare themselves with others. Society views getting married as a pinnacle and those who aren't may feel lonely or somehow less than."

The wave of doom sweeps in at her words, and I slowly deflate.

Olivia's eyes darken and glimmer with an unidentified emotion before she blinks it away. "But, Olivia says, with all things in life, we only see the grass as greener on the other side. And, because you and I are single, we don't have to answer to anyone. We get to live for ourselves and love the person who deserves it the most—ourselves. So, we're partying it up."

She leans in and whispers, "Think about it—we don't have to deal with the toilet seat cover being up, dirty socks on the floor, or loud snoring at night." She waggles her brows at me. "I mean, no brainer, right?"

I snort. "You're a riot."

Just then, I hear loud laughter nearby, and we turn our heads toward the commotion. Charles is standing next to the dance floor with *not* one or two, but *three* women practically draped over him. He's saying something, that damn charming smile on his face again, and the women practically melt in his presence. A brunette steps up and presses her hand to his chest.

"Ugh," I mutter. An uncomfortable pinch tugs at my gut. *Nope, not going to think about what that means.*

"What? You know him? Do we not like him?"

Charles is now gesturing in the air, each movement highlighting the muscles flexing under his tux. He twirls the brunette on the dance floor—one simple spin and dip.

My breath hitches. He carries himself with grace, his moves smooth and fluid—the man has had lessons before and he's pretty damn good at it.

I frown—did I just give him an internal compliment? I shudder in horror.

His harem giggles and I fight the urge to throw up at grown ass women acting like they are starstruck teenagers. The redhead waves her hand in the air next and he tugs her to him before he demonstrates a decent box step—a classic ballroom dance move.

Come on, who the fuck lives to be eighteen and doesn't know the box step? It's literally moving in the shape of a damn box. It's like saying you don't know how to make a grilled cheese sandwich.

My inner voice titters. *Someone is jealous, huh?*

Ack! Lochness Monster, go away!

His commanding presence draws the attention of everyone in the ten foot radius and more people join his little ménage and I roll my eyes. Then Ainsley and one of the little ballerinas walk up to him, both with hearts in their eyes. The little girl, still dressed in her tutu, waves to Charles and he chuckles, his eyes lighting up before he squats down and drops his ear by her lips, giving her all of his attention. My heart spasms at the scene before me. *He'd make a wonderful dad someday.* Another thought that comes from nowhere.

It has to be the effects of a wedding. Strange things happen at weddings.

That has to be it.

The little girl whispers something to him and he looks at Ainsley, who points to someone in the crowd.

Apparently getting permission from whoever she's pointing to, Charles sweeps the little girl up in his arms and twirls her around as she squeals in glee. I swear I can hear the ovaries of the women nearby exploding.

I tamp down the funny sensations in my gut and press my lips together in distaste. *Fucking showoff.*

"He's someone I prefer not to be associated with, to put it mildly," I answer Olivia. "What you see is *not* what you get with him. You should make him a case study. This," I wave a finger in his direction, "is a show he's putting on for the public. He's arrogant, opinionated, condescending, faker than a knockoff bag they sell on street corners, horrible—"

"Hm." A few long seconds of silence follow.

I frown and turn to her. "What?"

She arches her brow. "Oh—just that you're quite worked up over someone you don't like."

"Well, you won't like him if you know him too. And don't they say hatred is a strong emotion?" I glare at the golden prince and his gaggle of women.

Olivia chuckles. "They also say there's a fine line between—"

"Don't you dare say it!" My mouth drops open in horror and I shudder. Absolutely no way would I entertain any emotion of that nature toward him.

The music changes from a hip-hop song to something sexy and sultry—a song more suited for the tango and couples walk back to the dance floor.

I groan and stare forlornly at ladies in their glittering dresses, accompanied by their sharply dressed partners—I missed my chance to work out my jitteriness on the dance floor.

Suddenly, the air shifts, and I smell the intoxicating scent of cedarwood and bergamot. The hairs on the back of my neck rise to attention, and I feel a column of heat behind me. I close my eyes and brace myself for his taunting, raspy voice.

"Can't find a partner, minx?"

CHAPTER 23

THE UNMISTAKABLE MELODY OF Gerardo Matos Rodriguez's "La Cumparsita" sweeps into the dance floor, tantalizing all the senses with its sharp pauses and intense sexiness. There's a reason this piece is nick-named the anthem of tango. As soon as I heard the first strains of the music, I excused myself from the women to go to the restroom before I get looped into an unwanted dance.

They were all daughters or sisters of financiers and business partners, and I didn't want to offend them, but to say their advances were not appreciated would be an understatement. My jaw ached from smiling too much. But then, as I left the group, my gaze swept over the dance floor and I saw her.

My minx standing at the edge, fiery in her deep red dress and dark makeup, her arms crossed over her chest again. A temptress staring at the ruins burning at her feet.

But she had that damn look in her eyes again—hollow, like she was marooned on an island somewhere with no hope of rescue.

And obviously, I'm a masochist tonight because I thought it'd be a great idea to burn myself alive.

"Can't find a partner, minx?" I murmur, striding up to her.

She closes her eyes. Her throat ripples and I see a slight tremor in her body and heat sparks in my gut. She's not immune to this insanity between us.

"Go away, Charles. Even if I wanted a partner, it wouldn't be you." Her eyes are still closed like she's determined not to give me her full attention.

"I wasn't aware I was asking. I was just pointing out an observation."

A frustrated growl tears from her lips and my lips twitch in a smile. Riling her up may be the best part of my night so far.

"Go find someone else to bother—all those women fawning over you, pick any of them."

"Do I sense jealousy?"

"Please. As if I'd be jealous of women stupid enough to need dance lessons from the likes of you, you uncoordinated buffoon."

Her face flushes, the pulse on her neck fluttering harder. *You little liar, Taylor.*

Leaning in, I murmur, "Buffoon, huh? Did you learn that word from school?"

She snorts, finally opening her eyes and the dim glow of the strobe lights catches her gray irises, highlighting the small striations. And for a moment, I forgot what I was going to say, rendered speechless by the pools of quicksilver.

Her eyes darken as she stares at me. I watch her gaze drip over my face, landing on my lips before moving back up, and I find myself doing the same.

Heat curls around my groin, my cock clearly not getting the instruction we're not supposed to be interested in this madwoman.

Damn weddings—makes even the sanest people go insane.

The sultry strains of the song fan the flames between us, and my eyes snare at the rapid pulse beckoning me on her slender neck and suddenly common sense seems overrated.

"I bet I could out dance you," I rasp, "this song. The Argentine tango."

Her eyes widen and those voluptuous dark purple lips part. "*You?* Out dance me? A professional dancer?"

I lean in. "Want to bet? Appearances can be deceiving."

Couples sweep by us, the ladies hooking their legs around their partners' in a dance resembling passionate sex. My fingers twitch at my sides. I want to touch her—skin to skin—dig my fingers into her smooth flesh, feel her fire straight from the source.

Taylor falters, her mouth now panting quick breaths. Her nostrils flare as she stares at my lips again. My cock jolts in my pants.

Fuck.

I hold out my hand. "Is the badass ballerina scared? I won't bite. Unless you want me to, little girl."

"Don't 'little girl' me." Indignation flashes in her scowl and she jams her hand in mine and pulls me on to the dance floor.

"Do you prefer brat?" My lips cock up in a grin as I snake my other arm around her and pull her flush against me so that every inch of our bodies is pressing against each other—her soft curves against my hard planes. Her breath hitches. I swallow the ball in my throat as awareness throbs between us. She steps away and I pull her back harder.

"I don't think so, minx. I lead in the tango," I murmur in her ear, and she fucking shudders, her body becoming pliant. *She'd take it all so well, this inner submissive streak of hers. She just needs someone to get her out of her head.*

Blood rushes to my stiffening cock. It's a fucking hopeless cause. I have a beautiful woman in my arms. This is just biology. *Yeah, keep telling yourself that.*

Sliding my hands to her hips, I guide her into a figure eight position as she steps forward, her movements hitting each beat of the music, but her head is still held too high, arms too graceful.

Too indifferent, much like the makeup she wears to hide herself from the world.

I snap her toward me.

"That's the *ocho*. And this is tango, Taylor. Not ballet. Do I need to teach you how to feel the music in your blood?" I smirk before pushing her away and following her retreat.

Her muscles tense and she hurls a seething glare capable of murder my way. This time, when she makes her way toward me, I see the fire in her steps with every stomp on the floor.

Much better.

"Do they teach tango along with acting lessons at the fancy-ass prep schools for billionaires?" she hurls back at me when we come together.

I breathe in her scent—sweet, addictive nectar—and it fans the flames in my chest.

Every part of me awakens as I pause on the dance floor, watching her slowly circle me like she's a predator and I'm her prey.

A true predator will lull their prey into a false sense of security. "That's the *corte*, and much, much better, Taylor," I rasp.

Playtime is over.

Charging forward, I watch her eyes widen as she is forced to follow my lead and I maneuver her in a new direction. She submits to me...so fucking beautifully; I don't think she even realizes it. Her body is mirroring every single move from me, like we were made to dance together.

"*Sacada.* And no, I learned dance because my uncle is a world-renowned choreographer who encouraged my siblings and me to love the art of physical movement."

The music swells and retreats, much like the changing distance between us. Taylor spins in a series of twists before I pull her back to me. Her eyes widen, her face flushed, her mouth parted as she rakes in breath after breath, exhilaration bathing her features.

A sweltering image enters my mind—her same expression. Us in bed, our bodies entangled. Her shattering around my cock after I rain a few well deserving slaps on her ass. Her eyes glazed over, in complete submission to the beast inside me. My nostrils flare, hot blood flowing straight to the semi in my pants.

I wonder if every interaction between us since that blistering punch has been some sick and twisted foreplay.

But she had to ruin the moment by opening her mouth.

"Something about your uncle rubs me the wrong way. It's a gut feeling. I don't know what, but I'm going to find out." Taylor throws out a seething glare.

Anger churns through me. "What happened to you? Why are you so bitter and furious at the world? My uncle is a good man—one of the best Vaughns in our family. Why are you creating shit out of thin air?"

Her eyes darken at my rebuttal, and she dodges my attempt at pulling her back to my side. She spins around and walks away, not answering my question. Running away again.

I don't think so.

In a few strides, I catch up to her, grab her wrist, and twirl her around. "Do you just need to blame someone for hurting you in the past? What better person to blame than your new boss, who might not promote you because you're clearly not ready for it?"

She lets out a growl and hurtles toward me, but I counter her movement with a dramatic sweep of my leg.

"*Arrastre* and then *volcada*," I heave out the moves as I keep her off balance so she has no choice but to lean on me or else she'd fall flat on her ass. "I looked into my uncle, Taylor. There's nothing. You're holding onto something that doesn't exist."

Her face turns red, moisture gathering in her gray eyes, and the sight of her tears hurts more than any hit she could've inflicted on me. "You don't know *anything* about me and what I went through."

She slams her hands on my chest and pushes me back across the dance floor. "You think I'm just an immature brat who's making shit up for attention." I catch her hand on top of my chest as I stomp on the floor, rooting myself in place.

She circles me slowly before stepping into my space and pulling my head down, all to the beat of the music. "You know nothing about me!"

I growl, unable to stop myself as I charge forward and sweep out my leg, forcing her to lean against me once more. "Then tell me. Tell me why you're hot and cold, angry one minute and vulnerable the next. What are you hiding, Taylor? What happened to you? *Tell me so I can fix it!*"

The words tumble out from my mouth with no forethought, but as the blood rushes in my ears and my hands tighten against hers, I realize how true they are.

I want to know what caused her to be like this. I want to find out so I can destroy whoever made her this way.

"You like the idea of fixing me, huh? Fix the poor, traumatized ballerina because Mr. Rich Guy has nothing better to do with his time?"

My hand tightens around her waist, and I pull her toward me. The fucking minx. Maddening. Stubborn. I'm getting through to her, and that's why she's fighting back so hard. I want to break down every single one of her walls and find out what she's hiding. I want to see that sweet smile I saw earlier at the ceremony when she was teaching the little kids.

Taylor gasps, her body surrendering when her mind wouldn't. Her back dips toward the ground, but I catch her at the last moment. My arm snakes around her waist as her leg bends and lifts. My other hand slides up her slender calf, dragging the soft fabric up her supple thigh before hooking her leg around my waist as we dip together, her warm heat pressing against my hard groin.

"Have you ever considered you're wrong about me?" I rasp into her ear.

She lets out a moan. So soft I could barely hear above the music, but I feel every vibration, and it sets my body aflame. She dips her head back, her chest arched toward me, hard nipples saluting me through the fabric.

"That some of the wealthy are actually good people—like your brothers and me. That we actually care about you, even though there are days when I wonder why I even bother." *It's because she's real, unapologetic. She doesn't care what others think of her. She's brave. She's everything you're not.* "Ask yourself, why do you push us all away?"

I press my lips to the outer edge of her ear and there it is...that alluring tremble again.

She melts in my arms, her body curving backward, and I chase her motion, unable to resist the lure of her pulse fluttering in her neck like a hummingbird's wings. My nose dips to the crook of her neck and I inhale deeply and close my eyes.

The sweet scent of vanilla and something darker, nuanced and layered like this maddening woman in my arms. My fingers dig into her smooth thigh, kneading the muscles there—so strong yet so feminine—and pull her body up so she grinds on me, every inch of her plastered against my front.

Another moan. This time, louder, her body moving against mine, her leg clamping tightly around my waist, hips arching, gyrating in a sensual rhythm, melting under my dominance.

"I'll find out...I'll get it out of you one day, Taylor," I vow before dragging my nose down her neck. Unable to stop myself, my teeth make an appearance, scraping the throbbing pulse point. She lets out another wispy moan, her fingers digging into my neck.

She thrusts her tits up at me—an action I'm sure is involuntary. My mouth waters. My minx is a sensual goddess hidden under the cold facade.

"W-What are you doing to me?" Confusion laces her voice as I press home my point by sucking the bite marks on her neck. "Oh God," she whimpers, her hips thrashing, gyrating, rubbing that delectable pussy against my raging, hard cock.

A groan rumbles in my throat at the sharp sensations—the flames licking up my spine.

"No. It's Charles," I whisper, my mind clawing with need for this intoxicating woman in my arms. "Call my name when you're with me. Scream it. Moan it. Just know it's me making you feel this way, that maybe your body knows something your mind doesn't."

My body moves with her, my mind only focused on this vixen and her pleasure. My cock threatens to tunnel itself out of my pants, the throbbing intense as sparks gather along my shaft. I want to touch all parts of her—the soft curves, the enticing divots, every part she wants people to see and all the parts she wants to hide.

Thunderous applause erupts in the room, jolting me back into reality as the sensual haze slowly clears.

My lungs drag in one desperate breath after another and I watch as Taylor slowly comes to her senses. Her chest is heaving, her stormy eyes widening, the pupils bleeding into the irises. She quickly untangles her leg from my waist, but I hold on, kneading, digging tightly, memorizing her curves with my hand. She intakes a sharp breath, her eyes flaring at the pleasurable pain before she grits her jaw and yanks her leg away from me.

"Stop being such a relentless bastard." She stomps off, strands of her thick black hair tumbling out of her updo, and I can only stare at her retreating, my thoughts in disarray, my nerves ending raw. It felt like the most erotic sex I've ever had and my mind doesn't know what to make of it.

A few wolf whistles pierce the applause, and I whip my head toward the commotion, my hands automatically smoothing out the lapels of my tux. Ethan has his brow hiked up, Rex grinning and mouthing something suspiciously like *"I knew it."* Maxwell levels a warning with his glare.

Parker Wellington, who is the best dancer in my friend group in LA, smirks and makes an exaggerated bow at me as Steven's siblings, Jess and Emily gape at me, their mouths hanging open. Even the cold and sardonic Adrian Scott, Emily's husband, known to the public as The Shark for his shrewdness in business, shakes his head, his lips twitching in obvious amusement.

Shit—I completely forgot I'm in public. This woman has made me lose all common sense and control.

But I've never felt more alive.

Maybe this is why my parents are so wrapped up in each other—this addictive, intoxicating high.

My heart lurches at the thought and for a moment, I think I'm going to be sick.

But now fully aware of the hundreds of eyes trained on me, I force my lips to curve in a grin and sweep my arm out before dropping into an exaggerated bow. The demonstration is met with more raucous laughter.

And I fight every impulse to run after the fiery woman whose imprint I can still feel in my arms.

Shit. Shit. Shit. Shit.

What the fuck just happened there?

I stare at my flushed face in the bathroom mirror, my heart racing a mile a minute.

The spot between my leg pulses and for the first time ever, I want to reach down there and touch the tender flesh—not that I'd know what to do—so that I could feel the explosion I'd felt only once before in my life again. Because the pressure bottling up inside me, the tension, the intensity, like I'm on the verge of something and I need...I need...

Swallowing, I grip the sink, desperate for the cold porcelain to shock me back to reality. My mind is a mess, my body is out of control, and my heart is sprinting off to an unknown destination. I feel restless, unsatiated, my mind only filled with images of him—the blond devil, the man I'm supposed to hate.

The man I *do* hate.

Yes, I hate him.

My pulse ratchets up and my hands tingle with a thousand pinpricks. I stare at my face again, my bright eyes, the healthy glow, my swollen lips. I look ravished, pleasured...and I look like I want a repeat performance.

The heat between my legs pulses and wetness seeps out of my panties.

I hate him. The futile words whisper in my mind, but feel like a sultry caress. I want to say my body betrayed me again, that I didn't want any of the overpowering physical sensations coursing through me right now.

But that'd be a lie. Because I felt alive in his arms.

His muscular body wrapping around mine, contorting my limbs to his will. I wanted to melt into his arms and be swept up in his strength.

I felt safe, like I'd never felt in a long time.

"Have you ever considered you're wrong about me?" Have I? A voice deep inside me knows the truth—I just don't want to admit it, because admitting it would open my heart up to pain.

I want to experience sex and pleasure, the real thing on my terms, but my heart, my emotions, those are out of bounds.

"What are you hiding, Taylor? Tell me so I can fix it!"

For one weak moment, I wanted to tell him what I'd told no one else other than Alexis and Camden. Because I wanted to rest on his sturdy shoulders.

I wanted him to fix me.

It was then I knew this man could break down the walls I'd painstakingly built around me—each brick a testament of survival and strength.

And if he toppled my defenses and ended up hurting my battered heart, I didn't know if I'd have the strength to stand back up again.

CHAPTER 24

Charles

DRIED LEAVES OF GOLD and brown scatter around me as I push through the double doors to ABTC a few weeks later. I rub my hands together, icy from the sudden chill descending into the city. It's only the beginning of September, but it appears fall has arrived. I check my watch—I'm still early for my meeting with Uncle Ian to discuss the progress of the tour as we prepare to leave for Paris in mid-October for the first international stop.

It doesn't matter, I'll just work in the VIP lounge upstairs to wrap up some contract approvals I didn't get to finish in the office.

My dress shoes squeak against the marble floors as I make my way into the opulent main hall. It's only seven in the evening, but with the sun setting earlier, the space is shrouded in an eerie darkness, punctuated by occasional murmurs from dancers out of sight.

This building is a statement of old-world grandeur and mystery, completed with vintage lighting fixtures and massive crystal chandeliers, which are currently turned off, no doubt to conserve energy. I clamber toward the grand staircase spiraling upward from the center of the hall.

Reaching the lounge, I push open the door and step inside. But instead of the usual tranquil silence, I'm met with faint sounds of giggling and conversation. Frowning, I look around, not seeing anyone in the room.

"Stop it, Tay. You're messing with my design," a voice complains from a far corner in the space.

"You don't know what you're talking about. I've been doing this a lot longer than you and trust me, there are no plums on the Sugar Plum Fairy costume."

The hairs on my forearms rise at the familiar sardonic voice of Taylor, the woman who has interrupted in my sleep too many times—my fevered mind always imagining her sprawled on top of the pristine white sheets on my bed, her raven hair spread over the pillows, her dark eyes glowing like embers as I rammed into her.

Over and over again.

"More!" she'd scream at me.

"Don't you hate me?" I'd growl, the pleasure rising like a tsunami. I could practically smell her sweat and tears.

She'd respond by digging her nails into my back, drawing blood.

But I'd wake up before my release, my cock throbbing to the point of pain. And nothing would satisfy it even as I'd fuck my cock in my hand to memories of the dream or of us on the dance floor.

How long does insanity last? Or is this affliction permanent?

Frustration lances my insides as I walk toward the voices, past the burgundy velvet armchairs scattered throughout the room, not bothering to turn on the brass sconces in the darkened space.

A door designed to blend with the dark mahogany paneling is popped open in the back of the room, a warm light filtering out into the main area.

I quietly stand by the entrance to see what's going on in there. Taylor is with Ainsley and a few other girls I don't recognize.

A loud sneeze echoes in the room.

"Dang, Tay. You don't look so good. Do you want to go home and rest?"

"It's nothing. Let's get this done. You guys don't have much time left."

Taylor is on her hands and knees, her hair piled on top of her head in a messy bun. A pile of used tissues is scattered on the floor near her. The hem of her loose gray shirt has ridden up, exposing a large swath of milky white skin. She's hovering over a sparkly costume, her fingers nimble as she works a thread and needle over the dress. Blood rushes in my ears as I drag my eyes down to her tight ass, perfectly displayed in the soft black leggings she has on.

My dick jumps in my pants and images from my lurid dreams pop into my mind.

Fuck.

"There, it's done. It'll fit better and we don't need this plum appliqué to distract from your dance for the showcase." Taylor sits up and tosses her supplies into a container on the side.

"If you're sure," Ainsley muses, her voice sounding doubtful.

"I went through the showcase at another academy when I was your age. If you do well, you may get a few more sponsors for scholarships. Tons of rich people like to take artists under their wings. It makes them feel important. They don't really care about us." She shakes her head in apparent distaste.

I frown. Is this what she thinks of the wealthy, of people like me? I know from Steven that she and Grace had a rough go in childhood before they were reunited with Linus. They lived in the Bronx and Grace worked multiple jobs so they could get by, but I didn't know it was this bad.

"Men like you just know how to take what's not yours. Because you know you can get away with it. You're all one-dimensional. So how dare you lecture me on emotions!"

Her words from the Met Opera slip into my consciousness.

No. There's something more to her hatred than being poor. Maybe it has something to do with the person who hurt her.

My hands tighten into fists as the fire I try to keep leashed inside me threatens to erupt.

What happened to you, Taylor?

Taylor grabs a glass of thick orange liquid that doesn't look like orange juice and takes a sip. *What on earth is she drinking?* I wince as I watch her down the glass like she's playing beer pong. She lets out a loud burp of satisfaction.

My lips twitch in amusement. She's a walking contradiction. How is this woman one of the top ballerinas in the best ballet company in the nation?

Ainsley blanches. "Carrot juice—it's revolting, Tay."

"It's the best thing on earth. Carrots. Soooo delicious." Taylor grins, the smile transforming her entire face, and I blow out a breath. This woman has so many facets to her, I'll never understand them all.

But damn, I want to read every fucking page of her soul and learn all her secrets.

Ainsley sighs. "Now we just have the backdrop to finish." She motions to a large cardboard and paint supplies tucked away in a corner. "Maddy flaked on us today—I don't know why. She was so worried about the showcase. She needs the scholarships the most, you know, with her mom being sick and on disability."

"I thought I saw her earlier in the halls. She looked sad—did something happen?"

"I don't know. For the past two weeks, she's been moping around. I asked her if things were okay at home, if her mom's fibromyalgia was getting worse. She picked up extra shifts at the bodega too. But she kept saying everything was fine," Ainsley murmurs, her lips tipped in a frown.

Taylor sighs and looks out the window, appearing deep in thought. "I should check in on her. I know how tough it is to be in her situation."

"But you're on the other side now! An Anderson too!" Ainsley nudges her.

Taylor gives her a sad smile and shakes her head. "In some ways, things were happier back then—even though we didn't have a lot." Her lips tremble and she swallows, clearly overwrought.

I lean against the doorframe and clear my throat.

The girls startle. Ainsley beams and leaps to her feet, a small blush on her face. "Charles! What are you doing here?"

"I'm early for a meeting with Ian and thought I'd get some work done in here, but I heard you guys." I look around the small alcove, completed with a few bean bags and a tiny circular window. "I didn't even know this was here."

"They said it was a hiding spot for the Underground Railroad during the Civil War," Ainsley exclaims, her eyes bright. God, she reminds me of Firefly so much—the same bright energy, the same excitement about life.

"History buff, aren't you?" I murmur, setting down my briefcase. I eye the dark-eyed minx who still hasn't acknowledged my presence and is doing everything she can to not look at me.

Slowly, I approach the girls and take a seat near them, my back against the wall. Ainsley introduces me to her fellow dancers in the trainee program—Shelly and Tia.

"My sister loved history too. Her favorite time period was the Renaissance," I murmur quietly and stare at the half-completed backdrop, half dusted in glitter and fake snow, no doubt a scene from the dance of the Sugar Plum Fairy. "And the Regency era," I shake my head, memories of Firefly swarming in my mind, "and World War II. She had too many interests for her own good."

"Was?" A soft question uttered on an exhale. Taylor finally looks at me, her brows pinching.

I shouldn't think of Firefly in the past tense. Shouldn't I, as her brother, give her my strength and hope?

The uncharacteristic concern in her gaze slices me inside. *I don't deserve your concern, Tay.*

"She's still alive...barely." My voice catches on the last word and the sudden wave of grief threatens to pull me under. "She has been in a coma for a long time." I try to dislodge the lump in my throat as the heaviness that has receded in the background since Steven's wedding comes roaring back.

I shouldn't give up on Firefly, especially when I'm the one to blame for what happened to her.

But the whisper in the back of my mind, the one I've shoved in the darkest corner, hoping it won't ever surface, makes an appearance.

I feel like I've been saying goodbye for a long time and with each passing year, with each pristine, unopened gift I place in the drawer of her nightstand, I'm leaving a piece of myself behind, and a new gash appears on my heart.

A slow death. Painfully bleeding out and no one notices.

I gnaw on my lip, a sharp pain spearing me when my teeth pierce the skin, but I pay no attention, lost in the world of what-ifs and regrets.

"Girls, don't you need to go home? It's getting late," Taylor says, her voice soft with concern. I feel her gaze on me, but I don't look at her.

I'm afraid she'll see my sins on my face.

CHAPTER 25

SHELLY AND TIA GATHER their things and scurry out the door, followed by Ainsley, who hesitates as she crosses the threshold. She turns toward me. "I'm sorry, Charles. I hope she wakes up."

Forcing out a smile, I nod at her. There's no reason for me to air out my problems to a teenager. "She will because she's a Vaughn and we're a tough bunch to break."

Ainsley relaxes, and I give her a wink. She flushes again before darting out of view.

The smile slips off my face as I stare into the empty VIP lounge. If Firefly were here, she'd insist on tagging along and helping with the tour. She'd call it an adventure. The Vaughn siblings against the big bad press.

Maybe she'd even drag Liam here to do her bidding. He'd come if she asked—tattooed, piercings and all, looking completely out of place in the world of pink tutus and classical music.

"You know, you don't need to smile and pretend everything is fine," Taylor mutters. She hands me a tissue.

My brow hikes up and she motions to my lip. I lick the wound and my taste buds register the familiar metallic taste of blood. Taking the tissue from her, I press it against the cut.

Slowly, she sits down next to me, her sweet scent of vanilla flooding my nostrils. She sneezes and grabs another tissue before wiping and tossing it on the ground.

It's disgusting.

Yet, refreshing.

She truly doesn't care how the world views her.

"Ainsley isn't a kid and the real world is a tough place. There's no point in hiding that from her. The sooner she learns that, the better," she murmurs.

"Why make others uncomfortable when there's nothing they can do?" I close my eyes and rest my head against the wall, listening to the quiet sounds of her breathing. "In my world, it's better to keep things close to your chest. Vulnerability is a weakness, something people can exploit. Connections are made based on how you make others feel—trust, acknowledgment, confidence."

"I'm just hearing you use fancy words to describe insincerity and wearing a mask. Maybe it works in the business world." She scoffs, and I can feel her body move next to me, even though we aren't quite touching. "I wouldn't know. Your world is smoke and mirrors to me. Rich getting richer and poor getting poorer. But for the people who care about you, you aren't doing them any favors. I doubt they want to see you like this—hiding away."

"Isn't that what you're doing, minx? Hiding away just like me?" Perhaps that's why I've always had a strong emotional reaction whenever I'm around her.

Like recognizes like.

A gasp slips from her lips. "I'm not. I wear my emotions proudly. You're the one to call me a brat and other names for expressing myself freely."

I chuckle, my eyes opening, and I turn and stare at her, finding her facing me. The soft light from the lamp renders a beautiful silhouette of her face—the delicate nose, her skull piercing telling me she's probably in a foul mood today, the glow catching her mesmerizing eyes, which are now intent on mine. Unlike other times, there's no vitriol in her gaze, only curiosity.

Like she cares about what I really think of her. Under my mask and forced smiles.

My heart clenches as I take a good look at her. In this quiet moment, I don't want to lie.

"Maybe it's because you're getting too close," I whisper, "tearing down my masks like they're nothing, torpedoing my defenses. Why you?"

Her lips part, a flush crawls up her face. Her eyes dart to my lips and her pink tongue slips out and I swallow a groan.

"I have a feeling you hate me because I see through you," I murmur, fascinated at the way her pupils slowly dilate. "And you don't really hate me."

"N-No?" she asks, dazed. I graze her lips with my thumb.

"No. You've wanted to let someone in for a long time. Didn't you tell me bottling up your emotions is unhealthy? Surrounding yourself with loneliness...that'll kill you slowly, Tay." I would know.

Her breathing quickens, a flush crawling up her neck, and there's that tongue again, wetting her luscious lips, the sweetness I can almost taste.

Fuck.

I want more.

"Let me in, minx," I rasp.

I want her to stare at me like this—vulnerable, defenseless, trusting. I want her to look at me like I'm someone she can take a chance on, someone she can depend on, someone who won't disappoint her.

Unable to help myself, I reach out and tuck a few wispy strands of hair behind her ear, relishing her soft shiver when my finger grazes her cheek. So soft. So silky.

She's so goddamn beautiful.

The air in the room thickens with tension. The fluttering in my heart morphs into a maddening rhythm as my pulse riots in my ears.

I want to hold her and kiss her—watch her come apart in my hands.

"You and I both wear masks—yours are made of fire and mine of ice," I whisper. "What would it feel like if we take them off...together?"

Her dark lips part. Those perfect plump lips, made for kissing, biting, tugging. I want to smear her dark lipstick on her pale skin—I'm the artist and her body is my canvas.

Taylor swallows, her face flushed. "I'm not wearing a mask," she whispers as I lean in, drawn to her like a moth to a flame.

"It's okay, you'll tell me when you're ready," I murmur. "I understand."

How would it feel to be burned alive? Was this how the moth felt when he stared into the enticing glow of the intoxicating flame?

Her eyes widen before dipping down to my lips. She lets out a shuddering exhale, a small sound escaping from her throat. I feel that vibration all the way down to my stiffening cock. Reaching out, I glide my hand over her arm, skimming the goosebumps pebbling her skin. My other hand curls around her nape, my fingers digging into the tender flesh.

Taylor whimpers, her eyes fluttering shut, and with a guttural groan I seal my lips over hers and taste the fire at the source.

Fuck, she tastes like heaven. Sweet and addictive.

Her hand flies out and clutches my suit jacket as I angle my body toward her, afraid to spook her, afraid she'll fly away if I push too hard. My lips tangle with hers—a slow dance—the beginnings of our own sensual tango. Her fire spreads to my veins and the blood inside me simmers, then boils.

She lets out a sweet moan—the same one I heard when we were dancing the Argentine tango—and I take advantage and lick the seam of her lips before invading.

I need more. I need everything.

Grunting, I curl my arm around her waist and haul her on top of my lap. I fist her hair, tugging it out of her bun and wrapping it around my wrist as I deepen our kiss.

"Minx. You drive me insane," I mutter as we break for breath. My other hand clamps her round ass so she sits on top of my lap, aligning her legging clad pussy on top of my aching cock. "I've fantasized about this for so long, kissing these dark pouty lips, and nothing compares to reality."

Taylor whimpers, her sounds driving me wild. Her hands flutter to my chest, and I pull her tighter against me as I take control of the kiss. The beast inside me roars to life, its talons extending, clawing, needing more.

Conquer. Obliterate. Immolate myself with her fire.

I swallow her whimpers and give in to my urges. My hips thrust up into her pussy, moving against her automatically, my tongue simulating the fucking I want to give her, and the kiss quickly spins out of control.

She moans some more and I growl, deepening our connection. Molten lava floods my veins and I could barely hear anything other than the hammering pulse in my ears. My heart thrashes, as if wide awake after a long slumber, and my cock is so hard it almost hurts.

More. Fucking more.

My mind is swallowed by a storm of lust and heat as our bodies gyrate against each other...harder, quicker, the pleasure climbing. I angle her head to the side, taking the kiss deeper, swallowing every sound from her as madness churns inside me.

But out of nowhere, she yanks her hand free and slaps me across the face.

Stars appear in my vision as shock rears through me. I quickly let go of her and she clambers off my lap, her lithe frame trembling—no, shaking.

I watch in horror as I see the moisture pooling in her eyes, her lips bee-stung. She clutches her hand over her chest and backs away.

Terrified.

As if I took her unwillingly.

"Have you been paying attention, Charles?" Liam's words barrel into my mind.

I'm oblivious. Swept up in the tide of emotions and ignore what's in front of me.

Again.

Horror slams through me as a thought registers in my mind, and I hate myself for not figuring this out sooner. The answers were in front of me all along. Her hatred of men. Her baggy clothes and how she hides herself from the rest of the world.

The terror in her eyes right now.

She was abused by a man. Perhaps sexually.

And I just ground myself against her without a care.

I'm a fucking bastard.

My throat closes like invisible hands are choking me alive. I can't breathe, my mind a riot of panic and gut-wrenching terror, quickly chasing away the heady arousal dominating my body moments ago.

One minute he was kissing me and I was one second away from ripping off his clothes, the intense pleasure catching me off guard. We were two twisted souls feeding off the darkness no one else could see.

I told myself this was just physical, that he wasn't getting into my heart. I wanted to experience the sexual attraction I'd never felt before. It felt normal, what a woman my age should feel toward a handsome man.

For a blessed moment there, my mind shut off completely, the sensations in my body quickly taking over. I felt the dominating scrape of his hands on my arms, the possessive grip on my nape. The way his mouth moved expertly over mine—my first kiss since I was sixteen, delivered by a real man who knew what he was doing, not a boy. The way he effortlessly lifted me off the floor and deposited me onto his lap.

Instead of revulsion, it felt like a drug—a heady, sweltering sensation I quickly lost myself into.

It felt freeing, exhilarating. I couldn't stop touching him, wanting, no, *needing* the physical sensations I'd been deprived of for a long time.

But then he ground my hips on top of his. For the first few seconds, it didn't register, the pulsing in my clit delivering the highest of highs. I wanted to chase it, to take control of the pleasure this time because I didn't know when I'd feel this way again.

Then, I registered the bar of steel—far bigger than anything I'd ever felt before—hitting me at precisely the right angle, the throbbing in my pussy intensifying, hurling me toward the edge of a cliff.

Much like that night.

And the ugliness crept in.

"Fly, Harriet."

"Look at her...she's enjoying this."

"She's going to come, isn't she?"

Images of the monster moving above me barged into my mind. The clinking of belts. Peppermint. The pain which morphed into something else—something I still can't admit to myself to this day.

I feel dirty, disgusting, the throbbing in my pussy reminding me of my body's betrayal that night. I need to get away, far away from him, from those monsters in my brain.

I'll never be normal. I want to reclaim my sexuality, but is it a hopeless cause? *I can't think that way. Talk back to your fear, Taylor. This is a trauma response. You know that.*

Dry heaving, I'm dizzy, sick to my stomach, as I put as much distance between myself and Charles. The words aren't sinking in.

He quickly staggers to his feet and reaches for me. "Taylor, I didn't mean... I thought you were, I—"

"Stop!" I scream. I hate the terror in my voice. I hate how I can't seem to stand upright. "Stay back. Stay the fuck back!"

Charles stares at me in horror, his face completely leached of color. His hair is in disarray and I realize I must've mussed it up in the heat of passion just now. His throat works, his eyes brimming with guilt and regret as he holds hands up in surrender.

He must think I'm crazy. Pathetic. He must regret kissing me.

My eyes well with tears. A headache forms at the base of my spine as I try to blink away the evidence of my fear. I can't cry. Not in front of him. Not in front of anyone.

Charles looks devastated. Completely gutted. The arrogance and mask nowhere to be seen. "Taylor, I-I'm sorry, I—"

I swallow and do my best to even out my breath. My hands itch. My fingers twitch, wanting to find a needle and plunge it into my thigh, to feel the pain I can control instead of these horrid emotions I decidedly can't control.

"I don't want to hear it." I cut him off and spin around. I can't take it if he stares at me in pity. If he takes one look at me and figures out how messed up I am.

My hands tremble as I gather my jacket from the floor. "This never happened."

I dart past him, past the one man who was able to make me forget, just for a minute, the one person who made me feel normal. It terrifies me to the core.

Grief slams into me—the precious moment felt like a success, but then it was wrenched away. *Progress isn't linear.* The words swirl in my mind over and over again. A sob chokes in my throat as I slam the door shut behind me, leaving him behind, my fingers swiping at the moisture pooling under my eyes.

I won't cry. I can't cry. I don't want to fall apart again.

I'll never fall apart again.

CHAPTER 26

THE APOCALYPSE IS UPON US.

At least, that's my first thought when I open my eyes to the sound of loud pounding—a wrecking ball has slammed into my apartment.

"Shit," I mutter, trying to sit up on my bed as a blistering headache unlike anything I've ever felt makes itself known.

The daylight streaming in from the windows is a bright beam straight into my eyes and I wince, the need to retch up the chicken noodle soup I had for dinner last night soon to follow. The world swirls around me, and sweat has soaked through my tank top and shorts.

I feel like I'm dying.

Pound. Pound. Pound.

The wretched sound is back. I clap my hands over my ears, but the motion hurts like a right hook to my face.

"Minx, open up! Open the damn door before I break it down!"

Huh?

I feel my forehead. It's burning hot like the rest of my body. I must be delirious, hearing things. Because there's no way—

"Taylor Peyton-Anderson! You're in there. Open the fucking door. The doorman said he never saw you leave."

Charles? What the fuck?

Groaning, I stagger off the bed and head toward the door, my legs threatening to collapse as the ground swirls with each step. I'm seasick in the middle of a hurricane and none of this is happening.

Peering through the peephole, I blink the dots away from my vision as a head of familiar blond hair comes into view. With my remaining strength, I unhook the safety chain and disengage the lock before sliding down to the floor.

I plaster my body on the cool marble tiles and close my eyes. The surface feels so good to my overheated body. Everything hurts and throbs.

The door slowly opens in a soft creak, but I barely have the energy to look at him.

"Fuck," Charles mutters, and a wave of bergamot and cedarwood hits my nostrils and I greedily draw in a deep breath.

Anything that doesn't smell like death is welcomed.

"What the hell, minx. I went to ABTC today, and Ainsley and your friend, Lisa, were worried sick about you, saying you blew off mandatory rehearsals for Paris."

He pulls me up from the floor and into his arms. "You look like crap. Why haven't you called anyone?"

"You woke me up. I didn't get a chance to call," I mumble.

God, he feels so good—the smell, the heat, the deep timbre of his voice. I snuggle into his hard chest, my hands seeming discombobulated from my body, but I still try to touch his pecs.

I've been dying to know what they feel like. I didn't get to touch them during the kiss, the kiss I still dream about because I wish I could go back in time and experience it again. But without the fear or terror. I knead his muscles. They are so hard, so strong, just like the rest of him. Is this how normal women feel? Craving the body of a man without fear?

His pecs flex under my sporadic motions.

"That's so fucking sexy," I mumble, my mind woozy. I wouldn't be surprised if drool is dripping from my mouth. I wish I wasn't sick so I could enjoy this. He's all man—every hard inch of him.

A deep chuckle reaches my ear. "You're definitely sick."

A barrage of random thoughts slam into my mind as a wave of nausea thrashes in my gut. Covering my mouth, I dry heave before finally looking at my golden archangel, cradling me like I'm precious.

Beautiful. Unmarred. Worthy of love.

An overhead light renders his face in half shadows, like he's wearing a halo. It's fucking ridiculous, but I swear I can hear the angels sing.

"Charles," I murmur, my vision blurry, but I see his glorious golden blond hair, ruffled and unkempt, his scruff longer. Those piercing blue eyes darken like the stormy sea. "I'm dead, aren't I? Is this hell and you're here with me? That would be the hell I've imagined—trapped with you for eternity. But why would you be in hell? Aren't you an archangel?"

He lets out something suspiciously like a growl and a snort.

"A *grort*." I stifle a delirious giggle. "You just grorted."

"Oh fuck, what am I going to do with you?" he murmurs, affection in his voice. I have to be hearing things because why would he be treating me like I'm precious? He stands up and lifts me into his chest like I weigh nothing. My heart skips a beat and something flutters in my gut.

He starts moving; the motion jostles my head, and the stabbing headache worsens.

"You're going to stay in bed. No complaints from you."

"You're a tyrant. You can't boss me around. I'll do what I want."

"Watch me, brat."

"What are you going to do? Punish me?" I mumble, completely exhausted. Snuggling deeper into his hold, I listen to the steady thumps of his heartbeat—powerful, reassuring, a safe harbor. I'm so tired but in this moment, I can finally rest.

"No, you'll be awake and well when I punish you. And you'll be asking for more." Is it my imagination or his voice carries a rougher edge? A frisson of awareness slithers through me, but I'm too sick to think much of it. "You need rest. Lots of it."

But something about his words earlier finally register in my mind. I open my eyes. "N-No, I'm not sleeping. There's so much to do. The trainees' showcase. It's n-next week. They aren't ready. They need this to get their scholarships for next year. And I need to practice for Paris."

I can't afford to mess up Paris, my first performance as Odette—the first test to see if I'm ready for a promotion.

Struggling in his arms, I push at him, but it's like trying to move a boulder. He holds me tightly.

"Not happening. You're no good to us in this state," he mutters, and my eyes shut again. Everything is so bright—too bright, too noisy. So much pain.

"Shit, this place is a pigsty," he complains under his breath. "How the hell do you find anything?" I hear him kick something out of the way—it better not be the new box of self-help books that came in the mail yesterday.

He drops me onto the bed, and I groan from the pain throbbing in my head. I hear him move about the room and a moment later, a draft flows in.

"Too cold, close the window," I grumble.

"It smells bad in here. Go rest. I'll call Ian and tell him you're out sick."

I drift in and out of consciousness as sleep threatens to pull me under at any second. I hear his deep voice on the phone, rumbly and reassuring.

My eyes drift open and I see the blurry visage of him striding over, lines of concern marring his face. He hovers over me and for a brief second, my pulse kicks up as I'm reminded of that dark night, but as soon as the thought drifts in, another thought quashes it.

I'm safe.

Charles does something to the bed, and the next thing I know, I'm beneath the covers, tucked in tightly.

"Go to sleep. I'll take care of everything," he whispers, and my eyes drift closed once more. His finger grazes my cheek and I shiver.

"Right," I mumble, "or else I'm no good to you all." A hollow ache appears in my chest. Dancing—he's only concerned about the performance. *But it's okay, Taylor. You don't want emotional entanglements, anyway.*

Darkness overtakes me.

The next time I open my eyes, it is pitch dark and I wake up in a panic, my head burning hot. *Charles. Where are you?*

"Liam, I wish you'd pick up my call. I...I worry about you. Ethan told me you're fine. You're in Japan now?"

He's still here. Relief hits me and my fevered pulse settles as I listen to his voice emanating from the living room, his words temporarily distracting me from how sick I'm feeling.

"I'm sorry. I know I've said sorry too many damn times and none of it matters. If I could turn back time and undo it all, I would. I wish I were the one in a coma. I...I miss you, brother. Fuck." A choked sound escapes his mouth and my heart clenches.

I want to climb out of my bed and go to him, wrap my arms around his waist and take him away from what clearly are painful memories, just like how he's rescued me from mine during the kiss...albeit temporarily.

But the aches in my body, the heaviness of my limbs, the exhaustion weighing on my eyelids are too strong, and soon I drift back to sleep.

The rest of the night passes by in snippets—a slideshow of chills, fever, and body aches. My sleep is turbulent. I'm drifting in the dark ocean again, but this time, the waves are as tall as me as a violent storm rages around me. There's no moon, no stars, no sign of life.

I'm all alone.

"Help!" I cry out, my voice hoarse.

Another wave crashes over me, the icy water choking the air out of my lungs. I can't breathe.

"Help—"

"Shhh..." the ocean rumbles and wraps its icy tendrils around my body.

"No..." I struggle, but the waves are too powerful.

"Shhh... You're having a nightmare, Tay. Just a nightmare. You're safe," the dark waters whisper again. "Take your medicine. You're going through the worst of it."

Suddenly, I'm lifted upright and the grinding headache stabs me again.

"Shhhh..." The deep voice is back and I feel my face being tipped back when I open my eyes, seeing him, my nemesis. *Is he still my nemesis?*

"Charles?" I'm delirious—this can't be him. *Why would he still be here? How much time has passed?*

"Yes, minx. Take this," he murmurs, his voice gentle as he puts two pills in my mouth, then places a glass up to my lips. "Drink up. Dehydration makes everything worse."

"W-Why are you helping me? Don't you hate me?" I whisper after taking a few gulps of water. "I rejected you that day."

He freezes, and a thick lock of blond hair falls over his forehead, hiding his arresting eyes from view. I want to brush it away so I can look at him, but I don't have the energy.

"You make me feel so damn much, Tay, so fucking much. I *should* hate you," he says, his gaze falling on mine. Under the dim glow of the hallway light, I see a muscle twitching on his forehead, his eyes glowing, drawing me in.

"But?" Exhaustion slams me and I shiver, the sudden chill sending my teeth clattering. I'm having a fever, but why am I so damn cold?

The dark ocean beckons me again, but I don't want to go back.

But I'm so tired. Bone-deep weary.

"C-Cold, Charles. I'm fr-freezing." I shake uncontrollably, my body desperate for the blankets to smother me once more. Curling myself into a ball, I tremble in bed, wishing I could be unconscious and put out of misery.

"Fuck." I feel an icy hand on my forehead. "Burning. You're fucking burning. If your fever doesn't improve within the next hour, I'm taking you to the hospital." I hear rustling noises, the clanking of a belt buckle, something resembling a zipper being yanked down, a few muffled huffs.

My body fights at the familiar sounds—the same sounds from that night—and just like that evening, I can't move. A scream makes its way up my throat.

"Shhh..." he whispers and his familiar scent floods my nose, enough to stall the panic threatening to join the chaos.

Then suddenly, the mattress dips next to me and a pillar of heat appears at my back.

"It's me, Taylor. You're safe. I'm just keeping you warm, okay?" The words are gentle, reassuring.

He's asking for permission. My fevered mind registers. The terror slowly subsides and I moan my acquiescence.

Strong arms appear around my waist and I shudder, but this time I'm not sure if it's because I'm cold or if it's something else.

Charles pulls me tightly against his front and surrounds me with his heat. He tucks my icy feet in between his and twines his large hands with mine before resting them on my stomach. Amid the headache, the shivers, my mind registers I'm plastered against him, his head resting on top of mine, his entire body enveloping me.

His naked, hard body.

Sparks of panic threaten to reignite as his intoxicating scent makes its way to my nose. My pulse kicks up, my breathing quickens. *I need to get out, I need—*

"You're okay," he murmurs, his voice raspy, and a soft shiver coasts down my sweaty body. "Safe with me. Always."

He hums under his breath and I feel a pressure on my sticky hair, like he's pressed a soft kiss there.

"Little firefly flying against the wind, buzz, buzz, buzz, I'll never let it win..." he sings under his breath a familiar hymn—a song I could've sworn I'd heard before but that couldn't be true, since it wasn't a nursery rhyme Mom sang to us.

"My grandma used to sing this to us when we were sick," he murmurs, curling his arms tighter around me.

"Tell me a story, something, a memory, anything," I mumble, not wanting this moment to end. My mind is blissfully empty, even though my body is in pain.

I feel so treasured right now.

I hear a smile in his voice. "My sister loved to dance. I think you would've liked her. She was fiery, mischievous, full of life. She always told me she felt like each day was a present and we weren't guaranteed the next day, so why live with constraints?"

Snuggling deeper into his hold, I feel my panic slowly receding. "You must miss her a lot."

"Yeah. I do. Every fucking day. I used to tell myself I worked so hard for her and Liam, so they could do whatever they wanted with their lives without worrying about anything. So they could live without constraints. After all, someone had to do the boring stuff—running a large company. And I didn't mind it. I liked the business."

He rubs my arms, the gentle motions sending frissons of warmth inside me. "But I never listened to them. That's not what they wanted from me. They wanted a brother who was present for them, but I was too deep in my mind to know...until it was too late."

I fight the sleep threatening to overtake me. I want to know what happened, what made him hide behind this mask no one seems to see but me.

"The last time I didn't listen to them, I lost them both. Firefly in the hospital, and Liam...he barely speaks to me anymore. I haven't seen him in years. If it weren't for Ethan, his best friend, I wouldn't even know he was still alive. And that...that..." His voice catches.

"That kills you, doesn't it? The people closest to you not seeing what you're hiding in your heart," I whisper, slowly turning toward him, even though the motion is making me seasick.

My body is clammy, and I'm sure I look disgusting, but the look in his eyes, the intensity, it threatens to unmoor me.

There's pain, guilt, aching vulnerability.

And love. So much love for his family.

He rakes in a ragged breath, his hand sliding up to cup my face. I close my eyes, relishing the heat of his palm.

"How could they not see you?" I whisper. "You wear your heart in your eyes."

You're a good man, Charles Vaughn. If I'm not careful, I may lose my heart to you.

I hear a sharp inhale—it could be his or mine—and he cradles my head against his chest like I'm the most important thing in the world.

And in this weak moment, with my body battling a virus, my nerves and head on fire, I don't want to fight the emotions swirling inside me.

I want to let him in, and I know that should scare me, but I'm too sick to care.

I want one selfish moment to remember forever.

Pressing a soft kiss on his strong chest, I feel his muscles tensing. I murmur, "I see you, Charles Vaughn. One day, they'll see you too."

My energy spent, my muscles slowly loosening, I let sleep overtake me.

This time, there are no nightmares, no dark ocean.

Only reassuring, peaceful sleep.

The next morning when I wake up, he's gone. I'm about to question if everything is a figment of my imagination—my loneliness inventing someone to care for me.

But then, when I make my way out of the bedroom to a sparkling clean apartment, I find a beautiful bouquet of roses sitting next to my newly unpacked self-help books on the coffee table.

Healing from Darkness, the critically acclaimed memoir of a rape survivor, is on the very top of the stack, its shiny black cover beckoning me.

A wine-red rose, its thorns shorn, lies on top of it, along with a note.

My heart pinches at the smooth stem of the flower, wondering if anyone will ever love the rose with its prickly thorns before I pick up the small card and read the masculine scribble on it.

Taylor,

I hope you feel better today. Perhaps we're two sides of the same coin—both wearing masks to face the world. But if you're game, if you're brave enough, step into the light. With me.

Without darkness, there'd be no light.

You're not alone.
Charles
P.S. I'm sorry for scaring you that night in the lounge. I never meant for it to go that far and I apologize for misconstruing your consent. Please forgive me.

A sob tears from my throat and I clutch the note to my chest.

CHAPTER 27

THE CLOUDS ARE HEAVY and gray, the humid air clinging to my skin long after I escaped the elements. I stare out the window of the town car as my driver heads toward ABTC. The city never stops—rain or shine, thunderstorm or hail—us New Yorkers forge on.

Much like the woman I can't get out of my mind.

Battle weary and full of invisible scars, her thorns and attitude are defense mechanisms hiding a damaged heart. Last night, as I held her in my arms, I got a glimpse of the tenderness and vulnerability behind her walls. Followed by an answering surge of protectiveness pulsating inside me.

I think back to the way she reacted when I kissed her the last time I was here—the lust and passion quickly spiraling into devastating terror, the way she flinched when I closed in on her last night, wanting to give her my body heat because she was shivering like a leaf, to the stack of books I saw in her opened box this morning when I was tidying her apartment.

Healing from Darkness.

When Words Aren't Enough.

Why Won't They Believe Me?

Each volume was a gut punch to my soul. The fury, sadness, and outrage were a wildfire charring my insides—a beast wanting to level everything in its path.

It didn't take a genius to figure out the truth. The God awful truth that I suspected since the kiss, but didn't realize the extent until

I browsed the books on her shelves. And now, I don't know what to do next.

Taylor has been raped. There's no doubt about it. The details, I don't know, but she has endured a horror no woman should ever experience. I clench my hands tightly as murderous rage fills me.

I want to flay the skin of whoever did this to her. Dismember him body part by body part. And that still wouldn't be enough.

Expelling a heavy breath, my mind grabs onto something I didn't want to think about for the longest time, because the alternative would be unbearable.

Her reactions to Ian—the fear in her eyes when she first saw him at ABTC. Even though she doesn't seem to know my uncle, why would she have such a strong visceral reaction toward him?

The car lurches to a stop and I hear the driver mutter a curse and an apology as he blares the horn at whoever cut in front of us.

Acid boils in my gut and I want to crank open the windows and throw up.

It can't be Uncle Ian. There's no way he has anything to do with this. I've looked into him, haven't I? He wasn't in the States back then. He was in Europe, choreographing ballet.

It was a cursory review, Charles. You only did a cursory review. Photos can be faked. They don't document every second of his days.

My hands shake as I remember growing up in the cold, empty mansion, knowing I was raised to be the heir of the Bank of Columbia fortune because my parents couldn't be depended on. My absentee parents I saw once a month if I was lucky.

The fights. The black eyes on Mom's face. The public spats when our rare public outings devolved into an argument over another woman or man and I'd hide behind the nanny in embarrassment, wishing I were anywhere but there.

The joy I felt when Uncle Ian would show up after I called him. He'd take one quick glance at me and would know what happened. He'd whisk me away to the Met Opera or Central Park, where he'd buy me all the ice cream I wasn't supposed to eat. He'd take Liam, Firefly, and me to Coney Island for rides and roller coasters and tell us we were loved.

It can't be him. Can it?

But the terror in her eyes. The way blood drains from her face whenever his name is brought up. I sense uncertainty in her voice as well, because if she knew for a fact it was him, she wouldn't stay at ABTC. I'd bet my life on it.

"Sir, we're here."

My troublesome thoughts stay with me as I exit the car and climb the steps of the building. A small group of paparazzi are gathered outside. I couldn't focus on work today—meetings with investors, the PR team, my new finance team, which now includes an interim CFO, the permanent CFO position we're still recruiting for—I couldn't recall a single thing that was discussed. My assistant probably wants to kill me right now.

I only had a single thought today. I need to help Taylor, however I can.

"Mr. Vaughn! Can we get a comment about your opinion on the Patterson trial?" Reporters holler at me, but I ignore them. Sixty counts of sexual assault. Ten counts of rape. Patterson can rot in hell for all I care.

"Charles! Does your silence mean you're on his side? What about the victims?"

I freeze, the last man's words echoing in my head. I think of Taylor—the terror in her eyes, the books on her shelves.

Fury singes through me.

Whipping my head around, I grab the phone from the reporter who tossed out that question. "You want a statement? Fine, you got one. Patterson, if you're seeing this, you are the fucking scum of the earth and I sincerely hope you get what's coming to you."

The reporters gasp as I shove the phone back to the idiot's face. I growl, "Happy now?"

Ignoring the rest of them, I hurry up the steps and enter the lobby. Fuck, I should've controlled myself better—the press is going to have a field day with this.

But I don't have it in me to care. My mind only swirls around a certain ballerina and the terror in her eyes when she met Ian for the first time.

Pulling out my phone, I dial a number—one I swear I wouldn't use, but dammit, I'm becoming another cliché.

"Charles. Well, this is unusual," Elias Kent's low voice drawls on the line. I hear the familiar clicking of the ornate lighter he carries with him everywhere, even though he doesn't smoke.

I exhale a frustrated breath. "I need your services."

The clicking sounds stop, followed by a few seconds of silence. I stand in the middle of the main hall, impatient for his response.

He laughs.

The fucking bastard is laughing so hard, if anyone were to tell me this sound came from the infamous mobster, the king of the underground, I would've told them they were nuts.

"First Steven, then Ryland, then Maxwell, and now you." His laughter fades into low chuckles. "You billionaires sure have a lot of problems."

"Shut up. You're probably richer than all of us combined—we just don't know because you hide everything in the shadows."

The clicking resumes. "So, let me guess. This has to do with a woman? A certain ballerina?"

I frown. *Am I that obvious to everyone?* "You don't need to know the why. I just need you to find out if Ian ever left Europe a few years ago."

"Why can't you ask him yourself?"

"It's complicated. And," I swallow as dread slithers around my rib cage, "I don't know if I can trust his answer. Will you do this for me? This should be a cakewalk for you."

"You know my price, right?"

"A favor for a favor, yes." I feel like I'm signing my life away. A blank check written to Elias Kent can be dangerous—we never know when or what he'll want us to do when he cashes it.

But he's useful, smart, brains behind the villainy. Nothing gets past him, and he has helped my friends in the past, getting them out of sticky situations and, in Maxwell's case, even in life and death situations.

They trust him, and that's good enough for me.

"Send me the dates you're interested in, and I'll be in touch. I *am* curious why you're asking."

"And I won't tell you." I know Taylor wouldn't want me to tell people what I suspected happened to her. "Call me when you have something."

My thumb hovers over the end call button, but I quickly add, "Thank you, Elias. Favor or not, thank you."

A heavy silence fills the line.

He clears his throat and murmurs, "I'll be in touch."

Ending the call, I jog up the main staircase and head straight to the VIP lounge, where I'm met with quiet conversations from the back room again.

Quickly, I make my way toward the hidden room, shrugging out of my jacket and tossing it on a velvet chair along the way. The tie follows, then the cuff links. I roll up my sleeves and knock on the door.

Two pairs of eyes greet me—Ainsley and a brunette I vaguely remember from Steven's wedding.

"Charles?" Ainsley sits straighter and looks at her friend. "Do you have a meeting with Sir Ian? Or Taylor? Taylor's out sick and isn't here today."

I shake my head. "No, I'm not here for them. I'm actually here for you guys."

The girls frown, looking confused.

I explain, "Taylor told me you had a showcase coming up and are behind on finishing the set designs. Thought I'd lend a hand." Smiling, I motion to the half-completed boards lining up the walls and the floor.

Ainsley beams at me. She gestures to her friend. "This is Maddy. She's another trainee in the program." I vaguely remember them talking about her absence the last time I was here. "And we definitely need your help. The showcase is next weekend and we're way behind."

"Why isn't anyone helping you?" I squat down and pick up a paintbrush and start working on a landscape painting—the drawing is already rendered and the colors half done, so it's easy for me to follow the pattern.

If Maxwell, the artist in our group, saw me now, crouching over a board, painting trees and grasses for teenagers, he'd never let me live it down.

Maddy sighs, chiming in as she works on her set piece. "It's a trainee showcase—the least of the priorities for the company. It doesn't generate ticket sales and usually the folks who attend are our families or important people who want photo ops. So, they don't give resources to it."

"That's just the way things are. But it's also an opportunity for new scholarships from the wealthy patrons who show up—we need sponsors each year for scholarships. We have pledge forms there," Ainsley adds, her voice forlorn, reminding me what Taylor said about the wealthy before and how no one truly cared about those on the other end of the wage gap.

"That's rough," I murmur, my face heating as shame creeps inside me. I grew up in a gilded cage, surrounded by privilege. I never had to worry about the necessities. I should do more, much more.

I sneak a glance at the girls, both can't be older than sixteen, and take in the determined glint in their eyes, their paint-splattered hands, the faded clothes they're wearing. There's a thread of world-weary grit laced with innocence. Was Taylor like this at their age before her trauma?

Out of the corner of my eye, a beautiful backdrop catches my attention. Carefully, I set down my paintbrush and walk toward it. It's a floral scene—pastel flowers dusted with glitter in front of what appears to be a confectionery castle. But what catches my eye are the clusters of roses spaced throughout the backdrop.

Dark red petals, sharp thorns dusted with gold glitter.

Interesting that the glitter is on the thorns and not the petals.

"Taylor made that. Burgundy roses are her favorite flowers," Ainsley says. "This is a scene to be used in the waltz of the flowers."

My finger grazes the glittered thorns, so lifelike and realistic, I can almost feel its sharp edge cutting into my skin.

Something about the thorns beckons me to stare at them. They are so beautiful—the sharpness a perfect balance for the soft petals. Beauty with edge and character.

They elevate the flowers.

I think about the roses I left for her this morning, the ones with the thorns cut off, the way most florists prepare them. I wanted to give her a spot of brightness when she woke up. Perhaps as she was reading her books and trying to heal her broken soul, she'd know she wasn't alone.

Then I remember the way she scowled at the roses at Grace and Steven's wedding, followed by a haunting sadness when she touched the stems of the flowers, which, I'd bet had their thorns all shorn off because they were professional arrangements by florists.

Was she feeling this way, then? Sad? Unseen? Thinking the world only appreciated beauty when it was perfect, not when it was marred with something rough and gritty...something like thorns?

Roses are more beautiful with thorns.

"Really, now," I murmur as I examine the flowers in a different light, my heart clenching.

"I know she probably seems like a tough cookie on the outside, but Tay is really sweet. She's the only one who really cares about us. Everyone treats us like annoying wannabes, outcasts wearing hand-me-downs and here because management wants to look good for politics and do performative community outreach," Ainsley says.

"She teaches us on the side when she doesn't have to. She even sponsored a scholarship last year, and she told us she would've done more if her money wasn't locked down by trust fund rules. We owe so much to her," Maddy adds. "Hopefully, someday, we can pay her back."

"Not with money though, since she's an Anderson and everything," Ainsley says. "But maybe we can fulfill a dream or something."

"What do you think she'd want?" I ask, a sizzling energy pulsing inside me. What would make my minx happy?

Your minx? What are you talking about?

I shove the thought to the side.

The girls talk among themselves, arguing about what they think would make Taylor happy. She doesn't seem to need much and isn't one for fancy clothes or materialistic items.

"Oh! Tickets to see *Swan Lake* at the Bolshoi Theatre!" Ainsley's eyes glitter with excitement.

"Yes, you're right! Isn't that her dream? To go to Moscow and see the performance in the homeland of Tchaikovsky?" Maddy nods, then frowns. "There's no way we can afford that. Those tickets cost an arm and a leg, not to mention the flights and hotel costs."

The girls deflate.

"Never say never. I have a feeling you guys will go far." I make a note to gift anonymous scholarships earmarked with their names when I get back to the office.

Maddy smiles sadly. "I hope so. Then everything will be worth it." She swallows and whispers, "Everything we put up with." For a minute, the same haunted look I see in Taylor's eyes shows up in hers.

My brows pinch, a curl of unease unraveling in my gut, and she quickly adds, "You know—the usual bullying and stuff. It'll be nice to do something for Taylor later. She's really special."

"I'm realizing that," I murmur. Taking one last glance at the roses, I say, "Roses are much more beautiful with thorns."

Why didn't I see that before?

CHAPTER 28

SWEAT DRIPS DOWN MY forehead, my legs extended in an arabesque, as Dev lifts me high into the air. My heart pounds like a battering ram, the spotlight singeing my skin. Everything seems different, and I'm never more aware of the fraud that I am as I finish our inaugural performance of *Swan Lake* at the iconic Palais Garnier in Paris.

I feel the audience's eyes staring at me, scrutinizing my every move, picking apart each pose.

Look at how rigid she is as Odette.

Did they send in an amateur to do a professional's job?

An average performance. What a disappointment.

I can't breathe.

Dev, perfectly playing the part of Prince Siegfried, gently lowers me to the ground and I collapse into his embrace.

"Almost done. You're doing well, Tay," he murmurs, his face turned to the side, out of view of the audience.

After giving him a small squeeze of acknowledgment, I push him away—the moment when Odette decides to end her life to break the curse.

This pain, the hopelessness the beautiful white swan must've felt—this I can portray.

I think about my broken dreams as a child, the happiness I thought I'd experience once I make it on to the world stage, only for my innocence to be ripped away by reality. I think about the horror on Charles's face when I slapped him across the face after he gave me a kiss I very much wanted.

Swallowing the lump in my throat, I collapse on my knees, my arms stretching forward, the music in its sorrowful crescendo descending around me.

The death pose.

I rest my head on the floor—the moment Odette leaves this world in a tale of tragedy. Soon, Dev wraps his arms around me as he joins me.

The prince and his swan queen separated while living, reunite in death.

My breathing is loud as I try to contain my emotions. This is the moment I've been waiting for my entire life ever since Mom took me behind the stage at the Met Opera. This is the pinnacle—playing the white swan in one of the top ballet companies in the world on the prestigious international stage. I'm supposed to be elated, tears of joy streaming down my face, but instead, I'm met with soul-crushing grief.

Because it's all wrong.

Everything is wrong.

I still can't fix myself, even as I try, try, and fucking try.

I can recite the books I've read. I know everything I'm going through is normal, that the path forward sometimes requires a few steps backward.

But I'm tired. So damn tired.

I hear the gentle swish of the curtains drawing closed and polite applause ringing out in the large auditorium.

"It's done," Dev says gently as he pulls me up. "Not too shabby for your first lead performance." He grins.

"It was average. You and I both know it." I strain a smile at my friend.

My Odette was still too stiff, the emotions on my face other than the final scene feeling forced. Judging from the polite cheers and gentle applause, no one was swept away by my performance.

Soon, we make our way back onto the stage for our obligatory curtain call. Flowers are strewn, the camera flashes blinding. Out of the corner of my eye, I see Sir Ian smiling at the audience, but his expression is strained. He's gripping his ruby pen like it's his worst enemy.

He isn't pleased.

"You guys were excellent!" Lisa rushes up to us backstage before throwing herself at her boyfriend and the lovebirds engage in a passionate kiss.

Feeling awkward, I thank her before moving out of the way and heading toward the dressing room, where we have to change and get ready for the gala on site to celebrate the successful international premiere of the ballet.

How am I going to pull this off for the next few months?

My thoughts weigh heavily on my mind as I push open the door to my private room. I blow out a breath and check my phone to see if Emerson has an update for me or if I have any messages from the girls. Anything to distract me from my thoughts.

Inbox zero. I sigh. I know investigations take time, especially in a case this cold, but now that I started on the journey, I want to see it through. I want to know what happened and if I still can, put those bastards in jail.

I want closure. Maybe then I'd be able to dance Odette again.

A knock sounds at the door but before I can even say "Come in," it swings open.

"You were terrific!" Grace squeals, ambushing me in a tight hug. "That final segment—I had tears in my eyes, Tay!"

Chuckling, I pull away from her. If only she knew why I could dance the last part well. "Sir Ian is kinda pissed. I'm sure I'm in for it later."

"Pssh." Grace scowls. "What does he know?"

I snort. "He's only one of the best choreographers and dance directors in the world, so he knows a lot."

Grace narrows her eyes. "Well, I never—"

"Seriously, bravo!" another voice chimes in.

My head whips toward the second voice, finding Olivia grinning from the doorway.

"What are you doing here?" I laugh, pleased to see the girl who is quickly becoming a close friend.

She strides over and wraps me in a light hug before motioning to Grace. "I begged your sister for a ticket. I had a medical conference here last week, so I just extended my trip."

Olivia steps back and scans my face, like she's searching for something. "You know you were astounding, right, Tay? You're always too hard on yourself. Speaking as a friend and a shrink, celebrate those wins."

My heart clenches as I stare at the two beaming faces before me. I'm so thankful I have these girls in my life.

"Damn right," I rasp.

Grace claps her hands together. "Okay, let's get ready for your gala! Belle gave me explicit instructions when she sent over your gown. She told me the requirements—champagne dress and light makeup. I'm so excited, Tay! It's been ages since I've seen you in anything other than dark colors."

I roll my eyes as dread coils in my gut. The outfit requirements came from the top—from Sir Ian and the board of directors, according to Lisa's insider information. This gala is not only a celebration for the premiere but also an event where who's who with deep pockets in Europe will show up. Deals will be made, contracts will be signed. It's important to put up a good front for politics.

And apparently, as lead dancer, they want me to portray an air of elegance and radiance, not doom and gloom.

"I think I look awesome in dark colors. Dark and mysterious, don't you think?" I waggle my brows.

"Light—let there be light!" Lisa's faux snotty tone last week when I grumbled my complaints barges into my mind.

I feel naked already and I haven't even changed yet. I eye the form-fitting gown Belle chose for me and while I trust her impeccable tastes, the idea of being out in the real world without my loose outfits and dark makeup makes me want to retch.

"Chop, chop. No time to spare. We'll make you beautiful!" Grace announces and grabs the gown off the hanger.

I swallow as blood drains from my face.

"Tay, you okay there?" Olivia furrows her brows, her brown eyes glinting with sharp awareness.

Huffing out a laugh, I wave her off. "Let's get the fucking show on the road."

CHAPTER 29

I CAN BARELY KEEP my jaw from dropping to the floor as I stand at the entrance of the grand foyer in the opera house. Everything is washed in gold—the columns spanning the large space, the intricate gilded ceilings, the heavy tasseled drapes, the light from multi-lay-ered chandeliers glinting off the tall windows and mirrored accents.

It's like Midas has made himself a home here and never left.

A string quartet plays classical music in one corner, and the space is ablaze with a quiet energy. A soft hum of conversation and the clinking of champagne flutes fill the air as I stand to the side, feeling extremely uncomfortable in my dress.

Belle said the dress was fit for a starlet, and as I look at my reflection in the dark windows, the sun having set long ago, I know she's right. It's a beautiful one shoulder gown made of tulle and satin in a mermaid silhouette with a thigh high slit. The material molds to my body and the color makes me appear almost nude, but tastefully. The bodice is covered in crystals and a small train sweeps out on the ground. The sweetheart neckline is modest, but low enough to see the swells of my cleavage.

Grace and Olivia hemmed and hawed when they saw me in the gown, with Grace making joking comments about why I couldn't wear something like that to her wedding. She arranged my hair into a loose updo with wispy strands framing my face and dangling over my bare shoulders. My makeup is a simple cat-eye, no dark eyeshadows or thick liner, but my lips are in a dark red shade I like.

That was the concession I made—I got to pick the lip color as long as it wasn't purple, and the nose stud stays—a small crystal to match the dress.

I look unrecognizable.

I look like the sixteen-year-old girl with dreams of love in her heart, the girl who wore a beautiful dress to her first ballet function with her best friend, who didn't know hours later, her life would change.

My breath quickens as I stare at my reflection, desperate to hold on to the present.

The past is in the past, and I survived.

I not only survived, but I thrived. I didn't let that night ruin my life. And here I am, standing inside the opulent Palais Garnier in the middle of fucking Paris, playing the role of Odette.

You're a badass ballerina, Taylor Peyton-Anderson.

The thought stays the rising panic inside me, and I take my first steps into the room.

Immediately, I sense their eyes on me—the women eyeing my outfit up and down, some with awe in their eyes, others with their noses pointed in the air. But it's the men's gazes I feel the most—the malicious intent, the way they slowly examine me from head to toe as if I'm cattle to be purchased.

The nausea immediately makes an appearance and beads of sweat appear on the back of my neck. *This is just your trauma making you feel things, Taylor. Not reality.*

Then the searing heat of his familiar gaze settles on me.

Looking up, I find *him* in the far corner, a few businessmen surrounding him. They're trying to get his attention, but he isn't looking their way.

Instead, his attention is all on me.

Charles in a tux should be outlawed—a capital offense. He's standing tall and regal, like he owns the place. His powerful body, which I've briefly felt that fevered night, is stretching against his tailored attire. His blond hair is artfully swept up, a slight wave in the thick tresses.

But those eyes. Those piercing blue eyes.

They are burning hot. Smoldering. I feel myself bursting into flames from his intense perusal.

My heart skips a beat as we stare at each other.

Should I say hi? I texted him thank you for taking care of me, but that was the extent of our interactions.

The girls told me he had swung by to help them with the showcase and for that I'm grateful. Then there were the *Gossip Times* articles I read online about him nearly punching a reporter in the face in front of ABTC when they asked him if he sided with his former CFO on his assault trial. It caused an upheaval for a week before the press moved onto the next piece of juicy gossip.

I remember the clamoring in my chest when I watched that video clip of him—eyes blazing with fury, teeth bared, snarling as he gave his two cents about his CFO. A rare moment of public emotion from him. It was like he was unraveling at the seams, and I couldn't help but wonder why. What changed?

The public apparently agreed because Charles Vaughn suddenly appeared on a lot more internet searches and billionaire heartthrob lists.

I was wrong about him before. I shouldn't put him in the same group as the other rich men who take without asking. He treated me like I was precious that night. He made me feel normal.

Maybe my radar is just messed up—like how my body reacted to Sir Ian before, who has never been unprofessional toward me.

I think back to the latest update from Emerson on the case—he ended up texting me after I finished getting ready for the gala, much to my relief. He told me he located a suspect from that night, a financier from the UK, and he's chasing that lead down. He mentioned nothing about Sir Ian.

A beautiful brunette in a red dress walks up to Charles and drapes her arm on his shoulder. He holds my stare for one more second before turning to her and unleashing his dazzling smile.

An ache settles in my chest before an unsettling anger burns in my gut, and that is enough to jar me back to reality.

He took care of me because I'm their lead dancer in the ballet tour to save the reputation of his company. *Don't think too much of it.*

And the betrayals from Camden and Alexis still cut deep. *You don't want any emotional entanglements, remember?*

The brunette is now trailing her fingers over her cleavage and making moon eyes at him and, to his credit, he keeps his gaze on her face. I narrow my eyes in distaste.

"You were wonderful tonight." A large hand slides around my waist.

I jump and stifle a scream when I see Steven's dark brown eyes peering down at me. "Holy shit, warn a girl next time."

He frowns. "I did. I called your name. I thought you heard me."

A muscle in my cheek twitches—a half-assed attempt at a smile. "Oh, I was thinking about my next performance. There are some things I need to fix."

Steven stares at me for another beat before his shoulders soften. "Well, Grace tells me you're too hard on yourself, and she's right. To my untrained eye, you were perfect."

He smiles and presses a brotherly kiss on my hair. He glances over to the far corner, where Grace is drinking champagne with Olivia and laughing. His eyes soften and fill with affection. "She's so proud of you, you know. She tells me she only knows random facts and how to crunch numbers, but she doesn't have an artistic bone in her body, and she definitely isn't changing lives with her art."

A lump thickens in my throat. He turns to me. "Grace told me she had a dream about your mom last night—that she was so happy and proud of the woman you've become. All your grit and sacrifices paid off, and you're the most beautiful swan she has ever seen."

But it's fake though. The swan is a disguise. I feel like an ugly duckling underneath the feathers and tutu.

"Thank you, Steven. Grace is lucky to have you," I whisper, my voice hoarse.

He squeezes my shoulder and nods toward his wife. "Going to get a dance out of her before we leave. Have fun tonight, Tay. You deserve it."

I watch him as he strides toward my sister and pulls her in for a brief but intimate kiss. A flare of envy strikes me in my chest, and I unwittingly look for a tall blond man wearing a charming mask, but I don't see him anywhere.

I wonder if the sexy brunette took him somewhere for a quick romp.

The thought causes a pang in my heart I refuse to analyze.

A waiter comes by with a tray of drinks and I watch him pour water from an unopened bottle, satisfied it hasn't been tampered with, before taking a glass. Walking around the room, I do my best to channel my inner Belle, who grew up in the glitz and glamour of high society functions.

I smile at patrons and make small talk with a few who approach to congratulate me on a successful debut. They quickly scurry away after our conversations die down fast—I'm a dancer, not a socialite. Small talk is not my forte. I prefer moonlight and quiet, not humans as company.

My toes ache from dancing and the four-inch gold strappy heels I have on. A headache threatens to form at the base of my spine. I see Lisa with Dev, chatting with some stuffy-looking old men with gray hair, no doubt networking, which is what I'm supposed to be doing. Couples whirl on the dance floor and I just want to take a breather—somewhere I can hear myself think.

"No! I said, no!" a soft voice says.

"That wasn't the deal, we said…" The words trail off when I turn around, trying to locate the source of the argument.

Maddy darts out the door, her face splotchy and eyes shining with tears, a man trailing after her. The hairs rise on the back of my neck as alarm churns through me.

Quickly, I set down my drink and follow them out of the hall down a long corridor. Their shoes click and clack on the marble floors and I try my best to keep up and not make too much noise behind them.

I make a right and enter a dark, empty circular room, but they're nowhere to be seen.

Fuck. Where are you, Maddy? My thoughts flash to the shadows of men crowding me that night, taking what didn't belong to them.

No one would miss you, little beauty.

Predators target the weakest prey, and there's no one weaker than a poor girl with no one to miss her at home.

I can't let anything happen to Maddy.

Panic seizes me as I quickly rush around the room, past the tables and various boxes and furniture they have set up in here. Moonlight streams in from the tall windows, rendering the shapes inside the room as looming shadows.

Menacing. Dark. Just like that night. Sweat beads on the back of my neck as I navigate the maze, desperate to find the girl who's almost like a little sister to me.

I'm sure they went this direction—where are they?

A slap rings out in the dark space, followed by a choked sob. I gasp and head toward the commotion. After creeping past a tall cabinet, I see two shadowy figures standing behind a bookshelf with Maddy.

"Arrête, ce n'est ni le moment ni l'endroit," one man says to the other, his voice too soft for me to hear.

Damn it, why didn't I pay attention in French class in high school?

"Cette garce doit apprendre à connaître sa place. Tu sais ce qui se passera si elle le dit à tout le monde?" the other man replies as he tugs his hair, appearing frustrated. Something *bitch* and something *tell the world*. I growl in frustration under my breath.

"Elle ne le fera pas. Je vais lui parler. Calme-toi, Laurent," the other man murmurs.

I will talk to her. And the angry man's name is Laurent. I can't make heads or tails of this conversation.

Maddy sniffles, her words echoing in the room. "I don't want to do it anymore. I don't care what I promised, I don't—"

I fist my hands tightly, my eyes on the small trembling shadow of the person huddled in the corner. I don't care who these people are. How dare they hurt a young, defenseless girl like Maddy?

A girl who has her whole life ahead of her.

A girl who probably dreamed about dancing the white swan role as she ate plain bread for dinner.

A girl who believes in love.

A low growl makes its way up my throat, and I charge forward, wanting—no needing—to save Maddy, to give the men a piece of my mind, to—

A hand clamps around my wrist and pulls me into a recessed alcove, and another hand smothers my scream.

Terror races through me and I thrash in his arms. I won't be doing this again.

This isn't happening. I'll die before I let him hurt me again.

I raise my stiletto heel and am about to slam it on his foot when the mystery man says, "Shh... It's me. Stop struggling, minx."

CHAPTER 30

THE DRAPES FALL SHUT, and her body stills as she registers my words. I know the exact moment when she recognizes it's me behind her. Her breath hitches and her muscles relax before she turns around and stares at me.

"Charles?" she whispers, clearly in shock.

My voice deserts me when I take in her face under the pale moonlight streaming in from the arched window. Her large eyes are guileless at the moment, charcoal pools I want to dive into and never resurface. Her perfect lips, painted in the color of her favorite burgundy roses, are now parted.

She dips her tongue out and heat rushes to my groin. My eyes greedily absorb the sight, roving from her midnight hair piled high, a few strands teasing those creamy shoulders, to her delectable body clad in a stunning gold dress that makes me want to kneel and worship at her feet.

Then there's the sweet, intoxicating scent of vanilla swirling in the air, making my mouth water.

My breathing quickens and my hands tighten around her waist, my fingers digging into the thin fabric. I can feel the heat of her body and I'm sure if I trail my fingers up to her neck, I'll find the rapid fluttering of her pulse.

"Charles? What are you doing here?"

Her question draws me out of the sensual haze, and I quickly remember why I'm in here, hiding under the cloak of darkness with her. The black envelope in my pocket digs into my skin, reminding me of the unpleasant conversation I had in the ballroom ten minutes ago.

An older man with dark hair and piercing eyes approached me when I was taking a break from socializing. "Monsieur Vaughn, finally get to meet you in person."

I stiffened as he guided me to a darkened corner of the room, away from prying eyes. "You have me at a disadvantage."

"Laurent Archambeau, chief of police of this beautiful city."

"And to what do I owe the pleasure?" There was something in his voice that was unsettling. I'd heard of him before—it took a certain ruthless personality and reputation to rule one of the major hubs in Europe with an iron fist.

He arched his brow and held my gaze for a few seconds, as if assessing something. Apparently, I passed muster because he murmured, "I was told to give you this."

He retrieved a black envelope from his tux and handed it over. On it were two words in gilded, cursive text. *The Association.*

Grandma's words and Maxwell's comments whispered back into my mind and the hairs on my forearms prickled to attention.

"What's this?" I asked, even though there was a sinking sensation in my chest.

"An invitation. You want to take Bank of Columbia to greater heights or cleanse your hands from the pesky public image problem your former CFO has handed you or perhaps make sure that certain CFO doesn't talk anymore? All you need to do is ask. But of course, nothing comes for free." With a secretive smile, he tipped his head and walked away.

I opened the envelope and found a simple black business card inside with a single phone number.

Something told me the price of this favor would be too hefty to pay. The warning bells in my gut blared loudly—if there was one thing I prided myself on, it was listening to my intuition.

What do they want with me? Theories ran through my head as I stared at the crisp card, feeling its ominous weight. Minutes later, out of the corner of my eye, I saw Archambeau following Maddy, with my fiery minx trailing after them, looking all too suspicious.

Taylor growls and shoves me deeper into the alcove, trying to make a break for it again. I hold her tighter against my chest. "Shhh. I'm saving you from yourself."

Taylor stiffens, her eyes now flashing with ire. "What the fuck are you talking about? I need to save Maddy. These men are hurting her! I need to—" Her voice rises in volume. Fear rips through me. If Archambeau is part of The Association, then he's dangerous.

I can't let him know Taylor is here and eavesdropping.

I quickly clamp my hand over her mouth again and she mumbles her complaints into my palm.

"Hear me out. If I let go, will you be quiet, please?"

She struggles in my hold, and I bite back a growl of frustration.

"Please. Please, Taylor. Just listen to me." I heave out a big breath. *Please let me protect you.*

She stills, her eyes scanning my face before she slowly nods.

I take my hand away and murmur in her ear, "That man in there, the one with the louder voice. That's Laurent Archambeau, the chief of police. He's a very powerful man in the city and he's dangerous, involved in some shady business we definitely don't want to take part in. You *do not* want to cross him. The other guy I didn't see, so I don't know who he is. But he's probably someone important as well."

Her eyes widen before they narrow at me. She shakes her head. "I don't care who the fuck they are. Maddy is crying. I heard a slap."

"Did you see them hurt her? Because accusing the chief of police on his home turf carries severe ramifications. Not to mention, the man is dangerous. I don't want him to have you in his sights."

Taylor's eyes widen in horror, then she swallows, her breath rickety. "I...I-I didn't see...but I heard it, I swear!"

"Look at what I'm seeing right now." I pull open the drapes slightly and let her peer through.

Maddy is smiling as another girl greets her in the room and the two of them leave, arm in arm. Her complexion appears clear, no reddened cheeks to indicate she was slapped. The two men stay behind, whispering furtively to each other.

Taylor stiffens, and I can almost see the dark cloud hovering over her head. She turns around, a deep frown on her face. "I swear I heard it. Something is wrong, Charles. This doesn't add up."

Gently, I place my hands on her forearms, my fingers tingling from the contact. "I believe you, Taylor. I really do. But I want to protect you too."

She stills, her eyes wide and searching mine. Her breathing slowly evens out and I take it as a sign to continue. "If you charge out there and throw out accusations when you have no proof and you didn't see anything, you'll definitely be on Archambeau's radar. I don't want to think what problems that'll cause, especially when you have a few more shows in the city. What if—"

Taylor scowls, her nostrils flaring. "Of *course,* this is about the damn shows to you. My God, why did I think you'd be different? Why am I so *stupid*? Of course you don't care about Maddy, the poor scholarship student. You only care about lining your pockets and your precious company. You—" She raises her hands, her face flushing.

Before she shoves me again, I catch her wrist in a tight clasp. This woman drives me mad.

This is why emotions terrify me. They make you lose your sanity.

But I know she's so used to being alone, of protecting herself. She's probably doing this as an automatic reaction.

"Calm down, Taylor. That's not what I'm saying at all. Stop twisting my words." I close my eyes and exhale because in this moment, I just want to shake her to get her to understand the ramifications. "I'm only suggesting you ask Maddy what happened. She's safe right now. She's not in the room with these two men. That's what you're worried about, right? It makes no sense for you to burn your bridges on the most important tour of your life and get in the crosshairs of someone dangerous and powerful in the city."

Her chest heaves, her eyes wild, but she slowly deflates as my words take root.

"Ask Maddy," I whisper, still aware of the two men in the room, "and if they did something to her, I promise you, I won't let that go. I'll do whatever it takes to dole out the punishment they deserve."

Taylor still doesn't speak, her gaze snared on mine. Her breathing is loud as her lips tremble. She shakes her head, strings of nonsensical words slipping from her mouth. "I can't let them... No, she has her future ahead of her. Maybe I'm looking at her and s-seeing my—" She swallows, not finishing her sentence, but she doesn't need to.

Herself. She was seeing herself before her trauma in Maddy. The grief and anguish in her voice are unmistakable.

Tears slowly well in her eyes and the same ache I felt when I saw her look at Grace at the wedding comes back tenfold. Desperation burns through me and every muscle in my body tightens. The sight of her splitting at the seams is unbearable. The pain she's holding in, a dark well I assume runs very deep, is overflowing, and I'd do anything in my power to stop it.

"I promise you, Taylor. You aren't alone in this." *Not anymore.*

Tremors appear in her body, her breathing ragged and tortured. She's staring at me with those beautiful, watery dark eyes, like she's imploring me to save her.

She clutches my arms tightly, fingers digging into my sleeves, and her face crumbles.

A lone tear slips down her cheeks. Followed by another, and another.

My heart lodges in my throat as pain stabs me in the chest.

The sight of her tears unmoors me.

I want to destroy whoever caused her this unspeakable agony. Whoever flayed this warrior with their weapons and left her with permanent scars.

I hear the faint sounds of the men leaving the room, but I don't care, because the woman in my arms is unraveling. Deep sobs wrench from her throat as more tears slip out, the liquid melting the liner from her eyes into rivulets of black.

Rivers of darkness streaking down the pale ivory of her skin.

"You're *not* alone," I say again, my voice rough. Unable to help myself, I hold her trembling frame tightly in my arms, wishing I could take an ounce of her pain away.

I'd do anything to make her happy again.

Anything to hear her snarky comments and to see the fire in her eyes.

Anything to turn back time and prevent the bastard from hurting her.

Her sobbing soon slows, her tears no doubt making a mess of my tux, but I don't care.

Slowly, she lifts her face away from my chest, her face a painting of black against white—of her grief against her strength.

"I must look like shit," she whispers, the wispy moonlight lovingly caressing her face.

"Never," I rasp, my heart pounding out of my chest. My thumb lightly grazes her cheek, swiping away at the evidence of her pain. "You're breathtakingly beautiful."

Taylor's breath hitches, her lips parting. She looks astonished, like she can't believe I think she's beautiful.

"Roses are much more beautiful with thorns," I murmur, emotion clogging my voice.

She inhales another sharp breath, her nostrils flaring, and a second later, she pulls my head down and crushes her lips against mine.

CHAPTER 31

CHARLES FREEZES FOR A second before his body leaps into motion. He snakes his arms around my back and tugs me flush against him as his mouth pillages mine.

Here in this private alcove, with the lonely moonbeam as our only witness, I want to forget.

About the darkness in my past or the uncertainty in my future.

About my fears and nightmares, heartbreak and heartaches.

I want to be the breathtakingly beautiful woman this man in front of me sees. This man who's protecting me, calming me down when panic swirls inside my mind and I can't even think straight.

"Roses are much more beautiful with thorns." His words echo in my ear as the heat ratches up between us.

He hears me. He sees me. He thinks my thorns are beautiful.

The scattered thoughts send more tears falling as if all the tears I've held inside for all these years are finally unleashed, because they need a safe harbor.

Because I need someone strong and tall, someone who infuriates me as much as entices me to hold me while I rest in his arms.

Because I'm so damn tired.

A sob collides with a moan as I throw myself into the kiss, accepting his tongue as he slips it between my lips. My skin is hot, sensitive—I'm throbbing everywhere—my nipples, my clit. I rub my legs together, the piercing sending an extra layer of sensations, shocking my senses like live wire.

He groans against my mouth, his hands buried in my hair, tugging the strands to the point of pain—oh, so pleasurable pain.

"I can't get you out of my mind," he rasps as we pull apart for air. "You intoxicate me. Turn me into someone I don't recognize."

His eyes are dilated. I can barely see his irises anymore. His blond hair is disheveled and I realize I have my fingers buried in his thick strands too. He looks ravenous and desperate.

And somehow, just like the last few times, I'm still not afraid.

The thought sends a sizzle of excitement.

I'm not afraid of him.

"You drive me nuts too," I whisper, pulling his head toward mine.

"Let's fall into madness together." Charles takes my lips between his and his teeth make an appearance as he peppers small bites on my bottom lip, the tiny pinches direct caresses to my core.

Wetness seeps out of me and the pulsing need climbs between my legs—higher and higher. I'm like a bomb seconds away from detonating. My body is not mine anymore—I'm a slave to the sensations rioting through me. I want to flee from them. I want to burn with them. I want to pull him closer so I can't tell what parts belong to him and what parts belong to me.

Clamping one leg around his waist, I grind into his hips, wanting more friction, more heat, more of the electricity sparking in my veins.

He growls, sliding his hand down and kneading my bare thigh as I move against him. Searching, seeking, needing to see the end of this.

An unmistakable hardness prods at my stomach and for a moment, that makes my motions falter.

Fly Harriet.

"*No!*" I attempt to shove the thoughts away. Taking Charles's other hand, I close it over my aching breast.

"Fuuuck," he grunts, his fingers squeezing over the sensitive mound. He thumbs my sensitive nipple, which sends a sharp current of pleasure to my pulsing core.

"Look at her thrashing. She's going to come, isn't she?"

"Go away. Stop it. No!" *Don't ruin this for me. I'm feeling normal, wanted, needed.* More tears slip down my cheeks.

I grind myself against Charles's cock, needing to fan the flames again. This time, I get to decide when to explode.

I get to choose this. This elusive pleasure I've been deprived of since that night.

But after a few seconds, I realize he's stopped moving, his hand clamped on my thigh like a vise, the other hand curled around my waist. His lips are still on mine as puffs of air hit my face from his heavy breathing. He's trembling—the vibrations so subtle, I almost don't notice it.

I tilt my head up and what I see on his face makes me gasp in shock.

Charles looks furious. The same violent god of thunder I saw that first day at ABTC, except this time, I'm within searing distance of the scorching anger radiating from his body. A vein bulges on his temple, his nostrils flaring as a muscle tics in his jaw.

"I'm going to kill him." A low, gritty rasp.

Goosebumps appear on my arms. Heat circulates through my body. "What?"

"You were crying 'no.'" My breath hitches, and I realize I must've spoken my thoughts aloud. Charles dips his forehead to mine, his voice a lethal whisper. "I'm going to kill the bastard who hurt you. I'm going to cut his dick off and make him swallow it as he bleeds on the ground before you."

My heart slams itself against my rib cage, like it's desperate to escape, and to my horror, my pussy pulses at his words, the murderous intent in his voice, the wrath and fire in his eyes.

My archangel will avenge me.

I swallow, knowing everything I'm thinking or feeling is probably illogical right now as I'm riding high on my emotions.

But I don't care. My mind is mad with desire.

"Make me forget, Charles. Make me forget," I plea, taking his hand and resting it over my breast again.

Raw determination shifts over his face and, with a guttural growl, he slams his lips over mine.

And he takes, takes, and takes, plundering my mouth like a pirate coming across a forbidden treasure.

I give back as good as I get from him. I bite, suck, and swirl at his lips, his tongue, his salty and masculine skin. I allow him to take from me, to obliterate my senses.

This time, I get to choose.

My body. My life. *I want this.*

His fingers pinch my hardened nipple and I tear my lips away from his to draw in a ragged breath before arching back, needing more of the same sensations. I need his touch everywhere. I want him to take me to nirvana.

"Goddess. You're a fucking goddess," he mutters while he plays with my nipple—rubbing, rolling, kneading, the sensations sparking my body into mini convulsions. "I can spend days upon days worshipping you and it won't be enough."

He follows suit with the other side as I writhe against him, desperate for more, for both this maddening torture to continue or to end. His cock lengthens, hardening unbearably behind his slacks, each drag of his turgid length hitting my barbell, what used to be an instrument of pain, but now only fans the pleasure gathering in my pussy.

Charles slides his fingers under my dress and up my thigh, the slow graze a sensual torture. He stops as he reaches my underwear.

"You sure?" His fingers play with the cotton, snapping the cloth on my skin. "We don't need to if you don't want to do this. Just say no and I'll stop."

I look at him, finding his eyes intent on mine. He's breathing heavily, his abs rippling through his shirt, the necktie of his tux nowhere to be seen. He looks like he's seconds away from exploding and taking me down with him.

"I'll stop and it'll be okay," he repeats himself. His body trembles and a muscle tics in his jaw. "A true man doesn't take what is not given."

I wet my lips, a sultry warmth spreading from my heart to the rest of my body. He's already taking care of me in his own way. How did I ever not see him? This passionate, sensitive Charles Vaughn underneath the veneer or his forced smiles and surface-level charm?

"I'm sure," I whisper, arching my hips forward. "Over my underwear?"

A muscle twitches on his temple and his jaw works. He dips his head into a curt nod and seals his lips over mine again.

Our tongues duel and I savor the taste of fine whiskey in his mouth. His hand finds my breast again and resumes his tortuous ministrations as his other hand slowly glides over my thin underwear, my only barrier between his fingers and my pussy.

He touches the spot between my legs, his head bolting up when he feels the piercing protruding from my panties. His eyes darken and burn, and nostrils flaring.

"It's supposed to be for pain," I murmur, knowing I'm probably not making any sense to him.

But somehow, I think he understands, because he doesn't question further. Instead, he flicks the barbell, sending a sharp wave of pleasure through me.

I moan and arch my head back, baring my throat. *Kiss me. Make me forget.*

"Fuck. Fuck me. You're going to be the death of me," he rasps.

Charles buries his face in my chest, kissing my cleavage, the divot around my collarbone. He drags his nose up my neck before laving at the pulse points, all the while his fingers unleash fury on my clit.

I'm wet. So wet. Wetness seeps out of me and I'm helpless to stop it. The sensations are building, the throbbing so intense, I'm lightheaded. His expert fingers flick, then circle, then tug at the piercing, then return to my swollen clit.

Lewd moans and whimpers echo in the room and I belatedly realize they are from me.

But as the sparks coalesce and I creep closer and closer to the edge of the cliff, the voices come back.

"She's going to come, isn't she?"

My body seizes, my mind trying to fight for control and give in the pleasure because I own this. This is *my* pleasure and not someone else's. I can't let them steal from me anymore.

"Come, minx. Look at me. Don't think about anything or anyone else. It's just me and you." Charles's sharp command snaps my eyes open, and I'm trapped in his mesmerizing pools of glacial ice again. "You're so fucking wet, I can feel you through your underwear. You drive me wild. You and your thorns undo me. Come for me, minx. Give me more of your cum. Let me feel you flood my fingers."

His words send me over the edge and I scream. An explosion unlike anything I've ever felt before slams into me like a freight train.

"Fuuuck," he grits out, his fingers quickly circling my barbell and clit, unleashing another wave of sparks. My mind blanks as I shake against his body.

I claw at him, wanting to push him away as the sensations become too much and also wanting to fall into the flames with him again. And again. And again.

Before long, the throbbing intensifies and my mouth drops open, my eyes rolling back as I fall limp in his arms.

"F-Fu-Fu-Fuck," I mewl.

"Yes. Fuck yes. You can give me another one." His finger ghosts over my opening before dipping in slightly through my panties.

I fly headfirst into another orgasm, my world shattering around me, the sharp pleasure spreading rapidly from my pussy to the rest of my body. Uncontrollable shakes rip from me as I thrash in his arms.

Charles captures my lips with his and smothers my cries. He groans as he moves faster, rolling his hard muscles against my sensitive body. He removes his hand from between my legs and rubs gentle circles on my back. I collapse on him, my head resting on his hard chest as I slowly coming down from the excruciating high.

Tears stream down my face—catharsis, relief, grief, exhilaration, and too many other emotions for me to name. I sob into his warm chest as I reel from the second and third orgasms I've ever experienced in my life.

The only orgasms I choose for myself.

As my breathing slowly calms and I can finally hear the rapid thudding of his heart, I notice the hard length resting on my stomach.

He hasn't come.

He hasn't pushed me to give him satisfaction. His sole purpose was to give me pleasure.

Roses are much more beautiful with thorns.

The thoughts send my heart into a tailspin—and I don't want to contemplate what that means. Fear suddenly shakes me to my core as I remember Camden's harsh words and Alexis's betrayal. I can't do this again—make my heart vulnerable. Is it possible to give in to physical pleasure without giving away my heart?

I can't. I can't feel *anything* for him.

Panic swirls in my mind, chasing away the remnants of my orgasms.

And so, like a coward, I push him away and run from the room, desperate to escape the new and intense emotions rushing inside me.

CHAPTER 32

"Sir Ian, what are your thoughts about your Parisian performances? The reviews were lukewarm—are you disappointed?"

There's a quiet murmur from the press—pens scratching against paper, the shutter sounds from cameras, whispers and furtive glances. I look at my uncle, finding him sitting tall in his seat behind the long table where we're having our first international joint press conference in Prague, the second international stop of the tour, between ABTC and Bank of Columbia to discuss the tour and the donations we've raised so far.

Ian appears to be smiling, but it doesn't reach his eyes. This is the smile he taught me when I was young—lips tilted a fraction, eyes slightly squinting to fake the genuine thing.

A muscle twitches on his forehead, but his expression doesn't waver.

He's mad—Ian Vaughn's performances are never mediocre, they are always spectacular.

"The company has undergone a lot of changes recently, with me joining as the director and with our lead dancer getting injured. A slow warm up is to be expected, so no, I'm not disappointed. I'm actually..."

I don't pay attention to the rest of his words. My gaze trails to the woman next to him, her lips in her signature dark purple, her thick glorious hair in loose waves—hair that I finally got to wrap around my wrist as I made her come and shatter in what was the most erotic experience of my life.

I don't even want to think why that is the case when I typically prefer sex to be rough and raw, pain and control.

Taylor's shoulders are hunched forward, like she's weighed down by Ian's disappointments. She's fiddling with the silver bangle I've seen her wear often. I wonder what the story is behind it and if she'll tell me someday.

I frown. Something tugs at me in my mind, but it disappears before the thought crystallizes.

Look up, minx. Where's that badass I don't give a fuck ballerina?

As if she heard me, she glances my way, and her gray eyes widen before she quickly looks away.

Taylor did ask Maddy what happened in Paris. Maddy said she promised to perform for a private event for some businessmen to earn money on the side, but decided not to do it at the last minute. There were some arguments, but she was fine. Taylor was obviously relieved and gave me an update, knowing I was concerned as well.

But other than that, she has been avoiding me since that night in the alcove—darting in the opposite direction when she sees me walking down the corridors of the hotel or the rehearsal studios, or leaving the room when I enter.

It's maddening as fuck.

"Why are you doing this, Taylor?" I cornered her in her dressing room after the last performance in Paris.

My patience was running low after yet another TV interview about the bank's re-haul efforts, but at least I hadn't seen any more picket lines. Ironically, the public seemed to have warmed up to me after my unhinged outburst in front of ABTC over the Patterson trial, which was still ongoing. I shredded the invitation from The Association, deciding to heed Grandma and Maxwell's warnings. We'd weather the trial the old-fashioned way. We Vaughns lived with honor, and I was sure anything to do with that mysterious organization was anything but honorable.

"Doing what?" She moved about the room, her hands fiddling with makeup brushes and random items.

"Avoiding me."

"I'm not. Just because of what happened doesn't make you the boss of me. Don't get your panties all up in a twist."

A muscle pulsed in my jaw. "I never took you for a coward."

She whirled around and faced me, her eyes narrowing. "Fuck you. I'm not a coward. I just had a moment of weakness and you happened to be there. Nothing more, nothing less. Don't think so highly of yourself, Charles Vaughn. Nothing happened—nothing important, anyway."

I stepped toward her and watched her throat rippling as she swallowed. "Nothing important, huh?" A bolt of heat shot up my spine and I wanted to reenact that night to see if she'd say the same thing after she came apart in my arms again.

She backed up a few steps as I continued my pursuit.

"So you didn't come and leak all over my fingers that night?" I rasped, the fury in my veins slowly turning into something else as heated blood gathered in my cock. "I still remember all your whimpers and moans when I flicked your little piercing, minx. Your sweet smell and taste as you asked me to help you forget the past. Then I wiped your tears away and every inch of me wanted to murder the man who put them there."

Taylor pressed her back against the vanity table, her pulse fluttering wildly in her throat. Her lips parted, beckoning me to kiss them, to bite them, to get another fix of the addiction I was never supposed to have.

I leaned in and whispered, "Do you remember that? I do...every night before I close my eyes with my hand wrapped around my aching cock, wishing you were there with me, because I knew it meant something to you that night, just as it did for me. And fuck if I know why that is, but at least I'm not a coward about it."

Our lips were inches apart. I could almost taste her honeyed sweetness. I wanted to give her more pleasure, to chase out the pain of her past.

Suddenly, she pushed me away and pointed toward the door. "I need to change and I'd like to do it alone. Please leave."

"Mr. Vaughn, what are your thoughts on the matter?" a reporter's voice draws my attention back to the present.

Heat rushes through my body and I fight the impulse to tug on my tie as I reply, "Sorry, can you repeat the question? I've been thinking about our successful tour and how meaningful the donations will be for the organizations—always multitasking." I finish my remark with a grin and a wink.

The reporter flushes before speaking, "Sir Ian mentioned some hiccups at the beginning are to be expected. What are your thoughts?"

I clasp my hands together. "I completely agree. I have one hundred and ten percent faith in Sir Ian's direction and Ms. Peyton-Anderson's abilities. The best is yet to come. Mark my words." I feel the weight of her stare on my face.

"Is the Bank of Columbia still firm on their commitment that all proceeds will go toward victims' rights organizations?"

"Definitely. That is the least we can do for the victims."

"What is your response to your former CFO claiming his relationships with his underlings were sanctioned by the company?"

Closing my eyes, I tamp down the anger forming at the base of my spine. That spineless idiot is trying to bring everyone down with him because we washed our hands clear of him the moment the allegations came out.

Gritting my teeth, I reply, "That is categorically untrue. I wouldn't put stock in the words of a predator."

The reporter nods as she flips to another page in her notebook. She looks up and asks, "The scandal has sparked a debate on whether it is appropriate for a person in power to engage in a relationship with a subordinate or someone in a lesser position. What is your stance on this?"

Sweat beads on my forehead, and I fight the urge to look at Taylor, the dancer in the ballet company I'm sponsoring, who falls under the definition of 'someone in a lesser position.' My mind flashes back to the lurid images of us devouring each other in the darkness, my hands on her tits, her cum soaking her underwear as I pushed her over the limit.

I reply, "It isn't recommended but not forbidden as long as there's consent and the relationship is adequately disclosed to human resources."

"But aren't human resources always on the side of the company? Do you think having this policy could've prevented Patterson's alleged crimes?"

The tie cinches tightly around my neck and I drum my fingers on the table. I eye her name tag. "It'd be archaic for us to forbid human emotions in the workplace, Candace. Hence my position—such relationships aren't recommended."

What a load of bullshit, Charles.

Leaning forward, I add, "And I can't comment on what could've happened to past events. I'd like to keep us focused on the ballet tour, please."

My palms grow sweaty and I maintain my calm smile as Candace finishes jotting her notes and sits down. Another reporter stands up, this time directing his attention to Taylor.

"Ms. Peyton-Anderson, are you satisfied with your performance so far?"

Taylor wets her lips before replying, "I can do better." Her words carry a steely edge and she sits up straighter.

"There are rumors you got to your position because of the alleged sabotage of the previous lead dancer. Are they true?"

Her skin turns red. "No. Definitely not true. And why are we talking about this? I thought this was supposed to be a conference about the tour and the proceeds to the assault victims. This is a strange line of questioning, don't you think?"

My lips twitch even as I groan inwardly. The minx has no finesse.

But fuck, that's what you like about her.

Chuckles erupt in the room as the reporter purses his lips. "We ask questions the public is interested in." He clears his throat, a predatory gaze in his eyes. I see Taylor flinch at his attitude change. "The ballet world was plagued with a few high profile scandals in the past—sexual harassment by management or company doctors. As one of the highest ranking female dancers at ABTC, you must've seen a lot in your career. Is this still rampant in the industry? Have you experienced it yourself?"

Gasps and murmurs arise from the crowd, and Taylor pales. Her chest rises and falls rapidly as she opens her mouth to reply, but nothing comes out.

"I...I—" she whispers, "I think—"

The seconds feel like eternity as I ball my hands into fists on top of my lap.

Quickly, I click on my microphone. "Ms. Peyton-Anderson, you don't need to answer that question."

I turn toward the reporter, a muscle pulsing in my jaw as I watch his lips twist into a smug grin. The bastard wanted to put Taylor on the spot to get back at her for embarrassing him. "We've entertained your line of questioning long enough. We're hoping this tour will shine awareness on the rampant harassment and sexual assault women face in their daily lives and you, sir, by putting a dancer on the spot with your ridiculous questions, is the definition of *not* being an ally. As men, we need to do better. We need to create safe environments for women—victims or not—to speak up, not hostile environments."

Standing up, I turn to the rest of the crowd, noting the shocked expressions on their faces and force myself to smile. *Calm the fuck down, Charles.*

I want to strangle the asshole in front of me.

"Time's up and the press conference is over. We're thankful for your support of this important cause." I button my blazer.

Catching Taylor's eyes, I watch the color returning to her face and she rakes in a shuddering inhale. She rolls her lips inward as she stares at me, the same vulnerable expression I saw that night in the alcove on her face.

Gritting my teeth, I tear my gaze away from her and leave the room as reporters hurl questions at my back. Anything to not draw more attention to her, even though I want nothing more than to walk up to her, take her hand in mine, and haul her out of this room, away from the soulless leeches.

But what will people think? CEO in a tainted bank in an illicit relationship with a ballerina under his sponsorship?

The last vestiges of rational thought hammer in my brain, reining back the emotional impulse. I'm starting to understand why my parents are swept up in their feelings.

They burn and consume until common sense ceases to matter.

I can't become like them.

Or maybe it's already too late.

CHAPTER 33

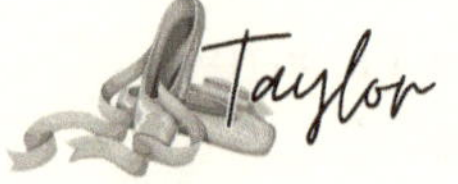

I STARE OUTSIDE THE window in the rehearsal room at the historic Estates Theater for our last performance in Prague in late November, barely paying attention to the moody scenery outside—wet cobblestone streets, streetlamps illuminated but barely making a dent in the dark night, gothic spires half-hidden by a blanket of fog as the chill sets in at night. My mind is filled with thoughts of what transpired in the last two weeks since the press conference.

Charles knocked on my hotel room door that night, his hair in disarray, his towering frame clad in a casual sweater and dark sweatpants. His cologne hit my nostrils, and I fought every urge to launch myself on him and snuggle in his warmth.

What's wrong with me?

"Yes?" I eyed him, my pulse quickening.

He rested his arm on top of the doorframe and I fought a shiver at how manly he looked and how small I felt next to him.

"I want to apologize for the reporter's questions."

I fiddled with my T-shirt. "It's not your fault. You weren't the ass-hole. Why are you apologizing?"

Charles swallowed, his blue eyes darkening. "I know he brought back bad memories. My team should've vetted him better." His voice was quiet, calm, but I saw a muscle twitching on his forehead.

Does he know what happened to me? Has he guessed everything? Panic rushed inside me. "I...Charles, it isn't...I—"

"You don't owe me any explanation. You don't need to tell me any-thing you don't want to," he murmured. His jaw worked, then he added,

"Real men don't force women into unwanted situations. But Taylor, I just want to tell you…if you ever need someone to talk to, someone to shoulder your burdens, I'm here. I'm strong. I can take your pain."

A sad chuckle escaped his throat as he shook his head. "Despite what you may think of me, I care about you, and I meant what I said in Paris." He looked up, his eyes intense. "You aren't alone anymore," he whispered.

His words burrowed deep into my heart, and part of me wanted to throw open the door to let him in, because damn it, I wanted to have normal relationships, to fall in love, have sex, to do all the things other women do without thinking.

But deep down, I was still terrified. I didn't want to get hurt again. I'd gotten so used to the fear lurking inside me, I didn't know how to be free of it. I thought I could separate physical pleasure from love. I thought I could try to have sex without being emotionally involved.

But it was impossible not to feel anything for him. I felt too damn much.

And so instead of telling him, I murmured, "Thank you."

I moved to close the door, not missing the slump of his shoulders as he walked away.

"Charles." My heart slammed into my throat. I wanted to be brave, for him, for myself, just for one second.

He paused and turned around, his eyes alert.

"If it could be anyone, it would be you," I whispered before quickly shutting the door, not wanting to see his face or hear his response.

I blow out an exhale, watching my breath fog up the window in front of me, wondering if I made the wrong choice that night.

But it's probably for the best. Charles is the nephew of my dance director, the best friend of my brothers. If things don't work out between us, it'll get ugly on multiple levels.

If I want to try having sex again, to reclaim my pleasure, maybe it's better if I find someone harmless, unassuming, someone I don't feel anything for.

It's safer.

Plus, I haven't seen the man very much these days. Charles has been busy with business meetings and events for the past two weeks, or perhaps he's giving me the distance he senses I need. The only time I ever saw him was backstage in passing or I'd catch a glimpse of him in one of the private boxes during our performances.

Even through the distance, I'd feel his gaze on me, the intensity, the reassuring warmth.

And I'd feel comforted.

Because I wasn't alone.

Riiiiing.

I startle and quickly take out my phone, my body freezing at the caller ID.

Emerson Clarke

My pulse quickens at the name of my private investigator. I left him a voice message yesterday asking for an update on the case.

Quickly, I answer, "Emerson? Do you have something for me?"

"Someone has taken great pains to hide their trail, Taylor," he says.

"What do you mean?" I grip my phone tightly.

"The financier I told you about, he was arrested and thrown into prison for embezzlement three years ago, but he was killed in a scuffle shortly afterward. There were no witnesses. The murder was suspicious."

My breath freezes in my throat. *Murder? What?* "W-Why do you think he has something to do with that night?"

The silence is heavy and grim.

"What? Just tell me, I can take it."

"Shit. I didn't want to tell you this until I could take care of it for you. But...there are photos...photos that came from his phone with a geotag."

My heart lurches to the floor, and I sway on my feet. "Photos of..." *Please don't tell me, please, I beg you.*

"Drunk girls in compromising positions at the hotel lounge you were at that night. It's bad. I won't sugarcoat it for you. I'm running facial recognition right now, so that's taking a while."

I place my hand on the window, trying not to throw up at the news. "A-Are there p-pictures of...o-of..."

I couldn't get the words out. But thankfully, Emerson takes pity on me.

"No, I haven't come across photos of you yet. There's still a lot to comb through. The photos were found on the dark web and there are places my team hasn't searched yet, but I want to be transparent with you." His voice turns urgent, as if he's upset he isn't having this discussion in person. "We're going to get these motherfuckers, okay?"

Closing my eyes, I focus on my breath, my teeth clattering as the hazy memories of that night swallow me whole like a tidal wave. How many of them were there?

When will this nightmare end?

"O-One more thing...were you able to locate Sir Ian?" I whisper, hoping this one memory I have—blond man, blue eyes—this one is false. That there is no reason for the nervousness I feel in his presence.

Because if he's involved, I won't be able to continue dancing at ABTC. I will fight like hell to get him arrested, to get the justice I deserve. It'll be chaos, a dynamite thrown into our circle of friends and family at home.

And Charles, his nephew, the only man who's ever been able to get close to me...I'll have to cut ties with him. Because there's no way he'd choose me over his family.

My pulse pounds rapidly in my ears as a hollow ache spreads inside my chest.

I can get through this. I'm Taylor Peyton-Anderson, take-no-prisoners badass. I can survive this.

"I can't match the geotags of the photos to his phone yet." My breath whooshes out, the sudden relief letting me rake in a much needed inhale.

"But his credit card statements and cell phone records show no activity for that night and the days before and after it. Nothing on social media either, so no alibi yet."

"So we can't rule him out." I blow out a deep breath.

Clicking sounds come across the line, like he's typing. "I'm sorry I don't have better answers for you."

Heavy footsteps echo down the hallway outside. "I-I got to go. Keep me posted, Emerson."

I don't wait for his response before I hang up and slide the phone back into my pocket.

"Taylor, I've been looking for you. I want to discuss the final lift with you. I think if you angle your leg—" Sir Ian frowns and cocks his head to the side, his startling eyes crinkling in obvious concern as he steps into the room. "Is everything okay?"

I shove my hands behind my back. "F-Fine. Everything is fine. Just a little homesick on Thanksgiving, that's all."

His eyes soften. "I'm so used to traveling around the world, I completely forgot today is Thanksgiving. I'm sorry you don't get to spend it with your family, but Happy Thanksgiving, Taylor."

My nostrils flare, my heart still racing too quickly inside me, but I think about Grace and Steven, who're celebrating in LA with Steven's family. Millie is also there because her shrewd billionaire brother, Adrian Scott, is married to Steven's older sister, Emily. Belle and Maxwell are with the rest of the Anderson crew and Olivia has plans with her parents in Brooklyn.

I wish I were there with them.

"It's okay. I should get used to this," I square my shoulders and look him in the eye, "because if I'm going to be a principal ballerina, I will travel throughout the year as well."

Sir Ian quirks his lips into a smile and I startle—the expression reminds me so much of Charles. "I like your gumption and spirit. Come with me." He waves his hand, motioning for me to follow.

I quickly fall behind him. *Focus on the dance, the performance. The past is in the past. Don't let it control your future.*

"I've seen improvement on your Odette. So, good job on that. I think you can do better, though. As I said, your lift should be..."

Discreetly, I power off my phone, needing to close the lid on the nightmare threatening to resurface.

The past is in the past.

But I can't help but feel it'll somehow taint my future.

CHAPTER 34

"CHEERS!" LISA THROWS HER arm around my shoulder and hefts up her glass, the alcohol sloshing over the rim. "Oops," she giggles, eyeing the large red stain on her white tube top, "I look like I got shot."

I shake my head and hand her drink to Dev, who slides in next to us at the crowded bar top. "You're so drunk, Lisa. Dev, save me from her."

Dev chuckles, his eyes shining with love as he bends down and kisses his girlfriend, and that uncomfortable twinge in my chest makes a reappearance. "You're such a cute drunk," he murmurs.

You can have that too if you take a chance. Someone wants to take off his mask with you.

My pulse kicks up at the thought of Charles, who I haven't seen since we wrapped up our last performance two hours ago. I distinctly remember seeing him in his usual box right before the performance, the fervor in his stare setting my skin on fire.

His lips curved into a ghost of a smile when he caught me looking at him before he turned to his companions in business attire.

Like all the times before, I felt reassured and comforted because of his presence. Somehow, I knew things would turn out okay.

The performance itself was uneventful, and while I wasn't blowing anyone away with my Odette, I knew I was doing a great job as Odile. I was met with thundering applause at the end of my thirty-two turns.

During the curtain call, my eyes drifted over to Charles's private box. He stood there clapping, a soft smile on his lips as he mouthed, *"Good job."*

I felt the compliment right in my flurried heartbeats and wondered if, despite my efforts to keep my distance, to protect what was left of my broken heart, if he'd already snuck in and stole it away.

He left with his group after the performance, no doubt to some business dinner, then to the airport. I overheard from Lisa earlier that Charles had to go back to New York to take care of some business. I wouldn't see him again for a few months.

I fought the aching disappointment settling on top of my chest.

Why didn't he let me know?

Probably because you insisted on keeping him at arm's length.

Isn't this what you wanted, Taylor?

Annoyed at myself and needing some distraction, I went with Lisa and Dev for a quick bite of dinner before heading to a trendy club near the restaurant.

My eyes sweep over the throngs of people on the multicolored LED dance floor in this club on Dlouhá Street, a few blocks away from Estates Theatre. It's close to midnight on Friday and the atmosphere is electric as people celebrate the end of a workweek.

"Let's dance!" Lisa shrieks, grabbing Dev's hand and pulling him toward the crowd. "Tay Tay, come with!"

My feet are sore and I just frankly want to go back to the hotel to reacquaint myself with the clawfoot bathtub. I shake my head. "You guys go ahead! I'm sitting this round out."

She pouts, then sticks her tongue out and the two of them disappear into the masses.

I bop my head to the loud music, the bass heavy, vibrating into my bones. Getting another glass of a nonalcoholic citrus cocktail from the bartender—they unfortunately don't have carrot flavored anything here—I take out my phone and swipe to the text messages.

Olivia

> Look at our Thanksgiving chicken! Mom's not a big fan of turkey, unfortunately.

Belle

> We have tons of leftovers! Turkey, stuffing, the works. The Andersons go all out during this holiday. Want some, Olivia?

Olivia

> I'll never say no to free food. *smiley face*

Lana

> How's my little sister doing all the way in Europe? Meet any hot European men yet?

Grace

> You tell her, Lana! I've been trying to get her to date. She doesn't listen.

Lana

> I have single guy friends over there. Total catches! Just say the word and I'll call them up to take you around. *grinning emoji*

I smile and type on the phone. Lana is always busy, flying around for work and I don't see her as often as I see my brothers, but she's a blast, and I'm thankful Grace and I have a smart and kind older half sister.

Taylor

> Why don't you hook up with these "great catches," Lana?

Lana

> Who says I haven't? *wink* Just kidding. Maybe I'm waiting for a certain someone.

Grace

> *Squeal* Lana! You can't drop that without giving us more details!

Grace

And Tay Tay, I hope you had a great performance today. We miss you a lot! We'll do a
makeup Thanksgiving when you're back.

She sends over a photo of her and Millie with Steven, his siblings, and Millie's brother, Adrian, in the background.

Grace

Millie misses Ryland a lot. She won't admit it
though.

Belle

Well, she's in for a surprise then.

Belle

Ah crap, I wasn't supposed to say anything.
Dang it, pregnancy brain! Millie, act surprised
when someone rings your door in an hour.
wink wink

She sends a photo of her and Maxwell at the Anderson Estate with the entire gang minus Ryland. Belle is a picture of radiance in her navy dress, her hands cradling her cute baby bump. After experiencing some fertility issues, she and Maxwell went through IVF and got pregnant.

Grace

You are glowing, Belle! OMG I can't wait to
find out if it's a boy or a girl! Auntie Grace will
pamper the shit out of him or her!

Belle

You're next, Grace. I'm saving all the cute stuff
I buy for you guys.

The girls talk about Belle's pregnancy and baby showers. I'm re-minded of the hollow loneliness I felt at Grace's wedding, akin to standing in the middle of a busy street, feeling lost while everyone dashes toward their next destinations.

My fingers hover over the keyboard, and I swallow the lump in my throat.

Taylor

> Happy Thanksgiving, girls. Wish I was there with you guys. I'm partying it up though!

I attach a photo of my drink and the club, hoping they won't worry about me.

"Is this seat taken?"

Startling, I glance at the guy standing next to me. He looks a few years older, medium build, kind eyes, floppy brown hair. He smiles, looking uncertain, and waves to the stool vacated by Lisa.

My initial reaction is to reject him, to tell him my friend is sitting here, but then I look at my texts again—my friends happy and moving on with their lives at home—then I glance at Dev and Lisa, who are all over each other on the dance floor. I eye the guy, taking in his appearance again. Button-down dress shirt and jeans. A casual messenger bag. He looks friendly enough. A decent-looking nerd.

Nonthreatening.

My body doesn't heat in his presence, my heart doesn't skip a beat.

Unlike how it reacts to a certain god of thunder.

Maybe this is a good chance for me to put myself out there with someone who doesn't make me feel too much.

"It isn't taken. Go ahead," I reply.

"Great." He sits down next to me and extends his hand. "I'm Jan. I haven't seen you around here before."

I arch my brow, a frisson of discomfort flowing through me. "Tammy." No way I'm giving him my real name. "You come out here a lot?" *Appearances can be deceiving.* Charles's words before he danced with me at Grace's wedding echoes in my ear. What if this guy is just like the businessman from all those years ago? That guy didn't look threatening, but look what happened?

Breathing in, I push the thought away. I'm not inebriated. My friends are here. I'm in a public place. I can handle this.

Jan chuckles. "It's a popular spot to decompress. What's the saying? 'Work hard, party hard?'"

I smile, setting down my drink on the table. He's leaning toward me, a charming grin on his face. Shaking my head, I reply, "It's actually 'work hard, play hard.'"

"Ah, sorry. My English is so so."

"I understand you just fine." Something occurs to me and I frown. "Hold on, how come you know I speak English? You didn't speak to me in Czech first." The unease flares up in my gut again.

"Ah. I have to confess, I was looking at you for a long time. You stand out, you know? You have a beautiful aura." He waves his hand over my face. "I heard you and your friends speaking in English."

I exhale. *Completely reasonable explanation, Taylor. Not everyone is bad. Don't overreact.*

"So tell me, what do you do?" He leans in, clearly interested.

We make some small talk, and slowly I relax again. He hasn't made advances toward me, but only talks about how he wants to visit New York City and try the pizza there. We have a few rounds of drinks—my nonalcoholic cocktails I got for myself.

I find myself laughing more than I usually do with strangers as excitement simmers inside me. Not because I'm attracted to him, but because I feel fine. This is what a twenty-something-year-old girl should be doing—going out, meeting new people, having fun.

Not being afraid of life.

Jan downs a shot and cracks another joke. They're getting more horrible by the minute.

"Okay, get this. I have a friend in the city who's good at chess. Do you know what I call him?"

My lips twitch as I shake my head. This is so ridiculous.

"He's my Czech mate." Jan busts out laughing and pounds the bar top and I snicker, because his smile is infectious. His phone rings and he holds up a finger. "Excuse me, I have to get this. Save me the seat, okay?"

I nod, and he heads toward the entrance. Bopping my head to the music, I let out a satisfied sigh, thankful I'm relaxed and relieved at how my panic hasn't appeared tonight.

Suddenly, I feel someone's gaze drilling into my back and my pulse speeds up.

I know it's him before he whispers seconds later, "Him, really? Why?"

My heart lodges in my throat as I drag my gaze to Charles, who looks like he hurried here from wherever he came from, his golden hair slightly unkempt, tie loosened around his neck. My core clenches—he looks so good—a virile fallen angel.

His jaw tics as he stares at me with his stormy eyes.

The peace and calm I felt in Jan's presence are completely obliterated by the turbulent heat emanating from the alpha male towering over me. Every atom in my body thrums and vibrates as I fight an impulse to touch him—the enticing scruff on his jaw, the vein protruding on his forehead. Then I want him to hold me in his arms as I listen to his thudding heartbeat.

This is why I can't do this with him. My emotions are too involved.

"You disgust me. I-I just can't be with you. I can't forget. I just can't," Camden's voice whispers in my mind and I inwardly flinch.

He loved me too. And I liked him a lot. Look how that turned out.

"Why him, Taylor? Why do you trust him more than me?" Charles's raspy voice draws me back to him. His breath hitches, his voice pained. My heart throbs in my chest, desperate to throw myself against him.

I've never felt this way about anyone before.

If Camden could hurt me so much, imagine what Charles could do.

I swallow a few sips of my drink. "We were just chatting, Charles."

"He's into you. Even the blind could see that. He was all over you and you were—" He stops himself, his voice hitching.

"What are you talking about?" I shrug nonchalantly.

A chill befalls his features and a muscle tics in his jaw.

"I see." His voice is quiet—too quiet. "I told myself to be patient. I knew you were scared because of what happened to you in the past. I was ready to wait for you because I knew you felt the connection between us, but I guess," he scoffs, "I'm just stupid for thinking a self-professed badass would come to her senses."

Fuck, the man always knows exactly what to say to rile me up. Ignoring the twinge of guilt inside me, I narrow my eyes. "Or maybe you aren't as memorable as you think you are. Don't think so highly of yourself."

Charles's eyes flash, a muscle twitching in his jaw. "Oh yeah? Well, I bet he can't make you feel this way." He leans in, his breath ghosting over my neck, and I bite my lip to keep from moaning and leaning into him.

He rasps, "Your breathing is fast. I see the goosebumps on your neck. Your eyes are dilated. And I bet if I were to slip my fingers between your legs, you'd be soaking wet."

My pussy pulses at his erotic words. His sexy cologne wafts to my nose, and all my senses heighten in awareness.

He presses a light kiss at the tender spot where my ear meets my neck and I shiver, heat churning through my veins. "Only I can make you feel like this," he whispers.

I want to lean into him, to touch him, kiss him, to say yes to taking off our masks and being naked with each other. Physically. Emotionally.

I also want to dry heave on to the floor and I wonder if this reclaiming my body and pleasure thing is too much for me. If I'm not ready.

I push him away. "Not. Interested."

He steps closer into my space, our bodies inches away. My resolve weakens by the second. "You're scared because you know what you're feeling is real. Admit it," he grits out.

"Is this man bothering you, Tammy?" Jan appears next to us, his brows furrowed.

Tearing my gaze away from Charles, I reply, "Yes, he is. Let's dance."

Slipping off my stool, I grab Jan's hand and pull him to the dance floor, completely aware of Charles's lasered focus on my back the entire time.

As I move to the music, with Jan dancing next to me, I can't help myself but look back at the bar.

Charles stands there, his hands fisted at his sides, his eyes anguished. He looks completely gutted. He shakes his head and chugs down a drink before slamming the glass back on the table and storming off.

The hollow ache from earlier spreads inside me. *What am I doing? Why am I sabotaging myself?*

Jan grins, giving my arm a squeeze. "A beautiful girl like you shouldn't be frowning. I'll make it my mission to help you forget your troubles. Let's dance your worries away."

He pulls me against his chest, which feels completely different than the strong, muscular frame of the man I can't forget, the man I want to run to this moment, the man I very much regret hurting.

I need to find Charles and tell him I'm sorry.

My feet move toward where Charles was standing moments ago, but Jan drags me back to him.

"Tammy, having fun?" His hands slide around my waist, gliding lower and lower.

And lower.

"Get your hands off me!" I shout, but the words are drowned out by the loud music.

Panic rises inside me as my heart pounds rapidly inside my chest. I shake my head, my hands trying to dislodge his from around my waist. He doesn't back off, but pulls me flushed against him, and I feel a distinct bulge at my back.

He's hard.

Horror churns through me.

Danger. Run.

I struggle, but Jan is stronger than he appears. His fingers dig into my hips.

"Come on, baby. You were enjoying yourself earlier. We were having fun, right? Don't be shy." His breath reeks of alcohol.

No, this can't be happening. Not again.

Snippets of my nightmare barrel into my thoughts.

The charming dark-haired man in an expensive suit handing me, a sixteen-year-old who didn't know any better, a flute of champagne.

"This is a secret between us, okay?" He winked.

My skin warmed, and I shyly took the drink from him, even as a small pinch of guilt settled inside me for thinking this man was hot, even though I had a great boyfriend in Camden.

But hey, that's just a normal biological reaction, right? Just because I'm happily taken doesn't mean I'm blind.

"Here's to our future prima ballerina, Taylor. You'll go places," the man whispered, clinking his glass with mine.

He stared at me as I took a drink, his eyes darkening.

Minutes later, the world spun around me, my limbs growing heavy.

Jan grabs my ass and groans in my ear, shocking me back to the present. "Having fun, Tammy? Relaxing yet?"

No, motherfucker.

Over my dead body.

"Let me go."

Gritting my teeth, I spin around and knee him in the balls; the movement causing me to almost trip as the strobe lights flash into my eyes. I vaguely hear his screech of pain as I break into a run, my body pitching, my arms braced in front of me, pushing anyone in the vicinity out of the way. My pulse roars against my ears, icy adrenaline coursing through my veins.

I try to focus on the crowd before me, but their faces merge into one. There's no way I can find Lisa or Dev in my current state.

I look back, finding Jan's face flushed with fury, hot on my heels.

Fuck.

Panic joins the chaos inside me, my breathing sawing through my lungs too fast, making me disoriented. I push people out of the way, my legs carrying me as fast as I can through the crowds toward the entrance where the bouncers are. The lights are flashing too brightly, the music too loud; a few bodies smash into me, slowing me down.

Terror curdles inside my gut. I need help. Shit. Fingers trembling, I take out my phone and press a few buttons.

I call the only person I trust.

CHAPTER 35

"Fuck!" With a rough yank, I pull off my tie as I sit inside my town car on the way to the airport. Not that it does anything to the heartache and betrayal coursing through me.

My mind is filled with images of her laughing, flirting with a random guy she just met—a guy who probably doesn't even understand the beauty of thorns on roses.

How could she deny everything between us? Did all of it mean nothing to her?

I was supposed to head back to New York right after a business dinner tonight to take care of some bank business that couldn't be done remotely, and frankly, I'd been away for too long, delaying my departure because of a certain minx. I told myself to just leave. Maybe the distance was what we both needed to think through things. After all, she was the youngest sister of my best friends. Things could get messy.

But the itch to see her only grew throughout the dinner. I *needed* to see her before I go. I wanted to tell her how proud I was of her.

Her Odette, while still flawed, was beautiful in her own way.

The strength in her turns and lifts, the fierceness in her eyes.

To dance a role that challenged you, knowing the public was scrutinizing your every move, but still putting yourself out there, night after night, ignoring naysayers, gossipmongers, and critics.

There was strength, and yet, there was also an underlying vulnerability.

It made her white swan unique.

I wanted to tell her before I hopped on my jet, knowing I wouldn't see her for a few months, knowing I'd miss her and hoping she'd miss me, even though I knew she wouldn't admit it.

But what did I get instead?

"Fuck, fuck, fuck!" Anger makes an appearance, joining the pain. *Another person you care about who has no interest in you. This is why you don't do emotions, Charles. This is fucking why.*

I stare out the window, my mind a swirl of madness when the phone in my pocket vibrates.

My minx.

The immediate thought crossing my mind is concern because she never calls me. My anger quickly set aside, I answer, "Minx."

"Ch-Charles?"

The hairs rise on the back of my neck. She sounds terrified. I rap on the center divider and instruct the driver to turn back.

"What happened?"

She shrieks. Something's wrong. "H-He's chasing me. God, I-I'm so scared. I'm sorry for everything. I need you—"

She needs me. I'll fight an army to get to her.

"Stay on the phone, don't turn it off. I'm on my way."

Five minutes later, I dash into the club, my heart threatening to rip out of my chest. Scanning the space, I try to spot the most beautiful woman among the crowds. Fear curdles inside my gut as desperation rips the breath out of my lungs.

Fuck. Where is she?

"Sweetheart, I'm here. Where are you?" I try to keep my voice even. She can't hear my panic. She needs me to be calm for her.

Silence greets me. I look at the phone. Damn it, it disconnected.

I push people out of the way, my feet carrying me into the throng.

Desperation carves me in half. I need to find her. I won't be able to live with myself if anything happens to her.

Just then, I hear a commotion on top of the usual club ruckus. My feet pivot toward the sizable crowd huddled around the restrooms.

"Get out of my way!" I push through the bystanders and my heart nearly plummets to the floor at what I see.

The fucker is approaching Taylor, who is cornered and screaming. I hurtle toward them just as she bares her teeth and delivers a sharp elbow strike to the bastard's face; the crowd reacting to her move with a roar.

The idiot howls in pain and staggers toward her. Her eyes are wild as she drives the heel of her palm into his nose.

My lungs heave in rapid breaths of oxygen, my heart beating against my rib cage.

Awestruck. I'm fucking awestruck. That's my minx.

The crowd roars and some idiots even whistle. The bastard's nose is bloody, and he charges toward her, obviously pissed off.

Torture. Maim. Murder. I'm going to strangle the life out of him.

Quickly, I reach them in a few strides. I clamp the asshole by the collar, serve him a right hook to his face, and fling him away from her. Then I pull her into my arms.

She screams, her arms flailing, the horror clear in her voice, "Let go of me!"

"It's me, Tay. Me. Charles. Shhhh. You're safe." I hold her tightly, feeling her lithe body trembling in my embrace. God, she's shaking so much.

Growling, I whip my head toward the asshole on the floor, who appears to be disoriented. I'm going to fucking kill him.

"Ch-Charles?" She looks up, her shaky voice drawing my attention back to her. Her gray eyes are glazed over, her lips trembling. Then her body slumps against mine, like I'm all she needs in the world. "You came. You came for me."

Mine. Possessiveness curls around my chest.

"Always. I'll always be here for you." *Always. Whenever she calls.* I crush her in my embrace, floored by the intense emotions flooding my body.

"Charles, I want to go back to the hotel. Please." She wobbles on her feet. A few bouncers head in our direction.

I lift her up in my arms, ignoring the stares and cell phone cameras pointed at us. "You're safe, my little minx. You're safe."

Taylor moans, her body trembling, and she snuggles deeper into my hold. My heart fucking breaks. She looks so vulnerable.

"I kicked his ass, didn't I?" she whispers.

My lips twitch up, a spark lighting inside me. My feral little kitten. No, she's not vulnerable or fragile. She's a fucking fighter.

"Damn right you did." I press a kiss on her hair and carry her away.

"I'm safe," she mumbles. "I'm always safe with you."

A heady warmth floods my chest, my heart racing, pulsing, coming alive inside me.

Mine.

And it's then I know, I'm already in too deep.

CHAPTER 36

I WAKE UP TO the darkness, a sultry ache pulsing through me, lingering on my nipples and pussy. Everything is so sensitive, my body hovering at the edge of ecstasy, like I just had a sexy dream I can't remember.

Sitting up, I feel the cool air of the air conditioning graze my skin, goosebumps forming soon afterward. My senses are heightened, my skin hot to the touch. I glance around, finding the dark shape of a man sleeping soundly next to me.

Startling, I swallow my scream as fear slams into my chest, but then I recognize his form—the light hair, the strong build, his muscular arm slung over his eyes.

Charles.

The events of the night come rushing in like a slide show. Clubbing with Lisa and Dev. Arguing with Charles. A nice looking guy striking up a conversation at the bar.

The guy chasing me, and me fighting back. The terror I felt thinking I'd go through what I experienced at sixteen again.

A thought niggles my mind. I gasp. *I fought back. I kicked his ass.*

The worst didn't happen because I. Kicked. His. Ass. I controlled the situation with my body and my power and turned it around.

A blistering energy flows through me—a laser burning through chains I've felt around my rib cage ever since that night. My fingers tingle, my lips curving into...a smile?

Looking at the slumbering man next to me, memories of the rest of the night flood in. Charles came, no questions asked, even after I picked a fight with him because I was terrified of my feelings for him.

Always. I'll always be here for you.

My heart doubles in size, the warmth spreading, joining the ache blossoming in my pussy.

I had an adrenaline crash in the car and barely remember him tucking me into bed.

But now, I'm wide awake, my mind crystal clear, blissfully empty of dark memories and fear.

In this quiet moment, in a dark hotel room in Prague, staring at Charles, the man I once thought I hated, but now realize that was probably never the case, I know one thing.

As opposed to giving myself to another man who doesn't make me feel so much, why can't I have sex with him? He'd take care of me. It wouldn't be painful with him.

Roses are more beautiful with thorns.

My clit throbs and I clench my thighs together, biting back a moan threatening to escape.

My clothes are too restrictive, too rough on my sensitive skin. The scent of bergamot and cedarwood wafts to my nose and I shiver, desperation burgeoning inside me.

It's him all along.

My mind made up, I slowly slip out of my pants and shirt. I swallow a whimper at the pleasurable sensations lighting up my nerves. Wetness seeps through my panties as I stare at Charles's slumbering form again. I take in the sexy map of veins on his arms and hands, the well-defined pecs and abs, the trail of hair leading to the sizable bulge in the sweatpants slung low on his hips.

I swallow, my pulse thready as I climb over him because this is something I've never done before. I don't even know how he'll react.

Slowly, I settle over his torso and bite my lip as my pussy comes on top of his heated body. I carefully slide my hands up his chest, biting back another whimper at all the manly muscles underneath me. I lean forward...and forward...until I'm hovering over him, my lips inches away from his ear.

"Charles?" I whisper.

He groans, his hips automatically flexing under me, his hands clamping my ass, and I moan in pleasure.

"Charles, you awake?" Unable to help myself, I pepper light kisses on his jaw, relishing in the hard scrape of his scruff on my skin.

So that's what it feels like. I rub against him like a cat in heat.

I know the moment he wakes up. His muscles coil in tension as he stills.

"Tay?" His voice is hoarse and deep. So fucking sexy.

My tongue dips out as I lick his jaw, the salty taste addictive, and I moan again. "I need you, Charles."

My body is on fire, my nerves burning for him. I want to fall into madness with him.

"Fuuuck," he grunts, thrusting up, his hard cock hitting my piercing through our clothes. "Shit."

I whimper, my hips moving of their own accord. I don't know what I'm doing, but apparently, my body knows this dance and is taking over.

"Minx. Fuck," he rasps as I gyrate harder, moving my underwear clad pussy from the base of his cock to the tip. More wetness drips out of me.

It feels so good, too good.

"Minx," he tries again, "you have to stop. You were attacked earlier. You're probably still running on adrenaline and not thinking straight."

I bite his neck and he lets out a sharp hiss, his fingers gripping, digging into my ass cheeks to the point of pain.

It feels so good.

"I've never been more clear-headed," I murmur into his ear. "You were right. I was scared. Scared of feeling anything real because...because of things that have happened to me in the past." My voice is thick, but I push myself to continue, "But I don't want to let the past control me any longer. I want to move forward."

Lifting myself up, I pause my movements and stare at his face, half shadowed in the darkness, only illuminated by the pale moonlight streaming in from the windows.

The answer was in front of me all along.

"And I want to have sex and I want to do it with you, Charles."

His nostrils flare, and even in the darkness, I see his eyes sharpen with intensity, emotions flitting across his face—too fast for me to decipher. He swallows.

"No," he rakes in a ragged inhale. "If we're going to have sex, I want you to be completely sure. I don't want you to regret it later."

Leaning down, I kiss his lips. The ache pulsing between my legs is now an incessant throb. I gyrate harder on his cock, a fission of pleasure shooting up my body.

I moan, "I'm sure. I *need* this. I need you. Please, oh God, I need you. I'm going to die if I don't come."

I rub harder against him, the sparks quickly burgeoning, and a guttural groan tears from his mouth, the sound a direct hit to my clit.

Yes. Yes. Yes. Quicker. Faster. Chase the inferno.

I'm burning, and I need him to relieve me. *Light me on fire.*

My senses are flooded with everything that's Charles Vaughn. My fucking sexy god of thunder. My archangel. My avenger who dropped everything to save me.

Gripping his face with my hands, I kiss him, my tongue licking his lips, my mouth sucking, taking any part of him inside me. He slips a finger into my mouth and I lave at it like it's the best tasting lollipop. I'm drunk from him. Delirious from want. I crave his addictive taste. Salty. Smooth. Masculine.

"I'm going to hell." He moves his hips under me, hitting that sensitive spot over and over again.

I moan around his finger before I take it out and find his lips again.

He shudders, his breathing harsh in the silence. Not breaking our kiss, I shrug out of my bra, my breasts heavy and tender, and I let out a pleasurable sigh as my hard nipples graze his chest.

"Fuck me," he rasps.

We break apart for air and I see pitch-black eyes snagged on my heaving tits, my pebbled nipples thrusted forward, needing him to touch them, play with them, kiss them.

His nostrils flare, his tongue swiping his lips as he stares at my tits. "Shit. Fuck... You're testing every limit I never knew I had, minx."

"Play with me," I moan, clasping my breasts in both hands, offering them up to him.

"Fuck. Fuck. Fuck." Madness swirls in his eyes, his control clearly close to snapping. I tug at my nipples and whimper, my hips moving again, the sensations overbearing, almost becoming too much.

"I need this, Charles...I need to know what sex feels like when I want it," I whisper.

Something about my words causes his body to still. A muscle pulses in his jaw and he looks at me.

No, he stares at me, his intense eyes seeing through all my layers to the darkest parts of me, the sides I never want the world to see.

He must've concluded something because slowly, he sits up and pulls me snug against his body as if I weighed nothing.

He can break me in half if he wants to.

But somehow that doesn't scare me.

"I won't have sex with you tonight, Tay. But I'll pleasure you. I'll show you what it's like between a man and a woman who want each other."

He curls his hand around my nape and brings my head toward him. His lips touch the whorl of my ear. "And when you're ready to take off your mask with me in the daylight, I'll make love to you. Fuck you hard. Make you forget every man who has ever touched you before, because all you'll remember is me."

CHAPTER 37

MY COCK IS THROBBING, leaking at the tip for her. I've never been this hard before, not even in the most depraved scenes at The Orchid in my younger, anything goes, days.

And we haven't even done anything yet.

This alone should scare me. The fact I want nothing more from her other than giving her pleasure and chasing away her pain. I'll be happy holding her in my arms, kissing her, watching her come apart over and over again because she trusts me to take care of her afterward.

It's an honor.

My lips tangle with hers, my tongue dueling, lashing, swiping inside her mouth, tasting the sweetness that's the most addictive drug. She's moving on top of me, her body in a natural rhythm—a fucking sensual goddess rubbing her hot little pussy on my aching cock like it's the only thing she wants in the world.

I want to bury myself deep inside her, feel her tight muscles wrap around me, sucking the cum out of me. But I don't want her to regret this. I know this isn't casual for her. It's a big milestone. I'm betting this will be the first time she has sex since her trauma.

I don't want her to regret it later.

And so, I'll satisfy myself with relieving her ache. I move my lips down the slender column of her neck, biting her throbbing pulse, listening to her hiss, then feeling her grind against me harder.

She likes the pain. My little masochist.

Growling, I grip her luscious tits in my hands—fuck, they're perfect creamy handfuls. Her nipples are hard and I suck on them, listening to her moans and whimpers as a guide on what she likes. She shakes on top of me, and I clamp my teeth lightly around the tip.

"Charles!" Taylor screams, throwing her head back, her body pulsing on top of my cock before she slumps forward.

Fuck, she came already, just from me kissing her and playing with her nipples.

My minx is so sensitive—the things I can do to her. Lurid thoughts of her on her knees, metal clamps on her nipples, me controlling every inch of her body—cum leaks out of me and I stifle a growl.

"You like me biting you, huh? Pain was torture for you before, but not anymore. I'll teach you how pleasurable pain can be."

Wrenching her off me, I toss her to the bed. Her eyes widen as I hover over her and trail more kisses over her heated body.

"Fuck, Charles, please fuck me," she whimpers, tugging my hair.

I hiss at the sensations, my cock leaking into my underwear, and I bite my lip—anything to stave off the need to come right now. "No. Not tonight."

Trailing my mouth over her smooth belly, I make my way down her body until I reach her thighs. My nose flares at the sweet scent of her arousal. Fuck, I can't wait to taste it.

Parting her legs, I bury my nose into her pussy, pausing...needing one last confirmation before I continue because I know this is all new to her.

She tightens her thighs around my head like a vise and arches her hips up. "Charles. I feel so...I need..."

"I know damn well what you need." With a growl, I pull off her panties and take my first swipe of her wet pussy.

Fuck, she tastes delicious. Sweet honey, like heaven.

"Fuck me," I mutter before lifting my head and staring at the piercing that has starred in my most depraved dreams—the perfect little barbell taunting me above her clit. "This piercing, Tay. I've wanted to see it for so long. This naughty little secret hidden in a place only I can see."

Biting the barbell, I give it a soft tug and she screams, her thighs clamping tighter around my face, almost strong enough to cut off my oxygen. I swipe my tongue around her clit.

Taylor thrashes, her legs trembling. Pulling her legs apart, I hold them down as I suck her clit into my mouth, circling it with my tongue, tapping it, my fingers pulling at the piercing at the same time.

Her breathing quickens, rapid bursts mixing with the lewd moans from her mouth. My hips buck against the bed, needing friction, feeling like I'll burst at any second.

I break the pattern with a tortuous lick down her pussy, lapping up the sweet juices flowing out of her. I'm addicted. High on the taste of Taylor Peyton-Anderson. My cock burrows deeper into the covers as I go back to her clit and take it into my mouth. Then I slowly slide a finger into her opening.

"Charles!" she cries, her pussy clenching against the invasion. She's so tight, so wet. I lap at her clit and play with her pussy some more and I feel her slowly relax as my finger slams all the way in.

Quickly, I start off a rhythm, thrusting my digit inside her, curling it so it grazes that sensitive spot and she grabs my hair, her hot body writhing on the bed.

"Fuck me, fuck me, fuck me," she chants, her voice delirious. "Oh my God, what are you doing to me, oh fuck, oh fuc—"

"Minx, you're so fucking tight, I can't wait to get my cock inside you. You'd take it so well. Shit, your greedy pussy wants more, huh?"

I insert a second digit, and before I can thrust a few more times, she falls apart.

"Charles!" Her cries join the lurid sounds of my fingers moving inside her. Her body arches up, liquid spurting from her pussy and she trembles uncontrollably, but I don't let up, kissing, tasting everything she's giving me. So fucking delicious.

The sparks spread from my heavy, aching balls up my throbbing shaft.

With a grunt, I kneel before her and tug down my underwear, my cock springing free. I grip it tightly as she stares wide-eyed at me, her face flushed, sweaty, her eyes glazed over with pleasure.

"Watch what you do to me, minx. My cock is leaking for you." I tug myself harder, fucking my fist like it is her pussy.

Holding my stare on hers, I watch her lips parting, her tongue darting out as she moves her hips on top of the bedsheets like she's imagining me inside her. I grow harder.

"Like what you see, my feral kitten?"

I groan, the pleasure reaching a boiling point. Black dots form in my vision, my pulse roaring in my ears.

"All for you, minx. All fucking for you. This is what you do to me."

The dam bursts and I fall into oblivion, my hand gripping, moving faster as ropes of cum shoot out of my cock, spraying over the sheets, landing on her belly and tits.

Molten fire spreads through my veins at the sight of my cum on her—marking her.

She's mine.

Taylor moans as she stares at me, her face flushed and breathing rapidly. She trails her fingers to her heaving tits and swirls the digits over my cum. Then she slowly brings them up to her lips and licks her fingers, tasting me.

She moans and closes her eyes before sucking her fingers like she can't get enough.

Fuck me. Tugging my cock a few more times, I wring out every drop of cum, every pleasure I can get in this moment, hoping in the light of day she won't regret any of this.

"Shit," she whispers, her eyes opening and staring at my cock again. "You weren't kidding at ABTC about your inches."

Her lips twitch and it takes a few seconds for me to remember what she's referring to—that day at the steps, which seems so long ago, and I bark out a laugh. This woman.

"Fucking minx," I rasp, watching as her eyes glint with laughter.

Gripping her neck, I haul her to me for another kiss and soon, intense passion chases away the humor. She melts against me, not caring we're a mess of cum and sweat. My tongue tangles with hers, her nails scraping down my back. My cock stirs, wanting another round, wanting to be buried inside her this time.

With my last ounce of restraint, I tear myself away from her, but not before pressing the softest kiss on her lips.

"This is how it should be between two people who want each other," I whisper to her parted lips. "The tip of the iceberg." I press another kiss on her mouth and rasp, "I won't rush you, but I want you so damn much. All your thorns. All your scars. Every inch of you. Step into the light with me, Taylor."

Her eyes fill with tears as her throat works. She's rendered speechless. But it's okay. I know what she's thinking, even without words.

She once said my heart is in my eyes.

But really, she's talking about herself, because I want to be the man she's staring at right now...in shock, awe, and all the heavy emotions I've tried to ignore most of my life, thinking they are beasts I should tame.

I want to unleash them with her.

"You're never alone. Not anymore," I murmur.

A few tears slip out of her eyes, and she throws her arms around me. She cries into my chest, each sob carving a new wound on my heart. I curl my arms around her shaking body, anguish tearing up my insides. I hold her close until her shudders calm and I feel her body relaxing.

"Charles?" she mumbles, her voice sluggish, like she's seconds away from drifting off to sleep.

"Yes, minx?"

"I'm fucked up. Why do you like me? Give me a reason. Any reason..." Her voice drifts off.

I frown and look down at her, finding her fast asleep, a frown marring her forehead. It's torture to see her like this, beautiful but scar-ridden at my feet. The helplessness of not being able to take away her pain. The rage threatening to swallow me whole.

Leaning down, I kiss her forehead and smooth out the wrinkle there. She lets out a sigh and snuggles deeper into my hold.

I want to know what happened; I want to fix her.

Someday, she'll tell me everything and I'll chase away every single shadow in her eyes.

Her demons are mine, her enemies are mine.

I'll destroy them, whoever they are.

CHAPTER 38

THE AIR IS FRIGID early December in Edinburgh as I walk along the Water of Leith, a river cutting through Dean Village. It's a neighborhood dating back to the 12th century, which used to be known for its grain mills, but is now a quiet residential area famous for its cobbled streets, stone bridges, and medieval style architecture. The rest of the company went out to celebrate after wrapping up the Edinburgh performances.

Lisa swore she wouldn't leave my side this time. She felt so guilty after I told her what happened, leaving out the part about Charles coming to my rescue. I told her it wasn't her fault.

But nevertheless, after what happened in Prague, I declined the group outing. Instead, I find myself walking the quiet streets, breathing in the chilly late afternoon air. I want to think through some things.

Taking a seat at a bench by the river, I hold the small bouquet of roses up to my nose, smelling the sweet scent, and I smile. A dozen burgundy roses, thorns intact and tipped with gold glitter, carefully wrapped in black parchment paper. I read the note card affixed to it for the hundredth time.

To My Minx,

Congratulations on yet another successful performance. I wish I was there to watch you dance.

Stay warm in Edinburgh.

Yours,

Charles

P.S. Reason number twenty-one: Your fascination with carrots. Now every time I eat something with them in it, I automatically think of you. But then, I don't need help with that. I think of you far too often.

My heart skips a few beats as I imagine him munching on a carrot at a restaurant inside The Orchid, his thoughts on me.

Charles left early morning after our night together in Prague. He gently roused me on the bed, the softest caress and the gentlest kiss, and said, "Minx, I need to go back to New York to take care of some things at the bank. I was supposed to go back last night..."

He didn't finish his sentence, but I knew he stayed for me.

My brain is foggy from the events of the prior evening, after which he and I took separate showers before he wrapped me in his arms as sleep overtook me.

I was cocooned in safety. No more nightmares or shadowy whispers.

And so, that morning, I lazily blinked open my eyes and smiled at him and I saw him catch a breath, his beautiful blue eyes darkening, his jaw clenching before releasing.

"Thank you, Charles...for everything." *For being here, for letting me feel pleasure again. For being patient with me.* "Safe travels."

We stared at each other, not saying anything more, because honestly, I'd no idea where we stood. My emotions were a mess, my mind still trying to process everything in the light of day. He was right. I needed to think things through before we took things further.

But I know my body is ready now. I just need to open up my heart.

He swallowed, not pushing me. "If my schedule permits, I'll try to be at the last performance in St. Petersburg. But if not, I'll see you back in New York."

Leaning down, he pressed a kiss on my cheek and whispered, "You're not alone, Taylor. Not anymore."

His words echo in my mind as I stare at his note, one from each day I'd receive from him. The first bouquet arrived the day after, tucked with a note of something he thought about during his day. He'd always end the note with a postscript...a reason why he thinks I'm wonderful.

Reason number one: The fire in your eyes when you dance—I feel like I'm chasing your dreams or vanquishing your demons right alongside you.

Reason number two: Your wit and dry sarcasm. Do you know they say sarcasm is the highest form of intelligence?

Reason number three: Bravery. Whenever I think of that word, I think of you. The way you face the world, no fucks given, the way you don't let your past keep you down, the way you are clear in what you feel...love, hate, everything written on your face.

The notes go on and on, arriving early morning with a bouquet of burgundy roses, the thorns intact.

Roses are more beautiful with thorns.

The walls around my heart crumble. He's wooing me with actions.

As always, I take out my phone and send him a text message to thank him for the flowers, and include a photo of what I'm seeing in front of me.

Taylor

Thanks. The performance went well. It's a gloomy day in Edinburgh. I'm at the Dean Village. But my day is made brighter by your flowers.

After taking a quick selfie, I attach it to the text message and press send.

A few minutes later, he replies.

Charles

Go to Stockbridge after your walk. There are some great cafés and bakeries there. They might even have carrot cake.

I smile and type back a reply.

Taylor

What are you doing now? Is the bank doing okay? Has the press calmed down?

As far as I know, while my performance has been average, the international tour has been decently received. Belle kept sending articles about the press raving about my Odile, the strength in my thirty-two fouetté turns in the most famous part of the ballet, the Black Swan pas de deux.

I may not be the ideal white swan, but my black swan is shining, the dark feathers gleaming under the spotlight. But now, I'm wondering, why am I so focused on Odette when I do Odile well? The black swan's routine is more technical, more difficult, more famous.

Am I focusing on the wrong thing?

Charles

The bank is doing fine. We've sent the first wave of proceeds to the organizations, which is the smallest thing we could do. And the press is giving me a break. The Patterson trial is wrapping up soon, and I was able to quash the photos from Prague.

My muscles tense at the mention of that night at the club. Charles texted me later he didn't want me to worry about the photos taken by bystanders. That he'd take care of them.

Those photos could've put us in a bad light, even though I was the victim and he was my knight.

The press is ridiculous.

Taylor

Thanks.

Charles

I'm at the hospital visiting Firefly, then I'll head to The Orchid to meet your brothers for drinks.

Frowning, I know from our text messages the last two weeks he's taking it hard around the holidays because it's his sister's favorite time of the year.

Taylor

How is she? Still no change?

Charles

No. I've never told anyone this, but there are days when I wonder if it's hopeless. If I'm selfish for holding her here for me, and not really for her. After all, I don't think she'd want to be hooked up to monitors and tubes. But I can't let her go.

My chest clenches in pain. I can't imagine losing Grace or any of my girlfriends. I remember the agony it was to lose Mom, to get the call from the cops telling me there'd been an accident and she was killed on impact. It's a pain I wouldn't wish on my worst enemy, not even the bitch Carla.

But to have this torture dragged out for years...losing hope and yet feeling guilty about it?

> Grace believes in shooting stars. She told me they were the gods peeking down from the heavens and that's when they'd grant wishes. The next time I see one, I'll make a wish for her and for miracles.

Three dots appear, disappear, and reappear.

> It's almost Christmas. The city is beautiful—all decked out in lights. How is it possible to feel alone in a place with over eight million people?

I grip my phone tightly, wishing I were there with him, because I know exactly how he feels—lonely, but never alone.

> I miss you.

My heart spasms as my fingers hover above the keypad. I want to respond and text him, *I miss you too.* But something holds me back...I feel naked, even though I'm bundled in a black turtleneck sweater and a thick puffer coat.

But I'll get there. I'm sure of it. I'm a fighter and I've taken so many strides forward. I've just gotten so used to protecting my heart, to being alone, it'll take time to rework my thoughts.

Emerson has been quiet on the case. Two weeks ago, he texted me the photo of the financier who was killed in jail and I remember my phone clattering to the ground when I saw it.

It was the charming man who gave me the champagne. Emerson is on the right track.

Other than the photo, the last update I have from him is, he has located a few more suspects, all powerful people in elite circles, and he's chasing them down. I'm just thankful so far, there are no photos of me and nothing on Sir Ian, who has been completely professional and kind. He's taken it upon himself to give me more coaching on Odette.

"Work with what you have. Don't force something you don't have. Use your emotions as a source of power for your dance. Channel them. Harness them into something greater. Vulnerability can come in many forms, Taylor." That's what he told me last week.

My muscles still tense whenever I'm around him, but I've come to terms with that reaction. It has to be a trauma response not grounded in reality.

Swallowing the lump in my throat, I slide my phone back into my pocket and clutch the roses tighter in my hands. I look at the surrounding scenery, soaking in the gloomy atmosphere. The Victorian style streetlamps flicker on and off, casting long shadows on the wet cobblestone pathways. The trees are barren, twisting against the gray skies.

Kids laugh and their parents murmur something as they walk hand in hand, wearing colorful coats. A little girl giggles as her dad hoists her on his shoulders.

I stare at the families, my heart pangs.

Leap. Odette did it with Prince Siegfried. You can do it with Charles, the wind whispers.

I take out his notecard and read it again. They say distance makes the heart grow fonder, and I think it's true.

He has stolen parts of my battered heart with each angry glare and snarky retort, with his heated glances and blistering kisses.

I have already given him power to pulverize the rest of me without realizing it.

But he makes me feel safe. When he's there, the monsters don't come.

And I miss him.

CHAPTER 39

Ethan stands by the windows, his back toward me, a glass of Scotch in his hand. Quietly, I walk into our usual private room in the gentlemen's club inside The Orchid. We're meeting the others in an hour, and I want to get some time alone after a week of grueling meetings. I didn't tell Taylor it took me ten calls and twenty million dollars to buy out every copy of unflattering photos taken of us at the club in Prague.

I also didn't tell her I had a private investigator tail the asshole who assaulted her at the club. He caught him doing the same thing to another woman a week later. His new victim reported him to the police.

The fucker is in lock up now.

The work at the bank hasn't stopped since I left Prague—press conferences, financial reporting, new corporate initiatives, forecasting. It's relentless, and normally, I'd live for the challenge, since I have no one waiting for me at home, but now... I just find myself fucking annoyed at it all. But at least the stock price is finally stabilizing and my name or the Bank of Columbia doesn't appear in newspapers or gossip rags as often now.

I've also thrown myself into interviewing for the permanent CFO role.

This time, I'm vetting out every single candidate myself, reviewing all their background checks, not letting any detail escape me. I haven't found the right fit yet, and with the interim CFO only assisting in bare minimum tasks, my workload has increased significantly in the meantime.

But through it all, I miss her. I know her sister and girlfriends flew to Edinburgh to spend Christmas with her, but I couldn't get away—investor calls, all the fucking work landing on my lap as we close out another calendar year, not to mention the almost mandatory networking to be done at the infamous Christmas Ball at The Orchid.

Other than our texts, each of which I've read and memorized by heart, and sending her the roses I know she loves, I haven't seen her or heard her voice.

I often wonder if that night we had together scared her. If she's keeping her distance on purpose. But I told myself she'd been through unspeakable terrors, that patience is the name of the game now.

Today, I thought I'd get an hour of quiet just to sort through everything, but it seems like I'm not the only one who needs alone time.

Ethan is dressed in a dark suit, his profile still as he stares at the sea of white outside the window. It isn't a January day in New York City without a snowstorm.

"How is she?" he murmurs, still not looking at me. The cold light renders his face into half shadows.

I know he's talking about Firefly.

I pour myself a drink before I stand next to him. "How did you know I visited her?" It was the first snowfall of the new year—a blizzard at that. Firefly would always be so excited when that occurred.

"Her favorite time isn't Christmas. It's after New Year's. Everyone fucking hates that time because all the festivities are over, but she loves it. She once told me January symbolized new beginnings. She loves the fresh snow." An anguished smile appears on his face.

Hearing him talk about Firefly makes me feel shittier as an older brother.

He's using present tense.

"Maybe this will be the year when she wakes up," he adds before taking a sip of alcohol.

"You've never given up hope?" A thousand pound weight sits on my chest.

"Never." He turns and stares at me, and I see the determination in his gray eyes, the same dark eyes of the woman who's constantly in my mind. "Don't beat yourself up for it, Charles. We all grieve differently. Perhaps I'm the one who isn't facing reality."

I've always wondered why Ethan hasn't gone after Firefly—it's obvious he cares for her a lot, but he'll deny it if I ask. I wonder if it has anything to do with Liam being his best friend. Him and I aren't as close—I hung out more with Maxwell and Ryland whereas he spent his time with Liam when they were growing up.

In times like these, I wonder if his feelings run deeper than I originally thought. But Ethan Anderson, despite being the youngest son of the family, reminds me of his oldest brother Maxwell. Quiet. Holding all his cards close against his chest.

"If I took her seriously all those years ago, she probably wouldn't have gotten into the car. That's the reality I face every day." I toss back the whiskey.

"We all make mistakes, Charles. She wouldn't want you beating yourself up. She'd hate it."

I know she would. But that doesn't lessen the guilt.

"Did you ever find out what she wanted to talk to you about that day?" he asks as he sits down in front of the fireplace.

It's one mystery that has been nagging me ever since her accident. All I knew was, it was an emergency, but it wasn't life-threatening. She wanted to talk in person.

I never knew why she wanted to meet.

And to this day, other than the guilt of putting her in the position she's in right now, I also feel I've failed her as a brother.

She needed me, and I wasn't there.

"Charles, you have a moment?" A low voice startles me and I turn toward the doorway, finding it propped open. Elias Kent is leaning against the doorframe.

The man moves without a sound. I suppose that makes him good at whatever he does in his criminal activities.

He smirks as he straightens up and tugs on the lapel of his expensive suit before he nods to Ethan. He motions outside and slips away.

I take it as a sign to follow him.

I find him in a hidden alcove around the corner. The small space is lit up by a few flameless candles, which only draw attention to his dark hair and the long scar spanning his face. He turns toward me before I reach him.

"I have news," he murmurs.

My pulse ratchets up. "Ian?"

He nods. "Before I tell you, I have to let you know there are other interested parties. It's a race out there."

"What do you mean?"

He takes out the lighter I've never seen him use again and stares at the gold chain attached to it. "There are people who are very interested in the same thing you're after. Have you heard of The Association?"

I freeze at the name of the organization, the hairs on the back of my arms rising. "An elite network of powerful people, something like that right? I've been warned to stay away from it."

Elias's eyes search mine, as if checking to see if I'm telling the truth. Unease slithers up my spine.

Something is very, very wrong here.

"Whoever warned you is wise." He snaps shut his lighter. "And it's something like that. I won't go into the details with you, but it's an organization of concentrated power—politicians, scientists, billionaires who thirst to dominate their markets. Once you're in, you can control whatever realm you want to dominate—get into the Senate? Done. Lead the World Bank? Done."

"Why do I feel like there's a catch to all of this?"

He scoffs as he sways the lighter in front of him. "There's always a catch. The Association is formed on blackmail of illegal deeds. You get power, but once you're in, you're a slave to it."

The air thins as I put the pieces together. This was why Grandma said I should avoid it—she knew about the ugly fine print. This was the reason behind Maxwell's cryptic comment before.

"And Ian is…" I whisper.

"A member."

Nausea sweeps through me like a sudden storm. "What does this mean?"

Fuck, please tell me this isn't what it means.

"A member was found dead in the prison three years ago. On his phone was a photo of him and Ian in New York City during the time you asked me about. They were in a lounge and there were women. Intoxicated women. I saved a copy of the photo when I found it and deleted the original."

The floor swirls around me and I knot my hands around the lapels of his suit. "What are you saying? Spit it out, Elias. Enough of the cloak and dagger shit."

He stares at me, his green eyes unfazed. "I'm saying he was in the city and he's a member of an illegal society. And he was at a party where *women*," he swallows, a muscle twitching in his jaw, his eyes flashing with ire, "women were getting taken advantage of."

Elias yanks my hands off him and shoves me, his face turning red. This is personal to him. I don't know why, but this investigation has struck a nerve. "I don't know why you're looking into Ian, but you *fucking* put the dots together."

He takes a deep breath and his face is once again the chilly mobster we've all come to know. "Our deal is done." He takes a photo from his jacket and hands it to me. "Remember, you owe me a favor. Anywhere, anytime. I'll be in touch when I want to collect."

Without another word, he walks away, leaving me reeling with the news.

My uncle—the harmless, loving man I often wished was my father instead of my real dad—is in a society formed on blackmail? Why would he need to join such a thing? He's a Vaughn—we're in the top one percent of wealth in the country. He can get whatever he wants without resorting to clandestine methods.

Questions hammer inside my mind, the nausea churning, the waves higher and higher. My fingers shaking, I turn over the photo.

And there he is, his face flushed, tie askew, hair mussed, his arms slung around another man.

I make out the small logo on the cocktail napkin in his hand.

Hotel Renegade, New York City.

The time stamp, October 5th, seven and a half years ago.

CHAPTER 40

THERE WERE NO FLOWERS this morning, and he didn't respond to my messages.

Dressed in my Odile costume while the makeup artist helps with the final touches of my black swan getup, I quickly open our text message thread. The last messages are the ones I sent him yesterday.

Taylor

> I love the roses. How did you find them in the dead of winter?

Taylor

> Will I be seeing you tomorrow for the last performance in St. Petersburg?

Taylor

> I miss you.

Taylor

> Reason number one. You chase away the monsters in my dreams and I want to fall asleep in your arms.

My heart pounds as I reread the message, heat creeping up my face as uncertainty threatens to swallow me whole. I debated whether to text him about my feelings. I wanted to call him, but it felt too intimate...too vulnerable. Too foreign.

I'm used to making snarky comments and flinging out curse words, not laying my soul bare.

But in the last few months, away from family and close friends, outside of Lisa and the brief visit from Belle, Grace, Millie, and Olivia during Christmas, I've realized something.

For the last seven and a half years, I told myself I didn't need anyone, that men were more trouble than they're worth. I was doing fine on my own, and I was finally learning to accept myself—my version of Odette with my past and my present.

I told myself love was for suckers, and there were so many more rotten apples out there than good ones; it was better to depend on myself and frankly not eat apples at all. Carrots were better. Much better.

But with every bouquet of roses, every note card and text I receive from the man who hides his true self from the rest of the world, he has given me bravery—the last little bit to push me across the finish line.

I dream about his kisses and the rough scrape of his hands on my skin.

I think about his deep, raspy voice and the way he tells me my thorns are beautiful.

I invent imaginary arguments I can have with him when I see him again because our fights are our strange form of foreplay and our love language.

Step into the light with me, Taylor. His words are louder with each passing day, and my decision becomes stark clear.

I miss him, and I want to be in a relationship with him. Not just sex, but the real thing—emotions, my heart, all of it. I want to be vulnerable with him and tell him my darkest secrets, the pain I've silently endured for all these years.

So, I worked up the courage to text him yesterday and to tell him the first reason he's special to me. Now, it has been over twenty hours of radio silence, and I'm trying to fight both the embarrassment and disappointment flooding me.

This is what you get for trying again, the damn Lochness Monster whispers. *Haven't you learned from your past?*

Oh shut up, you. He's a busy man!

"We're all set. You look great!" Sally, the makeup artist, pats my shoulder. "Have you seen Maddy? I saw Carla talking to her earlier, but I need to redo her makeup. Is she okay?"

Her words shake me out from my thoughts, and I frown. "What do you mean?" Maddy has been quiet these days, and she said I was overly concerned about her when I asked. Ainsley thinks she's homesick, which I don't blame her.

Sally shrugs. "She was crying earlier. I need to fix her makeup." She leans in. "I heard she came into some money recently. I thought she'd be happy. She wouldn't need scholarships anymore. But I must be wrong."

Unease prickles my insides. None of this makes sense. Ainsley or Maddy would've told me if some earth shattering change was happening, right? Why wouldn't they tell me?

"Anyway, I'll find her myself. Good luck, Tay. Last performance before we head back home! I can't wait." She grins.

"Right? I never thought I'd say this, but I'm getting sick of traveling. Craving a good hot dog about now." I strain a smile, my mind still on the trainees who are like little sisters to me. I need to find them to figure out what's going on.

Sir Ian waves me over. It's showtime.

I close my eyes and channel my inner black swan. Seductive. Enticing the men around her.

Seducing the white swan's true love.

Have you ever been in love?

Madame Renoir's question from almost two years ago comes barreling in. But this time, my heart spasms, images of him flooding my mind.

I know how it feels now.

Use my emotions as a source of power for my dance. Channel them. Harness them into something greater. That was what Sir Ian told me. I didn't understand before, but I do now.

The atmosphere inside the Mariinsky Theatre in St. Petersburg this cold February evening is electric—perhaps the crowd senses this will be a special performance, because it's the last one before we head back. But the place seems incomplete, like the hollow in my chest.

I know it's because I've been searching for that familiar blond hair in the audience, not seeing him.

I feel incomplete.

I've missed him in every performance since Prague. His intensity. His electrifying gaze. How he wears his banked emotions in his startling blue eyes.

I'm not performing for you. I once told him in Sir Ian's office.

But I want to perform for him now. Because whatever happens, he has awakened my heart, and because of him, I feel something.

I rake in a deep breath before smiling at Dev, taking on the persona of the seductive, strong black swan who pretends to be the white swan the prince actually loves. I often wonder what the black swan's true motive is, what Mom was trying to tell me all those years ago.

Dev tugs me into him, our dance second nature by now. We move from the slower adagio movement to the faster allegro. I imagine he's Charles, the man I've been missing, and this is my way of telling him I miss him and want him. My grazes become bolder, my pirouettes and leaps stronger. Out of the corner of my eye, I see Dev's eyes widen, no doubt wondering what's gotten into me.

Then comes the thirty-two fouetté turns—thirty-two nonstop turns that are one of the most difficult moves in the ballet.

I'm a fighter...a survivor. I am alive and I'm fucking thriving.

My body thrums with energy as I throw myself into the turns, one after another, embracing my dark past, the black feathers sprouting from my skin.

I'm flying. With or without anyone, wherever my future takes me. I am flying as Odette and Odile.

Breathless exhilaration rushes through me as I come down from the difficult sequence. Dev's smile widens—there's awe in his gaze, and

I hear loud applause breaking through the audience—normally, they'd wait until the dance was over.

Tears glimmer in my eyes, my heart pounding with a bittersweet joy.

I am Taylor Peyton-Anderson, almost twenty-four years old. Yes, I've had a difficult past, but I've risen above it and I accept myself now.

I am free.

My eyes sweep over the blurry crowd as I move into the final pose.

And I see him.

His passionate eyes trained on me from where he stands in the box closest to the stage. He's clapping like the others, his lips curved into a smile.

He's here.

Happiness rushes through me, giving me a high much more powerful than the cheers and applause from the audience. I bite my lip before smiling back and I see the acknowledging smolder in his gaze. But there's something else in those eyes I've grown to love.

Something heavy and undecipherable. I frown.

The rest of the performance passes by without a hitch and we're met with a standing ovation at the curtain call. Sir Ian glances at me and gives me a nod of approval.

"Excellent," he mouths.

I know I'll never be the Odette from the stage all those years ago.

But it's okay.

I can shine as Odile. I can embrace the black swan. A weight has been lifted off my chest and I can finally breathe.

After changing out of my outfit and giving Lisa and Dev quick hugs, I dash out of the dressing room to backstage, then to the lobby, searching for a tall man with blond hair and icy blue eyes, a man I used to hate but am feeling very much the opposite emotion right now.

The lingering crowd gathers around me in excitement, notebooks and writing pads thrusted at my face, Russian and English requests blurting from their lips. I smile absentmindedly and sign autographs, my eyes still roving over the opulent marble interior, trying to find him.

I couldn't have been mistaken, could I?

But he isn't here.

After security escorts the crowd away, disappointment weighs inside me as I head out the side door, where a van would pick us up to take us back to the hotel.

As soon as I step outside to the frigid cold in the sea of white, I see him...

Charles Vaughn, holding a bouquet of burgundy roses, a soft smile tugging his lips.

CHAPTER 41

THE BRISK WIND RUFFLES his hair, a lock of it falling over his forehead. There's something different about him than last time, even though he's looking as hot as always in his fitted black suit and black coat, his hands clad in dark leather gloves.

We're standing a few feet apart, people walking around us, oblivious to the thickening tension in the air. My heart flutters in my chest as I rake my eyes over him—starving, famished for the sight of him I've missed in the last few months.

It's the vulnerability in his gaze. That's the difference. The way a muscle twitches in his jaw, his chest moving up and down like he's struggling to breathe, just like me. The way his hand is clutching the roses like they're his lifeline.

He's not wearing his usual mask.

Charles's eyes darken as the seconds stretch into minutes and a surge of energy, which has been gathering inside my heart since I saw him standing there, rushes through my body, kick-starting my muscles.

This beautiful asshole.

Grinning, I run to him and leap into his arms.

Low chuckles reach my ears as he catches me. I curl my arms around his neck and bury my nose in his chest, inhaling the scent I've missed so much—cedarwood and bergamot. A voice tells me I shouldn't do this in public, where anyone can see us. What will the press think? What will Carla and the other bitches think?

But I couldn't care less.

The man I couldn't forget came back for me.

"I've missed you, minx," he murmurs into my ear and I shiver at the husky rasp of his voice.

Gently, he sets me on the ground and looks at me with tenderness. He frowns and slowly tugs off his gloves, the motion sensual, and he slips my hands into them, one at a time.

I belatedly realize in my rush to find him, I'm not wearing my coat or gloves, and it's frigid out here. He then shrugs out of his coat and places it over my trembling body.

"I can't leave you alone, can I?" he murmurs, his bare hand scraping my face, and my eyes flutter shut, my nerves alighting at his touch. "You'll freeze to death without me. You know, it's a sign of low IQ to be outdoors in Russia in February without proper attire."

I snort, opening my eyes. The damn bastard.

"Well, Mr. Vaughn, it's a sign of low EQ to leave a girl hanging after she texted you." I arch my brow.

He barks out a laugh and bites his lip.

"Fuck, I've missed this." He leans in. "And for your information, I was busy wrapping a bunch of stuff up so I could fly over here and make it in time." He hands me the flowers.

My lips twitch, clearly failing at smothering a smile. I take the bouquet—two dozen glorious, perfect roses with all their beautiful thorns intact—and hold them up to my nose to take a whiff.

"You never told me how you got these flowers in the last few months. They aren't in season."

I look at the bouquet, trying to find the card I usually see, but there isn't one.

"Reason number one hundred six," he murmurs. "You're secretly living your year of yeses because you wake up every day, ready to fight whatever monsters come your way. You may think you're failing or you aren't trying hard enough. But you are excelling. You remind me progress isn't linear, that you can have your year of yeses even if certain days are just...not yet."

My breath catches in my throat as my lips part.

He smiles. "Maxwell told me about Belle's year of yeses and how you gave her a book that inspired it all. And to answer your question, I find greenhouses in each city and pay a ridiculous amount to buy all of their roses offseason."

A warmth fills me, butterfly wings flapping in my stomach.

Charles leans in, his eyes glittering, his thumb stroking my cheek. "Reason number one hundred seven. Your apartment looks like a tornado hit it, but it's because you don't sweat the small stuff. You don't need to control all aspects of life because life is chaotic. It is messy."

Tears well in my eyes as my heart sprints a marathon inside my rib cage.

His voice thickens as he continues, "You'd rather spend time and energy with your friends, your family, quietly supporting them on the happiest days of their lives while you're grieving in secret. You'd rather spend the few hours you have outside of practice to read books to heal yourself, because you're a fucking fighter."

"Ch-Charles," I whisper.

His eyes take a fierce glint and he whispers urgently, "I may have been born with money and you may have come from poverty, but I'm awestruck by you. Floored by you each day. Your wealth isn't in dollars and cents, but in your unbeatable, fighting spirit. You are a breath of fresh air in a world tainted with pollution. Reasons one hundred eight, nine, and ten."

My hands shake—I can't control the flood of emotions rushing through my veins like a shot of adrenaline to a dying heart. The flowers fall to the ground, dark red petals scattering among the sea of white.

"Does this answer your question? Why I wanted to tell you in person instead of texting you? How much I fucking missed you...your annoying barbs, your sarcasm, your fiery emotions, everything I've tried to avoid, but realize your absence has been slowly killing me inside... Do you know now, Taylor?"

Words desert me. Instead, I do what I do best, let my body, my movements tell him what I'm feeling—just like how ballet is a love letter without words.

I pull his head down and crush my lips against his, swallowing the groan emanating from his throat. He curls his arms around me, his hand snaking up to angle my head so he can take our kiss deeper, closer, our tongues and teeth making an appearance.

He exhales, and I inhale. He attacks, and I retreat. His hand kneads my back, sparking a thousand little fires inside my body.

An icy gale blows by and I know I should be cold, but instead, I'm burning hot for the man holding me to him like I'm a life jacket in the middle of the ocean. I moan as he rakes his teeth down my neck, eliciting a pinch of pain that is a direct caress to my clit. I need more. I need—

A car honks in the distance and we spring apart, belatedly realizing we're still standing outside the door, in full view of everyone. Thankfully, the crowds have thinned out, but out of the corner of my eye I see Sir Ian's eyes widening as he steps into the van with the other dancers. Carla sneers at me and Lisa has her mouth on the floor as Dev smirks and pushes her inside the vehicle with the others.

The cat's out of the bag.

I *should* care about this. I *should* worry about what other people will think.

But I don't give a fuck.

A small smile appears on Charles's face as his eyes dart to the company van as well. He arches his brow at me, as if daring me to complain.

"You did this on purpose, didn't you?" I mock shove him. "You knew they were watching."

"You pounced on me, minx. I haven't moved from my spot."

I cringe as I remember running toward him—he's right.

"Don't get used to it, mister."

He chuckles and tugs me to his side. "Let me take you back to the hotel. It's cold out here. And I think we have more to talk about, don't you think?"

CHAPTER 42

MINUTES LATER, WE SIT in the back seat of the town car, the center divider up, so we're enclosed in this small cocoon of privacy. My feet bounce on the ground. Perhaps it's because we're shrouded in the darkness in this small space, I'm compelled to do something I'd never done before.

Another first with him.

"Charles," I whisper, my eyes staring at the black divider in front of me. "I w-want to tell you what happened to me."

His breath hitches, and he reaches toward me, gently clasping my hand in his. Before I draw down the bridge and let him storm the castle, I want to tell him the truth, the story I've never told anyone other than Alexis, Camden, the cops, and the school therapist.

I want to be brave...and I want to know if he'll look at me differently.

If it is a mistake to open up to him.

He links his fingers with mine and gives it a squeeze before pulling me to his side, but I feel the tension radiating from his frame.

Blowing out a breath, I begin, "When I was sixteen, I was a trainee at a top ballet academy. I was a scholarship student, because back then, it was just Mom, Grace, and me. Mom wouldn't tell us who our father was, so it'd always been just the three of us. Mom worked a lot. Grace also took on additional jobs outside her classes because fuck...everything in New York City was expensive, even if we lived in the shittiest place in the Bronx."

My nose prickles as I think of the past, which seems a world away, and yet I can remember as clearly as if it happened yesterday. "I wanted to quit ballet too. It was expensive even with the scholarship. The shoes, the outfits. The extra fees. I could've gotten a job to help my family out. But Mom and Grace insisted I continue, because I had talent and I loved to dance. And I do...it was...*is* my life."

I focus on the reassuring graze of his thumb on my hand as I get to the next part. "Things were going well. We didn't have much, but we were happy. I was doing well in ballet. My instructor thought I was going places. But everything changed one night."

I rake out an exhale, nausea starting to swirl in my gut. "There was a celebration—the end of a successful season. Like ABTC, we relied on the funding from rich sponsors and this was an event all of us were expected to attend. After all," I scoff, "the sponsors wanted face time with the people they were spending money on."

The car slows to a stop and Charles slides open the divider and murmurs something to the driver before leaning back. A second later, the driver's door open and he leaves, leaving Charles and me alone in the car.

"You don't have to do this for me. Only if you want to," he murmurs.

I still don't look at him because I'm afraid if I see him staring at me in pity, I wouldn't be able to continue.

And I want him to know. If there's someone I want to trust with this ugly truth, I want it to be the man who thinks roses are more beautiful with thorns.

"My best friend dressed us up. I was secretly excited because Grace and I never got to go anywhere—we couldn't afford to. I wanted to see how the other half of the world lived—the women in pretty dresses and nice shoes, men in their expensive suits and shiny watches, just like the damn TV shows. The academy covered all the costs, and we had a blast. We stayed behind after the event ended because we didn't want the night to end."

I unlace my hand from his, my palm sweaty. I close my eyes, not wanting to see or hear anything, as I purge my memories of that night. "I had a boyfriend then, he was a dancer too, but Camden had to help out at home and couldn't come. I got separated from my group and...b-but I was...I didn't care. I was at the bar, feeling so very grown up."

Fighting the urge to dry heave, I continue, "An older man came up to me—he looked like he stepped straight out of a fashion magazine, or a stock photo for a hot successful businessman. He congratulated me on my performance. He was charming, nice, didn't treat me like a little girl."

I tug the hem of my sweater. "I fell hook, line, and sinker for his smiles and charisma. I even felt guilty for being attracted to him when I had Camden."

Shaking my head, I murmur, "I wasn't going to do anything. I was just so excited. He asked me about my hobbies, my family—he seemed so genuine and interested in me. I thought nothing of it when he handed me a flute of champagne."

My voice trembles as anger and self-hatred carve a fresh wound inside my chest. The argument I've made in my mind a thousand times since that night. "How could I have been *so stupid?* Lesson 101: don't take food or drink from strangers. They teach that to toddlers. But I didn't remember."

I shudder and focus on Charles's presence next to me. "I never had champagne before. Fancy stuff, you know? I felt like a new person, not the poor girl from the Bronx. I didn't think...I shouldn't have drank it. I remember thinking champagne didn't taste that good. It was weird to have bubbles in alcohol."

My cheeks are wet with tears, but I don't bother wiping them away. "Then the world swirled around me and my nightmare began. I couldn't move. I could barely speak. Everything was in fragments. Painful, terrible fragments. The next thing I knew, I was in a dark room, and there were multiple men there."

"Fuck," Charles mutters under his breath. I hear the horror and fury radiating from his voice. "Taylor, I—"

"No! Let me finish, or else I won't have the guts to tell you the truth."

He quiets, but he grips my hand in his, his fingers tightening almost to the point of pain. His forearm trembles on my lap, but he doesn't say another word.

"I suppose it was both a blessing and a curse to be drugged, because I don't remember everything. But then I also didn't remember enough to ID the bastards and put them away. I didn't know how many of them were there that night. I just remember hearing the sounds of men undressing, grunting, my dress being ripped from my body. The sensations, the pain, probably made worse b-because..."

I sob loudly, my tears free falling now. "It was my first time. I was saving myself, you see. I went somewhere in my mind, far away from it all. I didn't know how long or how many times h-he, th-they...I don't remember. I just remember one of them the most...light hair, light eyes, raspy voice. The smell of peppermint. It's his voice I hear when the monsters in my mind come now. And do you know what the fucking cherry on top was?"

I swipe my tears from my cheeks, but they keep falling down. My chest is being cleaved in half, the pain so visceral I wonder if I'll ever feel normal again.

"That monster did something to me, and my body betrayed me. He made me feel pleasure—it was cruel. I came even though I didn't want to. My first orgasm. It took me by surprise and I felt disgusted, sick."

Charles intakes a sharp inhale but stays silent. His grip is painful on my hand now, and I focus on the pain, the grounding pain, so I can continue.

"When I came to a few hours later, she shook me awake. I was naked in the back room of the lounge and she...sh-she took one look at me and ran off. She was supposed to be my best friend!" I pound my fists on my lap, experiencing her betrayal all over again.

"I remember the revulsion in her eyes. She was so disgusted. But she came back. She gave me some clothes she found somewhere then dropped me off at my apartment. She told me she was quitting ballet. I never saw her again."

I begged Alexis not to quit when we were parked in front of my apartment. I needed her. I didn't want to tell Mom or Grace what happened. I felt ashamed. Stupid. Dirty. But Alexis just shook her head.

"I fell apart, and I took a steaming hot shower afterward, wanting to clean myself of those monsters. But I couldn't stay in the shower for too long or else Grace would suspect something was off. So I told her I caught a nasty bug and felt sick, and lucky for me, she bought it."

Closing my eyes again, the tides slowly recede. The rest of the story is painful, but we're reaching the end. "Then, the next day, Camden came by. He looked furious. He said he was worried about me going to a hotel lounge and he stopped by, hoping to surprise me. He...s-saw me with them through a small gap at the door. He didn't even notice how wrong the situation was. A-And he said it looked like I was enjoying it."

Fury replaces the earlier anguish—the sudden flood of emotions disorienting. I scream into the dark, "Like I enjoyed being *raped* by monsters!"

The R word. The first time I've used it in almost eight years. It feels cathartic and yet an avalanche of grief, betrayal, and anger slams into me. My breathing saws in and out of my lungs, and for a moment, I couldn't speak. But I need to. I want to finish the rest of my story, even if that means he'll leave me after this.

Because he'd be repulsed by me.

"Camden dumped me. He didn't believe me. He asked why I didn't go to the police if I was a victim. The truth was, I didn't think. I just wanted to go home, to get clean and pretend nothing ever happened, but that was impossible. I did eventually go to the cops, but they took one look at me and said I didn't have any evidence because I washed it all away."

I scoff, my voice raspy. "As soon as they heard I had alcohol, and I was underage and from the Bronx, they probably wrote me off as some gold-digging delinquent. They didn't believe me. I tried talking to the school therapist, who didn't do shit. She kept focusing on the fact I couldn't remember much. Was there a chance I made parts of it up?"

I shake my head and slump on to the seat, my body exhausted, my energy depleted. *"Nobody* believed me. My best friend and boyfriend both left me within forty-eight hours of the worst night of my life. He quit the academy the following month and cut off all ties with me. He never even apologized to me! Since then, I couldn't dance Odette. I couldn't be the beautiful white swan. I couldn't let anyone close to me. I buried my anger and trauma into the deepest part of my heart. I was grossly violated, but I swore I'd protect myself in the future. I wouldn't let my body or my heart be hurt again."

The next words come out in a whisper. "I guess there was a silver lining—I didn't get pregnant or catch any diseases. I never told my family, my other girlfriends, or even Lisa. Nobody else knows. I don't want them to look at me differently, like I'm damaged. I don't want them to feel sorry for me. I'm not the only woman this has ever happened to. Shit happens in the world and this just happens to be my pile of shit. I don't want to be any different... I want the old Taylor Peyton to live on in their eyes."

Slowly, I unlink my hand from his and fold my arms over my chest, my eyes still squeezed shut. "You once asked me what happened to me, if I hated myself, and I lashed out at you because," a lump forms in my throat, "because you were too close to the truth. So now, you know everything. You're the only person who knows all the ugly details. And to this day, those bastards are out there living their lives and I-I'm trapped."

Pain tears my insides as I whisper the rest of the story, "I still hear their voices, the awful things they said to me. They mocked me, saying I must be enjoying my first cock since I was thrashing under them. They said no one would miss me. They called me little beauty. I didn't want to be beautiful anymore. They called me Harriet. 'Fly Harriet.' For the longest time, I'd obsess over these phrases, trying to figure out what they mean, trying to make sense of why this happened to me. But it was useless. I realized there was no way to rationalize what these monsters did to me."

I brace myself for judgment, for the same words of betrayal and cold revulsion I heard from Camden, the horror I saw in Alexis's eyes, or the pity from the cops or the therapist. I wrap my arms tighter around myself, needing to brace for the inevitable.

But instead, I feel his large hands on my shoulders as he turns me toward him. His reassuring scent wraps around me like the sweetest embrace, and I want to cry. I want to melt into his arms, but I'm also afraid to open my eyes.

I've never felt so naked before, like a rose in the barren winter, all the beautiful petals gone, only the ugly thorns remaining.

Who would love me now?

Maybe that's the secret I've been hiding all along. The biggest fear in my lovesick heart. The reason I haven't let anyone close is because I won't ever have to be disappointed when they don't love me back.

CHAPTER 43

 *Charles*

HER EYES ARE DOWNCAST, her cheeks wet with tears.

She won't look at me.

For the first few seconds after she shared her trauma with me, I couldn't think. I was filled with murderous rage at the monsters who did this to her, the men who fucking clipped her wings. I wanted to find them, hack them into tiny pieces until there's nothing left of them.

But I forced myself to tamp down the violent urges because a stronger, much more powerful emotion coursed through my body.

Protectiveness—the need to make her feel better, to chase away the demons clouding her eyes.

Gently, I turn her toward me, my fingers shaking, my heart rioting inside my rib cage.

Swallow the rage, Charles. Feel the pain, which is only a fraction of her pain.

"Look at me," I rasp, my voice sounding unused.

Taylor shakes her head, her tears falling onto her lap. They're like bullets to my heart. I want to take them away—absorb all her agony and leave her unscathed.

I clasp her cheeks, my thumbs wiping the wetness as heartache spears into my chest. "Tay, you listen to me. It's not your fault. I'm so fucking sorry this happened to you. You're not broken. You...You're fucking amazing. I'm not worthy to be in your presence. I—"

"You don't need to say that to make me feel better," she whispers, but she slowly lifts her head. The grief in her stormy gray eyes unmoors me.

Words aren't enough. I don't have the words to express everything inside me. Instead, I haul her to me and crush her in my embrace. I tighten my arms around her, needing to feel her warm body, her vitality, her strength.

I want her to know I don't care about her past, I just want her future.

"You are a fighter. To have undergone everything you went through and still be standing before me, the most breathtaking woman I've ever seen... Trust me, Taylor. I beg you to believe me."

Her lips wobble as she pulls back and stares at me and it's then I notice she isn't wearing her nose piercing, nor does she have her usual dark makeup on her face. She's a mess of tears, her hair in disarray. But goddamn, she takes my breath away.

She's the person I want to share my future with.

"You don't think I'm damaged? So fucking messed up?" she whispers. "You don't think I'm dirty?"

The anger packed deep at the base of my spine rears to life and I want to jump on a plane and find those bastards who hurt her and eliminate them from this planet. *They did this to her. They violated her body and scarred her mind.*

"You're the strongest person I've ever met. I...I...*Fuck!*" I crush her in my embrace again, my words still jumbled in my brain. I feel useless, like nothing I do or say will ever make her feel better, because how can it? How can simple words take away a horror no one should ever experience?

"Ch-Charles," Taylor sobs into my chest, her lithe frame shaking in my arms. My eyes well with tears as I'm hit with a helplessness I've never felt before in my life.

"Let it out, minx. You've been holding it in for far too long. I'm here. I'll never leave you." I press kisses to her hair as she lets out her anguish, each cry a knife into my heart.

Sometime later—it could be minutes or hours, for time ceases to matter—I walk her back to her hotel room. Her fingers are clammy in my hand, my mind still in a daze, swirling with what she told me. Everything makes sense now—why she hates rich men in business suits, why she despises fake charm and smiles, why she wears loose outfits and hides herself behind dark makeup.

Then there's her reaction to Ian the first day we met.

Fuck. My uncle.

I think back to my conversation with Elias and how Ian is part of The Association. How he was in New York City all those years ago when he swore to me he never came back to the States then.

Hotel Renegade. The hotel logo on the napkin.

It can't be. There's no way. Unease slithers inside me, joining the inferno of anger, grief, and turmoil. *Charles, there were God knows how many hotels and lounges in the city, and this was years ago. Ian probably forgot he made a quick US trip. You travel a lot too; you don't remember everything, right?*

I cling onto my sanity, my mind desperate to believe Ian's appearance in the city had nothing to do with what happened to Taylor.

My pulse pounds in my ears as I usher Taylor into the elevator. She's quiet, her eyes bloodshot, her pale skin splotchy.

She's still the most beautiful person I've ever seen.

But the question in the back of my mind won't leave me alone. *Where was she assaulted?* I force myself to stay silent, because this isn't the time to ask. Instead, I wrap my arm around her shoulder, giving her my strength and support. She leans on me and heaves out a laborious sigh.

Soon, we arrive on her floor, and I walk her to her room.

Before she told me what happened, my heart nearly burst with joy at her text messages from yesterday.

She missed me.

She kissed me in front of everyone. She took off her mask in the proverbial daylight for me.

And now, as I watch her shrivel into her frame, her eyes taking on a faraway look like she's trapped in her past, I finally understand every outburst from her in the past and why she behaved the way she did.

No wonder she's terrified of men, sex, and love. And yet, she still took a fucking leap with me.

Chaos bombards my mind—violence, awe, fury, admiration—I can't process it all.

I can't think.

Her door unlocks, and I step into the room with her. I sweep her into my arms and she lets out a gasp of surprise as I carry her to the bed, chucking off her shoes along the way. She looks exhausted, weary to her bones.

I tuck her into bed before wiping her face with a wet towel from the bathroom.

Leaning down, I kiss her forehead and whisper, "I'm proud of you, Taylor. For being you. For being here. For fighting each day. Thank you for giving me the honor of holding your pain with you."

Her lips tremble and a stray tear slips out. I kiss it away, the scything ache deepening inside me. "Go to sleep. Don't think. You're a survivor, okay? You're the badass ballerina we all know, and you're not alone. Not anymore."

"Th-Thank you," she whispers, her gaze intent on mine, brimming with thoughts I couldn't decipher. The seconds stretch on as she stares intently at me like she's searching for something. I fight to maintain my composure, to not blow up in front of her because fuck, the fury is quickly taking over my body.

A sad smile appears on her lips, then she closes her eyes. "Good night, Charles. Thanks for flying out here to watch my last performance."

She is shutting down. It's not enough—I can't heal her. My words are meaningless to her. She doesn't believe me.

My chest is weighed down by an anvil, but I straighten up, my airway closing on me.

I need to get out of here—she doesn't need to see the violence in my blood right now.

"Good night," I murmur before exiting her room and closing the door quietly behind me.

My thoughts are in disarray as I beeline to the hotel bar on the first floor. I don't notice the crowds or the noises. Everything is a blur and I'm drowning underwater.

"What do you want, sir?" the bartender asks in a thick Russian accent.

"The strongest vodka you have." The anger I tamped down before burns through the restraints.

He sets down a glass and pours alcohol into it.

"Leave the bottle," I command before chugging the drink down and wincing at the burn singeing my throat.

My hand trembles as I pour myself another shot, my body blistering with rage, her words in the car finally burrowing deep into my consciousness.

Those fucking bastards. Unwanted images of her being brutalized fill my mind, and I grip the glass tightly, my knuckles stark white. Fury I've never felt before rumbles through my veins—I feel like an atomic bomb, seconds away from going off.

I'm going to kill them. I'll find every one of them and kill them. Then it still wouldn't be enough.

My vision turns red as the alcohol hits my bloodstream. I want to maim, destroy, burn the world down. *I'm going to kill them.*

I slam the glass onto the bar top and it shatters into a thousand pieces.

A sudden hush descends on the room, and belatedly a sharp pain radiates from my palm. My eyes refocus and I realize a shard of glass has embedded itself into my hand and blood is flowing out of the wound.

"Sir, are you okay?" The bartender rushes over and hands me a stack of napkins.

I curl my fist around them and hiss at the pain. It's a superficial cut. It hurts like a motherfucker, but I won't die.

As I watch the river of crimson spread on the napkins, I'm hit with a sudden realization—this blood, this pain—it's only the tiniest fraction of what Taylor has been dealing with all these years.

Alone. With no one by her side. Abandoned by two people she thought were in her inner circle. Doubted by authority figures.

What the fuck am I doing? I should be with her instead of being here.

Tossing a few hundreds on the table—they'll figure out the currency conversion themselves—I stand up.

Ignoring the stares leveled my way, I stride toward the elevators as fast as my feet could take me.

An urgency fills my veins, a desperation to be near her, to be the one pressing the bandage on her wounds and kissing her stitches and scars, loving them, caring for them because no one did that for her.

A few minutes later, I knock on her door, my heart racing a mile a minute.

I hear her footsteps, followed by her voice. "Who is it?"

"Minx, it's me. Open up."

CHAPTER 44

"You don't think I'm damaged? So fucking messed up? You don't think I'm dirty?"

I stare at the dark ceiling as my questions to him echo in my ears, my fingers trailing over Alexis's friendship cuff on my wrist.

He didn't answer me.

I try not to let the hurt in—it was an emotional moment, and while he suspected something happened to me, I knew he was shocked at all the details. It was a rude awakening.

It would be a lot for anyone to take.

And maybe he couldn't answer me because he didn't want to hurt my feelings.

Maybe he'd never look at you the same way again. Now he knows all my dark secrets, the grime I can't scrub away no matter how many showers I take.

My eyes burn and I clutch the blankets closer to my chest as I replay our conversation over and over.

"I'm proud of you, Tay," I whisper to myself in the dark, needing to hear those words. "You let someone in. That's damn b-brave." A shuddering exhale escapes me.

Thump. Thump. Thump.

I frown. It's late. There shouldn't be anyone.

Thump. Thump. Thump.

Panic seizes me, but another thought slips in. *Could it be him?*

Quickly, I scramble off the bed and walk toward the door, hoping, no, *wishing,* the person on the other side is the only man who's ever made me feel completely safe, the man who used to say I was breathtakingly beautiful.

I wonder if I'll ever hear those words from his lips again.

"Who is it?" I call out.

"Minx. It's me. Open up." The unmistakable rasp. The possessive tinge. My pulse quickens.

I throw open the door and there he stands, his chest heaving like he ran up the stairs to get to me. His face is flushed, his eyes wild with passion and intensity, a blazing fire that's too strong to contain.

"Charles?" I whisper, staring at him, my nerves lighting up in his presence.

He expels a ragged exhale. His arms shake as he grips the door-frame above him.

Like he's one second away from tearing into me.

"I'm a fucking idiot," he rasps. "I shouldn't have left you here alone. I was in shock. I knew something bad happened to you. I suspected you were assaulted. But it was one thing to suspect something and another thing to know."

His throat ripples, and he thumps the wall for emphasis. "I left because I fucking wanted to raze the world. I wanted to burn everything and everyone who'd hurt you. I c-couldn't control my emotions because I fucking hated how helpless I was. How I wished I knew you when you were sixteen, how I wished I could be there for you to protect you so you wouldn't have to go through what you did. B-Because, I...I..."

Charles's eyes burn, lightning in stormy skies. "I *crave* you. The way you make me feel alive. The way you challenge me. The way you call me out on my bullshit. And now, knowing what happened to you, and seeing you still standing tall, proudly each day, I'm fucking obsessed with you. It's terminal. Uncurable."

I clutch my sweater, my pulse rushing in my ears. What's he saying? Is he saying—

"I realize I never answered your question. It's not because I couldn't answer you, it's because I was too damn stuck in my own head. I was dying inside when I thought of what happened to you."

He huffs out a ragged breath, his voice deepening, his nostrils flaring. "Taylor, I swear to God, I'm going to find every single bastard who hurt you that night. I promise you. I'll make them pay, and I'll—" His chest rises and falls, a cyclone approaching me at breakneck speed, but I don't want to leave.

I want the storm to take me with it.

"You're not damaged. You're not messed up. You're not dirty. You're a warrior, a queen. Those battle scars make you more beautiful in my eyes because they are a testament to your strength. You, Taylor Peyton-Anderson, are the most fucking breathtakingly beautiful woman I've ever met."

Tears escape my eyes and I rake in one inhale after the other.

He sees me. Truly sees me. Thorns and all.

He *still* thinks I'm breathtakingly beautiful.

Charles's eyes sharpen, a growl rumbling out of his chest, and with one quick stride, he steps into the room, hoists me to him, and slams his lips on mine.

His kiss is savage. Feral. It's messy and violent. Wetness streaks across my face as his hand cups my cheek before he pivots and slams my back on the closed door.

I pull back and touch my cheek, gasping when I see the red liquid. Blood. I quickly look at his hand, and I see the same crimson essence seeping out of his fist. "Charles, what happened?"

"Just a cut. I don't fucking care." He pulls me back to him and swallows my next words with his talented mouth.

The temperature rises, the inferno overtaking us both. He pulls my hair, I bite his lip, he digs his fingers into my ass, I claw his back. He shrugs out of his coat and his tie. His suit jacket crumbles to the ground.

His tongue duels with mine before he swipes it up from my chin to my temple, like he's tasting and kissing away my tears. I moan, the sound foreign to my ears. My body burns as I grasp his dress shirt, needing it off him. I hear fabric tearing, buttons pinging on the floor, but I don't care.

Charles wrenches my sweater off me.

"More," I moan, baring my neck to him as he sucks and scrapes the tender spots down my throat. "Fuck, I need more."

"I'll give you more, minx. I'll give you everything." He yanks off my bra and my nipples prickle to attention. He snarls and bares his teeth as he stares at the hardened points before he sucks one of them into his mouth.

A sharp current hits my clit and I curl my legs around his waist, my pussy already pulsing from the sensations he's wreaking on my body.

"So fucking sensitive," he rasps, "a goddess." He suckles my tits, biting, licking, flicking his tongue in a way that drives me wild.

His hands grab my leggings and with a rough yank, he tears them off me and I curl my legs around his waist again, his hard cock hitting my pussy. I shudder and gyrate against his hard length.

"Not enough," I whimper. "I want everything." I want us naked, skin against skin, feeling every inch of our bodies plastered against each other.

Growling, he holds me tight against him, his lips making their way to the whorl of my ears as he carries me to the bed. He tosses me on to it, his breathing harsh in the room. I rub my overheated body over the cool sheets, my nerves raw as more wetness seeps out of me. I need more. My touch-deprived body needs everything.

His lips twitch as he slowly unbuckles his belt, the clinking sound sending a frisson of panic inside me.

"Look at me," he rasps. "It's me and you. No one gets to have this moment except us."

His commanding words stave off the fear and I nod, my hands traveling up my body before I cup my breasts, my eyes fluttering shut as my fingers play with my nipples.

So sensitive. So fucking sensitive.

"Eyes open. Keep them on me, minx."

My eyes flutter open and I stare at him, watching as he slowly takes off his pants and underwear.

"Good fucking girl," he rasps.

I swallow a whimper.

My mouth runs dry when I see his hard cock curling around his stomach. It's thick and long, an enticing vein running along the side. Its tip is swollen and red, liquid dripping from the slit.

"Look at my cock weeping for you," he grunts, his hand curling around his cock and gives it a tug. Charles hisses in pleasure, his eyes growing molten as I press my thighs together, eager to relieve the ache in my pussy.

Slowly, he prowls toward me, his hands sliding up my legs to my thighs, eliciting a thousand sparks on its path. Pressing them open, he trails kisses on my skin, stopping at areas I didn't even know were sensitive to begin with. It's like he has mastered the instrument of my body, like he knows it better than I do.

Suddenly he pauses. His grip becomes borderline painful and I look at him, finding him staring at my parted legs. What is he looking at—

Fuck.

I try slamming my legs shut, but he holds them open and a muscle tics in his jaw. "What is this, minx? What am I seeing?"

I bite my lip and fist my hands on the sheets. The last ugly side I haven't shown him. The tiny little scars on my inner thighs. But he sees them now. I might be a warrior. I might be brave. But I'm also hurting myself because I can't cope.

"I-I...I stab myself when the flashbacks become too real. Needles. Just the needles. No drugs. No one can see them because they're on my inner thighs. But the pain...the pain and the hot showers stop the memories. They stop the voices. I know I should be stronger. I know I shouldn't hurt myself. I know—"

"Fuck what you know or think." He presses his lips over my scars. "You're dealing with everything the best way you can. You had no one to care for you, to *take* care of you." He suckles my scars and a thousand sensations course up my legs and settle on my pussy.

Charles slides my underwear off me as he continues his sensual assault on my needle marks. His finger flicks my barbell and a loud moan escapes my lips.

It sounds lewd. Horny. I'm burning for him.

"It makes sense now, what you told me before. This little piercing was for pain and punishment, not for pleasure before, isn't it?" His mouth travels to my barbell and he licks the piercing along with my clit, his tongue flicking the area in strong, rapid movements.

"Charles!" I scream, my body nearly careening off the bed if not for his firm hands holding me in place.

He alternates between sucking, flicking, swirling, all the while playing with my barbell. His finger dips into my wet entrance. I tense up automatically, but soon, another gush of wetness flows from me as he tugs my clit into his mouth and feasts on it.

My eyes roll back, my muscles locking in tension. "F-Fuck, I'm going to c-come!" The sudden onslaught of pleasure becomes unbearable. Fireworks explode between my legs and I shatter into a million pieces as he sucks and laves at my juices like it's a taste he couldn't get enough of.

My legs spasm against his face, and his scruff is abrasive in the best way.

"One day, I'll teach you pain for pleasure, not for punishment." His voice is hoarse, a dangerously low whisper.

I shudder, the aftershocks spreading through my body, hazy images of that evening in The Sanctuary floating into my mind.

I now interpret that scene completely differently.

My thoughts are muddled, my body pliant as he climbs on top of me after he rolls a condom on himself. He braces himself over me with his forearms. His eyes are dark, the irises nowhere to be seen, his beautiful light hair raking over his forehead.

He's like a fallen angel. A deadly heavenly creature.

His cock settles on my stomach. It's hot, throbbing and I shift underneath him, watching in fascination his eyes flaring, a hiss escaping his mouth.

Charles Vaughn's restraint is seconds away from snapping. The man prides himself on his meticulous control—his appearance, behavior, mannerisms are all perfectly crafted.

And he's about to unravel because of me.

A sultry pride sweeps through me and I move again, watching as he bares his teeth into a snarl. "Minx, you don't want to unleash the beast. Trust me, you don't want to."

Emboldened, I move my hands down his muscular back, my fingernails digging into his muscles before I wrap my legs around his backside again.

This time, nothing separates us.

For a split second, fear threatens to spark as he gives me more of his weight, pressing me into the mattress. I grit my teeth, the familiar sensations of panic unfurling from the cavern in my chest.

I can get through this. I can do this.

Taking a deep breath in, I force myself to calm. *I can do this. I want this.*

"Tay," Charles rasps, drawing my eyes back to his.

His brows are furrowed, and he cups my cheek again. Of course he can read me like a book. It has always been this way with him and maybe that's why I was so against him in the past, because I didn't want him to see through my layers.

"Are you sure?" he asks. I know it's taking every ounce of restraint inside him to hold back. I feel it in the coiled tension of his body, I see it in the muscle throbbing in his temple.

I nod. "Yes."

I want this.

His nostrils flare as his thumb trails circles over my cheek. A loving caress.

"*This* is your first time," he whispers, and those five words unlock a wound inside me, a loss I've never let myself grieve. My first time stolen by monsters. Tears well in my eyes again and I curse myself inwardly for becoming emotional yet again in his presence.

"My sweet, darling minx. This...This is your first time. Anything before doesn't count. They're meaningless. This..." he links his fingers with mine, our hands locked with each other and my heart throws itself against my rib cage, "is everything. I'm here with you. Always. Every step of the way. You're not damaged, you're not dirty."

My breath freezes as he leans down and presses his lips against mine.

He rasps, "You're perfect."

With those words, he enters me and I whimper at the pleasurable pain and he lets out a guttural groan, his fingers tightening against mine.

"Fuck, you're so tight. So wet. You're doing so well, taking every single one of my inches like a good girl."

He presses the last few inches in and he's burrowed as deep as he can, our hearts beating as one, our breathing in sync. Charles kisses me, his lips moving over mine in a tender embrace, his hips beginning a sensual rhythm—a dance of our very own.

Soon, I feel myself relaxing, the pleasure gathering between my legs as his cock scrapes against a tender spot inside me. There's no more pain, no more terror, no more dark voices.

There's only me and him.

My first time.

The thought unmoors me and I move my hips, joining him in his rhythm, kissing him back with everything I have inside me, thanking him without words for this gift he's giving me.

Tears slide down my face, but I don't care. My heart is mad for the man above me, the man loving me with every thrust, every piston, the man raining kisses over my eyelids, nose, and lips.

"You're doing so good, minx. You're fucking made for me."

The pressure climbs from a spot deep inside me, his cock gyrating harder, hitting that sensitive spot with every movement and soon, I thrash underneath him, urging him faster with my hips, chasing the high only he can give me.

It's different this time. The sparks build from deep within, the pleasure burgeoning into something I can't control.

I grip his hand, my nails digging into him. "Charles, it feels...I f-feel... Oh my God." My legs tremble, and I'm pushed to the edge of a cliff, nirvana gathering in my veins.

"You're going to come, minx. You'll come so hard. Your pussy is strangling my cock. Fuck, you feel so good."

The shudders erupt from my legs and travel up my thighs then to my chest, my tits becoming even more swollen and sensitive, my nipples scraping against his hard chest in the most delicious way. The pleasure grows and grows and soon, his gentle thrusts become a punishing hammering, the slaps of skin hitting skin loud in the room.

Charles clamps his teeth on my neck and I detonate.

"Charles!" I shriek, black dots blurring my vision and a low growl rips from him.

"Fuuuck," he roars, his hips snap into me a few more times, his cock throbbing as he follows me into ecstasy.

My blood roars in my ears, our moans and grunts a lewd symphony. My pussy tingles as he gyrates his body on top of mine, sending sharp aftershocks through me. We're a mess of sweat and tears, our skin no doubt full of scratch and bite marks.

Everything is too sensitive in the best of ways.

I open my eyes, finding his startling gaze on mine, concern radiating from those brilliant blue pools. He's worried about me. I truly am not alone anymore.

A smile breaks across my lips, and I see a myriad of emotions crossing his face—relief, awe, and finally, happiness.

He chuckles before he settles himself on top of me, sealing his lips with mine. We're still connected—both physically and emotionally.

"Happy Valentine's Day," he whispers, and I startle. I didn't realize today was the international day of love, for I never had anyone to celebrate it with.

Charles smiles, as if he knows what I'm thinking. "Why did you think I dropped everything to fly halfway across the world today, minx? My Valentine."

My Valentine.

My lips hike up in a smile. "What if I said no to you outside the theater? You drive me crazy, after all."

He chuckles and presses a soft kiss on my forehead. "I'd find a way to convince you. I'm a relentless bastard, you know." He winks, no doubt thinking how I called him that when we danced the Argentine tango.

Warmth fills my insides and I kiss him with fervor, my heart thudding resoundingly. I've never been good with words, my body has always been more proficient at speaking for me.

And it appears he understands, because he kisses me back with passion, with the same desperation my lovesick heart feels. But this time, the hole in my chest is filled, and I throw myself into the madness he's created with me.

My life stopped when I was sixteen. Now, at almost twenty-four, I'm resurrected.

CHAPTER 45

I can't get enough of her.

"Yes! Oh my God, yes!" She bounces on my lap as I grab her tits with both hands. I stare at our reflection in the mirror—us perched on the edge of the bed, her moving her tight little pussy up and down my cock, her little barbell winking at us with every motion.

The storm batters the windows to the sound of my cock pounding into her from below.

"Charles," I rasp, my fingers playing with her rosy nipples, squeezing them hard and feeling her inner walls strangle me some more. "Remember what I told you on the dance floor—it's Charles, not God. Moan my name, curse it, scream it when you're with me."

Taylor shudders. Her body arches back so her tits are thrusted upward, and her head rests on my shoulder.

"Ch-Charles, shit... Is this what I've been missing?" she moans again as I slide my hand between her legs and play with her piercing.

That little barbell drives me wild.

We've sequestered ourselves in the hotel room for the last week as a blizzard blows through St. Petersburg. The rest of the tour company left before the storm hit, but Taylor and I were more than happy to indulge ourselves with each other in our little slice of paradise.

Other than a few mandatory work calls and a terse exchange I had with Elias telling him I'd contact him once I was back in the city, because I know I'll need his help if I wanted to find the assholes who hurt Taylor, I've spent every waking moment with her.

I told her about my family and how much it devastated me that Liam had written me off from his life since Firefly's accident. How I missed the happier days of the past. How tired I am with acting like everything was fine. She listened and didn't judge me. She shared stories about her childhood and her mom. How she felt like ballet had saved her life at her lowest.

I've never felt closer to anyone else before and I think she feels the same way because in the last seven days, the darkness I typically see in her eyes is gone.

Then there's the sex.

While I haven't introduced her to the rougher side of sex yet, because it's far too soon for that, sex between us has been transcendent. As if by telling me her past, she's unlocked a part of herself long hidden, and now we can't get enough of each other. It's not just physical pleasure coursing through me, but a possessive need tugging at my heart.

I can let go of everything with her.

My cell phone has been pinging nonstop, my PR manager sending me article after article of photos taken of Taylor and me outside of Mariinsky Theatre, with headlines ranging from "Hypocritical CEO? Inappropriate relationships at work?," "Is Bank of Columbia a breeding ground for illicit relationships?," to "Anderson ballerina taking golden bachelor off the market!"

I should be concerned. The stock has gone nuts—plummeting one moment and rising the next—the public not knowing how to react to the news of a Vaughn kissing an Anderson. The old Charles would be disappointed in himself. My actions were impulsive and emotional, not driven by logic and strategy. This takes us back a few steps, especially given what I said in Prague about unequal power dynamics in relationships being frowned upon.

But I don't give a shit.

Logic flew out the window the moment a certain black-hearted ballerina flew into my arms and kissed me in front of everyone. I was ready to give her the world then and now, after she told me what she went through and how she survived?

Screw everyone else.

"Look in the mirror," I rasp. "Look at how sexy you are, your tits swaying, your pussy sucking in my cock so well."

Taylor whimpers, her eyes fluttering open as she stares at our reflection. Her motions falter.

I drag my teeth down her neck before sucking the sensitive spot under her ear. My fingers pluck at that naughty little piercing as I slam into her from below, each thrust loud into the room.

Her mouth drops open, her eyes rolling back, and she grips my arms for dear life.

Fire burns up my spine as the pressure gathers in my balls. I bite her neck and pinch her clit. She screams, her juices gushing out of her—my minx likes a little pain in sex—I don't think she realizes it yet, but I intend to teach her, to have her love the different sensations coursing through her body.

"Oh fuck," she mewls, coming down from her orgasm, but I don't stop. Instead, I pound harder, feeling her walls throb and clench around my dick.

"To answer your question," my breathing is loud against her ear, "you are missing sex. That's true, but it's *never* like this."

I place her hands on top of her tits and curl mine over them, our fingers interlocking as she thrashes against me. Gritting my teeth, I force myself not to come even as my cock lengthens inside her.

"It's so good, oh fuck, Charles!" she cries, her legs shaking again, and I know she's close.

Black dots form in my vision and this time, I let the final restraints holding me back snap. Clasping her tightly against me, I heft her up and walk the few steps to the mirror before setting her down.

"Hands against the mirror, minx. Watch yourself as you flood my cock with your cum while I go feral over you."

Our bodies are slick, and I grip her thick black hair and pull as she arches her delectable ass against me, her hands against the shaking mirror.

Her beautiful eyes are wide with lust, her perfect lips swollen, her creamy tits slap against the mirror with each snap of my hips.

"*This* is what it's like between us, minx. Insanity, blissful fucking insanity." Fire races up my balls and my cock and I rub her clit before inserting the tip of my index finger inside her, on top of where we're joined, and that extra sensation sets her off.

"Charles!" Her legs give out from under her, but I hold her against me as I roar my release, my vision blackening, blood rushing straight into my head as waves of orgasm pull me under.

For a few minutes, I can't speak, can't think. All I can do is pull her onto the ground with me, our bodies heaving, sweaty, completely satiated. She melts, her head resting on my chest as she splays a shapely thigh across my torso.

My feral kitten is a softie underneath her scars and claws.

Just like I knew all along.

A surge of emotions clamor in my chest and a strong sentiment is perched on the tip of my tongue, but I couldn't say it aloud. Because deep down, I'm still afraid of admitting what I'm feeling—that little boy hidden inside me is still traumatized at how a four letter word is an excuse for his parents to neglect him and his siblings.

I push the thought away and smile at Taylor instead. She snuggles deeper into my chest and lets out a satisfied sigh. She's been smiling more.

The other day, she asked me why I was interested in BDSM and I told her it was an outlet for me, to let go of the day-to-day restraints I had on myself, that I enjoyed the control and valued the trust subs gave to their Doms. Her eyes lit up. She was curious and full of questions. I laughed when she pulled out her phone and started researching. Her face turned a cute shade of pink as she read about limits, safe words, and the different types of play. I promised her one day we'd explore it together.

She also told me she hired a private investigator to look into what happened to her because she wanted closure. She wanted the monsters to stop appearing in her dreams. A pinch of guilt landed on my chest when she mentioned that, because of what I found out about Ian and Hotel Renegade. And the occasional nights when I heard her moaning in her sleep, bathed in sweat, I'd wrap her up in my arms and tell her she's safe because I was there with her.

I'll fight her demons for her.

And so I can't bring myself to ask her, not when she smiles at me during the day, when those demons seem to have receded in the background and she appears happy.

Frankly, I'm afraid of the answer.

Lately, she's been talking about her dreams of the future. She wants to volunteer at sexual assault support groups. She wants to set up endowments for dance scholarships for kids from disadvantaged neighborhoods. There's a spark in her eyes I've never seen before and I need to keep that softness, that drive in her.

She deserves everything.

"It's only ever been this way with you," I murmur, watching a blush creep up her face. Her eyes flutter open, a smile tugging her lips. "I have a feeling," I play with her hand, intertwining and locking our fingers together, "I've been trapped in a cave, waiting for you to rescue me."

"Charles," she murmurs, "You're the one who saved me, not the other way around."

I shake my head and kiss her hair before pulling out of her. She has no idea how much she's changed me. After taking care of business in the bathroom, I gather her in my arms and deposit her on the bed.

"You aren't ready for another round again are you?" She eyes my torso dubiously. "Don't men need to rest between rounds, especially *older* men? That's what I heard before."

"Think I'm too old for you?" I smirk. I lean over and kiss those berry lips of hers. She moans and my cock stirs. "Don't tempt me, because I can definitely keep going."

She mock groans and throws her arm across her face, the pink flush spreading over her pale ivory skin. "I take back all the mean things I've ever said about you if you and your hard inches will spare me."

I laugh. "What did I tell you before? My inches are very much real."

Taylor snorts and shoves me before she rests her head on my shoulder. My phone buzzes on the nightstand and I groan.

"I don't want to know what awaits me," I murmur, reluctantly picking it up.

Maxwell

> Charles Fucking Vaughn, you better answer before I fly over to Russia. What are your intentions toward Taylor? You didn't even have the *decency* to let us know about it beforehand?

Rex

> I knew it. I knew it. I knew it. I knew it. I knew it. I knew it. I knew it. I knew it.

Rex

> That's it. That's my message. *Gloating in satisfaction.*

Lana

> I'm happy for them! They're cute together! Charles, don't sweat the PR stuff. I can help if you need me. We got this. We Andersons take care of our own, and you're officially one of us now.

Ryland

> I seem to recall someone sending a text last year complaining *he* is in this text group, even though he isn't an Anderson. Look how the mighty have fallen, dipshit.

Lana

Oooh! I am changing the chat name! "Charles is whipped." Simple and to the point. Has a nice ring to it, don't you think?

Rex

This is why I love you, Lana. You're my favorite—always know exactly what I'm thinking.

Grace

Hey! I thought I was your favorite! And Tay, I've been fielding messages from the other girls. You and I need to have a nice looooong chat when you get back.

Taylor snorts next to me, and I see her typing away on her phone.

Taylor

You're in deep shit, Rex, because you told me I was your favorite sister.

Rex

Well, well, well, look who's resurfacing from her love nest? Shit. Don't tell me. I don't need that image in my head.

I growl and add my two cents to this ridiculous conversation.

Charles

No one is imagining anything about Taylor. Unless they want to die a painful death.

Maxwell

You haven't answered my question, Vaughn.

Shaking my head, I set the phone on the nightstand as it continues to buzz.

"What are you thinking?" she asks as I stare at the sea of white outside the window.

While my heart is filled to the brim for this woman next to me, reality is knocking on our door, begging to be let in. I take Taylor's hand in mine and kiss her fingertips. "I need to talk to your family first. They deserve that. Everything else can come second."

"What are you going to tell them?" she whispers and I hear a twinge of fear in her voice. *That fucker Camden really did a number on her.*

Frowning, I turn toward her and answer, "That I'm head over heels crazy about a ball busting woman and with or without their blessing, I'm having her by my side."

Taylor swallows, her eyes misting again. "I...I really like you. You've no idea what you've given me."

My heart pounds at her admission because I know this is an enormous leap for her and I'm going to try my damned best not to let her down because the men in her life before she met her brothers have been sacks of shit.

Then a small kernel of disappointment surfaces. She likes me. That sounds so trivial compared to how I feel about her. *What are you disappointed about, when you can't even say the four-letter word yourself yet?*

I want to take the final leap with her, to have what my friends have with their wives and girlfriends. I want her to know my world and my history.

"When we get back, can I take you to see Firefly?" And Liam, if he'll return my calls.

"Your sister?" Taylor's eyes widen. "Yes...of course. I'd love to meet her, even if she's..."

In a perpetual sleep.

Pain slices through me as I think of Firefly's still figure on the hospital bed—a sleeping beauty who wouldn't wake up.

"Can you tell me more about her? About...what happened?"

How will Taylor feel about me once she learns the truth? Will she still look at me like I've hung the moon in her sky?

Panic seizes my chest and for the first time since we've opened our hearts to each other, I strain a halfhearted smile. "Of course. I'll tell you everything when we get back, but for now, let's not talk about it."

CHAPTER 46

"Thanks for meeting me. I didn't want to do this at The Orchid." Too many people I know are there, and I don't want to answer any questions.

I stare at the glass facade of Manhattan Memorial Hospital, watching staff and visitors strolling through the quiet courtyard at seven in the morning. "We have to make this quick, because Taylor is meeting me here in half an hour."

We are going to visit Firefly because I want the woman who's stolen my heart to meet my sister.

I wonder if Firefly already knows. I look up at the dark clouds hanging low, watching a crow soar past us. The air is humid and cold this April morning—the skies gray after an overnight drizzle. Much like my gloomy mood as I prepare myself to open a can of worms that may change everything forever.

The last month has been bliss—after some much deserved ribbing from Maxwell and his siblings, everyone has accepted Taylor and me with open arms. The press has been a different issue.

The market ultimately decided they didn't like our clandestine relationship even though she's an Anderson. Our stock plummeted five percent since the photos of Taylor and me in Russia blasted through all the major networks and gossip sites. My PR manager had been working overtime, with Lana lending her services even though she had a full workload with her Chief of PR position at Fleur.

Our teams scheduled strategic date nights and public appearances for us. Lana somehow even got the minx to wear lighter colors and makeup, claiming it'd make her look more like a woman in love, and a happy woman would do wonders for these scandals.

It's bullshit—what Taylor wears shouldn't affect how people see us—but appearances are important, as I was taught growing up.

A lump forms in my throat. Despite all these changes, there has been good news. Patterson was convicted of his crimes. He'll spend the next several decades rotting away in jail, and I know prisoners are not kind to rapists.

My relationship with Taylor has never been better. She has been so happy—her nose piercing is a rotation of red hearts and sunflowers these days. We haven't talked about her dreaded night again and it seems like she's finally moving past it.

With every single day that passes by, I fall deeper and deeper into what used to be that dreaded emotion with her.

Love.

Except, it no longer seems so terrifying. Not when it's with her.

But I know I need to find out the truth, not only because I want to punish the bastards who hurt her that night, but also because she deserves closure. She deserves justice.

Even if the truth may cost me my relationship with her.

Because Uncle Ian. Hotel Renegade. Seven and a half years ago. The potential outcome I don't want to face. The roiling nausea in my gut whenever I look at the photo I kept from Elias. The denial I'm clinging on to because the alternative is unbearable.

The man himself takes a seat on the bench next to me, his fingers fiddling with his lighter attached to its usual gold chain. He snaps it open and stares at the open flame, a spark of warmth on this dreary morning. "I was wondering when you'd contact me. It's been a month since you've been back."

Of course, he has been keeping tabs on me.

"Elias, tell me. What would you do if someone brutalized the woman you love?"

He snaps shut his lighter. "I'd kill them. But before that, I'd make sure their last hours on earth were misery, and death would be a mercy they'd be begging for."

Elias's voice is cold and apathetic, but when I look at him, I find his green eyes burning with anger.

Like he's imagining this happening to him.

"Even if the woman you love might leave you afterward?" I lock my jaw as a suffocating weight settles on my chest.

Elias stays silent for a few seconds before he replies, "Yes."

"I thought so," I murmur and take a sip of the coffee in my hand. "What I'm telling you here cannot be repeated. But I can trust you, right?"

"You wouldn't have called me if you had doubts."

I nod and force out the next words, "I need to know if Ian and Taylor were at Hotel Renegade at the same time." And I can't ask Uncle Ian because that'd alert him to my investigation.

He draws in a quick breath, no doubt connecting the dots on everything I'm not saying. "I should've known. I always wondered why you were looking into your uncle. It makes sense now. And you think—"

"I just need to know. I could ask Taylor, but she...she..." Her words flit through my mind and I know the reality of that night was much worse than what she described. Fury chars my insides and I crumble the paper cup, barely noticing the hot liquid scorching my hand and splashing onto my trousers.

"You don't want to re-traumatize her." He finishes my sentence, his voice a low rasp.

A few seconds pass by, heavy with tension. He turns toward me. "Charles?"

Gritting my teeth, I face him. The harsh morning light makes the scar on his face seem more menacing than usual.

"This one is on the house." His hands are white knuckled around his metal lighter. "I'm *not* a good man. But there is one line I wouldn't cross. Hurting women. And I *despise* monsters who cross that line. I'll get you your answers for free."

I heave out an exhale even as dark dread swirls inside me. But I can't run from the truth. I need to know. "Thanks. And one more thing."

He cocks his brow.

"Taylor had a best friend who quit ballet around the time of her trauma. She also had a boyfriend back then. I only know his first name. Camden. Can you find these two people for me? This could come after Ian. But there is some unfinished business."

I'll bury them too, for abandoning Taylor at the worst time of her life.

Elias gives me a curt nod. Without another word, he gets up and slips through the morning crowds. It's personal for him and if my senses are right, this extends beyond him knowing Taylor or Taylor being Maxwell and Ryland's youngest sister. I can't help but wonder if this last line of moral defense is why the Andersons work with him on running the Rose floors inside The Orchid. Those floors sell sex, lust, and would be ripe for abuse if it were any other establishment. But with Elias Kent at the helm, no one dares to step out of bounds.

A stiff wind blows by and I tug the lapels of my coat tighter against me, my mind spinning with scenarios about how this could turn out; all endings I have a solution for except one.

The ending I fear the most.

What if it is Ian? What if I don't really know him at all? What if the man who's practically a father to me is the monster who did unspeakable acts to the woman I love?

My tie restricts my airway and suddenly I can't breathe.

———·———

Ten minutes later, I'm walking down the busy corridor of the long-term care unit inside the hospital. My mind is still swirling from my conversation with Elias earlier. I loosen the collar of my dress shirt, my tie long stuffed into my coat pocket.

I have fifteen minutes to get my shit together before Taylor comes and joins me in Firefly's room. I don't want her to see me like this. She'll take one look at me and call me out on my bullshit.

I won't be able to lie to her if she asks me.

I vaguely notice people waving at me—nurses, custodial staff, admin personnel—but I don't have the strength to do what I usually do well.

To fake a smile and pretend everything is okay.

Instead, I ignore them as I stride toward Firefly's room, wanting to tell her what's going on in my life, hoping I can unload my worries before Taylor arrives. Maybe I'd feel better if I told someone everything, even if that person is my comatose sister.

"I'd never thought I'd see you like this," a deep voice says from in front of me. "Unkempt, troubled. Finally looking like a human."

My head snaps up and I see him, the other person I've failed—other than Firefly. My pulse ratchets up and I swallow my shock as I stare at my brother, my body not knowing how to react—anger at him for being MIA, relief at him being alive and well?

Liam looks so much older than when I last saw him. Gone is the lanky boy with piercings and tattoos who holed himself in his room, blaring punk rock music at two in the morning. In front of me is a man—cold, hardened, muscular, with more tattoos covering his forearms, which are showcased in the thin black T-shirt he has on. His dirty blond hair is mussed, his nostrils flaring as he stares at me.

"It's been six years. I thought you forgot about us," I mutter. "Couldn't bother to return a call or a text?"

His eyes flash with fury. "Fuck you. I wasn't the one who forgot about his family. You were. And I've visited Firefly all these years, just not when you were there, asshole."

"Are you going to hold this over my head for the rest of my life? You think I *want* her to be in there?"

Shocked gasps echo in the hallway and I belatedly realize how loud my voice is, but I can't find it in me to care.

I'm tired. Exhausted. Pissed off.

It's not healthy to bottle everything up. That's what Taylor always tells me.

Liam gets in my face and in this second, I'm hit with how my younger brother, the little kid who used to follow me around the gardens when we were growing up, who'd come to me when the girl he asked out in high school rejected him, is now a complete stranger.

It tears me up inside.

"No, I don't think you'd want our sister to be in a coma. Even you aren't that cold. But how much money did you spend to cover that up?" He shoves me back a few steps. "Tell me this, how many people in your circle even know you have a sister in a coma?"

I ball up my hands at my sides. He knows nothing. He doesn't know what it's like to be the crown fucking prince of an old money dynasty. And would telling everyone about the accident, having the press get up in our business and parked outside the hospital building help Firefly?

It wouldn't. She wouldn't have wanted that.

He barks out a laugh at my silence. "Because that'd be bad press for your precious company, right?"

"Fuck you!" I shove him back. "I served, so you guys didn't have to!"

"Bullshit! You liked the power and prestige of being the fucking CEO of the Bank of Columbia."

More shocked whispers and murmurs surround us. Chairs squeak. Footsteps pound toward us. I look around, finding Julie and the other nurses wide-eyed and aghast, security striding down the halls toward us.

"Are you happy now? Causing a commotion? You wanted emotions, right? Now you got them." I grab his T-shirt, torn between the urge to hit him for abandoning me all these years and the desperate need to beg for his forgiveness because I miss our days in the Hamptons.

"Go ahead, you asshole. Hit me! I don't fucking care!" Liam spits on my face.

My vision clouds in red as I haul him closer and raise my fist, letting the rage from this morning and the guilt I've carried for most of this past decade burn through me.

"Stop it! You guys, break it up!" A scent of vanilla fills the air.

Her.

Taylor.

She pulls me apart as Ethan steps up from nowhere and drags Liam back a few steps.

Liam fights and claws at his best friend's grip, and I wipe the spit off my face.

"I don't care what beef you have with your brother." Taylor stomps up to him and jabs her finger into his chest. Liam stares at her, his mouth dropping open.

She looks around, clearly taking in our audience, and steps back. "I don't know what happened with your sister but I'm a woman and I'm also someone's sister and I can tell you, the last thing I'd want if I were laying on the bed in a coma is to see the people I love going at it like enemies outside my door!"

Her words are a blow across my face and shame fills me. Liam's nostrils flare and a muscle tics in his jaw, but he remains silent.

Taylor points to me, then glares at Liam. "This man has so much heart inside him. He loves you guys so fucking much. You don't know how lucky you are. He's the best man I know." She swallows, her voice trembling. "Trust me. I know. So, I won't have you hurt him like this. If you want to go at him, you'll have to go through me."

A rush of emotions slams through me—the sticky shame from moments ago, the sweltering warmth of appreciation, the burst of pride, and so much fucking love singeing my chest I almost forget how to breathe.

My minx is fierce. The black swan ruffling her feathers under the spotlight, owning the attention of everyone in the room.

And she claimed me as her prince.

"Understand?" she asks Liam.

My brother swallows as he shrugs himself out of Ethan's clasp. His voice is thick and rusty as he rasps, "For your sake, I hope you're right."

He spins around and walks back into Firefly's room. Ethan holds my gaze for a second and mouths, *"I got this. Come back another day. Go cool down."*

Taylor steps in front of me and cradles my face. Her brows are pinched, lips pursed. She swipes the wetness on my face with her thumb, her big eyes wide with concern.

"You okay?" she whispers.

I stare at her beautiful eyes, my heart pounding a resounding beat and without another word, I clasp her nape and crush my lips with hers, wanting to tell her everything I'm feeling without words.

To thank her for seeing me, for standing up for me, for fighting on the same side as me.

Our kiss deepens as she relaxes in my arms, but soon a few pointed coughs break through the haze of my emotions.

I release a deep exhale and dip my forehead toward her. My past is catching up to my present. This is bound to happen. "Yes. I will be okay...because you're here. I'm sorry you had to witness that."

She pulls me into her arms and places her head on my chest. I relish her warmth and reassuring weight as I close my eyes. "That was Liam...but you already figured that out."

She nods. "I bumped into Ethan on the way up. He told me he was meeting your brother."

"They are best friends," I explain before pulling back to look at her beautiful face again.

Thick black hair piled up in a bun, barefaced without a stitch of makeup, a glittering red gem on her nose. She's wearing one of her black loose-fitting sweaters and leggings today.

She goddamn takes my breath away.

And her startling eyes are staring at me with such warmth and concern.

I wonder if that'll change after this.

"Come," I pull her to a seating area in the corner, devoid of people, "I want to tell you what happened. Liam's not wrong, you know."

Looking into her eyes once more, I take a breath, then utter the next words.

"It is my fault. I put her in a coma."

CHAPTER 47

Charles

Seven and a half years ago

"Get me London, now!" I holler to my assistant, my stomach plummeting as I watch the free fall of our stock price on one monitor—the red line associated with stock ticker BOC glaring at me—and the trading volume rising on the other.

It's a bloodbath.

Some bastard is trying to take over the company. A sneak attack, clearly months in the making—getting folks to sell their shares, causing the stock price to dip and then buying it all before we can do anything about it.

My office line is ringing off the hook, no doubt investors or the press wanting to know what the hell is going on.

I pick up the phone. "Yes?" I bark.

"Charles, is the situation under control?" Grandma's voice comes across the line and I look at the caller ID. Shit. Of course, she'd know about this. It's only been a few years since she's handed the reins of the company to me and I am royally fucking it up.

"Yes. I'm working with Patterson on some numbers and we will fight back. I got this."

"If you need help, call me, okay? Patterson knows what he's doing. I trust him, and I still have contacts at Deutsche and Barclays. They should back us up."

My cell phone buzzes and I groan. "Yes, will let you know. I have to go."

After hanging up, I eye the monitors again and holler, "Patterson, in here, please!"

He strides in, laptop in hand, his cell phone tucked against his ear. "Charles, I just got off the phone with Kenneth from Barclays. They are placing the bids to buy the shares being tossed out right now. We'll owe them, but we may be able to put a stop to this."

This is why Grandma asked me to keep him on. This man was one of her top recruits and he's been with the company since he graduated from college.

He's brilliant.

My assistant knocks on the door. "Sir, London is on the line."

Holding up my finger, I answer the call. "Joe, thanks for getting on. Yes, it appears someone's making a move. We have Barclays in our corner right now." I nod my thanks to Patterson, who tips his head in acknowledgment. "But I think we'll need more capital. Can you liquidate our assets at HSBC? Have them front us an emergency loan and we'll settle the next day."

My cell phone buzzes again as I listen to the head of finance halfway across the world talk numbers with me.

My mind is in a swirl. I can't let the Bank of Columbia be acquired under my watch. No fucking way.

My damn cell phone won't stop buzzing.

I pick it up, looking at the caller ID. *Liam.*

Rubbing my temples, I murmur, "Give me one minute, okay? A call is coming in."

I blow out a breath and answer my cell. "Liam, this isn't a good time."

"It's an emergency. I need your help. I can't get to her—I'm in the air right now."

I type an email out on my computer. "Who?"

"Our sister! She called me just now. She must've called you too, right? It sounds like an emergency. She wants us to meet her somewhere. Can you do it?"

"Liam, there's a hostile takeover at the company and I can't—shit!" Another ten percent dip in the stock price.

"Fuck the company, Charles! This is our sister. She'd never call an emergency meeting unless it was an emergency. Please, just check on her, okay? At least make sure she's fine."

I delete some words and retype—I can't think straight right now. My office phone rings again—who the fuck is it now?

"Fine. I'll call her. I really need to go."

"Thanks, bro. I can count on you, right? You're going to check on her?" Liam asks. I hear rustling in the background. "Because if you can't, I'll tell the pilot to turn back. But I rather not."

"Yeah, I will."

We hang up and I pick back up the office phone and redial London, because of course they hung up on me since I kept them waiting for so long.

"Sorry about that. The call went long. Yes, so I need you to move the funds from this account."

I fiddle with my phone and see the missed calls. Ten missed calls from Firefly. Three unread texts.

Firefly

> I need your help. It's an emergency. Please. I can't do this over the phone. Needs to be in person.

Firefly

> Charles? I tried calling and you haven't picked up. Liam is on his way to the airport.

Firefly

> I'm scared.

My brows furrow as worry prickles me. *What's going on?* Then I shake my head. Firefly is a passionate person. This is the girl who was scared of the dark until she was in high school. Then there was last week when she was scared about the strange noises in her apartment, which turned out to be a leaky faucet. She has inherited her fiery personality, along with all the detested emotional upheaval from our parents. *She's probably being dramatic.*

"Charles, Barclays said they got approved for half the funds. I think we need a second backer," Patterson murmurs from his seat across from me.

Shit. I knew this was going to happen.

I put London on hold and ping my assistant to get Deutsche on the line. I may need Grandma's help after all.

Flipping back to my call with London, I instruct, "Yes. The interest rate is fine—a small price to pay to keep the company safe."

My cell phone buzzes again and this time I ignore it.

Present Day

"I completely forgot about her. Didn't call her back or text her," Charles rasps as he stares at the floor in front of him, his eyes haunted.

A weight sinks on my chest as I put the rest of the story together. Obviously, something must've happened to his sister that day.

"That night, I got a call from the hospital. They found her trapped inside her car in the Hudson River. She was lucky because a Good Samaritan saw her car plummeting into the water and dove in and saved her. But she was nonresponsive—there was too much trauma—ribs, legs broken, internal bleeding, fluid in her lungs. It was a miracle she was still alive." His eyes glisten with tears.

"Shit," I murmur and wrap my arms around him. I would've never known he was carrying so much inside him if he hadn't told me.

He is wearing a mask—a damn good one forged by years of pain and guilt.

"I'm the oldest in the family. Growing up, it has always been us three. My parents," he scoffs, "are alive and well, but they never cared about us. I often think they had kids because that's what everyone else did. They didn't want us. And so, it had always been us against the world. Uncle Ian would do his best to be there for the big events in life—graduation, award ceremonies, playoff games—but we were used to depending on each other."

A tear streaks down his cheek and my heart breaks into tiny pieces. "I was supposed to take care of them. Put them first. Love them so they wouldn't even notice our parents were MIA. But I failed. Big time. And now she's in a coma, half alive, and Liam won't talk to me."

I wipe the moisture from his face and turn his head toward me.

His startling, expressive eyes radiate with so much pain, guilt, and so much love for his siblings. I wonder how everyone missed this side of him before.

How were we all so blind?

But you see him now, Taylor. Just like he sees you.

"You listen to me, Charles Vaughn. I don't know your sister, but I'm damn sure she wouldn't want you beating yourself up because of her. You didn't put her in a coma. You didn't cause her injuries. It was a tragic accident."

Charles lets out a derisive chuckle and shakes his head. "I tried telling myself that for years, Tay. *Years.* I don't believe it, nor does Liam. And he's right to be pissed at me. I convinced myself saving the company was more important than an SOS from my sister."

He leans his head on my shoulder, his hands gripping my waist, his hold borderline painful. "Liam called me, you know. He said he'd tell the pilot to turn around if I couldn't get to her, but I told him I'd take care of it. And I didn't. She told me she was scared. I thought she was being dramatic. I ignored all the warning signs. I'm not a good man, Tay."

He heaved out a heavy breath. "Over the years, I've wondered what happened to her that day and what she was scared about. The police said there was no foul play and the rain probably factored into her accident. I looked over the records and everyone told me it was not my fault. But I couldn't forgive myself."

Charles lifts his head up and stares at me, his gaze bleak. "You were right about me before. I survived on fake charm and charisma. I ignored my family in their time of need for shit that didn't matter in the grand scheme of things. I don't deserve forgiveness or you."

I shake my head. "It's not your fault. Yes, maybe you should've listened to her. Maybe you could've done more, but you had an emergency you were dealing with already. You didn't put her behind the wheel or engineered that accident. If you'd known what was going to happen, you would've dropped everything for your sister. You can't beat yourself up like this."

He pushes out a ragged exhale as his gaze roves over me like I'm the last lifeline he's holding onto.

Swallowing the lump in my throat, I murmur, "Didn't you tell me my darkest night wasn't my fault? When I was beating myself up for the thousandth time for taking a drink from a stranger, didn't you tell me not to think that way? If I made a different choice that night, a simple choice in retrospect, everything would've been different."

I wet my lips as a burn appears behind my eyes, my voice thick. "You told me it wasn't my fault, right? You said I was still breathtakingly beautiful, that I wasn't messed up or fucked up. So you listen to me, Charles. You're an annoying fucker sometimes, but none of this is your fault. You're a damn good man, the only man other than my brothers I trust. Nothing is going to change the way I look at you, you hear me? It's just a fucking pile of shit that is life. What happened to Firefly is not your fault, just like what happened to me is not my fault, okay?"

His jaw works, a muscle pulsing on his forehead. His eyes darken—turbulent like the skies outside.

"Fuck, I love you, minx," he rasps, and my heart flips and skips several beats.

Then he seals his lips with mine.

I love you too, Charles.

CHAPTER 48

I HUFF OUT A breath as I walk down the steps of ABTC juggling a bunch of green balloons and a diaper tower wrapped in cellophane. I love the city in May—spring is in full swing and the temperatures are balmy and comfortable.

Today, life feels especially hopeful, even though I had a doozy of a practice just now. Ainsley seemed at odds with Maddy, and Carla was bitchy the entire time, which wasn't a surprise. On a brighter note, Bethany visited the premises today and her ankle was doing much better, but she still has a few more months of rest before she can start practicing again.

So, I'll be dancing the finale performance at the Met Opera next month, then the show will be over.

Then I'll find out if I can sit for the promotion evaluation.

I shove the nervousness to the back of my mind as I tighten my grip on the balloons and the present for Belle, who's having her baby shower today.

But this time, the milestone doesn't bring with it a lash of envy or the pang of grief I'm used to experiencing whenever I think about the girls moving on without me.

This time, only joy lights up my chest, and I know who to thank for that.

"Better not let him know, or else he'll gloat," I murmur to myself, thinking of Charles.

After that day at the hospital, we've grown even closer. There's a lightness in his frame I haven't seen before. The weight of what happened to his sister must've been haunting him, just like how my past was always lurking in the shadows. While we weren't able to visit his sister that day, I was thankful he shared with me the trauma he tried to hide behind his charisma and smiles.

My sleep has been better and more restful. The dark eye circles I thought were permanently etched onto my skin have now faded. The monster's voice still occasionally haunts me when I least expect it, but for the most part, I've been able to keep my past firmly in the past.

My Odette is flawed, that much hasn't changed, but my Odile is as strong as ever, and I've come to terms with it. Perhaps I'm creating a new dance for other girls like me out there. Maybe a young girl with a checkered past is hiding backstage, watching me dance the white swan—beautiful but imperfect—and she'd feel seen somehow.

For the first time in years, I have a new feeling percolating in my chest...a spark of light, a twinge of excitement.

I have a wonderful boyfriend who doesn't shy away from the darkest parts of me, the ability to enjoy panty-melting sex, a relatively successful ballet tour in a lead dancer role under my belt.

Charles and I have spent every other day together, either in his place on the Upper East Side or mine. He'd complain about my choice of horror movies and taste in fried foods and I'd gripe about his penchant for foreign language films and his snooty love for fine wines from impeccable vintages.

"This is for you," he murmured last Saturday before wrapping his arms around me from behind when he stepped into my apartment. He started kissing my neck, his fingers grazing the swath of skin between my sweater and my leggings. The damn man has mastered all my erogenous zones.

"J'aime ton odeur, ton goût, tes sons. Ton corps me rend fou." He softly nipped me, and I moaned, my pussy throbbing from the sensations. The man had to be a vampire in another life.

"Not fair, you're breaking out French. I can't win this one." I leaned into his embrace, finding him already hard and poking at my backside.

He chuckled. "If I knew foreign languages would make you wet, I'd have broken it out a long time ago. I speak multiple languages—French, Italian, and some Welsh. And what I just said was, 'I love your smell, your taste, your sounds. Your body drives me insane.'"

Charles slid his hand under my sweater and grabbed my breast, thumbing the pebbled nipple. "Fuck, I can't get enough of you. You've made me an insatiable caveman. Netflix and chill is overrated, let's skip to dessert."

A snort tumbled out of my mouth and he froze, staring at me quizzically. "What?"

"You know Netflix and chill is code name for sex, not watching TV, right?" Reminded of the purpose of the date night—to watch the latest slasher film I'd been looking forward to—I pulled his hand out of my sweater and grabbed the bag from him. I peeked inside.

Carrot cake with cream cheese frosting from Estelle's. The best of the best. My mouth waters.

"What did you have to do to snag these? They are sold out by eight each morning."

I swallowed a gasp as he pulled me back against him and peppered kisses down my throat to my collarbone.

"I sold my kidney," he whispered, "and it was worth it to see that smile on your face."

Heat traveled up my body, and I rolled my eyes. "You're ridiculous."

"Only for you, minx. Only for you. So, Netflix and chill?" he murmured, amusement in his voice as he hoisted me up in his arms and walked us toward the bedroom.

I clench my thighs together as I remember the rest of the weekend when I indulged in a lot of carrot cake and a lot of him. I used to think Charles Vaughn was the god of thunder, but I was clearly wrong.

He's an incubus, a sex demon. Doling out orgasms like candy.

I'm thankful he's taught me to love my body again.

Baby shower for two hours and then fun times in the actual shower with him later this evening.

I giggle and clap a hand over my mouth.

I *so* did not make that noise.

"Someone is in *love*!" Lisa sidles up from behind me and I inwardly groan. Leave it to her to catch me mooning over my boyfriend, who isn't even here in person.

"Shut up," I grunt.

She claps her hands and squeals.

Loud footsteps pound behind us and a familiar brunette, clearly in a rush, bumps into Lisa.

"Maddy? Whoa. Easy there, you okay?" Lisa asks.

Maddy's face pales, and she swallows, her eyes widening in something resembling panic. The slither of unease I felt in Paris comes sweeping back in. She's been quieter since she got back from the international tour, and neither Ainsley nor any of us could get anything out of her.

We thought things were looking up for her. It seemed like she came into some money, even though she said it was only a small scholarship she got from a local charity. But I don't see her wearing thrifted clothes anymore. We presumed her quiet moods had to do with her mom and her illness. Maybe it got worse?

She looks behind us and shakes her head. "I...I'm fine. Sorry for bumping into you, Lisa. I have to run, okay?"

She flies down the steps without waiting for an answer and I look back, finding Ainsley staring at her friend, her brows furrowed and Sir Ian and Carla stepping out the doors. Ainsley looks crestfallen as she walks back inside the building. I make a note to ask her about it later.

"If you see Charles later, tell him to call me," Sir Ian murmurs, a smile on his face as he reaches us. "The boy used to make time for me at least twice a week, but lately, I'm lucky if I get a call from him once a month. I wonder why." He arches his brow and Lisa snickers next to me.

My skin heats and I kick my shoe on the pavement. "I'll let him know tonight," I mumble.

Lisa squeals again and Sir Ian laughs as he waves and walks away.

"Don't you think it's disgusting you are sleeping with the director's nephew to get a leg up?" Carla sneers as she bumps into my shoulder. She glowers and folds her arms across her chest.

I wait for the burst of anger to rise inside me—the indignation to make an appearance—but it never comes. When people are jealous, they react in two ways. One, they congratulate you and nurse their jealousy or sadness inside. Two, they try to destroy your happiness and drag you down to their pit of misery.

It's sad, really.

I shrug. "I guess some of us just have all the luck. Maybe if you stop being so bitter, some of my luck will rub off on you."

"Burn!" Lisa smacks my shoulder, and I grin as I make my way to the car idling at the curb.

CHAPTER 49

TWO HOURS LATER, I find myself enjoying the baby shower Grace and Millie put together for Belle in a private room within the ladies' lounge inside The Orchid. The luxurious space—the walls normally adorned with ivory floral wallpaper, pale gold and marble furnishings, velvet armchairs and curtains of blush pink—is now transformed into a sea of blue green.

Belle told me this unique shade is called atrovirens. Apparently, it's her favorite color. I can almost imagine myself in some magical fairytale forest surrounded by gauze, chiffon, and so many ruffles.

Lana is humming under her breath as she gleefully stirs some mysterious baby food into a shaker before dumping her concoction into martini glasses. We're playing a ridiculous game to figure out the flavor of baby food *after* it's been stirred into gin. "Okay ladies, try this one. There's no way you can guess."

She hands out the drinks to the group.

"This has to be pear!" Grace giggles after downing her drink in one gulp.

"No way. This is disgusting. I vote for some vegetable. Maybe beets." Olivia grimaces, her face pinking. She arches her brow at me and waves her finger. "I'm not drunk yet. This is the curse of the Asian glow." She points to her red face.

"Beets would've made the drink red, doctor!" Millie giggles as she slumps against Olivia, who's shaking her head.

"I thought this was a baby shower, not a bachelorette party. Why are you guys all drunk and I'm suddenly the designated driver...except we aren't driving?" Belle grumbles, but her hazel eyes are twinkling with laughter.

"Sorry, Belle. You're carrying a baby the size of a..." I scroll on my phone to the website I'm looking for, "cabbage?" I arch my brow as I eye her round stomach dubiously. "There's no way that's one baby then. You're fucking *huge*!"

The girls groan and Olivia smacks her hand on her forehead. "Tay, you aren't supposed to comment on pregnant women's bellies."

She leans over and waggles her brow, her eyes glazed. Oh shit, she's definitely one drink away from drunk, despite what she said just now. "Even if they *are* huge," she whispers loudly, and we snicker.

"I heard that...unfortunately, I'm completely sober!" Belle bemoans as we laugh again.

"God, this is more fun than I originally thought. Who knew baby showers could be so fun?" I smirk.

"Maybe because we're all halfway to being drunk!" Olivia shoves as we dissolve into giggles again.

Lana clears her throat and hands Belle a glass of water before raising her own glass of mystery flavored martini. "I want to propose a toast."

She turns toward Belle, who looks absolutely radiant in her lavender floral maxi dress. "Belle, thank you for joining our family and making my brother the happiest man on earth."

She swallows, no doubt thinking about the normally cold and aloof Maxwell, who's been through too much tragedy in his life.

"You saved him," Lana whispers, her voice trembling. "I was always so worried about him before...trapping himself in the estate, thinking he's doomed to live a lonely and loveless life. And then you came in and turned his world upside down in the best way." Lana's eyes tear up.

Belle sniffles and grabs Lana's hand.

Lana nods and wipes her eyes. "And now you're going to make me an aunt! You're fulfilling his dream of having a family of his own. Th-Thank you."

"You're making me cry!" Belle pulls Lana to her and the two hug.

Grace and I glance at each other, my vision blurry too, because how could anyone not feel anything in this moment?

"This makes me want to meet someone too," Olivia whispers next to me and I sneak a look at her, finding her staring at the scene with a forlorn expression on her face.

She quickly glances at me and smiles before shaking her head. "Ignore me. I'm an emotional drunk." She waves her empty glass in my face.

I smirk. "But I thought you said you weren't drunk."

My phone buzzes in the pocket of my navy sundress, part of my PR friendly attire Lana has assigned me.

Taking it out, I grin and read the message.

Charles

How's the baby shower? Maxwell is annoying me. He keeps asking for updates, but he doesn't want to text his wife and ruin her moment. The fucker doesn't want to let her out of his sight. Remind me not to be like that in the future.

My heart sprints laps inside my rib cage. *The future? Baby? Me and him?* An image forms in my mind—a little girl with blond curls and gray eyes wearing a pink tutu, giggling as I twirl with her in the studio. Charles leaning against the window, watching us, a grin tugging his lips.

I rake in an inhale. I'd never imagined this future for me before. It never seemed possible, but now...

Butterflies beat their wings in my gut as I reread his message again, bubbles forming inside my chest.

Yes, I want this future with him. I want to tell him I love him and I want this image in my mind to become my reality.

Wetting my lips, my fingers shaking, I type an answer.

Taylor

It's going well. I'm actually having fun.

My pulse kicks up as I wait for his response. It comes a few seconds later.

The warmth in my chest becomes an inferno and I exhale to keep myself from calling him and blurting out everything I'm feeling.

Biting my lip instead, I start typing.

"You're texting Charles, aren't you?" Grace snickers as she plops on the seat next to me.

I pause and slip my phone back into my pocket, cursing myself for not having a better poker face.

"Just giving him an update. He wants to make sure we're having fun."

"I like this look on you." Grace smiles. "You seem so much happier. It's what Mom would've wanted for you, but we just never knew how to reach you. It always seemed like you were hiding a part of yourself from us." She reaches over and grabs my hand. "You know, whatever it is, we're always here for you. But regardless, I...I'm glad you have him."

Suddenly, my dress seems too tight on my body and I swallow, trying to dislodge the lump forming in my throat. I want to let her in, to let all my girls in. I want to trust people again.

Maybe it's time to tell them.

Looking up, I see Lana laughing with Belle and Olivia chatting with Millie.

Not right now, though.

"Later, Grace, I want to tell you something. Something few people know about." I squeeze her hand.

She freezes, her eyes sharpening. "Everything okay?"

The scars on my thighs itch and the tendrils of the monster buried inside me struggle to get out. I breathe in deeply. The past is in the past, and it'll stay that way if I can help it. But I want to let my girls in.

I nod. "I'm fine. It's something I should've told you a long time ago."

Grace nods slowly, her dark blue eyes trained on mine. I give her a soft smile. For the first time in a long time, I finally feel like things will turn out all right.

My phone buzzes in my pocket, and warmth floods my chest. It must be Charles. He's behaving like Maxwell already and I'm not even married to him yet.

Smirking, I take it out and swipe to my messages.

Blood leaves my face as a sudden surge of nausea and horror pulls the rug out from under me.

Unknown Number

> You and your boyfriend need to stop investigating or this will be splashed all over online. And there's more where they came from.

A photo is attached.

A close-up of my face and naked chest, my dress ripped, eyes glazed, and mouth opened. My cheeks are wet with tears. A man's arm is in the frame.

The horror from that night, permanently captured in a photograph.

I drop the phone and hurl the contents of my stomach onto the floor.

CHAPTER 50

Moonlight streaks across my vision as I spin, spin, and spin on this nightmarish merry-go-round of my twisted mind. Cold sweat breaks out on my back as my pulse scatters in my veins. My calves scream in pain, my toes swollen in my pointe shoes, but I don't stop.

I. Can't. Stop.

I can't stop. I can't stop. I can't stop.

The image on my phone is seared into my mind. I can't get it out. I can't get rid of the feeling of ants crawling on my skin, of black grime sticking to me.

Fifty-five. Fifty-Six. Fifty-seven. The twirls continue. They are chaotic, sloppy, but I don't care. Because if I stop, I'll need to take another shower again. I'll have to find more needles to poke myself.

But I've already tried that—my usual coping strategies aren't working.

I thought I was over this. I thought I got better. I thought I was healed. I thought the past was in the fucking past!

A manic chuckle rips out of my throat. What will the girls think of me now?

The Taylor Peyton they thought they knew died a long time ago.

What will they think of this impostor? Are they disgusted with me? Will they leave me just like Camden and Alexis did?

Flashes of the ruined baby shower slam through my mind.

Grace's eyes widened in horror after she scrambled out of her chair to reach my side as I heaved onto the floor. The girls immediately rushed over to see if I was okay as my world obliterated around me. I remember seeing Lana's horrified face when she picked up my phone from the floor and saw the photo before handing it to Grace.

Dismay crossed my sister's face. Millie had her hand over her mouth. Olivia looked at me in pity.

It's over.

I can't hide anymore.

Everyone knows.

And unless I stop investigating, give up on finding out what happened that night to get closure and to put the bastards away, whoever this asshole is will leak the photos to the press.

Then the whole world will know. My career, my life...everything will be over.

I snatched the phone from the girls and ran out the door, my mind in a daze. I don't remember how I ended back up at ABTC. The first thing I did was to take a scalding shower and stab myself with a needle from my locker. It didn't work.

Nothing is working. The panic won't recede, but is spewing out instead—a cataclysmic volcanic eruption I can't stop.

Ballet. I'm ballet. Ballet is me. The pain and control I have as Taylor the ballerina...it's my last ditch effort.

Stop thinking. Stop it.

"You'll never be rid of me, Fly Harriet," the monster whispers before chuckling.

"She's going to come, isn't she? Enjoying your first cock?"

"No!" I shriek and fall to the ground.

My pulse riots in my veins and every muscle inside me protests as I stagger back up and throw myself into the fouetté turns again. Black swan. Odile. I'm the best Odile. I can be better.

Tears streak down my face as I hurl myself into more spins. Higher. Faster. My muscles cramp and tear, agony searing into me, but I don't stop.

"I'm Taylor *fucking* Peyton-Anderson, badass ballerina, and you won't beat me!" I holler at the darkness.

Suddenly, powerful arms snake across my waist and haul my body off the floor.

The monsters in my nightmare are here again. I won't let them take me. I'll die before I let them steal from me again.

I let out a bloodcurdling scream, my fists punching and legs kicking, hitting the beast behind me. A few deep *oomphs* reach my ears, the madness teeming in my blood, but I don't stop.

A hand clasps my chin tightly and I feel the monster's arm banding me flushed against his chest.

"Minx, minx. It's me. It's me. You're safe. You're always safe."

My heart throws itself against my rib cage, bloodied and battered. I finally make out the deep, raspy voice, the firm muscles I know intimately, the familiar notes of bergamot and cedarwood in the air.

Charles.

Sobs tear out of my throat, the manic phase of my mind quickly devolving into depression—a bottomless dark abyss. I'm sinking into the turbulent ocean, drowning under the moonless skies.

"I got you, minx. I always have you," he chokes out as he curls me tighter against him. I feel his lips on my cheeks, my hair, my eyes, and I realize my face is wet with tears.

"Ph-Photos...there are photos," I whisper as I turn around and bury my face against his chest. His rioting heartbeats are loud in my ear. "Th-They know. Everyone knows."

"Shhh...I got you," he rasps over and over again. "I'll find the bastard. I'll stop him. Fuck, when I find him, he'll wish he were never born."

Tremors rush through my body as I cry in his embrace. Chaos has taken over my mind, my pulse clamoring inside me, my breathing quickening as black dots form my vision. I can feel the monster's touch on my body again. His weight. His sounds. His words.

His fucking scent of peppermint.

Desperate, I grab at Charles's arms. I need to forget. I need more. I need everything.

"Charles? P-Please...Please..."

He tightens his grip on me, his eyes burning with anger and anguish. "What do you need? Please tell me what you need."

"I need to forget." I shake my head vigorously. "I f-feel him...them. I don't want it. I need to forget it all. I need to get out of my mind!" I claw at his arms, my nails digging deeper as a fleeting thought takes root in my head.

Arching up to look at him, I whisper, "D-Didn't you say you want to teach me pain can be pleasurable? Teach me. Make me feel pain. Get me out of my head!"

Charles stills, his muscles tensing. His eyes flare, and a muscle tics on his forehead. "What?"

The idea sounds better to me by the minute. *Yes, this is what I need.*

"What you did at The Sanctuary. I want to try it. I need it, *please.*"

A muscle pulses in his jaw. "A responsible Dom won't start anything with a sub when she's emotional. There are conversations to have. I need to know your hard limits, soft limits. We need to have safe words. I need to walk you through the process, the aftercare. BDSM isn't something to try when you're feeling this way, Tay."

He's rejecting me.

Somehow, the thought causes panic to seize my chest again. Is he regretting having a fuck up like me as a girlfriend?

I shake my head. "Please," I beg him. "Please save me from myself. From the monsters, please!"

A few seconds of tense silence passes by, his sharp eyes trained on my face like he's reading every single fear in my mind. "Are you sure? I need you to think through this. This can be triggering. Intense."

The rioting voices in my mind quiet for a few beats—long enough for me to consider his words. *I need this and I trust him.*

Nodding, I rasp, "Yes. I am sure. I need this. Please, Charles."

He intakes a sharp inhale and sets me in front of him before backing up a few steps.

"We won't do anything hard or intense. Only light BDSM. Now, I need you to listen to me very carefully." His eyes darken and I see a chill befall his features.

He's becoming the Dom I saw that night at The Sanctuary.

A burst of relief floods me. He's going to do this. He's going to get me out of my mind.

I nod eagerly.

"Whenever we're in a scene, you'll call me Sir. Is spanking, pinching, biting okay for you?"

My pulse careens off a cliff. "Yes."

"Light breath play? Degradation?"

I swallow. "Yes to all of it."

Charles nods and takes off his suit jacket. His hands slowly unknot his tie before he drops it on the floor. Then he shucks his shirt, baring all his rippling muscles. A new sultry heat fires up my insides as I see the thick veins rippling on his forearms.

His eyes are intent on mine as he says, "Red is stop. Yellow is slow down. Green is continue. Repeat after me. I need to trust you will remember them."

I focus on his words and repeat them. He stares at me for a few seconds—a sharp assessment.

"Good. If you can't speak, pinch anywhere on my body and I will stop right away. Is that clear?"

"Y-Yes."

His eyes are dark like the night skies outside. "Yes, what?"

A shiver tremors through me. "Yes, Sir."

Charles's eyes flash, a dangerous gleam reflecting at me. "I'm going to ask you again. Are you sure you want to do this right now?"

I back up slowly, an automatic reaction, until my back hits the bar on the wall. My pussy pulses as he stalks toward me, every inch the alpha male I glimpsed at the club. My skin heats, my breasts grow tender. I want to rub my thighs together to relieve the ache building inside me.

Quick exhales escape my lips. I need him, all of him, including his sadistic side right now. "Yes, I need this."

His lips twitch, his eyes darkening.

"Good. Now kneel."

Chapter 51

She slowly drops to her knees in front of me.

Blood rushes to my cock as I stare at the woman I love, bathed in the ethereal moonlight streaming in from the windows. She looks so beautiful in her purple leotard and skirt, her luscious raven hair flowing over her shoulders. Tears pool in her eyes and streak across her face, but she's still the utterly breathtaking vixen I met at ABTC, the minx who socked me across the face.

When Grace called me in a panic, telling me a disturbing photo of Taylor, naked and in distress, appeared on her phone, and she ran off in the middle of the baby shower, I about lost my mind. Luckily, Lana quickly tailed Taylor and saw her entering ABTC.

Maxwell rushed over to the ladies' lounge while I beelined here. On the way over, I called Elias, insisting on an update of his investigation because if Ian was behind all of this, I wouldn't rule out strangling him. Elias had someone hack into Taylor's phone to get the text and quickly do a trace to a burner phone located outside of the US, and so it doesn't appear my uncle was behind this.

After I arrived at ABTC, I rushed in, opened doors, and checked rooms until I bumped into Lisa, who told me Tay liked to dance in the rooftop studio alone. When I yanked the glass door open and saw her dancing under the moonlight, my heart shattered.

Pain, anguish, terror, and heartbreak flitted across her face like a slideshow. She was out of control, a broken wind up doll who couldn't stop.

Spiraling into madness.

And now, she's on her knees in front of me, looking at me like I'm her last resort.

Holding her gaze, I quickly discard my pants before striding toward her. Her haunted eyes widen and that enticing pulse flutters wildly in her neck.

Am I making the right choice?

It goes against what a proper Dom should do—to do this when a sub is so distraught. She isn't level-headed right now. But then I think about how I found her—mad with grief and hurting herself—I know this is the right choice.

I need her mind to shut down, to succumb to forces greater than her, to let me control every aspect of her so she can rest and just feel.

Stopping a few inches in front of her, I rasp, "Take out my cock."

Tay shudders and licks her lips. The sight of that pretty pink tongue hardens my cock even more. I can't wait to feel her around me. Her hands tremble as she pulls down my boxer briefs. I kick them out of the way. My dick is throbbing, dripping at the tip as she holds it in her hands before slowly pumping it.

Biting back a groan, I utter, "Suck it, minx. Put it down your throat. If I see any visible inches, you'll get a spanking later."

She whimpers and puts my cock in her mouth, and I groan when she sucks me in, her tongue lapping and swirling at me as she struggles to put all my inches inside her.

White hot pleasure burns through me when the tip of my cock hits the back of her throat. She attempts to swallow me down her throat. Tears overflow and wet her cheeks, her free hand playing with my heavy balls, sending more blistering sensations throughout my body.

Growling, I coil my hand around her hair and pull so she's staring up at me. "Look at my personal slut sucking my cock in like a champ. You like it, huh? Are you greedy for my cum?"

She nods, her teary eyes widening as a familiar glaze appears in them. Lust. Attraction. Love.

"Too bad, you still have three inches you can't swallow." I grunt when her teeth make an appearance. She bites and I hiss before pulling her hair sharply. "That'll earn you a few more slaps."

Whimpering, she slides her hand between her legs and I quickly snap her face toward me, jamming the last three inches down her throat. "I didn't say you can touch yourself."

Taylor gags as I thrust in once into her tight channel and I nearly come at the way her throat welcomes me in its warmth. Pulling out, I growl, "Give me a color."

"G-Green," she pants out, reaching for my cock again.

"My fucking insatiable girl." I grip her head again and slam my hips toward her again, my eyes rolling back as sharp currents of pleasure shoot through me. The control I wear outside of BDSM is slipping fast as I lose myself in the sensations of her talented mouth working me like I'm the best thing she's ever tasted.

She gags as I thrust into her again and again, gathering speed, the pressure quickly rising from the base of my spine to my balls before rushing up my cock. Tears slide over her face as drool drips from her mouth, but her eyes are hazy—the way she usually is in the throes of sex with me.

She isn't thinking now. I'm getting her out of her mind.

My legs tremble, her tongue working harder around my cock, swiping, swirling as I slam her repeatedly on me. My mind darkens, but I tell her, "Pinch me if it's too much."

More saliva drips out of her as she shakes her head and bobs faster to the rhythm of my pistoning.

"Fuck! You'll be the death of me, my little cum slut. You're such a good girl, kneeling before me, taking your Sir's cock like you were born to do that. Fuck, fuck, fuck," I mutter as the sharp frissons of pleasure coalesce into a singular beam of nirvana.

My muscles tense, my cock lengthening and twitching. "I'll give you my fucking cum, my naughty ballerina."

Pulling out as the first ropes of cum shoot out of me, I spray the rest of my cum on her face and neck. I tug my cock, the obliterating pleasure making the floor sway from under my feet. Taylor whimpers, and as the dots fade from my vision, I see her rubbing her clit over her tights, her tongue swiping out and licking the cum off her lips.

The feral minx.

My cock twitches when I take in the rest of her, my cum streaking across her cheeks, dripping down her neck, joining her tears and saliva.

She's fucking perfect.

Hauling her up, I grab her nape and slam my lips on top of hers, tasting a bit of me mixed with everything that's her, and that's enough to cause my cock to resurrect and harden, ready for another round.

"You make me insatiable, Tay, fucking insatiable," I rasp before swiping my tongue inside her, tangling, dueling, overpowering her mouth in the way my own inner beast craves.

She tastes so sweet, so addictive, so intoxicatingly mine.

Taylor mewls, her body softening, legs giving out underneath her as she submits to me, so perfectly like I knew she would, and I hoist her up and prop her against the bar by the mirrored wall.

Keeping my eye on her, I whisper, "Look at me. It's me doing this."

Yanking her legs apart, I gather her leotard at the neck and rip it, baring her creamy tits to the night air. Her tits jiggle from the movement, her hard nipples pebbling like eraser buds, and I feel myself leaking again.

I slap her breast. Hard. She screams.

"I seem to recall someone deserves a punishment for not taking all my inches in earlier."

I watch in fascination, a red flush appearing where I slapped her. Quickly, I smack her two more times in quick succession, her body twitching at each impact as she cries out some more, new tears sliding down her face.

"Give me a color."

Her eyes snap open, her lips tremble before she says, "Green. Fucking green."

Madness burns through my veins as I deliver slap after slap on her heaving tits, watching as her skin beads with sweat, pinkening under my torture. I pinch those hard nipples taunting me, then take one in, suckling it before biting it...hard.

"Charles!" she shrieks, her body bowing back. She clutches my shoulder for dear life.

"Color."

"Green, oh fuck yes!" She thrashes before me as I switch breasts and pinch her other nipple.

Blood roars in my ears. My throbbing cock curls tightly around my stomach as cum leaks out all over, dripping down the length.

I pull back and look at her, finding her body twitching, her hands limp at her sides, her mouth dropping open. Her long legs splayed wide, so she's almost sitting on top of the bar in splits.

Her tights are soaked between her legs, the wet spot beckoning me to tend to it next.

Leaning down, I listen to her harried gasps of air, and I lick up from her neck to her ear before whispering, "Look at you, my dirty little slut is leaking all over her clothes. Do you need to come, my darling minx?"

She nods eagerly, her hands running up my body, her nails scraping over my muscles.

"What are you thinking of right now?" I whisper before sucking on my favorite part of her neck, where her pulse batters against her skin.

Taylor whimpers, her tits arching up, head dropping back and hitting the mirror behind her as I suckle that tender area, nipping her the way she likes.

"Answer me."

Rapid breaths flutter past her lips and she rasps, "N-Nothing. Only you. Oh fuck, Charles."

I deliver a hard slap on her pussy, and she screeches and twitches. "Try again."

"S-Sir," she moans and I rub her piercing through her panties. Fuck, she's completely soaked through.

"Color?"

"Green. Always green with you." She grabs my face, forcing me to look at her. "Because you make me feel safe."

Raw possession buries me in a landslide, and I slam my mouth against hers, swallowing her moans, her cries, her words of love and trust.

I don't deserve her, but I'm a selfish man who'll take anything she'll give me.

My hands travel down her body, squeezing her heavy tits, scraping her smooth belly before landing between her legs.

"I need to get to your pretty pussy, okay?" I murmur, the remnants of logic in my mind remembering the trauma she went through.

Taylor whimpers and nods. She clutches me tighter.

With a rough yank, I tear the seam of the tights, the sound of it ripping fanning the inferno in my veins. Quickly, I tear off her lacy panties before throwing them to the ground.

My mind mad with lust and love, I step back, needing to admire my masterpiece.

Taylor looks shell-shocked, her face still wet with tears, sweat, and cum, her luscious hair tangled and sticking to her pale skin like artwork. Her tits are trembling, shaking with each breath, the moonlight rippling across her body, highlighting the scratches, bite marks, the pinkened areas where I slapped her earlier. Her leotard hangs loosely at her sides, tattered and torn.

My minx's legs are parted, her tights still fully intact except for the large hole ripped between her legs, which bares her beautiful plump pussy lips slick with juices, the little barbell glinting under the moonlight.

She looks depraved, debauched, and one hundred fucking percent mine.

Fisting my cock, which is thickening and lengthening by the second, I watch her eyes pinned on my movements, her pupils large and dark, that damn tongue sneaking out again, like she's imagining my taste.

"Are you on the pill?" I ask, suddenly remembering I don't have a condom with me. "I don't have protection. I'm tested and clear."

Taylor startles as she registers my question, and tears her gaze away from my cock. She nods. "I've always been on it ever since that night."

"I'm going to fuck you raw. Is that okay?" My dick pulses in my hand, eager at the idea of entering her with nothing between us. "I've never been with anyone without protection before," I add, watching her soften.

She swallows and nods. "Yes."

A fresh wave of possessiveness slams through me and I prowl toward her, my lips twitching before my teeth make an appearance. The chains of control running my everyday life snap and fall to my feet with each step I take toward her, the woman who consumes me so completely, I don't know how to live life without her.

Bending down, I push her legs wider, so she's balanced precariously on the bar, then I swoop in and taste her juices.

Taylor screams, her body shaking as I hold her hips so she doesn't fall over. My tongue laves the piercing before swirling over her clit. I lick all of her sweet nectar, then thrust my tongue into her sopping entrance.

"Fuck!" She grabs my hair and pulls, the pain adding to the maddening lust taking over my body.

"My perfect, beautiful ballerina is now my dirty cum slut made for me, to be used by me, to be pleasured by me." I bite her clit quickly and she cries, her body thrashing, thumping against the mirror behind her, her orgasm taking her over. A fresh torrent of wetness comes flooding out, drenching my face and I lick at it, swallowing, going back for more, because I'm addicted to her.

I swipe my hand over my damp hair before I climb back up her body and bend over her. Lining my dripping cock between her legs, I swipe the tip around her piercing before dragging it over her clit, then notching the tip right at her entrance.

My muscles clench, poised to detonate and power into her, a desperation I've never felt before. My hand slides up her slick body to coil around her throat before I give it a soft squeeze.

"Color?" I rasp.

Her mouth parts, her gaze drunk with pleasure as she tips her face up and stares at me. "Green," she whispers.

Growling, I tighten my clasp around her neck and slam into her. I swallow her scream with another soulful kiss.

Fire spreads rapidly inside me, my nerve endings raw as I piston into her. Her walls clench my cock so tightly, I feel like I might come at any second. It has never been this intense before, being without barriers inside her, feeling every single sensation and reaction from her pulsing pussy. Relaxing my hand slightly, I let her heave in a few deep gulps of air as bolts of electricity batter my veins.

Dipping my forehead against hers, her fluttery breaths caress my face as the sounds of our bodies smacking against each other echo in the room.

I'm on fire, every part of me clamoring to be closer, to be part of this woman before me, so our atoms enmesh and we become one.

Taylor's legs shake against the bar, her stomach tensing, her arms spasming as she arches back. I chase her movement, kissing her one more time before tightening my hand around her throat, not enough to cut off her oxygen, but enough to make things a little bit more difficult for her.

She thrashes against me, her nails raking over my forearms.

"You can pinch me and I'll stop, because you have all the power," I whisper, watching her eyes widen. "*You* are in control."

Tears fall down her face as she shakes her head, her mouth dropping open, her eyes rolling back as her limbs stiffen.

"You listen to me, Taylor Peyton-Anderson." I grunt, fighting with everything in me to stave off the orgasm threatening to erupt at any second. "You're a fighter, a warrior, and the world bows down to you. I fucking kneel at your feet. You're always the most breathtakingly beautiful woman I've ever seen, and I love you so damn much."

I release her throat and pinch her clit before pulling her piercing to the point of pain and she shrieks, her lungs drawing in much needed air. A gush of liquid spurts out of her as her pussy clamps tightly around me before pulsing wildly and I fall into ecstasy with her.

Black dots blind my vision, and fire burns up my body. Unending streams of cum unload inside her, my mind flooded with so much pleasure, I don't even know how to form words. Instead, I kiss her. Again and again, telling her my love won't change, no matter what the world throws at us.

Telling her she isn't alone anymore.

My cock stills inside her, pulsing from aftershocks as her inner muscles flutter around me, I slowly come down from my high. Pressing a soft kiss on her swollen lips, I graze her wet cheeks with my fingers, wiping away her tears and my cum. Taylor is quivering against me, her body pliant, her face against my chest, her arms looping around my back and clasping me against her.

"I love you so much, Charles Vaughn." Her words come out in a soft whisper.

I still, my heart seizing. She has never told me the words in person, even though I've felt them from every look, touch, and smile from her.

Gently, I swipe her wet hair from her face and tilt it up, so I can stare at those beautiful gray eyes, the darkness nowhere to be seen.

"I love you, your thorns, your dark feathers. Don't you ever change."

She hiccups, her nostrils flaring.

"We will get through this together, no matter what happens," I promise.

She doles out a wobbly smile and nods. The fierce glint is back in her eyes. She pulls my head to her and puts her lips against my ear.

"Yes. We'll get those bastards together. They can't hurt me anymore."

CHAPTER 52

"And so that's it," I whisper, looking down at my lap. "Now you guys know everything."

I shiver in my seat inside the expansive two-story library at the Anderson Estate. The space is filled to the brim with books and is dimly lit by antique sconces and the late afternoon lights streaming in from the lattice windows. Normally, I'd be all over the books, but now, I just want to hide behind one of the many bookshelves.

Charles spent the entire night with me after I fell apart at the studio yesterday. The experience with him at the studio was transcendent and emotional. He balanced the line between sadism and care perfectly, like he knew exactly what I needed to forget about everything. The pain he doled out grounded me, but also ignited the lust inside me until I couldn't tell the two apart.

After he took me to his place, he ran me a bath, spoon-fed me dinner on his lap, even though I told him I was perfectly capable of eating by myself. He tended to my new needle marks, his eyes anguished when he saw the bruising forming on my skin because I wasn't as careful yesterday.

"If you feel lost again, text me, call me. I'll drop everything for you," he promised me as he pulled me flushed against his chest last night in bed. "I don't want you to hurt yourself anymore because every wound you inflict on yourself is a wound carved into me."

Other than a quick text to Grace telling her I was okay, I ignored all the texts and calls for the rest of the day. I had no mental bandwidth to deal with anything else. But I knew I needed to meet the girls and have this long overdue conversation.

The ball in my throat grows as the silence stretches on. I grip the hem of my gray sweater. "I'm sorry for ruining your baby shower, Belle."

My pulse is rickety in my ears and I close my eyes, bracing myself for the rejection I felt with Camden and Alexis.

But it never comes.

Instead, a warm weight flies into my arms, landing on my body in a big *oomph*.

"You're such an idiot!" Belle curls her arms around my neck—well, as much as she could since her belly is in the way. "I don't fucking care about the baby shower. I care about you! And I'm cursing, so you know I mean it!"

A twinge of amusement joins the crushing relief at her words. Belle is the prim and proper lady among us, and she rarely curses. More sniffling reaches my ears, and I'm almost suffocated by the hugs from Lana, Millie, Grace, and Olivia.

They are all still here.

My eyes mist with grateful tears and I can feel my tensed muscles relaxing as I hug them back, even though I normally don't like prolonged hugs.

"I failed you," Grace whispers. She throws her arms around my neck. "I'm so, so sorry, Tay."

She sobs into my shoulder. "I should've known. You changed so much then, but Mom and I just thought it was hormones and heartbreak since you and Camden broke up. I sh-should've known something was wrong. I'm a horrible sister!"

Tears overflow and streak down my face as I hug her back. "You couldn't have known. I didn't tell you anything. I...I didn't want you guys to look at me differently."

"Stop it!" she growls before pulling away and staring at me, her eyes fierce. "None of this is your fault. Why would we look at you differently? Those *monsters!*"

Lana crouches at my feet and grabs my hand. Her striking gray eyes, so similar to mine, flash in something akin to murder. "Do you know how strong you are, Tay? How amazing you are to have gone through what you went through and still be standing tall each day?"

"You must've felt so alone." Millie's lips wobble. "I'm so sorry for not being there for you."

I shake my head at the girls, all wearing identical expressions of guilt on their face. "It's not your fault. I chose not to tell. I was too traumatized by what happened with Camden and Alexis. I shouldn't have kept this from you."

Grace snarls, her hands balling into fists. "That fucking bastard Camden. I'm going to find him and slice him into pieces and feed him to the sharks."

Lana nods. "I don't condone violence, but in this case, I'm more than happy to make an exception. And that Alexis girl, she's no friend if she dumps you at your lowest, Tay. It's her fucking loss."

Olivia hands me a tissue and tips my face up to look at her. "I'm speaking to you as a psychiatrist and a friend right now. I'm not an expert on sexual assault or trauma, but everything you've described is textbook behavior of assault and rape victims. Blaming yourself, replaying the what-ifs, hurting yourself to control and deal with the emotions that arise."

She squeezes my hand and murmurs, "You really should talk to someone. The past has already happened and nothing can change that, but what's up here," she points to her temple, "your wound hasn't been tended to and we can work on that. Heal it, learn the skills to deal with the flashbacks, to process the trauma and move forward with life."

My vision blurs as heartache slices into my heart again. It's been almost eight years and yet, everything feels so fresh. I thought I already healed and moved on, then this happened.

Will I ever heal? Can I ever move past this?

Olivia seems to read the questions in my eyes and she pats my hand. "Yes, you *will* heal and move past this, Tay. I'm sorry you had a terrible experience with your school therapist, but there are other professionals out there. You're my friend, so I shouldn't be your doctor, but I can recommend you colleagues and people I trust. We will be with you every step of the way."

I nod and look at Grace, who's wiping her eyes, Lana, her arms crossed over her chest like she's thinking of ways to avenge me, Millie, her lips curving in a small, supportive smile, and Olivia, her warm brown eyes reassuring.

And Belle, darling of the ball, who is still sobbing on my shoulder, her hand cradling her belly.

"Shhh... Don't cry. I hear the baby in your belly will cry with you." I rub her back.

Belle jolts up and sniffles. "I love you, but you really suck at comforting people."

I snort and the girls laugh. I may have purposely riled her up last year to distract her when she was going through tough times with Maxwell.

It works every time.

I look at my girls. All of them are still here. No one looked at me differently.

Biting my lip, I nod, a spark of determination flaring in my gut. Does it matter how the world views me if the people closest to me, the people I love whose opinions are the only ones that matter, don't give a shit?

I will get through this. And this time, I won't be alone.

"So, what are you planning to do with the blackmail text and photo?" Lana asks a few minutes later.

"Charles and I are going to join forces."

Rolling out the tense muscles in my shoulders, I tell them about the plan Charles and I came up with in the bath last night.

I won't bend over and take it. I've never been that girl and I'll *never* be that girl.

If that asshole thinks a photo and a text can stop me, he has another thing coming.

CHAPTER 53

It's a Western standoff.

I can practically see the tumbleweed blowing across the floor from my spot at the table in a private room inside MacGregor's Whiskey Library. Taylor stiffens next to me as the silence stretches on and I reach over and clasp her hand in mine, giving it a gentle squeeze.

Maxwell sits on my other side, his brow cocked as he eyes the scene before us. He insisted on coming because Taylor is his little sister and he *needed* to be involved to make sure things were resolved appropriately. The entire family would've come if we let them.

The two men in front of me continue their silent stare down. Elias, twirling his famous lighter and chain in his hand, his green eyes not leaving the cold blue ones of Emerson sitting across from him. Emerson glowers at the mobster, and Elias returns the favor with a smirk.

"You guys done measuring dick size yet? Can we get down to business?" Maxwell mutters, finally fed up with the two idiots.

"Emerson, it's been a while." Elias tucks his lighter back in his navy suit jacket. He props his leg up on his knee, a picture of complete nonchalance.

"Not long enough," the private investigator mutters, and rakes his hand over his golden brown hair. "I should've known you were fucking with my investigation."

Elias chuckles as if he's really amused. "So tell me, how's your brother doing? Still pushing paperwork at the Fed?"

"That's Special Agent Clarke to you, dipshit, and he's doing great in the *organized crime* unit. Should I tell him to pay you a visit?"

I roll my eyes. "Can you guys work together or not? Or did we make a mistake by bringing you together? This was supposed to save time, not cause more issues."

Emerson blows out a breath before twirling his index finger to get us to carry on.

Turning to Taylor, I kiss her hand before asking, "Do you want me to tell them, or do you want to do it yourself?"

She stiffens and sits up straighter. A rush of pride streaks across my chest at the fire burning hot in her eyes. *My fierce minx.*

"I've thought through things and decided I don't want to cater to the blackmailer's demands," she says. She grips my hand tighter. "I don't want to live in fear anymore knowing these guys are out there and they could come haunt me at any time. I want to find the bastards."

Elias stares unwaveringly at her, a flash of admiration in his eyes. "What if more photos or videos come out? We'll try our damned best to stop them, but there are no guarantees we can get to them before they're uploaded online, or if the press might get a hold of them and release them without our permission."

"It'll be payday for the press—an Anderson in a compromising situation in photos—especially since this Anderson is dating the heir to the Vaughn fortune," Emerson adds, visibly disgruntled that he's agreeing with Elias.

"Charles and I will take care of the press if it comes to that," Maxwell murmurs. He sneaks a glance our way. "Money isn't an issue here, Tay. The press just wants their payday. They don't care who it's from."

Taylor swallows, her eyes widening at the implication of me and her brother throwing what will be an exorbitant amount of cash at this problem.

"Thank you," she whispers, her voice catching at the end.

"Anything for you, minx. Nothing is too expensive."

Maxwell's gaze softens. "Tay, I'm sure the girls already told you this, but it's not just you and Grace against the world now. I know you're very independent and," his nostrils flare and a muscle tics in his jaw, "I wish

Dad reunited with you guys sooner. But you are one of us. An attack on you is an attack on our family. We *always* have your back."

Taylor's breath hitches, and she smiles. I tug her to my side, my eyes catching Maxwell's, and I give him a curt nod. I'm so damn proud to call the Andersons my best friends. Unlike most other wealthy families who don't take too kindly to illegitimate children born outside of marriage, the Andersons have welcomed Grace and Taylor with open arms. I didn't realize the extent of their commitment and honor until now.

"I have to ask you a question, Taylor." Elias clasps his hands in front of him. "Which hotel were you at on the night of your assault?" He sneaks a knowing glance at me as blood rushes to my head. He knew I couldn't bring myself to ask her, and he couldn't do it before now because Taylor didn't know he was investigating.

My palms grow sweaty as my pulse roars in my ear. *Please don't say it. Please don't say it. Please—*

"Hotel Renegade."

My heart plummets to the floor. The only scenario I don't have a solution for. The suspicion I had in the back of my mind, not wanting to face it. My uncle and Taylor in the same place, at the same time. I remember her eyes were haunted with terror the day she met him at ABTC. Her memory of a blond man with light eyes.

"And the exact date of your assault?"

The oxygen is sucked out of the room.

"October 5th. I'll never forget that day."

October 5th. Hotel Renegade. The words ring in my ears as my blood turns to ice.

Elias's eyes sharply dart to me as comprehension dawns on his face.

Betrayal sears into me. The final puzzle pieces sliding into place. The truth I didn't want to face. The man who was everything to me when I was growing up, the man who loved me, who taught me how to be a man not like my father.

That man is a *monster*.

I'm going to kill him. My mind swirls with violence as I grip Taylor's hand tightly, and she draws in a pained breath. Once I get confirmation that he was the monster who brutalized Taylor, I'm going to kill him.

"Charles?" She frowns as I shake beside her, unable to form words.

Emerson furrows his brows, his gaze bouncing between the two of us. "You guys know something, don't you? You're not telling us everything."

"Charles?" Taylor shakes me.

I turn toward her, staring at her beautiful face once more, taking in her startling eyes, now glimmering with concern for me, her pale skin I know flushes pink at the slightest emotion, her perfect cupid's bow lips that are pillowy soft.

It may be the last time she looks at me this way. Guileless. In love.

Because what she just said changes everything. Why would she stay with me if the monster who attacked her all those years ago and is now blackmailing her is my uncle?

I heave in one deep breath. And another. Slowly, I reach out and skim my thumb over her cheek, savoring the silky softness and her whispery inhale reaching my ears.

Swallowing, I murmur, "There's something I need to tell you."

Taylor freezes.

I caress her cheek again. I love this woman so damn much. "I'm sorry for keeping this from you. I couldn't bring myself to ask you before because I couldn't bear it if...if my worst nightmare becomes a reality. But Elias took care of it for me."

My pulse pounds in my ears and a headache forms at the base of my neck. "You see, when I asked Elias to look into your past, the first thing I asked him to search for is Ian's whereabouts all those years ago."

Taylor gasps, her face slowly leaching of color. Her hands slide out of my grasp and she crosses them over her chest.

She's slipping away already.

Dread lines my stomach and I feel like I'm suffocating in front of everyone. "He found a photo on the dark web of Ian with a few men at Hotel Renegade on the same day you were assaulted."

"No, no, no," she mutters, shaking her head. "It can't be. I couldn't have been working with him this entire time and I... No, it can't be—"

"Didn't you tell me one of them had blond hair and light eyes? And how you reacted to him the day we met? You were frozen in fear, Tay. I thought you were insane that day, but now I know better." My voice is hoarse, pained as I reach for her, desperate to feel her warmth again.

She shrinks away, her eyes darting around the room, her skin as pale as a sheet of paper. "I was mistaken, right? I told myself I didn't remember because I was drugged. The monster smelled like peppermint. But Sir Ian smells like oranges. There's no way," she stands up, her chair topping over in a clang, "I couldn't have been working with my rapist *this entire time* and not know it. Tell me it isn't true!"

Pulling my hair, I stand up too and haul her to me, crushing her in my embrace because seeing her standing there, looking so damn fragile and shell-shocked, has me wanting to burn the world for her. "I don't know, but we'll find out for sure, minx. Maybe your body remembered something your mind couldn't. Fuck, we'll find out the truth. I'm so, so sorry. If it was Ian, fuck!"

"No, no, no," she mutters over and over.

Closing my eyes, I shush her trembling body as we reel with this devastating clue.

"I'll always stand on your side, Tay. No matter what," I promise. *If you'll still have me.* "I should've told you when I suspected. I'm so fucking sorry for withholding this info from you. Will you forgive me?"

Taylor stills and looks up at her, her eyes searching my face. "I-I don't know what to think right now and I *am* mad at you for not telling me." She swallows. "I can understand the reason. But I won't put up with this shit in the future, Charles Vaughn. You need to talk to me!"

I heave out a sigh of relief. *She isn't breaking up with me.* Pulling her back in my arms, I murmur, "I promise. No more secrets."

She harrumphs. "Bastard, you better. And this doesn't mean I forgive you yet."

"We need to confirm it's him, of course. It's tenuous right now, with him being your dance director and the ongoing blackmail. If it *is* him, he obviously suspects we're onto him," Emerson murmurs, as I usher Taylor back into her seat after Maxwell uprights the chair from the floor.

"Everything is circumstantial. There were tons of people at Hotel Renegade that night. It could all be coincidence." Elias takes a sip of the whiskey, his brow arched high.

I don't believe in coincidences either.

"From where I sit, there are two ways to proceed from here. If the bastard is Ian Vaughn, and Charles confronts him, he will deny it and walk free because we don't have a shred of evidence. The photos or videos may be leaked online and we'll need to deal with that fallout." Emerson taps his fingers on the table.

He continues, "If it isn't him, we'll have caused unnecessary friction in Charles's relationship with his uncle and Taylor's relationship with her boss. Whoever is behind this may still find out we haven't given up and may still leak the photos or videos. Without concrete evidence, we'll never be able to verify if it is him."

"Or I can just torture it out of him," Elias offers, flicking open his lighter. "I just need half an hour. That'd be an overestimate."

"No!" Taylor sits up, some color finally returning to her face. "I need to know for sure before we do anything. Ballet is my life and Sir Ian is Charles's uncle."

She looks at me, her face crumbling at the possibility her rapist may be her mentor and the man I've looked up to my entire life. "I won't blow everything up until I know for sure. And I need to know what happened. I need to know the truth."

Elias snaps shut his lighter and sets it on the table. "If you don't want the torture route, then there's only one way to find out. But it'll be hard for you, Taylor. Are you up for it?"

CHAPTER 54

THE BLINDING FLASHES OF the cameras singe my skin, each trigger click feeling like bullets aimed at me. I'm standing behind the podium at Kensington Hotel, about to deliver a quaking blow that'll shatter life as I know it into a million pieces. The press gathers in front of me, a swath of grays and blacks sitting in orderly rows, their hushed murmuring and quizzical whispers echoing in my ears.

Elias's words three days ago sweep into my mind.

"The best defense is offense sometimes," he murmured, his piercing eyes pinning me in place as I brushed past him on my way out of the MacGregor Whiskey Library after our meeting.

I stopped and turned toward him. "Do you think this will work, Elias?"

He cocked his head to the side, the long scar on his cheek facing me. "You're taking control of the narrative."

I nodded. "How do you know so much about PR strategy, Elias? I don't think this is part of the usual curriculum of a mobster, is it?"

Elias smirked, his eyes twinkling, and he replied, "Strategy is part of everything."

He sobered and something flashed in his gaze. "And I learned from the best."

Blowing out a deep breath, I repeat my affirmations inside my head.

I can do this. I'm a fighter, a warrior, a survivor. The past didn't kill me and this won't either.

I bite my lip and think back to the revelation of Ian and me being at the same place that night. Maybe my body wasn't overreacting when I first saw him at ABTC.

Maybe I should've trusted myself. Deep down, I must have known the truth all along.

My body didn't betray me this time.

The thought, as strange as it may be, gives me strength.

I look at the front row and find Charles's eyes first. He sits there, clad in a formfitting dark gray suit, his posture deceptively relaxed, but I know his tells now. The muscle pulsing on his forehead. The slight crinkle between his brows. The strain of his forced smile. I nod at him and he mouths, *"I love you. No matter what."*

A flash of warmth burrows inside me. I've forgiven him for not telling me his suspicion about Ian. There are bigger problems to worry about and I really understand where he's coming from. He didn't want to believe the man he loves can be a monster.

I hope that isn't the case and somehow, this is all a coincidence.

My heart skips a beat as I scan the rest of the row, noting Maxwell, Ethan, Grace, the rest of my siblings, and my girls, minus Olivia, who has to see patients today, but she gave me the sweetest pep talk this morning. Even Belle is there, trying to fend off photographers wanting to take a close-up of her belly. The first Anderson grandchild is a topic of interest for the gossip rags.

The whispers grow louder; the crowd waiting impatiently for me to begin. No doubt they're wondering why so many Andersons are all in one place on a normal June afternoon.

"I'm ready to begin," I announce into the microphone and wince as the shrill screeching of feedback reaches my ears. A staff member adjusts the mic and motions for me to continue.

"Thank you all for coming." I grip the podium tightly as I stare at Charles, pretending only he's in the room. "I'm sure you're curious why you're here today."

I clear my throat. "One in six American women has been a victim of attempted or completed rape in her lifetime. Most victims experience PTSD or other mental disorders after their assault. In fact, every sixty-eight seconds, an American is sexually assaulted."

When I prepared for this speech, I decided not to make it just about my experience, but also to shine a light on this horrible reality. Too many victims live in silence, in fear, in shame. I won't do it anymore. If I have a platform, I'm going to make some noise.

A hush falls over the crowd as the tension thickens.

Nausea swirls in my gut, my sweat drenching the simple blue dress I have on. I take a deep breath to fortify myself and push out the next words.

"I am one of those women. When I was sixteen, I was drugged and raped."

Chaos erupts in the room as cameras click, the flashes a constant barrage of light searing my eyes. I close them as reporters bark out questions, their voices merging into one big roar in my ears.

"Silence! Let her finish!" Charles's loud voice pierces through the ruckus, followed by shocked gasps and uneasy silence again.

Opening my eyes, I find his gaze again. His jaw is tense, his hands fisted on his lap. He gives me a subtle nod of encouragement.

Keeping my eyes on him, I recite the words carefully prepared for me by Lana.

"It occurred at a hotel lounge after a ballet event. A man slipped something into my drink and I was assaulted. It was the worst night of my life. The assailants are still out there because I was too scared to pursue the case after the police ignored me. I was young, a poor teenager from the Bronx."

Heaving out a ragged exhale, I drag my eyes away from Charles to the press, taking in the horrified expressions on their faces, the mad scribbling of pens on paper, sympathy shining from some of the female reporters' eyes.

"I was powerless and silenced, like too many before me and, unfortunately, too many after me. No one believed me and I was forced to deal with the aftermath by myself. To live in fear, to be afraid of men, afraid of the world, my innocence shattered."

A spark of energy gathers in my gut and travels to my chest. These are words I've yearned to say ever since that fateful night and never realized how much it pained me to keep them inside. The physical wounds healed and are now invisible, but the mental anguish—that has never left.

And I couldn't tell anyone.

"But I won't be silenced anymore. Because this was not my fault. Because I deserved to be heard, just like other women in my unfortunate position. Regardless of my background—whether I was a poor girl from the Bronx or a member of the Anderson family—I deserved to be believed and be treated with dignity instead of doubt and suspicion. I hope by standing up here today and sharing with you my story, I'll inspire other women to come forward. To tell their stories. To tell them they can stand back up again."

A few people applaud, but I hold up my hand. "I wish I could tell you I'm doing this because of sheer bravery, but that isn't the case. I'm being blackmailed by one of the assailants."

Horrified whispers echo in the room and I force myself to continue, "This individual has photos and possibly videos of me and is threatening to disclose what they did to me if I don't comply with their wishes, which is to stop investigating what happened to me."

Leaning forward, I stare into the cameras aimed at my face. "I'm here to give *that bastard* a message. I'm not backing down. I'm not giving up. And I *know* who you are. I am coming for you."

My heart sprints circles inside me, a tornado of conflicting emotions gathering strength. "And to all of you in this room, I plead that you will be an ally to the women in my position. If you receive photos or videos of me from this criminal, I implore you not to post them, to respect my privacy, and not to play into his hands. I also want to remind you I was underage when this happened, and all images are illegal, considered as child pornography, and should never see the light of day. Thank you all for being here today."

My legs tremble as I walk off the stage toward the staff hallway. I hear the reporters hurling questions at my back, and I quicken my steps, fleeing the chaos behind me. Turning back to look at the room before I step inside the hallway, I see Charles and my siblings joining forces with the security team, blocking the reporters and photographers from following me.

Five minutes later, I make my way down to the side exit of the hotel where a car should be waiting for me to take me back to Charles's place. We figured it'd be best if I headed over there first before the word got out and more press surrounded the building. I'm lightheaded and dizzy, a jitteriness filling my veins like I'm having a sugar crash. A wave of relief at everything being out there, on my terms, unmoors me, followed by the crushing grief and blistering anger.

Curiously, one emotion—the one that has haunted me the most in the past eight years—is missing.

Fear.

I've taken the power away from the bastard.

He can't hurt me anymore.

Exhilaration joins the turmoil and I want to cry, to laugh, to sink to my knees and to tell that little girl who believed in princes and true love that she'll be okay.

Because she's a survivor.

I push open the door, expecting to see the black town car at the curb, but am met with a swarm of reporters instead. They must've found out from their colleagues inside the room. Glancing around, I find the town car parked across the street next to more press vans, no doubt because my side of the curb is blocked by traffic cones. There's no way I can make it over there without getting mauled.

"Ms. Peyton-Anderson, do you remember what the attacker looked like?"

"Ms. Peyton-Anderson, aren't you afraid of retaliation?"

"How many men were there? Are they old, young? Are they from your ballet company?"

"Taylor, look over here! Taylor!"

Blinding white lights flash in my face, the crowd converging toward me as I hold out my hands.

"Back up!" I yell, but they don't listen. They all just want the story, want an exclusive—men and women alike, waving their phones and notepads in the air, their cameras and microphones thrusted at my face.

Panic jolts my insides, my breathing coming in quick pants.

Then I hear the deafening roar of a motorcycle smashing past traffic cones before skidding to a stop by the curb. Snapping my eyes up, I see a man wearing all black on the bike. He takes off his helmet and shakes out his dirty blond hair, his familiar sky-blue eyes pinned on me.

Liam Vaughn. Charles's brother.

He twists the throttle again, the engine revving loudly. "Taylor, hop on!"

Quickly, I scramble toward him, throw myself onto his bike, don the helmet he hands me, and we speed away, leaving the crowd of reporters in the dust.

CHAPTER 55

I throw open the door to my penthouse apartment and rush inside. The fuckers ambushed us at the press conference. Instead of disbanding in an orderly fashion, they wanted more from a woman who had given up too much of herself already.

The soulless leeches.

Then, a hotel staff member rushed up and told us they had Taylor surrounded by the side entrance so she couldn't even get into the car. My heart nearly stopped when the staff told me she hopped onto a motorcycle of a random man before taking off. She hasn't returned my calls or texts—her phone must still be on silent.

Please tell me she's safe.

My feet come to an abrupt stop when I dart into the living room, finding Taylor sitting there with no one other than my brother.

"Liam?" I whisper, my pulse still clamoring in my veins.

He stands and smooths his hands over his leather jacket. "Charles."

"H-How?"

"Liam saved me from the vultures outside the hotel," Taylor murmurs as she strides up to me.

Relieved, I wrap her in my arms and inhale her familiar sweet fragrance of vanilla and patchouli. "Thank God you're safe. I was so worried."

"It'll take more than a few aggressive paps to get me," she mumbles into my chest and I chuckle.

Liam shifts on his feet before walking toward the door.

"Liam!" I holler and he stops and turns toward me. "Thank you."

He smirks. "I was in the area when they aired the press conference live and I had to swing by to make sure you guys were all right. It was the least I could do."

He looks at Taylor, his gaze softening. "You were a badass. Both at the hospital and at the press conference. My brother is a lucky fucker."

Lifting his hand in a half wave, he slips out of the penthouse and quietly closes the door behind him.

Inhaling my first real breath since the press conference, I look at Taylor. "You did a great job at the press conference. I'm so fucking proud of you," I murmur. "Are you okay?"

"I will be," she murmurs. "Do you think it'll work?"

Lead lines my stomach as I think about the plan Elias devised. The man scares me sometimes. You never know what's going through his mind by looking at him.

"His plan has merit. Emerson and Elias are combing through the dark web to look for photographic and video evidence of that night, but the bastard probably deleted them off the servers now that he knows we are onto him. Absent hard evidence, we need a confession."

Taylor swallows. "Because I washed everything away back then. There's no more evidence." Anguish fills her eyes.

I grip her shoulders, a fierce need to reassure her pulsing through me. "You listen to me. You did nothing wrong back then. You were a young woman who was just brutalized in the cruelest way. I read some books on assault victims and what you did was normal. You can't blame yourself for this."

She heaves out a deep breath as she nods at my words. I continue, "But to convict the bastard, we need admissible evidence. The bastard is obviously spooked since he's threatening you. And now, with the press conference, you've essentially told him to shove his blackmail up his ass. You've also told him you know who he is. He will act. And we'll catch him when he does."

Dread slithers inside me, slowly coiling around my windpipe as I imagine who that culprit most likely is. "And if it's Ian...if it's him, I know my uncle, he wouldn't be able to sit still and do nothing."

The man practically raised me. The laughter and smiles he gave us with his tower of presents over the holidays when Grandma was busy and we were alone in the mansion. The trips to Coney Island. The way he flew back to help me with the scandal, no questions asked.

How could this man be the monster who raped Taylor?

Part of me wants to hold on to denial even as the pieces of the puzzle slide together, but another part of me wants to know the truth once and for all.

Dipping my forehead against hers, I ask the question that has kept me up at night. "If it is him, would you still stay with me? The nephew of your rapist?"

Would you leave me too? Like everyone else in my family?

Taylor grabs my face and presses her lips against my mouth, her kiss turning ardent and passionate by the second.

Groaning, I hoist her up and deepen the kiss, unmoored by the passion in her body as she grinds herself on me, her talented mouth sucking my tongue before she nibbles my lips, jawline, and rakes her teeth down my neck.

"Fuck," I mutter, walking us into my dark bedroom, not even bothering to turn on the light. A slither of daylight seeps through the gap of the drapes as Taylor climbs down my body and pushes me into the black leather armchair I have in the corner of the room. "Tay?"

She backs away, and in the dim light, I see her eyes glistening with moisture. What's this? Was that a goodbye kiss?

Desperation flits through me.

Gripping the leather, I move to stand, but she points to the chair again. Confusion swirls inside my chest and I sit back down, wondering what the minx is doing.

Without another word, she slithers out of her clothes, leaving her clad in only a black lacy bra and panties.

My heart racing inside me, I move my body to the music inside my mind. Running my hands down my neck to my chest, I cup my heavy tits before sliding my hands to my stomach, then my hips. Charles's mouth drops open, his eyes darkening by the second. His throat ripples as he swallows, his fingers digging into the leather arms of his chair like it's taking him every ounce of restraint to not bolt up and come after me.

I dip down and stick my ass out before arching up, throwing in a whip of my hair for good measure. I hear a sharp, tortured inhale, the sound a direct caress to my clit.

"I once told you I was never dancing for you," I whisper, surprised at how hoarse my voice sounds. Brushing the straps of my bra down my shoulders, I watch his nostrils flare before slipping my arms out of the straps.

I massage my breasts, which are growing tender by the second, the bra slipping down so that we're one inch away from a wardrobe malfunction.

Charles shifts in his seat, his legs parting—the perfect man-spreading—and I see his glorious cock tenting up his pants. Beads of sweat gather on his forehead as he digs his nails into the chair.

"But I want to dance for you now, because you're the man who has awakened my heart. I thought I was dead inside. I thought I was doomed to live a loveless and sexless life because I couldn't let anyone get close to me. But you came in and smashed my walls like a wrecking ball."

Unclasping my bra, I let it fall to the floor and turn around and bend low, my hands grazing the floor, giving him a generous view of my ass, before I snap back up in a fluid and sensual motion.

Closing my eyes, I pluck at my nipples, needing the pain he doled out to me at the studio, the sharp pressure I can't seem to give to myself. My moans echo in the dark room, joining his ragged breaths. My pussy is wet, the piercing rubbing against my panties as I gyrate my body to the invisible rhythm.

Pleasure flutters into my veins, curling around my core, but it isn't enough. I need more pain, more aggression, more sensations.

Whimpering, I slip out of my underwear, kicking it to the side. I hear his sharp inhale as I drop to my knees and spread my legs. Arching back, I support my body with one arm, my tits thrusted in the air as my other hand travels between my legs and flicks at the piercing, pulling at it, then swirling my clit. Sparks continue to climb at my core, but the pinnacle is just out of reach.

I circle my clit harder, my motions growing more desperate as I thrash on the floor before him, letting him see how uninhibited he makes me. He vanquishes the darkness in my mind. The sparks come and go, the pleasure sharpening before receding.

Desperation climbs inside me and my lustful mewls echo in the room.

"Are you done yet?" A low, raspy growl.

I shiver. His words are like an electric current zapping through my body.

Opening my eyes, my vision clouded by a sheen of lust, I freeze at what I see before me.

Charles's eyes flashing in the dim light, his shirt unbuttoned, abs rippling, his cock fisted in his hand as his lips twist up in a half-snarl.

He looks positively feral, the god of thunder here to dole out punishment. Nasty, filthy punishment.

I whimper, wetness flowing out of me, slicking my fingers.

"Are you done taunting me, you brat? Did you forget who owns you in the bedroom?" His hand moves faster, his grip tighter, white knuckled around the throbbing weapon between his legs.

My nostrils flare as my mouth waters at the sight of him becoming unhinged in my presence. Perhaps this side has been hidden inside me all along, this need to be forced into submission, to reclaim my control by driving him insane. Biting my lip, I continue gyrating to the rhythm of my fingers, his searing gaze the accelerant I need to fan the flames around my pussy.

I whimper, the sensations climbing, morphing into a beast of its own. I creep to the edge of the cliff, seconds away from detonating and falling into the pleasurable abyss. Rubbing harder, my eyes flutter closed, my breathing coming in quick pants.

"Stop!" he barks, his voice sharp as a whip, and I flinch.

He crooks his finger toward him and points to his lap. "You don't get to come until I say you do. Get up here."

My blood vibrates at the violence in his voice, the aggression leashed down in the tense set of his jaw, and I quickly scramble up from the floor and climb onto his lap.

He flips me over in one fluid motion, so I'm lying ass up on his lap, my face by the leather arm of his armchair, my legs dangling midair.

"Charles!" I screech.

"What did you call me?"

My core pulses. "S-Sir." He rubs his palm over my ass, the sensations driving me wild.

Smack! Smack! Smack!

I scream as he rains hard slaps on my ass, one after another, in quick succession. My lungs seize and every atom inside me protests before the pain quickly blossoms into liquid heat, coalescing between my legs.

My mind mad with pleasure, I submit to him, to the man who has revived my heart and given me back ownership of physical pleasure. The man who wears his heart in his eyes even if the world doesn't see it.

The man who thinks I'll leave him if his uncle turns out to be the monster in my dreams. How could he think that? The sins of someone else aren't his sins.

Charles bends down and licks the whorl of my ear. "Give me a color."

I moan and jut my ass out, needing more of everything he's willing to give me. "Green."

His breathing is heavy as he rubs the pain away from my backside, then his finger travels between my legs, playing with the wetness there.

"Your body is mine," he rasps, his words thick with promise. "Your pain is mine, your orgasms are mine, and your enemies are mine."

He thrusts two fingers inside me and I thrash in his embrace, the sudden intrusion, followed by the hard pinches on my clit, a swift kick shoving me off the cliff as the world explodes around me. Stars appear in my vision as he continues his assault—the perfect blend of pleasure and pain.

Charles quickly gets up and tosses me back down on the armchair, his hands deftly arranging me into a position of his own liking—one of my legs is trembling on the seat while the other is perched across the armrest. I grip onto the headrest of the chair for dear life as my body quakes from the mind-blowing orgasm he just doled out.

I hear clothes rustling, the clicking of a belt buckle, a zipper being yanked down, a few buttons pinging on the floor. But these noises no longer cause a frisson of alarm because I know I'm safe. It's Charles, the man I love, the Dom I'm submitting to, behind me.

He'll take care of me. I'm always safe with him.

Then I feel his hot body plastered against my back, his long dick digging into my ass cheeks. He fists my hair and pulls my head back before he slams his mouth on mine, swallowing my gasp and moan.

"You're mine," he rasps when he breaks the kiss, "and I'm yours. You're a warrior. Even when we're in a scene, you're the fucking goddess and I'm the commoner. Don't you forget that, Taylor Peyton-Anderson. Don't you fucking forget that."

A rush of warmth spears into my heart as his fingers slip between my legs again, but this time, he swipes past my pussy, causing me to tremble before him. Then I feel a slight intrusion in my asshole.

"Has anyone taken you here?" He grunts.

I shake my head, my legs spreading, quaking at the idea of sharing another first with him.

"Someday, I'll fuck you here, minx." He dips the tip of his thumb in and the unfamiliar sensation adds to the inferno building inside me.

"Tell me you're mine." His other hand tightens around my hair.

My eyes flutter shut at the foreign sensations in my ass. *More. More. More.*

The thumb disappears and I whine before—

Smack. Smack. Smack.

I shriek from the sudden onslaught of pain as he slaps me.

"Answer me, minx." He rubs away the blistering ache and perches his thumb back against my asshole.

Gyrating my hips against him, I whimper, "Y-Yes, I am yours, and you're fucking mine, Charles Vaughn."

A guttural growl tears out of him and suddenly, he slips his thumb back into my ass as he spears his cock inside me at the same time. I scream, my voice echoing in the room.

"Color?" he rasps, his voice pained.

"Fucking green."

Before the words are fully out of my mouth, he unleashes a punishing rhythm, the sounds of skin against skin lurid, his thumb moving in the rhythm of his pistoning.

I feel full. So full. He drops my hair and pushes his body against me so the front of me is plastered against the chair. This gets him deeper, his cock hitting a sensitive spot inside me, making me see stars. The beginnings of another orgasm gather deep inside me—it's different this time—everything is more intense. Charles thrusts his free fingers inside my mouth and I automatically suck them in, my tongue swirling around them, biting the digits all the while my body submits to his thumb battering my asshole and his cock hammering inside me in a maddening rhythm.

"Look at you, all your holes stuffed by me, your hot body thrashing for me. Need to come, minx? Does this cunt need to come hard around my cock?"

My muscles tense, my mind blanking as a torrent of pleasure so sharp, so unlike anything I've ever experienced overtakes my body—the tsunami obliterating all my senses as I scream and shatter in his arms. My cum gushes out of me and I try to stop, but it's uncontrollable.

"Fuck yes!" He grunts, his hammering relentless. "You're so fucking sexy. I'm obsessed with you." With a few more deep thrusts, he lets out a raw, guttural growl, and unleashes ropes of cum inside me, the heat sending me off into another tailspin.

I don't know how many minutes pass by before my mind finally flickers on, my senses coming back online. The first thing I notice is the pulsing deep in my core, the final twitches and aftershocks. Then, it's his body heat and the dampness of his sweat dripping onto my back. Next are the quick puffs of air hitting my face from his ragged breathing. Finally, it's the soul-crushing warmth sweeping into my heart, a bright light illuminating all the dark crevices I've hidden inside me.

"I love you, Charles. No matter what happens with the investigation. If it turns out to be Ian, that'll never change the way I feel about you," I whisper.

He answers by sealing his lips on mine.

CHAPTER 56

"I'M ONLY A PHONE call away. Call me if anything comes up," Charles murmurs before giving me a quick kiss as the town car glides to a stop in front of ABTC. "Anthony stays with you at all times, okay?"

He motions to the tall bodyguard getting out from the front and opening my door. I don't like the idea of having a hulking man follow me everywhere, but I know it's wise and to refuse him would be the peak of stupidity.

I roll my eyes even as nervousness tremors inside me. This is the last full cast rehearsal of *Swan Lake* before our final encore performance at the Met Opera next week. It's also the first time I'll see Sir Ian after the press conference.

Swallowing the ball stuck in my throat, I strain a smile. "See my nose piercing?" I point to the skull stud I put on this morning. "I'm a fucking badass—they won't be able to hurt me anymore." I flip him a middle finger.

Charles throws his head back in laughter and unbuttons his suit jacket—today, it's a delicious navy three-piece that I want to rip off him later tonight. "You used to drive me nuts—the elegant ballerina with a bratty attitude and potty mouth, but God, I love it now. So fucking much." He slides over and grabs my nape, pulling me down before he leans in and kisses the daylights out of me.

My head woozy, my skin flushed, I pull back and grin. "You were just blind before, but now I'm glad your vision has been restored."

He smiles at me—the same charming smile I used to hate because it was fake, but now I can tell it's genuine. But then I notice his hand gripping the door handle tightly, his knuckles white with tension.

Gently, I unclench his hand before rubbing the coiled muscles, my mood sobering. "I doubt he'll be stupid enough to make a move right after the press conference. I know I won't. That's when everyone's guard is up. Don't worry about me. Plus, I have Anthony with me."

Charles nods and I give him a wink, faking confidence I don't quite feel as I walk into ABTC. When I step into the lobby, Lisa greets me with a hug before she nervously eyes the brooding man behind me.

I grimace. "Sorry, this is Anthony. He'll be my shadow for now."

"Of course," she replies before pulling me into a quiet corner, away from the other dancers rushing to the locker room or to run last-minute errands before the rehearsal.

Lisa's lips wobble and she pulls me in for another hug—this one so tight I almost couldn't breathe. I pat her back, trying to get her to ease up.

"S-Sorry! I'm just so overwhelmed. I saw your press conference, and I had no idea that happened to you! I couldn't go to Hotel Renegade that night and thought it was odd how sick you were afterward when you looked fine before. And then Alexis quit and you and Camden broke up, and I just didn't think those events were connected. I'm so sorry for not being there for you, Tay." Tears shine in her eyes as she grips my arms.

My chest pangs, a dull ache resurfacing. That night will forever be a part of my past, but at least now I don't have to hide anymore. I don't need to pretend everything is fine because what happened to me *wasn't* fine. And somehow, that makes it easier for me to breathe.

"It's okay, Lisa. I didn't let you in. Don't blame yourself. You did nothing wrong. I'm going to move on...finally."

She lets out a shuddering exhale as Dev appears by our side, his eyes shining with concern too. Wordlessly, he gives my shoulder a soft squeeze. "You're one tough cookie, and we're all here for you, Tay," he murmurs.

My lips curve up into a bittersweet smile as I pat his hand in acknowledgment. I nod toward the rehearsal room. "Come on, let's get going. Don't want to be late."

Anthony is stationed at the corner of the rehearsal studio, his eyes sharp and roving over all of us as the day drags on. I sense the other dancers' uneasiness—a tall stranger with an earpiece and a holster will definitely put you on edge. Guilt seeps into me as I force out a grin during a water break.

This is all fucked up, and it's because of me.

No, it's because of the asshole who put you in this position.

"You're brave," a soft voice says and I turn around, finding Maddy standing next to me, her brown hair piled on top of her head as she eyes the other dancers.

"It's borne of necessity," I reply. Motioning to Ainsley, who's chatting with the other trainees, I ask, "Are you guys okay now?"

Maddy stills, her eyes downcast. "I hope so. She doesn't agree with some things I did. She's disappointed."

Something in her tone gives me pause, and I turn toward her and look her in the eye. "Maddy, did something happen to you? I know I asked you the same question in France and you said everything was fine, but my gut tells me something is going on. You know you can talk to me, right? I know I'm not the world's most approachable person, but," I clear the lump in my throat, "you guys are like my little sisters. I don't want to see you get hurt."

Her eyes shine with wetness, and she wipes a stray tear away from her cheek. "It's too late for that, Tay. And no one will believe me, anyway." Her gaze flickers to me and she gives me a heartbreaking smile. "Maybe someday, I'll be as brave as you, but I don't think that day is today." She rises on her tiptoes and pulls me in for a light hug. "Thanks, Tay. You're the best mentor a girl could have."

Maddy walks away, her shoulders slumped, and the unease I felt when I saw the photo on my phone flares back up.

"Back to your positions. Starting at Act III." Sir Ian claps his hands. "Taylor, I need you to work on how you come down from the turns. I think you're overcompensating."

I startle, snapping my attention back to the familiar gaze of Sir Ian, my pulse quickening as I look at him for the thousandth time today, trying to identify new clues, or perhaps even new memory fragments—anything to tell me if this man in front of me is the monster from my nightmares.

Fly Harriet.

I shudder, and he cocks his head at me, his foot tapping on the ground. He points to his watch. "We don't have all day, Taylor."

"Yes, sir." Quickly, I scramble to my spot and get into position as the music streams in from the speakers.

Sir Ian frowns as he stares at me, his gaze giving nothing away. His finger is twirling the ruby pen he always uses. I'm thrown back to the first day when I met him, when I had a full-blown panic attack and flashback in his presence, when every atom in my body wants to flee from this seemingly harmless man.

The furrow between his brows deepens and I force myself to look away, because I'm supposed to act normal and be the bait. I'm tempting the monster to seek me out this time so I can gut him and chop off his head. Shaking out my tense shoulders, I throw myself into the dance, once again immersing my mind and body into the role of Odile, the black swan.

The rest of practice goes by uneventfully, all of us hitting our positions adequately and by the end of the rehearsal, there's a new-found excitement in the group as we look forward to finishing the encore performance and getting a break before preparing for the next show.

Chugging down a few sips of cold water from my bottle, I nod at Anthony just as his phone rings. I mouth to him I'm going to the re-stroom along with the rest of the girls and he eyes the group—safety in numbers—and nods before answering the call.

Lisa prattles on about her weekend plans as she hooks her arm with mine. As we make a turn after leaving the rehearsal studio, suddenly someone taps me on my shoulder.

Turning around, I see Ainsley chewing on her lip. A slither of dread coils around my chest as I take in her worried expression. I motion to Lisa and the others to continue without me.

"What's going on, Ainsley? Something is up, so don't bother bullshitting me anymore. Maddy is telling me cryptic things and you guys are behaving strangely."

Ainsley sighs and looks around the crowded hallway. She pulls me to the side and whispers, "Maddy will kill me if she finds out I told you anything. But I can't stand by and do nothing anymore. It isn't right. I'm not being a good friend if I know something awful is happening and I'm not saying anything."

Alarm rears through me and I lean in. "What the hell is going on?"

She bites her lip and looks behind me again before leaning in and whispering, "What you said at the press conference, I think the same happened to her."

My heart stops as her words echo in my ears. "What?" Of all the scenarios, this one didn't occur to me.

"The new clothes, the handbags, the money?" Ainsley shakes her head, her face flushed. "I think it's hush money. I saw her one day with an older guy—the businessman type. Her clothes were a mess, and she was crying. Then next week, all these gifts started appearing."

A growl slips from my mouth. Cracking my neck, I hear the joints snap. "That fucking bastard. Where's Maddy?"

"I saw her heading toward the VIP lounge." I take a step toward that direction and Ainsley grabs my arm, her voice in a panic. "Please! Don't tell her I told you. She'd kill me, but I just can't stand seeing this happen to her and doing nothing about it. I can't leave her with the scumbag!"

Memories flood my mind. Alexis and the horror in her eyes when she found me naked in the hotel. The terse silence in the car when she dropped me off at my apartment when I was bleeding between my legs and every part of my body hurt. When she told me she was quitting ballet.

The crippling betrayal I felt. The shame. The devastating loss.

Looking at Ainsley, I murmur, "You're doing the right thing. You're a great friend, Ainsley. Don't abandon her. She needs you."

Don't do what Alexis did to me.

Ainsley nods, her lips curving in a wobbly smile, and I quickly make my way to the second floor, my mind swirling with unwanted memories of how I felt all those years ago.

The loneliness, the guilt, the anger, the self-loathing. No one fought for me back then, not even the cops or the therapist, and I couldn't open myself up to trust anyone else.

I can't let this happen to Maddy. Maybe it's foolish to take on her problems when I'm still dealing with mine.

But I can't stand here and do nothing.

Taking a deep breath, I open the door to the VIP lounge and step inside, finding the space dark, the drapes drawn close.

"Maddy?"

I hear sniffling emanating from the back room.

Concern grips my heart in a vice and I make my way over there, to the girl who is feeling so alone right now, who probably thinks her world has ended and there's no hope for her in the future.

"Maddy? Why are you crying?"

I find her crouching on the floor, sobs racking her body. I shake her and she flinches, her eyes widening in terror as they settle on me. "Tay? W-Why are you here? You need to go now. Please. You can't let him see you talking to me. Go!" She gets up and pushes me toward the door.

What?

I push back. Something is horribly wrong. "No, I'm not leaving here until you tell me what's going—"

Click.

My heart stalls as the hairs on my neck stick up. Maddy's eyes widen with fear as she stares at something behind me.

"Why did you have to butt in where you're not wanted, Ms. Peyton-Anderson?"

<h1 style="text-align:center">CHAPTER 57</h1>

"THANK YOU FOR THE opportunity and I hope to hear from you soon," the man says before following my lead and stands before shaking my outreached hand.

"Thanks for coming in. We'll be in touch." I sit back down, watching the last candidate for the open CFO position leave my office.

It's been a year and a half of searching for the right candidate, and this one seems promising—sharp, a strong resume working for our competitors, and most importantly, a keen sense of integrity. He left his prior job because he unearthed a fraud that was ignored by the CEO and the Board.

Pinching the bridge of my nose, I close my eyes, exhaustion weighing on my eyelids. It's been a day of interviews and nonstop meetings, not to mention my old friends, the paparazzi hanging out outside the building, wanting to get a remark from me about Taylor's press conference.

The spineless idiots. But at least this time, the focus seems to be about Taylor's bravery in sharing her experience with the world and how she's standing up against her blackmailers. More stories have come out from countless women in all walks of life. Taylor told me that was the silver lining she'd hoped to see—to let others just like her feel less alone.

My heart doubles in size as I think about my minx, my feral little kitten—the silent strength, the don't fuck with me attitude, the gumption to face her emotions head on.

I honestly don't think I'll ever be deserving of her.

I wonder how she's doing in rehearsal today.

A pinch of worry sifts through me as I swipe open my cell phone, not seeing any calls and texts from her. But I remind myself she's a top ballerina rehearsing for a performance that'll determine if she gets to sit for a promotion evaluation. She's no doubt busy as hell.

My phone buzzes, and I quickly answer it.

"Anthony? Is everything okay?"

"Sir, Taylor told me she was going to the ladies' room, but when she didn't come out for a long time, I asked a dancer to check inside and she wasn't there. I'm searching the rest of the rooms as we speak."

"Why the hell weren't you stationed outside?" I roar, standing up and texting my driver to bring the car over.

"I stepped away for an urgent call and immediately went to the restrooms afterward. There were other people with her, so I—"

"Keep searching and keep me posted!" I rush out of the office, past my bewildered assistant and colleagues, who probably think I've lost my mind.

Alarm bells ring in my gut. This could very well be nothing, but my sixth sense tells me something is horribly wrong.

I get into the car and instruct the driver to get us to ABTC as fast as humanly possible. I try Taylor's phone.

Voicemail.

I try three more times, all the same results.

Then I punch in a few numbers and wait for him to answer.

"*Fy machgen*, finally have time for your uncle?" Ian chuckles.

"Have you seen Taylor?" Unease knots my insides. I close my eyes and listen to the sounds in Ian's background—any strange breathing or noises, any sign that something is wrong.

"She was at practice just now. I haven't seen her. Is this why you're calling me? To find your girlfriend? Here I am thinking you're finally missing your uncle."

My nostrils flare. Either he's innocent or he's a fucking good liar and with Ian Vaughn it's fifty-fifty.

Fuck, I wish we could unearth the bastard sooner than later because the little boy inside me really wishes for a miracle that the culprit isn't the man I've looked up to my entire life.

"I see. We should meet up for a drink sometime. I've been MIA." I keep my voice light, not wanting to rouse suspicion. If no one takes the bait we left at the press conference, I'm going to poke around Ian—ask him questions about Hotel Renegade to see if I can make heads or tails of his reactions.

"I'd like that. Glad to see you still remember me outside of your *cariad bach*." I hear commotion in the background and suddenly, he murmurs, "I have to go, son. Talk soon."

An unsettling silence fills the car as something niggles in the back of my mind. A phantom itch—like it's trying to tell me I know more than I think I do.

Closing my eyes, I sift through my memories—the damning photo of Uncle Ian at the hotel lounge when he was supposed to be across the world, the violent reaction Taylor had when she first met him, every excruciating detail of her painful recollection of that night, the photo on her phone from an unknown number in Europe.

The itch grows stronger. There's something here. What am I not seeing? Elias's investigation into Ian. His connection to The Association. The invitation I received in Paris.

I tap my foot on the floor as the car coasts to a stop. A suffocating heat wraps around my lungs, and I tug my tie loose from my neck as I exit the car.

What am I missing?

I toss the facts around in my head again as I climb up the steps and enter the building, looking for Anthony.

Fly Harriet.

I freeze, the door slamming shut behind me in a *bang*.

It's odd how she heard that, but she's sure the monster whispered that phrase to her.

Harriet.

Fly Harriet.

"Glad to see you still remember me outside of your cariad bach." Ian's words from the phone call echo in my ears.

Cariad. Welsh term for sweetheart or darling. My Welsh is rusty but I'm pretty damn sure an iteration of "my darling" is *"Fy Nghariad,"* with the "Fy" and "Ng" sounding almost silent and nasally, leaving *"Hariad."*

Fly Harriet.

Fy Nghariad. My Darling.

She's been hearing Welsh all along.

Fear slams inside me as I hurry up the staircase, needing to find Ian and demand an answer from him. Welsh isn't a commonly spoken language in the city. This is the piece connecting them together in one room, and I'll be damned if she works under him a second longer. I flick on the record function on my phone and search for the bastard.

Fury boils my blood as I fly to his office and throw open the door, but he isn't inside.

Motherfucker, where are you?

Gritting my teeth, I dash down the hallway, spotting Anthony coming out of a room and opening the door of another. I nearly plow into Ainsley, who looks equally bewildered and frantic.

"Ch-Charles! You *have* to help!" Ainsley tugs on my sleeve, her panicked voice causing me to freeze in my steps.

"Where's Taylor or Sir Ian?" I growl, not caring I'm probably scaring the shit out of her.

Ainsley points her finger toward a room. "Sh-She was checking on Maddy for me in the VIP lounge." I wave Anthony over and we run toward the VIP lounge, my breathing quickening. Ainsley calls after me, "I hear people arguing inside and it's locked!"

Bang!

Shrill screams pierce the air.

I flinch at the booming sound of the gunshot emanating from the room. My heart slams against my rib cage as bone-crushing fear threatens to decimate me on the spot.

No. Taylor. God no.

My chest tightens, icy adrenaline flooding my veins and I yank the doorknob, finding it locked as Ainsley said. I hurtle my side against the door and it barely budges.

More shrieks and cries come from the room, followed by muffled whispers.

Desperation carves inside me, the heavy weight of dread smothering my lungs. I need to get inside. My spinning mind is filled with only one thought—Taylor.

Anthony motions at me to kick the door at the hinges with him and in a synchronized effort, we deliver sharp kicks, and the door finally gives under our assault.

We burst in, and a shocked gasp traps itself in my throat when I see Ian holding a gun, pointed to a man on the ground, the distinct burning smell of a gunshot in the air. Taylor's face is leached of color, her arms stretched outward as she shields a quivering Maddy behind her.

She glances at me, her eyes widening in terror. My pulse riots inside me in fear and sweat beads on the back of my neck.

"Ian, put the fucking gun down," I growl.

CHAPTER 58

My heart seizes, my breath trapped in my lungs as I watch the man I love step into the room, his face twisted in fury.

"Ian, put the fucking gun down." His lethal rasp promises nothing but violence if Ian disobeys.

Charles stalks toward us, a vein bulging on his forehead, his face flushed and teeth bared.

Sir Ian stares at me and swallows, a muscle twitching in his jaw. He slowly raises his hands and gently sets the gun on the ground. Charles hurries over and kicks it away before grabbing his uncle by the collar. Out of the corner of my eye, I see Anthony charging forward to pick up the weapon, and I breathe a sigh of relief.

Maddy shakes behind me. I spin around and pull her into my embrace. "It's over, Maddy. It's over. He's dead."

My arms shake as I stare at the tall man lying at my feet, blood pooling onto the carpet from the bullet wound on the back of his head, his blank eyes staring at the ceiling.

Laurent Archambeau.

The Paris police commissioner, the angry man I heard in the dark room at Palais Garnier, before Charles pulled me into the hidden alcove.

One second he was threatening to kill me for continuing my investigation, and the next second, Sir Ian stepped into the room and shot him in the head, a cold-blooded lethality in his gaze I'd never seen before.

Tears stream down Maddy's face as she sobs, seemingly unable to speak. Then she shakes her head vigorously. "N-No," she whispers, "It's n-not over, no, no, no—"

"It was you, wasn't it?" Charles slams his uncle on the wall and we flinch as the windows shake. "You're a fucking monster."

Sir Ian stays silent, his lips twitching as he stares at his nephew.

"Tell me!" Charles roars.

What? I stare at him and at Archambeau, then at Maddy quivering in my arms. *What's going—*

My breath hitches. A chilly realization. The sensations of ants crawling on my skin are back and more vicious than ever before. Shaking my head, disoriented, I sway on my feet before backing up, away from the uncle and nephew glaring at each other, away from the dead man a few feet in front of us, away from Maddy, the dancer who reminds me so much of my younger self, who is now curled up into a ball on the ground, crying her heart out.

My back slams against the wall, my fingers stiff and icy. I watch the man I love confront the dance director I've worked under for the better part of the year. My body blares war sirens, begging me to listen to it this time.

Because Sir Ian is the monster in my memories.

"When did you figure it out?" Sir Ian murmurs, his voice resigned.

"You fucking bastard!" Charles slams a fist across his uncle's face and Maddy shrieks. "You thought we wouldn't find out, did you? Because she was drugged? Because she couldn't remember your face? You put on that innocent front, lulling us into believing it was all in her head when you were the one playing games all along."

He hits him again, and I close my eyes. My body can't stop shaking. I feel sick. I want to hurl my lunch on the floor. Flashes of that night morph into Ian's gentle voice as he guides me into various ballet positions this past year. Then his words of advice on how to improve my Odette echo in my mind. He got me to put my guard down. He got me to believe him.

"'Fly Harriet.' She told me she remembered that phrase from that night and it just occurred to me what she was hearing. You were fucking calling her 'my darling' in Welsh, weren't you? *Fy Nghariad.* You were calling her 'my darling' while you were raping her, you sick fuck!"

Charles hits his uncle across the jaw again and blood spews out from Ian's lips.

My darling. The words I heard, the sounds, the sensations from that night slam into me, and I dry heave on the floor, my body breaking out in a cold sweat.

"I regret e-everything," Ian rasps. "I was so desperate to get the director position in Paris, and I knew the academy was going to choose someone else. When The Association came to me, telling me they could solve my problem, I was blinded by ambition."

He grabs Charles's lapels. "They told me I had to commit a crime. But when I found out they wanted me to assault a woman, I wanted to back out. By then, it was too late. I knew too much. It was to be killed or to do as I was told."

Sir Ian looks at me, regret and guilt flashing in his eyes. The ruby on top of his pen tucked in his jacket pocket glimmers under the dim light. Another memory barrels into my mind. *The flash of red I keep remembering. It was his pen. Oh fuck, oh fuck, oh fuck.* I hyperventilate, my legs giving out from under me, and I slide down the wall onto the floor. My mind is scrambled, desperate to hold on to the scraps of memory I remember.

"Peppermint...but you smell like oranges," I whisper.

"You changed your fucking scent, didn't you? Because she called you out on it when she met you at ABTC!" Charles seethes, a muscle in his jaw twitching.

Ian grimaces and nods. I close my eyes, unable to look at him anymore.

He rasps, "I-I'm sorry, Taylor. One of them saw you at the bar, then had his associates run a quick background check. You were the ideal target—poor, no ties to anyone important in society. No one would believe you even if you went to the police or, worst case, went missing.

They would see you as a run-of-the-mill teenager who ended up making wrong choices in life."

"No. No. No." I feel seasick—tossed around by the high waves in the ocean.

"He drugged you and brought you to the back. There were other members there—it was an initiation of sorts. If I wouldn't do it, someone else would. And these bastards were brutal—their violence feeding off each other. What they did to some women, I couldn't even describe."

More unwanted memories force themselves into my mind. The men in suits grunting. My terror. But I hear more now. The screams. The horrifying screams of other women in the same room.

Ian pleads, "If I did it, I thought I could at least be gentler, to make you feel good. I made sure it was only me that night. No one else, even though those psychos wanted a piece of you. You were so beautiful, lying there. I'm a sick fuck. I'm so sorry, Taylor."

Nausea sloshes in my stomach. One monster. Only him that night. The thought doesn't comfort me. I want to claw my skin off and spend an eternity in the shower. An anguished cry rips from Charles's mouth, and I open my eyes just as he socks his uncle in the stomach.

Ian chokes, coughing up more blood, but he keeps his eyes on me. "Archambeau is one of their enforcers. They've been forcing me to identify girls no one would miss to 'participate' in the future initiation rituals—which could be any sadistic crime they wanted us to commit. Murder. Assault. Anything's on the table."

"You gave them Maddy," I whisper, my heart hollow. Maddy sobs louder, her cries reminding me so much of myself all those years ago, the last time I truly cried that night in the shower, feeling disgusted with myself.

"I tried to make things right—take care of her finances, but then Archambeau caught wind of it. He thought I was becoming a liability. He found out you and Charles were poking around the past and he needed to take action."

More clues pieced together—seemingly random events were all part of a bigger scheme. "Paris, at the gala...the other man in the room with Archambeau, that was you, wasn't it?" I don't even need him to answer because it made sense. The snippets of conversation I heard. The fluency in French—Sir Ian lived in Paris for a decade. Of course he'd be fluent.

Ian coughs, his face leached of color. "Why couldn't you guys leave it alone? After the press conference, he flew in because you two were officially liabilities to The Association, and no one messed with them and lived to tell the tale. He told Maddy and I to keep our mouths shut. But you had to go *public* and draw attention to them. They were going to make you two 'disappear.'"

Sir Ian's eyes are wild, and he glares at us. "I-I tried making it up to you when I saw you again. I knew you wanted Odette, but you weren't there yet. I coached you, didn't I? I gave you opportunities this past year that you wouldn't have gotten otherwise."

My heart plummets to the floor as his words sink in. A different betrayal carves through my bloody chest. All this time, I thought I had got to where I was because I deserved it. Staring at him, my words come out wooden, devoid of emotions. "It was you, wasn't it? Bethany's shoes. Her accident. You did it."

Everything is a lie.

Charles growls, his face mottled as he hoists Ian back up to his feet and pins him against the wall, his arm crushing against Ian's windpipe.

"Why?" Charles rasp. "You fucking bastard! And to think you were a champion of assault victims. What was that, guilt? You fucking hypocrite, claiming to be an ally when you were part of the problem, when you continued to feed The Association more unsuspecting women. I'm *disgusted!*"

He delivers another gut punch and Ian collapses into himself, clutching his stomach. "Why? You're a Vaughn. You could have any-thing you want. Why would you do this? Be involved with The Asso-ciation? Grandma warned us about it. *Why?*"

Baring his teeth, Ian's eyes flash with anger. He staggers back up and plows into Charles, the two men toppling to the ground. "She gave *everything* to you! She found out about my penchant for my students and cut me out of her will."

Anthony races forward, but Charles wheezes. "Stop. I got this. I'm going to kill this motherfucker myself." A muscle tics in Anthony's jaw, but he steps back, his hand curled around his gun.

Ian throws out a punch, hitting Charles on the chest, but Charles flips him over and delivers several quick jabs.

Spittle flies out of Ian's mouth. "Your father didn't give a shit about anything or anyone, including me, so I couldn't go to him for help! I would've ended up with nothing. The Parisian position would've solidified my place in ballet history and I would be set for life. You wouldn't understand. You're the golden prince of the fucking family. You—"

"You brutalized *her*!" A chill befalls Charles's features as he raises his swollen fist again. He delivers a loud blow across his uncle's face.

Smack. Ian slides to the ground, blood seeping out of his nose, his eyes rolling back.

"You made her life a living nightmare!"

Smack.

"You hurt the woman I love!"

Smack. Smack. Smack.

Charles doesn't stop, even as Ian stops struggling on the floor.

Tears pour down Charles's face as he delivers hit after hit, a violent madness overtaking him. Blood splashes onto his face, splattering onto his dress shirt and his golden hair—a brutal vision of betrayal and bloodlust. "I looked up to you! You were like my father. How could you do this? How *could* you?"

Maddy cries in her corner, her hands covering her ears.

Charles continues hitting his uncle, each blow violent and vicious. Loud sobs rack his body as he avenges me. "I'm going to kill you," he chokes out, his face wet with tears. "How could you hurt her like this? How could you?"

My breath hitches, my heart threatening to escape my chest, as I see the man I love devolving into a mindless beast, intent on revenge even as grief and torment carve an unhealable wound inside him.

It's tearing him up inside. He's killing himself with each blow he rains on his uncle.

I see it in the way his powerful frame shakes, the anguish in his voice, the soul-shredding pain and cutting betrayal conveyed in his words.

A new blistering agony carves through me.

I can't let him do this for me.

I can't let him kill the man he loved—the man who cared for him like his own. I hate Ian Vaughn with every breath inside me, but I can't let him steal Charles's life as well.

And he would if Charles kills him. Charles would never recover.

It would destroy him.

Tears stream down my face, and I finally find the strength to move. I fly to Charles and wrap my arms around his back, trying with all my might to stop him from delivering blow after blow to his uncle.

"Stop! You'll kill him. I don't want you to kill him for me. I don't want his death on your hands!" I cry, my vision blurry. "Please, stop for me, Charles. Please! Let him rot in jail for what he did. Don't do this for me."

A guttural roar rips from his throat, and Charles shakes in my grasp. I curl my hands around his face and force him to look at me.

Those beautiful sky-blue eyes I love, filled with so much pain. I want to take it all away, even as the horror of my past slams into my mind repeatedly.

My fingers trembling, I wipe the blood from his face, his hair, his lips. I dip my forehead against his as he chokes one ragged breath after another.

"I-I'm so sorry, Taylor. For what he did to you. For—"

"Shhh." I close my eyes, focusing on the sounds of his rough breathing, my heart splintering in half for the man before me. "It wasn't you. You couldn't have known."

An agonizing groan rumbles from his chest, and more tears slide down my face. "I don't blame you. I love you, Charles Vaughn. The past is in the past. We got him now."

Sobs continue to rack from his throat as he collapses in my hold.

Everything hurts so much—memories of the innocent sixteen-year-old living inside me, the all-encompassing emotions I feel for the man before me—it's almost too much for me to bear.

But amid everything, one voice rings true inside my mind.

I'm Taylor Peyton-Anderson, a fighter, a survivor, and my nightmare is finally over.

CHAPTER 59

The media is relentless.

"Charles, Taylor, how are you dealing with the fallout from Sir Ian being arrested?"

"How do you feel about him pleading not guilty and his claim that your partial recording is made from coercion?"

"Do you have a Plan B if the court throws out the recording?"

"Taylor, how can you stay with the nephew of your rapist?"

"Are you worried this case may impact your company?"

Gritting my teeth, I ignore the vultures as I help Taylor out of the car. The paparazzi have been relentless for the last two weeks after we finally learned the truth of what happened to Taylor all those years ago. We've both taken time off work to process everything.

Taylor connected Maddy with Olivia, who'd help the girl find a good therapist. My minx has also been calling Maddy every other day to check on her.

I sent my cell phone recording to the authorities. But unfortunately, it was a partial recording because my cell phone broke in the scuffle and that was all the tech guys could recover. Elias and Emerson are still combing through Archambeau's hard drives right now, no doubt hacking their way inside, but that may take some time. Maddy is willing to testify against Ian and her rapist, but our lawyers have advised us the defense may push back, saying she accepted monetary gifts among other things and didn't come forward when the assault happened.

They never believe the women.

That was what Taylor told me before, and seeing it unfold in front of me, even with the Anderson and Vaughn influences and resources, I know it was a hundred times worse for her back then.

It sickens me to the core.

There are still too many men from that night unaccounted for—the other sick bastards who did unspeakable acts to other women, but unfortunately, Ian has done a one eighty since he was arrested. He isn't talking. My guess is, he's afraid of The Association. After all, the bastard who spiked Taylor's drink was murdered in jail. Rumor has it he wanted to give up names for a more lenient sentence. And Ian killed Archambeau—The Association surely wouldn't be okay with that.

Taylor has been quiet these days. But sometimes, I'll catch her staring out the window as the news plays in the background, a haunted look in her eyes. The news has been reporting the latest updates on the case and the likelihood of Ian being convicted. I know she's worried.

It makes me wish I killed him that day. I know she didn't want his blood on my hands, but every time I think about what the bastard did to her, I want to break into prison and personally shove a shank up his ass.

Then, there are the other sickos still out there, hiding under the cloak of The Association, which will be impossible to take down given the group isn't even a legal entity. All these issues keep me up at night and I find myself tugging Taylor close to me as I stare at the dark ceiling, my mind swirling with fury and grappling with the recent events on top of the complete betrayal I have toward my uncle.

It's a devastation I can't describe, to find out you don't really know a person you thought you knew well.

How can someone so loyal and kind to me and my siblings also be capable of such horrific acts?

I don't think I'll ever understand.

But as I stare at the woman bravely facing the cameras, her head held high, her gaze defiant, I'm also hit with an overwhelming sense of love and admiration. This warrior, her soul crushed and body scarred, is still standing up tall. She has chosen to love me, to believe in me, to be with me.

Taylor glances at me, her brow arched high as she stops in front of the crowd of reporters. Narrowing her eyes, she snatches the microphone from the nearest reporter.

My lips twitch. Badass Taylor, no finesse as always.

"Aren't you guys asking the wrong questions?" she says as the cameras flash around her.

I stride to her and curl my arm around her waist, biting back a smile at the fierceness in her voice.

Taylor continues, "Am I the only person who's capable of understanding Charles is his own person and has nothing to do with the actions of his uncle? Why is this even a question?"

They hurl more questions at her but she raises her hand and says firmly, "I'm not done. The bastard has taken enough of my life from me and I won't entertain him taking more of my time. Your focus should be on the other women who have spoken up, the other victims who haven't had justice. Those are your stories, not me and Charles."

"Charles, what are your thoughts on this matter?" A lanky reporter waves his microphone in my face.

I tug Taylor closer to me, relishing in the strength and warmth emanating from her. *My fierce minx.* I look at the reporter in the eye and respond, "I echo everything this strong, brilliant woman next to me just said. We believe justice will prevail in the end. We've also set up a fund for legal, mental health, and investigation costs for sexual assault and rape victims to help them find the help they need in the darkest of times. My company will release more details next week. Thank you for your support."

Without another word, I twine my hand with Taylor's and we head inside Manhattan Memorial Hospital. Despite the insanity going on in our lives, the paparazzi doing a much better job than any bodyguard at shadowing our every move, Taylor said we shouldn't stop living our lives.

She wanted to meet Firefly and tell her what happened because she knew it would be hard for me to do it—to tell Firefly the truth about our beloved uncle.

Taylor's gruff exterior, her dark makeup, and prickly thorns, hide the most beautiful soul underneath. I don't know how I was blind to that for so long.

As soon as we step out of the elevators to the long-term care unit, we're met with pure chaos. Monitors are beeping loudly, the sounds jarring on the normally quiet floor. Nurses and doctors are dashing down the hallway, wheeling machines and carts, barking orders.

Frowning, I scan the commotion and see Julie coming our direction, her strides hurried, a determined pinch on her forehead.

"Julie!" I call out, and she whips her head toward us and skids to a stop. "What on earth is going on? Is everything okay?"

Julie's eyes widen, her lips curving into a smile. She grabs my arm. "I was just about to call you. She's awake!"

Taylor gasps and I feel her clutching my wrist.

My heart stops and the room blurs around me. I'm sure I misheard. "W-What?"

"Your sister! We've never seen a miracle like this before. She woke up fifteen minutes ago, completely out of the blue. Your brother is here and saw it happen. We are gathering a team to assess her." Julie's eyes shimmer with tears. "You've been waiting for this day for almost eight years—you were right about having hope. I'm so happy for you guys!"

My pulse roars in my ears, my lungs heaving in rapid breaths. Before I'm even cognizant of what I'm doing, I'm sprinting toward Firefly's room, Taylor quick at my heels.

She's awake.

The words echo and slam against my skull. Please tell me I'm not dreaming and if this is a dream, I don't want to wake up.

I burst into Firefly's room, finding Liam by the bed, clutching her hand. His face is wet with tears as he smiles—a wide smile I haven't seen from him in years.

He looks up at me and stands. "She's awake, Charles."

My palms grow sweaty as I slow my steps down and walk past the en suite bathroom, which blocks the view of her bed.

Excitement laces my blood as I step closer, taking in Firefly in still-framed snippets.

Her legs under the blanket.

Her slender arms and delicate hands.

And finally, her. My sister. Propped up against the headboard and *looking* at me. She gives me a tremulous smile.

Oh fuck. Oh fuck. Oh fuck. I blink my eyes and pinch myself, barely registering the flash of pain.

She's still there—still smiling at me, her eyes shiny with tears. "Charles," she whispers, her voice weak.

"Lexy!" I reach her in three strides and pull her frail frame into my arms, my body shaking as I bury my face in her hair. "You're awake. I can't believe you're awake. I've missed you so goddamn much."

She trembles in my arms, her voice, the sweet sound I haven't heard in *years*. "I don't know what's happening," she rasps.

I smooth my hand down her back. "Everything will be okay. We'll take it one day at a time. All that matters is you're back with us and this is the miracle we've been waiting for."

Pulling back, I stare at my beautiful sister—whereas for the past seven, almost eight years, her skin has been too sallow. Now, there's a faint rosy glow in it. Her blue eyes sparkle with life.

Then I hear a gasp and whispered words in the background.

Looking back, I see Taylor standing there, her hand pressed against the wall of the en suite bathroom as if she needs it to hold her upright, her face entirely leached of color.

Lexy shifts, no doubt wondering what has drawn my attention away from her.

She cocks her head to the side, bewilderment in her voice. "Lil' Tay, is that you? What are you doing here with my brother?"

CHAPTER 60

I STARE AT THE one person I thought I wouldn't see again, the person whose betrayal cut the deepest after my assault.

Alexis Evans. My best friend.

She abandoned me after the darkest night of my life. She looked at me with revulsion when she found me naked and battered in the lounge. She told me she was quitting ballet.

I don't understand. Nothing makes sense.

She stares at me, a quizzical look on her face as she cocks her head to the side.

"Lil' Tay, is that you? What are you doing here with my brother?"

My mouth runs dry as I stare at her, unable to form words, unable to calm the icy kick of adrenaline sending my heart in a tailspin.

I see Charles slowly getting up, the worry clear in his beautiful blue eyes. Eyes I now see are identical to Alexis's.

What on earth?

Alexis frowns. "I-I don't understand what's going on."

Just then the door sharply opens behind me, and I see my brother, Ethan, rushing in, his dark brown hair windswept, his eyes wild as he scans the room before landing on Alexis.

"Oh fuck," he mutters, rushing forward, ignoring all of us, and crushes Alexis into his arms. "You're awake, my nova, you're awake." His voice chokes up at the end. "I knew you were going to wake up. I've never given up hope."

A few seconds of bewildered silence pass by as I struggle to find my voice, to ask what the hell is going on. I see a similar confusion in Charles, who mouths something to Liam, who shakes his head and murmurs, "I don't fucking know."

Alexis stiffens, and she pushes Ethan back, her wide eyes scanning my brother's face. "W-Who are you?"

"What?" Ethan staggers back. "Lexy, you know me. Don't joke right now. Please, I'm going to have a heart attack. Please don't joke with me."

Alexis shakes her head and scurries to the edge of her bed, her eyes not leaving Ethan's face. Clearly sensing their sister's confusion, Liam and Charles gather around Alexis, as if protecting her from Ethan, who looks like he's been slapped across the face.

"Can someone tell me what the fuck is going on?" I step toward the group, my heart beating out of my chest, my eyes clearly taking in a scene my brain cannot understand. "How is my best friend, your sister?"

"Your best friend? The one who abandoned—" Charles begins, the color slowly draining from his face as he makes connections I still can't see. "Fuck. That's why she disappeared. Because your best friend is my sister. Holy shit."

Alexis stares at me again, like she can't believe what she's seeing. Her gaze darts to my wrist and I glance at our friendship bangle. "Our bangle? I don't remember. I don't—" She shakes her head, like she's trying to remember something, and she looks at her own wrist. "Where's mine?"

"Fuck," I hear Charles whisper.

My mind is still having trouble catching up as I turn my attention to him. He opens Alexis's nightstand drawer and pulls out her bangle, similar to mine, but in a different pattern. A matching set.

He shakes his head, clearly still in shock. "I should've known. I always thought your bracelet looked familiar, but I couldn't place it."

His words reverberate as logic finally turns back online. Alexis Evans dropped out of my life abruptly almost eight years ago. Charles's sister sustained traumatic injuries in a car accident, leaving her in a coma almost eight years ago.

I never heard from Alexis again because she was here, in a coma, all along.

Looking at Alexis, my emotions still reeling, trying to understand what this means in the grander scheme of things, I ask, "Your last name isn't Vaughn. It's Evans. Why?"

Alexis swallows. "It's our grandmother's maiden name. I never use Vaughn in my everyday life. It's too high profile. Why are you staring at me like this? Why do you look so different? Did I do something to hurt you, Lil' Tay? I don't get it." She looks around the room, the blood leaving her face again. "You all look so different."

A delirious chuckle threatens to rip from my throat. Did she do something to hurt me? That's an understatement of the century. Even as I reel from the news that my former best friend is Charles's younger sister, who was in an unfortunate coma until now, it doesn't erase the fact she left me on the darkest night of my life.

But maybe there's another reason for it.

A spark of hope flares up inside me. I replay her words in my mind.

Lil' Tay. She hasn't called me that since I was fourteen, and she was eighteen then. She treated me like a little sister until I grew older and we became best friends.

"You all look so different."

My breath hitches and I slowly approach her, watching the furrow deepen between her brows. "How old are you, Alexis?"

I hear a sharp inhale. I don't know if it's from Ethan or someone else. A sinking feeling sweeps in as I watch Alexis looking at me in confusion. "Sixteen. I want to say sixteen, but that can't be true, right? You guys look so much older."

"Fuck," I hear Charles mutter under his breath.

"So, you don't know who I am, Lexy," Ethan murmurs, his voice hoarse. He swallows. "You have no clue."

A knock sounds at the door and a group of doctors with nurses and technicians walk in. The one in the front, an older man with salt-and-pepper hair, looks at Charles and says, "I'm Dr. Carlson from neurology, and these are my colleagues from critical care, respiratory, and physical medicine/rehabilitation departments. We're here to assess your sister and to come up with the best plan of treatment for her. Can I ask you all to step outside and give us some space?" He motions to his colleagues—there are at least ten of them crowding the room.

"Of course," Charles murmurs and takes my hand. "Anything you need, doctor, just let me know. Spare no expenses."

Liam pushes Ethan toward the exit. My brother looks like he wants to stay behind. Liam mutters, "What's going on, dude? You're acting strange."

Ethan stills and lets out a half-chuckle that anyone with eyes can see is fake. "Just shocked." His nostrils flare. "Happy for you guys though."

"Lil' Tay!"

I stop, turning toward Alexis again.

Her forehead is pinched, and she's clutching her head like she has a migraine. "I don't know what's going on, but I need to tell you I have proof." She shakes her head and winces. "I don't know what that means. But I need to tell you that. A hiding place. I'm not making any sense."

"Ms. Vaughn, don't try too hard right now. Let us check your vitals first, okay?" One of the doctors gives me a sharp glance and shakes his head, as if to tell us to leave the room faster.

I pinch the bridge of my nose, a headache beginning to form at the base of my neck, and we filter into the hallway.

Proof? Hiding place? What?

"Thanks for coming, man. I knew you were worried about her, so I wanted you to see her in person. But it looks like her memory is jacked up and the docs are going to take a while in there with her. Go back to work. I'll call you if anything changes." Liam clasps Ethan's shoulder, giving it a squeeze.

Ethan nods, his eyes still looking gutted and lost. "Right." His lips curve up in a fake smile. He glances at me. "See you at the family dinner this weekend."

A heaviness sits on his frame as he leaves us, and I make a note to ask him about it later.

Liam shrugs on his leather jacket and shifts on his feet. Charles clears his throat. The brothers look awkward as fuck standing here. Rolling my eyes, I push them both toward a quiet seating area.

"You two need to talk. I'm tired of you being at odds with each other and I don't even know Liam that long. Your sister is in there and she needs you both. She has a long road to recovery in front of her. Get your shit together."

Charles smirks and shakes his head in amusement. He pulls me to him. "You're the smart one."

"No shit." I smile into his chest. I whisper, "Liam still loves you. I can tell. Just talk to him, be vulnerable. You guys will be okay. I'm going to head out. I need to do something."

Alexis's words sift through my mind like a riddle. A riddle I feel in my gut I have the answer to, and I know I won't rest until I figure it out.

"I love you," he murmurs before pulling apart. He gazes into my eyes. "You okay?"

I grin. "I'm not sure 'okay' is the right word for what I'm feeling right now. I'm confused as shit, but I know the answers will come. Don't worry about me. I'll call you later."

He nods, warmth teeming in his eyes.

I glance at Liam, who's sprawled in a chair, nervously bouncing his feet on the floor.

I smile inwardly as I walk toward the elevators. The brothers will be all right.

In the meantime, I have a riddle to solve.

CHAPTER 61

"I'M GLAD YOU DIDN'T give up on her," Liam murmurs when I take a seat next to him. We stare at the painting on the wall in front of us.

The deep azure of the ocean, the waves lapping on to the golden sand. Seashells scattered along the shoreline. Beautiful mansions and cottages in the distance.

The Hamptons.

"There were days when I wanted to," I whisper. "I thought I was keeping her hooked up on machines because I was too selfish to let her go, which would be in line with what you probably think of me."

Liam sighs and out of the corner of my eye, I see him adjusting the sleeves of his jacket, his silver rings gleaming on his fingers. "Charles, I don't think you're selfish. If anything, the selfish one was me."

The heavy regret in his voice causes me to turn toward him. Emotions flit across his face as he looks down at his hands. "I could've gone to her that day. I knew you were busy—I mean, a CEO for a large company had to be busy. But I was looking forward to my trip, and we were almost at the airport when she called. I knew you were much closer to her than I was. I...I just..."

He clears his throat, his nostrils flaring. "I shouldn't have pinned it on you. She called me first."

"But I was the one who forgot about her that day." Regret slices through me as I reflect on my actions for a thousandth time, wishing I could turn back time and make a different choice. Things would've turned out differently. She wouldn't have gotten injured. Liam and I wouldn't have had this rift.

All these years wasted.

"I was just angry. I hated myself for not listening to Firefly that day. That self-loathing was poisonous, and I wanted to blame everyone other than myself. I know you took on a lot for us. Mom and Dad are a joke," Liam scoffs.

"You were always the one looking out for us growing up. The mature one. The serious one. The one who followed the rules. The one with all the responsibilities. But if you didn't do that, who was Grandma going to rely on? We'd have to share the burdens. I know that."

The backs of my eyes burn as I listen to Liam's raspy words, sentiments I've ached to hear for the better part of this decade. Understanding. Compassion. Forgiveness.

But then, I haven't been honest with him either.

My voice is thick as I reply, "I should've talked to you more, Liam. Maybe if I shared my problems with you, we would've understood each other better. There's not a day that goes by when I don't regret not dropping everything to find Firefly. It's a miracle she's awake right now. We all know the statistics. The odds aren't in our favor. I can't help but wonder, if you and I just talked to each other more, if I didn't think I had to shield everything from you guys, if that would've made a difference."

Closing my eyes, I continue, "Maybe we would've made the same choices that day. Maybe Firefly would've ended up in that damn car accident no matter what we did. But at least we could've grieved together instead of..." A ball is stuck in my throat.

"Turning on each other," Liam finishes.

He reaches over and grabs my wrist, giving it a squeeze. "Taylor was right when she yelled at us in the hospital last time. The way I saw you that day, your walls down, I knew I was hurting you and your pain didn't make me feel better. It made me feel worse."

Liam heaves out a deep breath. "Forgive me, brother?"

A bittersweet ache sits on my chest—the pain of the past colliding with the warmth in the present. Opening my eyes, I stare at my brother—his tousled hair, his tattoos, the grittiness in his eyes—he's a different man than the one from almost eight years ago, but I recognize the teasing guy who chased Firefly around the grounds of our vacation home ten years ago.

He'll always be my little brother. We've both fucked up and we're given a second chance.

"Only if you'll forgive me." I stretch out my hand, palm up. Liam's lips tilt up in a half smirk as he puts his hand on top of mine and pulls me in for a hug, followed by a hard slap on my back.

A few minutes later, we are staring at the painting again, this time, a small smile on my lips. I think back to that day ten years ago, right before I ascended the throne as Bank of Columbia's CEO. The joyful laughter and shrieking from Firefly and Liam, the lightness in my soul. The way she was running after him, holding clothing scraps in her hands.

"What did you do to her that day? Why was she chasing you?"

Liam chuckles. Apparently, he knows exactly what I'm referring to. "I messed with her Sugar Plum Fairy costume. Stapled a bunch of dried plums to it. She was so fucking mad. She kept screaming how there were no plums in the Sugar Plum Fairy costume." He leans back and sighs. "It was because she carved her name on my guitar the week before."

I snort and shake my head. "You two."

We stare at the painting some more. Someday, we'll go back there. Maybe, this time, I'll get to run on the grounds with them. Liam and I spend the next half hour catching up on the milestones we've missed in each other's lives. There is anguish. There is laughter.

My phone buzzes, and I take it out.

Elias

> Camden Murphy. Currently single. Went back to school after quitting ballet. Lives in Brooklyn but works in Manhattan as a financial analyst.

He sends me an address.

Elias

> A little bird tells me he's currently eating lunch with his boss here.

I curl my hand into a fist, grinding my teeth together.

"Charles? What's wrong?" Liam asks.

I look at him and take in his whole bad boy getup. "Want to go on a field trip with me?" I tell him about Camden and what he did to Taylor back then.

Liam's eyes take on a dangerous glint. "Let's go."

You fucking motherfucker, I'm coming to get you.

⸻ ✦ ⸻

Twenty minutes later, Liam and I walk into Giuliani's in the Financial District. I spot the asshole right away based on a photo Elias sent me. Camden is laughing with an older man—his boss, Gerard Matthews from Matthews Investments, a small as fuck boutique firm I can put out of business in my sleep.

Liam and I yank out the two open chairs at their table before taking a seat.

"What on earth?" Camden asks, looking bewildered. "Do we know you?"

I hold up my hand and flag a waiter to bring over two whiskeys for Liam and me.

Turning toward Gerard, I smile. "Gerard, how is business treating you? Tim Riordan still letting you play with his money?" Based on my quick check on the way over here, Riordan, a mid-level millionaire, is their main client.

Gerard's eyes widen, and he lets out a nervous laugh. "Charles Vaughn, I don't think we've met before. To what do I owe this pleasure?"

A waiter comes by with our drinks and I take a sip, watching as Liam does the same.

I shrug. "Just a friendly visit to remind you to do a better background check before hiring people."

"What do you mean?"

Arching my brow, I motion to the asshole next to me, not even bothering to look at him. "Do you know there's a lot to be said about one's character, or lack thereof, when a man abandons his girlfriend after she was brutally raped? And then he had the gall to blame her for it?"

I hear Camden's breath hitching.

Keeping my eyes on Gerard, I swirl my whiskey in front of me. "I wonder how Tim would feel to know his money is being handled by a firm that employs such dubious characters."

Gerard swallows, a muscle twitching on his forehead. His gaze darts to Camden, then to me, and his expression hardens. "My firm would never knowingly employ such people."

I smile and sit back. "Glad to hear it." I raise my glass and watch his hand tremble as he clinks his against it. We take a sip of our drinks. "I think we're on the same page. Now, do you mind excusing us? We have some unfinished business with Camden over here."

He nods, quickly pushes out his chair, and takes out his credit card. I shake my head. "On my tab, because you answered correctly today."

Gerard expels a nervous breath before he addresses Camden. "Don't bother coming back to work." He turns around and leaves.

A small thrill sifts through me as I turn to the sputtering idiot.

"I don't care who the fuck you are. That's illegal, what you did there. He had no grounds to term—" Camden abruptly silences when I haul his chair over and set him next to me.

"You *hurt* my woman. You betrayed her at the darkest time of her life. What I did was the bare minimum of what you deserve." I can barely keep the fury out of my voice.

I lean into him and whisper, "Now, you're going to pack your bags and move out of this state. Your name is as good as animal shit in the financial circles in this city. You'll never get a job here. And you're going to write Taylor a nice apology or else I'll blacklist you everywhere else in the country."

Camden pales, his lips twitching. "Y-You can't do that."

I smile and watch him tremble. "Watch. Me."

I take out my wallet and toss a few hundreds on the table, more than enough to take care of the bill.

Suddenly, I hear Camden howling loudly, his body bowled over in pain. He's covering his groin, his face flushed as he struggles to catch his breath.

I look at Liam, finding him glaring at Camden. He glances at me and shrugs. "I think the statement needed a kick to the balls for impact."

Barking out a laugh, I stand up and watch Liam lean over Camden and slowly roll up his sleeves, displaying his tattoos. "Better listen to my brother, and don't let me see you around." He cracks his knuckles. "Or else, the kick to the balls is only an appetizer."

I hide a smirk. Looks like Liam's love for *The Godfather* has paid off. Just then, my phone buzzes again.

Taylor

> I found something. Can you come to ABTC? I'm at the rooftop studio. Bring a laptop.

CHAPTER 62

My hands shake as I stare at the tiny little USB drive in my palm. I place the white swan figurine on the ground, the tiny compartment on its back opened.

"I don't know what's going on, but I need to tell you I have proof... A hiding place. I'm not making any sense."

The agony on Alexis's face, the way she was grabbing her head like she was desperate to remember one thing, but she couldn't.

But it was important enough for her brain to hold on to it—apparently a memory from when she was twenty years old, when my assault and her accident happened, even though she clearly doesn't remember that time period.

She still thinks she's sixteen.

Her words bothered me as soon as she said them and I tossed them around in my mind, trying to unravel its meaning, to see the big picture with missing puzzle pieces, when it occurred to me.

Alexis, my best friend, knew about my hiding place at the rooftop studio. She made fun of it constantly, jokingly saying she was going to commandeer it and put her crap inside. I felt the truth in my gut. That had to be what she was referring to.

And so, I hauled ass to ABTC, hurried up to the studio, pried loose the floorboard, and examined every single memento I placed in there.

I felt around the hiding place, wondering if there was something else she could've hidden in there. I tapped on every single floorboard in the space, listening for the distinct hollow echo, to see if there were other hiding places here.

But there was nothing. Everything looked exactly the same.

Until I remembered there was one place I hadn't checked, because *I* never put anything in there.

The small storage compartment at the back of the beautiful white swan figurine my mom had bought for me at the Met Opera all those years ago. My most beloved memento from the woman I still miss every day. The woman who instilled in me the love of dance.

As soon as I clicked the unassuming button at the base of the figurine and the compartment opened, a small USB, light as a feather, tumbled out.

I've never seen it before.

Her proof. I'm sure this is what she means.

What's in there?

The door creaks open, and in steps Charles, his eyes roving the studio until he finds me. Afternoon sunlight streams in from the windows, highlighting the golds of his hair, the scruff on his face, the piercing blue of his gaze.

He strides over, his muscles rippling beneath his bespoke suit, a laptop in his hand.

"Minx, you okay? I came over as soon as I got your text. Why did you want me to bring a laptop?"

Wordlessly, I hold up the USB, and his gaze sharpens, his brow cocked in question.

"I-It's not mine," I whisper, my pulse beating against my ears. "What she said in the room...the proof, the hiding place. It could only be this spot here." I motion to the loose floorboard. "Only she knows about this place, where I store my precious knickknacks. I found this USB there."

A muscle pulses in his jaw, and he swallows, his throat rippling. He loosens the tie around his neck and sits down next to me, powering up the laptop.

After it loads to the home screen, Charles takes the USB and plugs it into the port. There are two video files on it.

We play the first one.

Alexis's strawberry blonde hair fills the screen. I squint, taking in her beautiful dress. It looks familiar—it's the same dress she wore to Hotel Renegade. It has to be.

Her eyes dart around—the background is dark, but I recognize the rooftop studio.

"Tay, Tay, I'm recording this for insurance, okay?" Alexis whispers. "I know you'll keep this safe because it's in your mom's gift to you. I hope you'll never see what's on this drive, because I'll get him to confess what he did to you."

Her voice chokes up and sobs rip from her throat. "I-I'm so sorry, Tay Tay. I'm so sorry I didn't get to you in time before it happened. I'll avenge you. You're my best friend, and I'll gut him for hurting you. But I need to talk to my brothers first. They need to know about this. They'll know what to do."

My heart drops to the floor as tears spring into my eyes. Is she saying what I think she's saying?

The clip ends, and Charles immediately clicks the next file.

Screams and whimpers fill the air, and I take in my writhing form on a leather couch. My clothes are torn. I'm clearly out of it. Ian leans over me, zipping up his pants. There are other women in the frame, all in equal states of distress, if not worse.

Nausea rolls through me and I sway.

"Fuck!" Charles pulls me into his embrace, shielding my eyes. He snaps shut the laptop.

"I need to know. I can handle it, Charles." I pry his hands away even as acid works its way up my throat.

I need to know what happened.

He clasps his hand on my cheek and turns me to face him. "Don't do this to yourself, Tay. I'll get this to the authorities."

I shake my head. "No. I *need* to know." I lost too much that day and not knowing is a hole in my heart.

A muscle tics in his jaw and he closes his eyes before his hand falls away from the laptop.

My fingers tremble as I open the lid and hit play.

"No," I hear Alexis whisper under her breath, horror and shock clear in her voice. "Uncle Ian? *What?*"

"Welcome to The Association, Ian. There's a recording of you raping this poor girl, but that is the price of admission." A man speaking in a heavy French accent appears in the frame, his back turned toward the camera.

Laurent Archambeau.

Ian spits on the ground, his frame heaving. "You motherfucker."

Archambeau laughs. "That's what they all say, but then the lure of power is too big to resist, no? And come on, you enjoyed it. We all saw you."

He slaps Ian on the back and leads him out of view.

Suddenly, the camera jolts and the screen turns black, but the audio is still on. I hear some hurried footsteps and Alexis's winded breathing.

"Young lady, this section is restricted," someone commands.

"I-I'm sorry, I lost my way. Was looking for the r-restroom." Shit. Alexis sounds so scared.

A few seconds pass and I hold my breath, not letting it out until I hear the man say, "It's that way. Don't come back here again."

"R-Right."

The video goes on for a few more seconds before cutting off.

I stare at the black screen of the laptop, the silence loud and heavy around us. Charles is stiff next to me, no doubt reeling from what we just saw.

Tears well in my eyes as a tornado of emotions hit me all at once—disgust, grief, and anger at what I just saw, which thankfully wasn't the act itself, but it was enough that I know I'll have flashbacks and nightmares in the coming weeks.

But then there's also the crushing sensation of relief.

I have proof. Video proof and confession from Ian. Definitive. No lawyers can get him out of this now.

And...Alexis didn't abandon me.

Silent tears slide down my face as I remember my best friend, the girl I looked up to as a bonus older sister who liked the same things I did, the girl who was fun, positive, and kind. The girl who loved singing, often humming songs I'd never heard of before.

"Little firefly, flying in the wind…" The memory of Charles singing the nursery rhyme to me when I was sick drifts to my mind. I cover my mouth. That's why it sounded so familiar. Alexis would hum it back then.

My memories of her aren't tainted.

She was true to me all the way until the end.

She was trying to avenge me when she got into her—

Smack!

Charles lets out an anguished growl, and he punches the floor with his fist.

"What on earth are you doing?" I quickly grab his hand, the knuckles swollen, blood flowing out of the scrapes.

His arm shakes, his breathing heavy and rapid. Then I hear it.

Tortured, restrained sobs. Even worse than what I heard that day when he nearly killed Ian in front of me.

Looking up, my heart breaks when I see the guilt and anguish on his face, the moisture clouding his eyes. His face is mottled, his body is throbbing with pent up tension.

"I could've helped you sooner," he rasps, his trembling hand reaching out to cradle my cheek. "If I'd dropped everything and went to Firefly that day, I would've found out what happened, and you wouldn't have had to suffer for years alone. No one by your side. You wouldn't have had to poke yourself with needles, hurt yourself, hate yourself. I would've gotten you help. I would've—*Fuck!*"

Tears slide down my face, and I shake my head before pulling him into my arms. "You can't blame yourself for this. You didn't know. None of us did. I don't blame you. Please, Charles, don't take this on. What-ifs will kill you. I know that. I've been there."

Minutes pass by as we hold on to each other, united in our swirling emotions and collective grief, and yet as the seconds tick by, I find it easier and easier to breathe.

The truth is out. All of it. Old wounds are finally being tended to.

I'm finally on the right path to recovery.

"I'm sorry, minx," Charles whispers when we pull apart. He wipes the tears off my face and I do the same to his. "Can you forgive me?"

I shake my head. "There's nothing to forgive." Motioning to the laptop, I murmur, "We got there in the end, didn't we? Ian is done for, and my best friend never left me."

Charles tucks a lock of my hair behind my ear, his eyes warm. "God, I love you so much, you brave woman. To think I could've met you sooner."

My lips curve into a tremulous smile. I close my eyes and kiss him softly before whispering, "We met when we were supposed to, when my heart was ready for you, and I'm thankful for that. I love you, Charles Vaughn."

Groaning, he seals his lips with mine and I pour my love into my kiss, my actions speaking far louder than my words.

I truly believe what I said.

Perhaps it's twisted how one little action, or inaction in Charles's case, caused ripple effects to multiple lives, but I've long come to terms with the bad things in life.

Sometimes, there is no logic, no reason our brains can grab onto. I'll drive myself crazy if I keep searching for the whys and what-ifs. The anger and grief will tear me apart and steal what's left of my time on this earth.

Yes, it's true. If Charles had ignored his company's hostile takeover, maybe he would've made it to Alexis on time.

Or maybe not. We simply wouldn't know.

And if he did, would I have gotten better sooner? The trauma had already happened and was carved deeply into my chest. Nothing would change that.

So the answer is the same. Maybe. Maybe not. I have a feeling, either way, it would've been a long road to recovery for me. Nothing could shortcut that.

But meeting him now, after clawing my way back on my own—shiny black feathers and all—I realize the timing was right. I couldn't have moved forward with him, with love, until I'd taken this journey alone.

And in this moment, I realize I understand what Mom was trying to tell me back then, all those years ago on the subway. The black swan was a survivor, her strength far surpassing her sister because she had been through the trials of life and came out the other side.

I've spent my life trying to run away from the black swan, thinking her feathers are ugly. Stained. Corrupted. But they aren't. They are beautiful badges of honor—medals decorating war heroes. Black absorbs all colors and doesn't easily fade. It's resilient and embodies strength.

Without darkness, there is no light.

Without my past, the present me wouldn't exist, the version of me that knows I'm strong enough to withstand whatever life throws at me in the future.

Because I'm a warrior. A fighter.

I'm the black swan.

EPILOGUE

Three Months Later

DEV JOINS ME ON the ground in the death pose.

I can feel the audience's attention on us, the enormous space completely silent during the last scene of our last encore performance of *Swan Lake*.

We were supposed to perform at the Met Opera for one last time two months ago, but the show was so successful, they extended it for a few more months. Normally, the curtains will close now, signaling the end of the ballet, the tragic love story of Odette, the beautiful white swan, and her Prince Siegfried.

But no.

Not this time.

I asked Lisa a month ago for an appointment to meet with her father and the rest of the board members. I told them I had an idea on how to shine a positive light on ABTC after Ian's involvement in mine and Maddy's assaults were disclosed to the public.

Ian ended up confessing once his team learned about the video Alexis had made. It was a smart move, because it closed the case faster, keeping him out of the limelight, no doubt for self-preservation.

Who knows if The Association will let him live?

The public rallied around Bank of Columbia's stock, the press spinning stories of how Charles Vaughn protected his girlfriend from a rapist, how he was a man of honor who cared about the truth and valued that over his family ties. From what he told me, he recently hired a strong CFO working under him now and they were getting back on track. Charles's parents are no-shows, as always. They visited Alexis in the hospital only two times. Charles is livid, but resigned—he's making peace with his dysfunctional family now that he and Liam are close again.

Things have been more chaotic at ABTC, since we're now without an artistic director. The board has been interviewing to fulfill the much needed position, but in the meantime, tickets to the show have been sold out.

I guess the public wants to see me, the poster child of assault survivors.

Tonight, on the last show of *Swan Lake,* I want to tell Mom's version of the story she never finished telling me before she died.

I know what the ending should be now.

The hidden happily ever after beneath the tragedy.

The board approved of the plan and here I am, laying on the stage with Dev as the corps de ballet surround us, the other beautiful white swans forming a circle, blocking us from the view of the audience.

Dev and I quickly dart out from the back of the circle, where makeup and costume staff greet me, changing me into a specially crafted costume—the softest, most beautiful tutu I've ever seen, the right side black, the left side white. Crystals adorn the bodice and the silkiest ribbons drape from the waist. The makeup artist draws on a thick black liner on the right side of my face, and applies a dark purple rouge to half of my lips so that half of me is Odile, the black swan, and the other half is Odette, the white swan.

We quickly enter the circle of white swans and assume our ending positions before the swans slowly twirl away.

The spotlight shines on me as I slip from under Dev's hold. The audience gasps when I turn around, showing them my black swan side. Smiling at the dark shadows, I spare a glance at the Vaughn family box front and center of the Parterre level, feeling Charles's intense gaze on me.

Arching my hip, I ruffle my black feathers, embracing the audacious and saucy persona of Odile. Staring straight at the man I love, who looks so delicious in his black tux and perfectly combed hair, I give him a wink and throw him a kiss from afar. His glittering eyes shine with love as his lips twist into a smirk. He holds up his hand as if to catch my kiss and plasters it against his heart.

The audience chuckles at my teasing movements and I turn back toward Dev, who's still lying on the ground. Before I head toward him, I prance toward the fallen sorcerer, Odile's father in the original story—a pure bastard through and through. The sorcerer, the schemer behind Odette's tragic death, is now shuddering on the ground, about to die himself after Odette and the prince decide to give up their lives to break the curse.

Slowly, I grab Prince Siegfried's prop sword from the ground and plunge it into the sorcerer's chest. The audience gasps as he flails dramatically before lying still. Then I hurry to Dev, and gently lift my leg high in the air as the front of my body bends down, all the while showing the black swan's side to the spectators. I reach for him and he slowly wakens before he gets back up and flips me around so that Odette, the white swan, is now facing the audience.

A few excited shrieks echo in the auditorium as the crowd slowly realizes what's happening. Odile, the strong black swan, the stunning fighter capable of the hardest moves and turns in the ballet, has planned this ending all along. She fakes the deaths of Odette and Prince Siegfried and kills their evil sorcerer father before resurrecting Odette and her love.

Dev lifts me high in the air as he spins on his feet. Exhilaration sears my blood before he sets me down. I perform another set of fouetté turns around him—faster and faster, so that my costume—the black and white sides blend and slowly blur into gray—the beautiful Odette with her sparkling white feathers merging with the daring Odile with her seductive black feathers.

I hear the roar from the crowd, followed by thunderous applause and the squeaking of chairs—a standing ovation—as I twirl and twirl and twirl.

Forty-eight. Forty-nine. Fifty turns, all equally strong and elegant.

Because I'm the best damn swan and I deserve to be standing here on this stage. And from the loud cheers and applause, the public agrees with me.

I'm controlling my destiny.

Slowly, I come down from my last turn and land in my ending pose as the curtains fall.

Chaos and commotion erupt backstage.

Lisa scrambles to us, Ainsley and Maddy close behind her, and the girls throw themselves on me.

"I had tears in my eyes, Tay. That was so beautiful!" Lisa exclaims. "Dad texted me and told me to tell you he wanted to schedule your promotion eval!"

My heart titters with happiness, the rush of satisfaction and joy practically stealing my breath away. I realize, at this moment, it doesn't matter if I get promoted to principal ballerina.

Because I feel like a winner already.

I finally understood what Mom was trying to tell me all those years ago.

"A happy ending for everyone. I'm so proud of you, Tay. I knew you could do it!" Ainsley grins, her eyes misty as well.

I thank them, but my attention is snared on the brunette standing quietly next to her best friend. The two seem to have made up over the last few months and have gotten closer. Maddy wipes tears from her eyes. Swallowing the lump in my throat, I pull her closer and whisper in her ear, "You're the black swan too. Fierce. Powerful, a fighter. Don't you forget that."

She nods. "Thank you, Tay. I don't know what I would've done without you."

"You would've survived and you would've been brilliant all on your own. And keep going to therapy. I'm doing that now too." I clutch her shoulders. "We'll chase away these monsters together with help."

I took up Olivia's offer, and she introduced me to her colleague, who specialized in healing from sexual assault. The sessions, while heavy and emotional, have been cathartic. The therapist is also using EMDR techniques on me, which help PTSD victims to reprocess their trauma and rewire the physical responses so they lessen over time.

Charles is also seeing a different therapist on his own to work out his issues—the guilt over what happened to Alexis and me, Ian's betrayal, his mending relationship with Liam. It's making such a big difference for him. The light shines more brightly in his eyes these days.

"Because we're survivors," Maddy says, and I look into her eyes, a jolt of pride rushing inside my chest when I see a flame spark in them.

"Damn right we are." I grin.

"So, plans for the break?" Lisa asks, her eyes twinkling.

"*Nightmare of the Dead* is playing, and I'm going to drag Charles to see it with me." I waggle my brows.

The girls laugh. They all know Charles is not the biggest fan of slasher films.

Someone shoves my shoulder and I glance back, finding Carla standing there, her arms across her chest, a flash of admiration in her gaze.

I arch my brow, waiting for her to speak.

"I never thought I'd say this, but that was good." She motions toward the stage, where the crew is beckoning us back for a curtain call. "You *do* deserve Odette."

Throwing my head back, I laugh as I head toward the front stage. "Odile. I shine as Odile," I hurl back at her. "And I'm damn proud of that."

At the curtain call, which is stretching twice as long as normal with the crowds cheering and clamoring for more, I smile, euphoria rushing through me. I scan the private Anderson box, seeing Dad standing, his eyes shining as he claps.

Belle is leaning over the railing, her baby son strapped to her chest, wearing the cutest little baby noise-canceling headphones. She lets out a shrill whistle as Maxwell hauls her back against him and shakes his head, a grin on his face. Ryland cups his mouth and hollers at me as Millie jumps in place next to him.

Ethan grins and I see him holding up his phone and my heart skips a beat because I know he's streaming this performance to Alexis, which technically isn't allowed, but no one gives a fuck when you're an Anderson. Alexis is still at the hospital, slowly recovering, but we will be there with her every step of the way.

Rex and Lana are making heart signs with their hands, and I see Olivia in a neighboring box with her family, clapping loudly. Grace and Steven are sitting with them as my sister practically climbs onto Steven's back, waving her hands in the air and I swear I can hear her scream, "That's my sister!"

I look for the one man who has awakened my heart—that gleaming blond hair I'd recognize anywhere—but he's nowhere to be seen. A niggle of disappointment pinches my chest, but I brush it away as I dip into another low curtsy before walking backstage and head to my dressing room.

As soon as I open the door and step inside, a strong arm yanks me toward him, his scent of bergamot and cedarwood sifting to my nostrils. I catch a glimpse of Charles's eyes, the color of the hottest fire, before he slams his lips on mine and kicks the door closed at the same time.

I barely notice the click of the lock engaging because Charles has his tongue buried inside my mouth—swiping, tangling with mine like he's famished for me.

"You were fucking amazing," he rasps, his voice rough. "A temptress on stage. I couldn't take my eyes off you."

His lips trail to my neck and he scrapes his teeth on my tender flesh and I whimper, the sensations shooting straight to my clit.

"Charles, oh shit. What's gotten into you?"

My mind grows hazy as Charles hoists me up and I clamp my legs around his waist, finding him already hard and throbbing underneath his tux.

"You. You're buried so deep inside me, I'm addicted. I take one look at you up there, owning the stage, setting everything aflame, and I want to kiss you, make love to you, tether myself to you. You set me on fire, minx. I'm burning for you." He tosses me onto a chaise lounge chair in the corner of the room before he climbs over me.

His fingers deftly loosen the ties at my back because he knows I'll kill him if he damages this beautiful costume. He smirks, as if he knows what I'm thinking.

"I'm not an idiot, despite what you might think," he rasps after the ties are loose and he yanks down my bodice, exposing my breasts to the air.

"That's debatable," I moan when his lips capture my nipple and he pinches the other one. A scream tears out of my mouth and he quickly slams his hand over my mouth.

"Naughty minx, what will other people think? Our prima ballerina getting railed after her performance?"

Wetness leaks out of me and I writhe under him, trying but failing to align my pussy over the bar of steel inside his pants.

Charles lets out a low chuckle and moves down my body, spreading my legs so one falls on the floor and the other is hoisted against the side of the lounge chair, fully exposing me to him.

He rips the seams of my tights and I whimper as he does the same thing to my panties. "How many pairs of tights are you going to ruin?"

"All of them, because I have a new kink now—fucking ballerinas in their costumes."

With a growl, he buries his face in my pussy, his talented tongue swiping at my folds before his teeth play with my piercing. The sensations quickly spark out of control as I arch against him, my legs trembling, my body quickly burning up when he spears his tongue inside me.

I bite my lip to keep from screaming, my eyes fluttering shut as blinding pleasure takes over my body and my mind grows hazy.

Smack!

The jolt of pain snaps me back to the present.

"Not yet," he rasps.

Quickly, I hear him unzipping himself, and he splits me in half in the next second.

My mouth drops open from the pleasurable intrusion as he slams into me repeatedly, fanning the flames inside me once more. My breathing comes out in quick pants and I grip his shoulder for dear life.

"You're fucking amazing, Taylor Peyton-Anderson. Breathtakingly beautiful in my eyes," he grunts, his face flushed.

He pins my hands over my head, his dominance something I crave now. His hips move faster, snapping against me in a punishing rhythm, hitting that special spot deep inside me.

Sparks coalesce into something greater, gathering deep inside me, and soon I'm perched on the edge, ready to explode.

Charles reaches down and pinches my clit and I scream as I burst into a thousand pieces, my body thrashing as my orgasm overtakes me.

He follows me over the edge with a roar, his cock throbbing, his hot cum sweeping inside me. His mouth swallows the rest of my cries as he continues to thrust inside me, prolonging our high.

The obliterating pleasure slowly fades into a crushing warmth. We're a mess of sweat and passion and I'm sure my makeup has melted on my face. He hoists himself above me, his blue eyes heated.

"I love you so much, minx. So damn much." He kisses me softly.

Smiling, I trail my fingers over his angular face—drifting over his perfect nose, his strong jawline, the enticing scruff that makes me want to rub myself all over him again. This man has stood by me through everything, never wavering.

"I love you too, Charles. You wear your heart in your eyes," I whisper, watching his eyes darken, "and now everyone can see it."

"Because of you." He takes my hand and places it over his heart. "This started beating when you walked into my life, and it will continue beating with you by my side."

Charles whispers in my ear, "Reason number infinity: You make me braver. You make me a better person. You make me fall in love with the thorns of roses, shiny black feathers, and rough edges. You complete me, Tay."

He pauses and takes a deep breath before continuing, "We've always been unconventional and I can't hold it in anymore. When I saw you on the stage, I knew I couldn't wait anymore."

Taking my hand and kissing the back of it, he stares into my eyes and whispers, "Will you make me the happiest man on earth and marry me?"

The bubbles gather in my chest—the same bubbles I felt that day at the Met Opera when I saw Odette and Prince Siegfried for the first time—but this time, they're a hundred times more potent. Butterfly wings flap in my stomach. I feel like I'm invincible and I can fly.

My lips twitch as I take in the ridiculousness of our positions, him on top of me, still inside me, my tights ripped and chest bare.

He cocks his brow, his eyes sparkling with amusement.

The damn man can read me like a book.

"Yes," I reply as the first giggles slip out of my mouth. "But this better not be your official proposal, Charles Vaughn, or I'd really have to kill you."

He barks out a loud laugh and kisses me softly.

A thought occurs to me, and I frown. I bite my lip, remembering the strange letter I received in the mail earlier. "Charles, did you have something to do with an apology letter from my asshole ex that I just got this morning?"

Charles tsks loudly and shakes his head. "Mentioning your ex while I'm still inside you?" His teasing eyes drift to my lips and he murmurs, "I can't tell you or I'd really have to kill you." He parrots my words back to me and smirks.

Heat flows through my chest. He definitely did something to Camden and my inner petty side squeals with glee.

I clench my core and move my hips, biting back a moan as he hardens inside me again. "You *bad*, relentless bastard," I whisper before curling my legs around his back and quicken my movements, the sparks quickly fluttering inside me. "I think you deserve a present."

He groans, his eyes darkening. "*Your* relentless bastard." He works his hips into a maddening rhythm. He rasps, "And I don't need presents, because I have you, and you're priceless. But I *do* have something for you."

I arch my brow and clench around him.

Charles hisses and lets out a rough chuckle. "Not that, even though my dick is all yours. Next month. Bolshoi Theatre. Special performance of *Swan Lake*. A private box just for the two of us." He winks.

I gasp, excitement surging inside me. *How did he know about my dream to see the performance there?*

He laughs and crushes his lips on mine, and we don't speak for a long time.

And so Odile, the beautiful black swan, has found a prince of her very own, and they live happily ever after.

* * *

Thank you for reading WHEN HEARTS AWAKEN. Hope you've enjoyed Charles and Taylor's story as much as I did writing it.

Bonus Epilogues: Want to go to the Bolshoi Theatre in Moscow with Charles and Taylor for a special "sparkly" surprise? These are the bonus epilogues you don't want to miss! Sign up for my newsletter to get **TWO EXTRA BONUS CHAPTERS**, new release alerts, exclusive bonus material, and more. Just click on the "When Hearts Awaken Bonus Epilogues" link on the website: https://www.victori-alum.com/bonus

Read Ethan's Story Next: Do you know Ethan and Alexis's story is next? Don't miss WHEN HEARTS REMEMBER, an angsty, romantic, brother's best friend, and amnesia romance. Read it here: https://gen i.us/whenheartsremember

Please Review: Please consider leaving a review on the retailer website and Goodreads https://www.goodreads.com/book/show/217147 073-when-hearts-awaken. Your reviews will really help this author out and will allow more readers to find this book.

THANK YOU

As a reader and an author, I've never shied away from tough topics, and *When Hearts Awaken* is no exception. Taylor has always fascinated me. When she first appeared on the page in the first book of *The Orchid* series, *When Hearts Ignite*, her tough, badass persona made me laugh and felt so refreshing. As I got to know her, I realized that behind her strength lies the story of a survivor. Like many of us, she puts up a front when facing the world, and she's no different. I hope her story serves as a beacon of hope for others in similar situations—no matter how dark the times may seem, there's always a glimmer of light to follow. You just have to keep getting back up and walking toward it. I'm fortunate that her experiences are not my own, and I can only hope I've done justice to her story.

Here's an interesting tidbit about Charles Vaughn: did you know he has appeared in every single book I've written so far, starting with my debut, *The Sweetest Agony*? This was completely unintentional, but I realized he's been waiting patiently for me to give him his happily ever after. Poor Charles has always wondered why he never gets the girl! Well, we find the answer in his story: he's been looking for the wrong type of women while waiting for Taylor, his perfect match. If you're new to my books—or if you've read them and don't remember Charles—it might be fun to reread my backlist and see where he pops up!

This story was a tough one to write—perhaps the most challenging one I've tackled so far, requiring countless rewrites and lots of late nights. But I love the themes of trauma, survival, and hope. Thank you for reading Charles and Taylor's story.

As always, thank you to everyone who has supported me. In no particular order:

My family: There aren't enough words to express my gratitude for your support while I locked myself away for hours on end, writing and rewriting Taylor and Charles's story.

My editors: Theresa Leigh and Amy Briggs, thank you for your guidance and encouragement.

Proofreader: Thank you, Virginia Tesi Carey, for catching all the errors that slipped through earlier rounds of editing.

My PA: Nikki Johnson, thank you for your constant help and support, as always.

Cover designer: To the talented LK Farlow of Y'All That Graphic, thank you for designing such wonderful covers.

Beta readers: Malia, Jenn, Jess, Denny, and Isha, thank you so much for your valuable feedback! Alicia, thank you for being my sensitivity reader—without you, I couldn't have done Taylor's story justice.

My ilLUMinati girls: You know who you are! I love you all.

My ARC and street team: You all rock! Thank you for your edits, DMs, and messages. I am truly blessed to have you on my team.

Fellow authors: So many of you have helped me on this journey—it's impossible to name everyone, but I appreciate each and every one of you.

PR firms: Thank you to Literally Yours PR, Truly Yours PR, and Swipe the Book PR for your promotional efforts and for helping spread the word!

My fellow readers: I love you all, and thank you so much for reading my stories. Without you, I wouldn't be an author

With love,

Victoria

ALSO BY VICTORIA LUM

Catch up on Victoria's backlist! Don't miss these swoony, romantic stories with all the sizzling spice and angst. All stories are standalones and can be read out of order.

LA Hearts:

The Sweetest Agony (James and Jess)

The Coldest Passion (Parker and Liz)

The Harshest Hope (Adrian and Emily)

The Brightest Spark (Jack and Sarah)

The Orchid:

When Hearts Ignite (Steven and Grace)

When Hearts Collide (Ryland and Millie)

When Hearts Surrender (Maxwell and Belle)

When Heart Awaken (Charles and Taylor)

When Hearts Remember (Ethan and Alexis)

About the Author

Victoria is a lover of all things romance, including movies, books, and television shows. A hopeless romantic since childhood, she is always dreaming up stories and happily ever afters. Caramel lattes are her fuel in the morning and she can usually be found reading anything she can get her hands on. She lives with her family and a beautiful Siberian husky in sunny California.

Keep in touch!
Sign up for her newsletter below:
Newsletter
Follow Victoria on social media:
Victoria Lum's Luminaries Facebook Group
Facebook Page
Instagram
Tiktok
Bookbub
Amazon
Goodreads
Scan the QR code below for all the links!